praise 1

Praise for DAISY Cl

A revelation. Just ... aster storyteller.

HISTORICAL FICTION COMPANY 5 STAR AWARD

Praise for MONTECATINI

A gem of a book. It interweaves a gripping plot with a topical subject.

Verified Purchase

Praise for THE ANNA PUZZLE

An enticing and timely tale of love, literature and espionage.

Tom Bromley, author, tutor at Faber&Faber

the anna puzzle

JUSTINE GILBERT

Published by Small Dog publishing 2026

Formatted with Vellum

I dedicate this novel to the Ukrainian women I have met: to their resilience, bravery, adaptability and hard-working ethics, in the hope they will soon see peace and freedom in their country.

Lana Sabishchenko
Lesia Hersymovych
Yanina Shvets

foreword

The characters in this book are fictional, but caught in real-life events.

In 2022, I read Andrey Kurkov's novel, Grey Bees, which showed me the trials and humour of the Ukrainian people, and I hosted Ukrainian guests under the Homes for Ukraine scheme. I have a deep respect for Eastern Europe and its efforts to remain free despite Russian brutality and meddling.

Although a story told from the European perspective, I am indebted to Merrilyn Thomas, an Honorary Research Fellow at University College London, an author and expert in the Cold War, who explained the history behind Russia's imperialist views.

But foremost, this is a love story, and such things are timeless.

contents

PART ONE

Unhappy Families 3
Prologue 5
1. London 9
2. London 18
3. London 26
4. Berlin 34
5. London 39
6. Berlin 45
7. London 50
8. Berlin 58
9. London 64
10. London 70
11. Berlin 77
12. London 83
13. Berlin 91
14. London 98
15. Berlin 107
16. London 112
17. London 119
18. Berlin 125
19. Whitstable 129
20. Whitstable 139
21. Goodwood, Sussex 149
22. Berlin 159
23. Goodwood, Sussex 165
24. Berlin to London 173
25. Goodwood, Sussex 180
26. Ukraine 189

PART TWO

The Tyranny Of Hope 195
27. Whitstable 197
28. London 202
29. Ukraine 211
30. Whitstable 220
31. London 228
32. London 232
33. Dover 240
34. Ukraine 247
35. Canterbury 252
36. Ukraine 260
37. Canterbury 267

PART THREE

Search & Find 275
38. Whitstable 277
39. Whitstable 282
40. Ukraine 290
41. Whitstable 297
42. Whitstable 306
43. Ukraine 313
44. Maternity Hospital, Kent 321
45. Mariupol, Ukraine 329
46. Whitstable 338
47. Berlin 347
48. Berlin 354
49. Berlin 362
50. Berlin 370

Now... 373
Bibliography 381
Acknowledgments 383
About the Author 385
Also by Justine Gilbert 387

part one

unhappy families

'All happy families are alike; each unhappy family is unhappy in its own way.'

The opening line to
Anna Karenina by Leo Tolstoy.

prologue

CAMBRIDGE UNIVERSITY LIBRARY

OCTOBER 1978

HE WAS CONSIDERING how best to bed the Professor's wife, for ethics mattered little in his line of work. The man was late for their meeting, which gave him cause enough and he quelled his irritation, wandering between the shelves in the Cambridge University Library. His attention snagged on some dusty editions of Anna Karenina, and he plucked one down to pass the time. The publisher had divided the novel into eight volumes, each featuring a title and Latin numeral gilded on the spine. Odd, he thought: he had never seen it in separate sections, but flipping a few pages, the puzzle grew. His English was excellent, if somewhat rough in accent, so the clumsy phraseology stood out. What an atrocious translation: he could have done better! A prickle of serendipity infused his fingers as he touched the calfskin-bound curios: they would be perfect as identifiers for covert meetings. With a stroke to their soft exterior, he slid them, one by one, into his briefcase next to his Beretta, looking around to check no one was staring. As usual, the English public avoided eye contact, and seeing as a Russian novel rightfully belonged in Russian hands, all was well.

His appearance in England was a consequence of the Soviet tanks rolling into Afghanistan. The KGB had tasked him with finding agents for a new cell to counteract any NATO interference, and Cambridge, the home of traitors, was a logical start. His group would require codenames, and these unexpected acquisitions offered a solution: he could use the characters in the novel. He had introduced himself to Professor John Blount and Annaliese Blount as a foreign academic, but would soon gather them into his grasp. The young wife – the one of his daydreams – had surprised him by launching into an eloquent speech about workers' rights and her belief in communism as an ethical alternative to corrupt democracies; she held a particular disdain for Ronald Reagan. He had watched in fascination as her mouth twisted enticingly. Those full lips! The breasts that heaved with each gesticulation! Not one to ignore a good bosom, he found it hard to avoid staring at the swell under her tight knitwear.

The book gave shape to his ideas. He could be known as *Vronsky*, and the Professor would be *Alexei*, making the wife, Annaliese, *his Anna*. What a poetic notion!

He imagined a future assignation with her in a seaside setting. Last month, an enemy of the state had offered him a hundred acres of good arable land near the coast on the Sea of Azov. A dacha. People offered all kinds of trinkets under torture, and this was near a town he'd never heard of – Zhdanov – which his Ukrainian victim called Mariupol. Apparently, it was no more than a day's drive to Crimea, a beautiful resort, and he smiled at the memory of the deal. All the KGB agents expected bribes, so he had allowed the man to write a note of transfer before finishing the game. In his line of work, guilt was an unknown word, which meant he could applaud his foresight; romantic beach holidays appealed to women.

Just as Vronsky and Anna Karenina's affair was famously passionate, so he conjured an image of himself and Annaliese's inviting smile, her curvaceous body in a swimsuit, the best vodka in a crystal glass, a clear blue sky and those lips on his. From what he remembered, the characters had never done this in the novel, but such details were unimportant, because Soviets made their own narrative.

A nearby chair scraped, and he looked up. Weaving between the tables, the Professor's pallid brow etched a rueful English apology; the drooping bottom lip accentuated his weak chin. He had never understood love, but even so, what did she see in him? Vronsky smiled, his fancies hardening into clear purpose and he extended a hand in greeting.

ONE
London

OCTOBER 2021

HER BROTHER'S request did not constitute a family crisis, but more of a conundrum. Alighting from the Kent coast, Anna changed from a south-eastern train to the London tube to reach her brother's house on the edge of the city. Stephen Blount, fifteen years her senior, had phoned to ask if she would stay at his home to reason with his wife. No – he had not asked – he had begged; a request she found deeply puzzling. But she had never understood her brother's marriage and sometimes wondered if she even understood love. As for passion – that was a foreign country.

Despite being the mother of a ten-year-old boy, Anna suspected her brother still saw her as the young child left in his care following their parents' fatal car crash in Berlin. The unexpected death of John and Annaliese Blount had caused Stephen to remain perpetually protective, which made yesterday's call even more peculiar. Never before had he sought her support.

She had grown up with the impression he controlled

everything, save perhaps his wife, Dolly. But now he was asking for her help, and gone was the normal paternal tone. Instead, he had spoken with urgency, and she had agreed to his request, more on grounds of curiosity than any sense that she might resolve their differences. This was Dolly he was talking about, and her sister-in-law had the DNA of a cat. No one made rules for Dolly except Dolly.

It was fortunate that the request came at a convenient time. Half-term meant her son Simon would stay with his paternal grandmother, a strident woman who clashed with Anna; and as her husband was away on business, she had no reason to remain alone in their large seaside home. London would make a change after the confinements of Covid.

The train screeched through tunnels before emerging into light. The route carved between suburban houses and blocks of flats, between rich and poor, shops and roads. Her husband's family was wealthy, and unlike many young women of her age, she had no money worries, which made her wonder if Stephen's anxieties were more economic than emotional. Were he and Dolly heading for divorce? It would affect their lifestyles, especially when she considered Dolly's spending habits.

Anna allowed her body to sway on the train, closing her eyes, deliberating what course of action might constitute *help.* According to her brother, his wife was having an affair. And this in itself was an odd statement, because hadn't she always been one to play away? And though Stephen might grumble, he usually ignored her ill-concealed lusts, for they had an open marriage – more open for Dolly than him. But what was different this time?

At nineteen, she had escaped their fractious house, fraught with Dolly's shouting and her young nephews' fights, to marry Alex, twenty years her senior. Okay, she conceded, her married life had proved less than perfect, and currently resembled trains on separate branch lines, but here she was, offering to act as the stationmaster. No. The whole thing was absurd.

With a touch of regret, she recognised even the word *flirtation* was too strong to describe her experience of premarital sex with Alex. As to her knowledge of *affairs* and heart-thumping passionate encounters – everything she knew came from her paid commissions, translating French romantic novels into English. No bed linen required. What, therefore, could she say to Dolly, her much older sister-in-law and poor role model, that might be construed as constructive?

The tannoy announcement made Anna jump. She opened her eyes with an irrational panic that nearby commuters might have heard her thoughts. Some passengers still wore their Covid masks, creating an element of menace, but the threat level heightened when three youths entered the train, their hoodies tugged over chins and brows. Like squirrels seeing a pack of dogs, commuters rushed to exit the carriage, giving the group a wide berth. Anna opted to swivel her knees in the opposite direction, relieved when a video absorbed their attention. Oblivious to everyone, they jostled and whooped, engrossed in their entertainment.

Further and further towards the east of London she travelled, and with each stop, someone exited. The carriage cleared, until only a man in a leather jacket remained at the far end. He held his khaki knapsack between his legs, fixing the group with a brazen stare. For a moment, he caught Anna's eye, but she looked away.

The boys' music rose, and they stamped trainers in

rhythmic appreciation, sending shudders along the floor. Fear forced her to walk towards the middle of the carriage, pausing at the doors, suitcase between her ankles, laptop strapped to her left shoulder. Holding tight to the rail, she focussed her thoughts on Stephen and Dolly; their lengthy marriage; their two sons, now both at university; their credit card lifestyle; Stephen's tendency to appease, Dolly's willingness to inflame – and the futility of her visit. The train shot out of a tunnel into the bright light, and she glanced at the teenagers. One more stop.

The train rocked and clacked and wheezed. The man with the knapsack scanned the platform for the station's name as the brakes screeched and the car park came into view. She exhaled in relief when the youths strode out. The danger was past.

Taking a moment to hitch the laptop strap higher over her shoulder, she clutched her overnight bag, before stepping out as the doors closed. In an instant, she realised they had dawdled and were there in front of her. Oblivious, a young mother trundled by, steering an empty pushchair in one hand and a protesting toddler in the other, while the gang gazed towards the car park, hands in pockets. Anna's nerves fluttered. At the far end of the platform, a London Transport guard rolled on the balls of his feet, back swayed, stomach out, blowing a whistle, as the train moved away.

She heard their footsteps at her side. Stepping to the right, she refused to let them catch her eye, but they blocked her, and one gave a vicious yank on the strap. Instinctively, Anna held on, but his tug dragged her to her knees, and a scream escaped her lips as she felt the sting of broken flesh.

'Stop!' She gasped in pain as the boys fled towards the exit.

The few remaining commuters parted in a tide of self-survival. Two of the boys jumped the barrier, but the third youth holding the case stumbled over an invisible hazard. With a decisive movement, the leather jacketed man grabbed the strap. Regaining his balance, the boy whipped out a knife, stabbing frenziedly at his assailant. Anna gasped and passengers recoiled and shrieked.

The station guard yelled. 'You're on CCTV, you little shit.'

The mugger moved to stab again and retrieve his booty, but the stranger dealt him a vicious kick. Staggering, the youth flashed the knife, but the man parried the blow with his arm. Shouting abuse, the empty-handed attacker jumped the barrier to run after his peers as Anna hurried towards her rescuer, gasping her thanks. He grimaced, bleeding from one hand but holding the laptop strap in the other. 'Is nothing. Is nothing.'

'Hang on, mate.' The guard growled into his phone.

She ignored the sting of her knees. 'My God, you're hurt. Is it serious?'

'Is nothing.' The blood from the back of his hand dripped in a pointillist pattern onto the grey station floor.

'Let me look.' She dropped her bag to examine his wound.

'Effing shits,' said the guard behind her. 'You good mate? And you?' He looked at Anna's torn leggings. 'I've reported this, don't you worry. Happens far too often. Those kids who live in the tower blocks down the bottom there. Always nicking mobile phones and whatnot. I'd round them all up and shoot them. Make my job a lot safer, I can tell you.' He wiped his brow as if he were the one who had fought the assailants.

Anna gushed more thanks. 'Hi. I'm Anna. Let me help you.'

'Here's your computer.' He had what she assumed was an Eastern European accent. 'Is broken? I think no.'

A silver pin-like scar ran from his eye to his cheekbone, and she had to stop herself staring. Whipping out some tissues from her pocket, she pressed them onto his wound. 'You could have been killed.'

'Not the first time.' His tone was light.

'You put yourself in danger. You shouldn't –,' she sputtered. 'Not that I'm not grateful, but – Please, tell me your name.'

'Oleksandr Vronskiy. I am glad to help.' His deep blue eyes crinkled without a hint of anger or distress.

'My computer is my life, but it's not right that you're injured.'

A grey-haired woman stopped. 'Hello love, I'm a nurse. Want me to take a look?' She examined the wound with an experienced eye pronouncing the cut too shallow for stitches. He thanked her. 'Have you had a tetanus shot? If you're visiting and you don't have a doctor, give it a good wash with soap and water, and put on a strong plaster. Or go to a walk-in centre. Are you a tourist? German?'

'No.'

'No? Sorry. Only I wondered if you have an EHIC ... Well, no matter. None of my business. It might wait until you get home.'

As she passed onto the platform, a police car arrived with a quick flicker of blue lights. Anna pictured Dolly waiting in her little red Polo, parked on double yellow lines.

Two uniformed officers clocked Anna's knees and the man's bleeding hand and one snarled, 'Has this man assaulted you?'

The London Transport guard butted in, his face a study in outrage as he described the actions of the boys.

'We're dealing with lots of muggings in this area,' the police officer remarked calmly, clutching the radio at his chest. 'Most in broad daylight. Phones and credit cards. That's what they're after. A new laptop would be a gift. Would you recognise them in a mug shot?'

'Not sure,' said Anna. Everything was happening so fast, she couldn't collect her thoughts.

In contrast, the foreigner appeared unruffled. He pulled out a piece of paper with an address. 'This is me. I stay here for two weeks. I will recognise them.'

'Well, Mr –.' The name defeated him. 'We need a formal statement for a crime number, so you have to go to the police station.'

Their intercoms bleeped in unison, and they jerked their heads towards the car. 'Sorry. There's been another incident. Fill out the forms. It's just up the hill.'

The guard puffed his cheeks at their departure. 'Yeah, yeah. The police station is up the hill, alright – in a nice leafy road. But all the bastards are down the hill. And me, muggins here, in the middle.' He turned, muttering curses, as another train arrived.

She grasped the Samaritan's elbow, urging him out of the path of the new arrivals, aware he smelt faintly of pine, as if he had just stepped from a woodland copse. A double-honk from her sister-in-law sounded from outside. Anna wanted to slow time, show her sincere appreciation, but Dolly would be too impatient for that, so she hurried to thank her rescuer once more, giving him her business card. *Anna Faver, translation services, no job too small.* 'Seriously. If there's any way I can repay you. Can we drop you somewhere?'

'I stay with my brother. He has medical kit.' The man looked at her credentials with curiosity. 'What language?'

'French, some Italian. Latin languages, and I suspect that's not yours. I'm so grateful you got my laptop – it contains all my work. It's my life, actually.' She gave a burbling laugh, unable to take her eyes off him and unwilling to walk away.

He patted the reddened tissue over his wound. Who was this man who confronted a knife-wielding attacker? She noted the rip on the jacket's sleeve. His actions deserved more than words.'Well if you're sure, Mr ...?' She couldn't remember his name.

He pointed to the semicircular row of shops opposite the car park. 'I stay there,' he said. Anna looked at the neon sign above the Continental Deli Cafe. Years ago, she remembered stopping there when it was a rundown tea shop. Now the slick European delicatessen glowed in anticipation of Halloween, and she wished she could stay with the Good Samaritan and buy him a good strong espresso. It seemed a ridiculously insignificant gesture to compensate for his wound.

'Sorry,' she added. 'I didn't catch your name.'

'Vronskiy.' He spelled it. 'Oleksandr Vronskiy. But everyone calls me Sasha.' Stubble softened the corners of his face, and it seemed to her that his features bore a classical beauty complimented by his broad shoulders, reminiscent of dusty marble statues from medieval churches: chiselled and scarred.

'You're Russian?'

A line creased between his brows. 'Ukrainian. Not Russian. I am here to see my brother.'

Apologising, she did not want to admit all Eastern European accents sounded the same to her, although mention of Ukraine prickled. Hadn't recent news headlines suggested something about Russia invading? But she never paid attention – she rarely watched any television, preferring to follow YouTube channels or to watch downloads of Friends. Her worries involved her cooling marriage, her son's happiness, and comments on Mumsnet about parking wars, and beach litter and how to be a good mother. Now she added Stephen's current dilemma to the list which left little room for world events.

Sweeping the tangle of hair from her face, she extended a hand in an awkward gesture. 'Goodbye, Sasha.' She swallowed as he smiled, but he ignored her palm. 'If I can help you in any way, please contact me.'

He shook his head, and outside in the car park, Dolly yelled. When he offered to carry her heaviest bag, she refused with a laugh. 'I couldn't – look at you. You're injured, and your jacket is ruined, and I'm responsible.'

'No. Is okay. And you have injury to you and clothes also. For me, is nothing.' He went to slip her card into his back pocket, but with a small hiss of pain, he dropped both the tissue and her details on the station floor. Together they swooped to retrieve it, narrowly missing heads, and Anna laughed breathily as Dolly's horn sounded with another double-honk. His smile showed even teeth and boyish dimples, and she felt his eyes lock on hers as new commuters swirled on either side. With another apology, she turned reluctantly towards Dolly, but a glance over her shoulder found him still staring after her, and she shivered. Déjà vu. Was she imagining things? Perhaps she had translated too many romantic novels, because she longed to see him again. His face was unforgettable.

TWO

London

THIRTY YEARS EARLIER: OCTOBER 1991

NEWS OF A PACKAGE did not constitute a crisis, but more of a conundrum. Alighting off the plane at Stansted, Vronsky took a taxi into the city towards his former landlady's house. She had phoned him about a parcel – *most likely a book* – with no return address or name. To him, the sender was obvious, and although he had never known love before meeting Annaliese, he understood it now. How he had missed her! But since glasnost, he had been forced to work crazy hours in Berlin, cauterising loose threads in the Anna Karenina cell, and of necessity, he had left Annaliese and her husband to get on with things in England, learning of their move from Cambridge to London.

This message-in-a-book suggested ... *Blyat.*

The old woman ushered him in with a smile, offering thick, strong coffee and hot blini. In return, she accepted a bottle of the best Siberian vodka, thanking him in Russian. Formalities completed, she withdrew to give him privacy. As he had suspected, it was one of the identifiers – Volume III of Anna Karenina. He smoothed the brown wrapping, recognising Annaliese's loops and swirls, and hastened to tease out the note secreted in the spine.

My darling Vronsky,
Problems.
Alexei was mugged. He's talking.
Come at once.
All my love, Anna.

He held the scrap of paper to his nose, inhaling her scent with its whisper of sex. When Gorbachev raised the Iron Curtain, agents were left scrambling in the void, and Vronsky knew he should have approached John and Annaliese sooner, but he had become embroiled with combined American/Russian operations on the former East German side. Change always came at a price, and for Vronsky that change had parted him from the woman he loved. He hankered for her warm body next to his; the tumble of hair; the Chanel perfume.

To clear his head, he took the 73 bus, sitting on the top deck, considering the implications of her message, which depended on what Professor Blount was saying. He gazed out through the rain-spattered windows and thought that, unlike Berlin, London appeared unchanged. Dog walkers crested the brow of Kensington Gardens; workmen climbed scaffolding, cleaning the exterior of the Albert Hall; and the weather was still miserable. In his opinion, the British were sluggish, inclined to introspection rather than action. Russia and Germany were where all the action took place, but he wanted to forget all that. Running a hand over the book's calfskin cover in his pocket, he felt that familiar stirring at the thought of *his Anna* naked, in his arms.

With one hand on the metal bar of the double-decker's

stair, he swayed, waiting for the bus to jerk to its stop at Kensington Gardens. Flattening the hair on his scalp, he touched his newly scraped chin, eager to appear a sophisticated Europhile, rather than a former KGB agent. His fingernails were clean, his cuticles trimmed; there was nothing to be done about his thickset hands.

Upon arrival, he stood a moment in the crescent where the four-story Victorian buildings, now turned into apartments, blended their cream and redbrick into the hues of dusk. He leaned against the black iron railings that encircled a private garden. It was currently empty, and all he could hear was the thrum of traffic along the parallel road of Kensington High Street. He lit a cigarette to calm his nerves, recognising such emotions as weakness.

On the second floor, a yellow illumination denoted life, and a woman came into view, dragging heavy curtains across the sash windows. He would know that silhouette anywhere; her shapely figure and the long curling strands of hair. He could imagine her painted nails scraping his back and hastened to cross the road, jumping up the three stone steps to the intercom to press hard.

'Yes?'

'Vronsky.'

'Thank God.'

He had never told her his real name, but now was not the time. The buzzer sounded, and he leapt up two flights of stairs to meet her at the door, his heart pounding. With relief, he saw that this last tumultuous year had not changed her physically.

She beckoned him in, putting a finger to her lips. 'He's sleeping,' she whispered. They went into the living room and kissed. His body stirred at her touch, and he was reluctant to release her, putting his nose to her neck. She still wore Chanel No. 5 perfume, the capitalist luxury she would never give up.

'What's happening? How is he?'

'Not good.' She took his hand, guiding him to the bedroom. Beneath sheets and blankets lay a figure he scarcely recognised as the Professor, breathing in shallow guttural spurts. Vronsky could make out a purple bruise and a large swelling obscuring one eye.

'*Blyat*,' he said, turning away.

'Yes. Fuck,' she agreed. 'Early onset Alzheimer's. The doctor diagnosed him some months ago.' She drew Vronsky back to the living room to offer a drink. 'Apparently, certain types of the disease act faster than others. Now, he's so disoriented, we can't go anywhere. You never know what he'll say.'

Vronsky swallowed the small vodka she offered, examining her trembling movements as she poured herself a glass of red wine. There had never been a formality to his relationship with Annaliese, and both had accepted its fluidity, although Vronsky made all the moves. If asked, he would say he didn't believe in love, that their affair was lust, but seeing her again like this, he knew she had captured his ungodly soul. So why had he not swooped on her at the first crumbling of the Wall? Why leave her when all he wanted was to insist they escape together? And he was certain she felt the same.

'I was in the flat above, talking to my neighbour about the faulty lift.' She stroked the glass. 'He must have gone out into the streets to look for me and become confused. Apparently, he was trying to stuff five-pound notes into his copy of Anna Karenina, shuffling along in bare feet. Then he began shouting for you. He was always shouting for you.' She gulped. 'Anyway, the police brought him back.

According to an eyewitness, someone punched him, took the money and left him on the pavement, clutching the book like a teddy bear. The policeman who tried to help came in for abuse. John called the man an officer of the Stasi and yelled about stolen microfiche and how Vronsky would be angry.'

'He used names?'

She drained her glass. 'Oh yes. Fortunately, the guy in the corner shop who does deliveries recognised him and told the police where we lived. Of course, they accepted that he was deranged, and listed it as a simple mugging.'

'And was it?'

'I don't know. Possibly. If you go waving money in the London streets ...' Her large eyes turned to him. 'What can be done? He's a liability, but I can't afford private care.'

Giving in to his longing, he drew her to him, pressing her body close to his. 'Glasnost changes things.'

'Does it?' she murmured. 'He's so vocal. Won't someone come to deal with him? And if they do, they'll deal with me, won't they? I've already sent little Anna away to her brother's. I can't risk my baby getting caught in the middle.'

His arms tightened around her, constricting both their breaths. She was right. The Cold War hadn't vanished; the parameters had morphed. With the Mafia surging in Russia, you either joined them or found yourself on a slab. Even for an agent such as himself, he walked a tightrope. Along with a few colleagues, he had joined Operation Rosewood where certain KGB assisted a group in CIA by handing over Stasi data. Put a foot in each camp, he had told himself, but obey rule number one: don't get caught on the wrong side – whatever that was.

'So. You sent me a volume, but you still have the others I left with you?'

'He's hidden them. God knows where. I've searched.'

'*Blyat.*' The Professor was only safe if he maintained silence and burnt the past; in this new peace, no government would risk embarrassing outages, and both sides accepted that former double agents had been left sitting in their homes wondering when their secret services might knock on the door with a cry of treason.

'I won't let you come to harm, darling.'

She pulled out of his embrace, her dark eyes holding him, just as they had the first time. 'But if he continues, can you really protect us? Or will I wind up dead in a convenient car crash while I'm driving him to a doctor? We know how many times that's happened.'

Her bottom lip trembled, and he longed to sweep her away to safety. He was no oil painting, but she had once compared him to a medieval statue. Would she agree to leave London and build a new life with him? It would be safest to leave her children behind.

'Vronsky,' she said, placing her hands on his chest. 'I'm not asking for myself, but the children must be safe. Promise me.'

'*Konechno*. Of course.' But his powers were waning. He kissed her fiercely, and felt her hips hard against his erection. His tongue probed her mouth, her hands meshed in his hair. A Judas kiss?

Returning to his landlady's place, he sat for a while in his boxer shorts, smoking three cigarettes, one after the other, lighting the next from the last. He let his thoughts swirl: how to save her and save himself. Seeing her once more, he realised he could not live without her. The KGB might dissolve, but Annaliese, *his Anna*, was the balm. A tentative plan formed, shrouded in cigarette smoke. Finally, he dressed and walked to a nearby pub run by a former sympathiser. In the safety of a back room, he made calls, the final one being to Sergeant Frank Dolomeyer. The agent was an American ex-military, with an enormous chip on his shoulder against his home country that Vronsky had fully exploited. Addicted to cocaine, Dolomeyer had chosen to remain in Berlin after the fall of the wall, accepting small jobs as a hired thug, and snorting his full. He could trust Dolomeyer.

'Hey, Mac.' The ebullient tone suggested he was coming down from a high.

The Americanism had always irritated him, which was probably why Dolomeyer used it. 'Loose ends,' Vronsky said. 'A can of worms needs closing. Alexei's sick in the head and shouting things he shouldn't.'

He heard the American's intake of breath and a quick chuckle. 'Gone doolally, eh?'

'Something like that.'

'Cool. Watcha wanna do, Vronsky? There's kids, eh?'

He checked his desire to swear. 'What do you mean?'

'C'mon Mac. I've done some insurance digging on those I met. Good thing, seeing as Gorby threw us to the winds. Alexei has an adult son, Stephen, and a little girl called Annette, Annie, Anna. Whatever! Whaddo they know?'

'For fuck's sake. Nothing.' He was only too aware of the American's enjoyment of violence: he'd made use of it often enough. 'The daughter's much too young to be aware of anything, and the son lives a separate life in East London.' He stopped. Dolomeyer didn't need more information. 'They're ignorant.'

'But the wife was one of us. So, is she gonna play ball?'

'Yes.'

'What makes you so sure?'

'Let's not talk over the phone.'

The American gave another quick chuckle and cleared his throat. 'Okay, Mac. Under a train? Car crash? Overdose? Venue? I'm assuming we can't do Kalashnikovs at dawn anymore, seeing as we're all one big loving family eating McDonald's.'

'Berlin.' For his plan to work, he had to take Alexei out of the country. Easiest to hide inconsistencies from relatives if the information came from abroad, and he still had contacts in that city.

'Both agents in one kaboom? You know what I always say: leave it to me for the usual fee.' Dolomeyer laughed.

The hairs on Vronsky's arms rose in protest. *Blyat*, no, he thought. Anything but that. He wasn't handing *his Anna* to anyone without a fight.

'Berlin,' he repeated. 'See you in Berlin, regular venue, and we'll sort details.'

THREE

London

OCTOBER 2021

THE VIOLENCE OF THE MUGGERS' attack on the platform had rattled Anna, but she did her best to hide this from her sister-in-law. As a child, she had experienced terrible nightmares, recalling how Dolly would enter her room with fuzzed hair and an irritated expression, insisting that sleep was precious. Would this incident cause a resurgence of old dreams? Despite never having seen the man before, the name, Vronskiy, held a ghostly resonance.

'What did the police want?' Dolly manoeuvred the car along the residential route, ignoring Anna's injuries. Her fingers bore chunky rings that clanked against the steering wheel like knuckle dusters. Anna hesitated. It took five minutes to drive from the station, twenty to walk. What should she say? The long road began with cramped bijou terraces and gave way to semi-detached and detached as it rose to a wooded triangle of land. Determined to be brief, she outlined the assault and rescue of her laptop, falling silent as they eased onto the semicircular driveway.

'Bloody kids on the estate.' Her sister-in-law flicked her fringe in exasperation. 'A couple of years ago, my sons got mugged for their phones. The police were useless.' She plugged the red Polo into the electric socket and raised an eyebrow. 'But you're okay, aren't you? You've got another pair of leggings?'

Anna stood with crossed legs as if her injury was a source of embarrassment, while Dolly unlocked.

'Why don't we go shopping so you can buy new? I'm sure your wardrobe could do with an upgrade. Fancy the mall at Stratford or Bluewater? Girlie day out? Lockdown made us sooo boring.'

Would retail therapy count as helping her brother's marital relations, she wondered? Her sister-in-law went through the familiar motions of throwing the car keys in the Japanese bowl on the hall counter, and shrugging off her designer jacket to examine her reflection in the large mirror. All Anna wanted to do was slump in a chair.

Ascending to the guest bedroom, Dolly launched into complaints about how Stephen had read some texts on her mobile, and how the whole situation had got out of hand. Was there no privacy in a marriage? He shouldn't have seen them; it was underhand behaviour, and she'd been in the bath. And how on earth did he know her password? Oh, alright, it was her date of birth, but even so. She warbled on, ending with: 'Your brother is so secretive, it wouldn't surprise me if he was the one having an affair.'

Exhausted, Anna put down her rucksack and placed her laptop on the white desk under the window. The room had undergone a transformation since the last time she'd visited, changing from mushroom to a periwinkle blue, and she gave the obligatory praise. Dolly smiled and it dawned on Anna, she must have botoxed her lips, but then, Dolly tended to change her appearance with the seasons.

In comparison, Anna's life was unchangingly flat. A house overlooking the North Sea, one beautiful son who preferred staying with his grandmother, an undemonstrative husband, Alex Faver, high-flying Foreign Office civil servant. On a CV, it sounded a success story, but when she turned thirty, she found herself envying bookish characters with their fervent declarations and passionate sex. She could imagine her Ukrainian Samaritan gathering her into his arms ... She blinked and strove to concentrate on how best to help her brother.

Stephen and Dolly were approaching their fifties, whereas Alex was past that milestone. As they all aged, the divide between Anna and her family had widened, with Alex staying in his London flat during the week to accommodate his long working hours. What could she say to her sister-in-law? That no marriage was perfect? That Stephen was a good man? So many well-worn phrases to pick from.

'Coffee or something stronger?' said Dolly. 'You're looking peaky. I thought you said you were okay?'

'I'm fine. Coffee, please.'

'Coffee first, then you can change. It doesn't look too bad: a shot of caffeine will sort you.'

With a quick wipe of her scraped knees, Anna trekked downstairs after Dolly, sitting on the bar stool to watch the theatrical show of grinding beans, harvested from some obscure mountain, costing double the price of supermarket beans. Dolly's jewellery rattled in tune to the whirring machinery.

'What about this new coffee machine?' Dolly said, tipping the pungent powder into a muslin sleeve. 'The only way to live is to imagine an audience awaits you. Buy expensive. Eat the best. Dress expensively. Hang around with the It Crowd.' These frequently repeated mantras had little effect on Anna. She considered her sister-in-law's comments to be motivated by jealousy for the Faver family fortune, and even though Anna had had to sign a prenuptial contract when marrying Alex, money did not concern her. Love was love. To which Dolly always replied: *But Love, like Butter, goes better with Bread.*

The machine bubbled.

'Well, don't be coy. Are you gearing up to be my marriage counsellor or not?' She sniggered. 'As I said on the phone, I'm not cross with you. It's him. The nerve. And if you mention menopause, I'll slap you. I may be fifteen years older, but I'm still only twenty-one.'

The machine hissed approval, and they took their coffees past the gleaming ash staircase into the living room. Since her last visit, Dolly had hired a painter to coat the walls in chalky white, and dot it with new art in coloured frames. Words like Sanderson, Farrow & Ball, Marks & Sparks flew into the conversation.

Anna wondered how her brother afforded all the treasures that popped up on Dolly's Instagram feed: the stylish new sofa, the gallery prints, the garden ornaments. He was a civil servant, working at a lower pay grade to Alex, and Dolly worked as a part-time conveyancer.

'Does Alex still spend every week up in London?'

'Yes, but it's okay. It works for both of us.'

'God, Anna, if you dressed better, you'd be a Stepford Wife.' She eyed the torn leggings.

Anna wilted. 'Actually, it does hurt. Do you have any plasters?'

'My dear! You should have said. You're such a martyr.' Dolly fetched a small first-aid kit from the cupboard and thrust it in her direction. 'I thought it was only your computer that was worrying you. Is it working despite having been in the middle of a battle?'

Anna felt the usual need to defend herself. 'Alex works under the Official Secrets Act, so I'm not allowed to back up documents on the Cloud. I use a hard drive at home.'

'And you live through that computer, don't you? At your age, you should live in the real world, not a virtual one.'

'I'm a mother and a translator, and I've got a website now.'

'Everyone's got a website.' Dolly's beads shook in disdain as she sipped her coffee.

Upstairs, Anna winced as she peeled off her leggings to examine the broken flesh on her knees, but the image of the silver pin scar and the bloodied hand rose like a ghost before her, and she hastened to clean and cover her superficial scrapes with a large plaster. Her laptop beckoned from its case on the desk. Had he rescued it or was it damaged? She watched as it fizzed into life, puffing a small sigh of relief; mentally sending a prayer of thanks to her saviour.

On her return to the living room, Dolly was texting in joyous rapidity while she laughed.

'By the way,' she looked up from the sofa as Anna entered, 'with all the brouhaha, I forgot to tell you. I found three copies of a novel with your father's writing inside. I don't know why Stephen kept them in his study, but I thought you should have at least one copy. A keepsake. You don't have anything of his, do you?'

'You found a book written by my father?'

'No. A translation of Anna Karenina in English, with notes all the way through in what I'm pretty sure is his handwriting. Given your line of business, I thought you'd be interested. According to Michel, some of the annotations are in Russian.'

'Michel?' A curl of consternation ran through her. 'That's him? He's the man? You let him go into Stephen's study?' Both Alex and Stephen had locked and secured their studies during Covid as part of the government regulations for those working from home, and it was now the norm.

A sly smile crossed her sister-in-law's face. 'We broke in while he was at work.' She laughed at Anna's expression. 'Michel's idea. I told him there's nothing in there, but Michel likes to play a game of smoke and mirrors, pretending he's a spy. He learnt to pick locks from someone in Paris, and I thought: what a hoot. So he opened the door, and we looked around, and he spotted the books. Fascinating!' She giggled.

Anna's sense of outrage fought with her curiosity as she fished for a reply.

'Haven't you ever read Anna Karenina?' Dolly raised her eyebrows in scorn. 'It's a classic, you know. The characters are Darya, nicknamed Dolly, who's Stepan's wife. And of course there's you, Anna. A married woman who has an affair with Count Vronsky. Spooky, eh? Perhaps you will succumb to my Michel's charms.'

'Vronskiy?' Anna echoed.

'Yes. That's Michel's surname, although it's spelt differently. And then there's Anna Karenina's husband, Alexei, like your Alex.' Bangles rattled as her hands rose and fell in gesticulation. 'Can't remember the whole thing, though. Dipped into it at uni. Seriously long novel.'

Speechless, Anna frowned at Dolly's levity.

'I can't imagine why Stephen had them in his study,' continued her sister-in-law. 'They've no value and it's only the three opening parts. God knows where the rest are. Did Stephen ever speak about them?'

'The books? No.'

Stephen had been the sole person to clear their parents' flat in Kensington when they died. As a child, apparently, she had had tantrums when he failed to rescue her stuffed bear. But when she grew up, he had little to add about their death. Whatever John and Annaliese Blount were doing in Berlin remained a mystery, with Stephen's only insistence being they wouldn't have taken a holiday as their father had advanced Alzheimer's. It was the unsolvable family puzzle.

Looking out of the French windows, Anna stared at the acer trees, branches waving wildly in the wind, their leaves red and smoky; changeling trees that went from forest green to magnificent reds to bare branches. In the autumnal gloom, her reflection ghosted across the pane.

Smoke and mirrors.

Dolly's mention of the Tolstoy characters, coupled with that phrase, once again, raised memories of her nightmares.

Annaliese. What are you hiding from me? Who is that child? Where is Frond Skis? Where is he? Smoke and mirrors, damn them. Smoke and mirrors.

In each nightmare, the words varied: sometimes her father wanted to kill *Frond Skis,* sometimes he wanted to talk to him, but *Frond Skis* was always missing behind a screen of *smoke and mirrors.* And she would find herself trapped in terror as her mother denied *Frond Skis* was there. The name was so bizarre, and yet her saviour had said: *Vronskiy.* Oleksandr Vronskiy. Not Russian, but Ukrainian. Not *Frond Skis,* but ...

While Dolly continued to text, Anna stood watching the

leaves whirl across the lawn, desperate to quell an irrational sense of panic. Her Samaritan, Vronskiy, was too young to have been an acquaintance of her father's. Was her sister-in-law's new man, also a Vronskiy, an old man returned from the past? And if so, why now? The conundrum joined the many pieces of her life puzzle that offered no easy explanation.

FOUR

berlin

NOVEMBER 1991

THE VIOLENCE of John Blount's attack in the hallway had rattled him. Nobody had expected the old man to fight so hard when they urged him into the car. Vronsky had made arrangements for Dolomeyer and Annaliese to travel by ferry and road, avoiding airports, while he flew to Berlin to prepare the ground. But Blount had flailed and punched when they attempted to take him from the flat, and Dolomeyer had had to administer a heavy dose of Oramorph, rendering him unconscious. Throughout Annaliese had wept, which was uncharacteristic for her. All in all, it wasn't an auspicious start to their plan.

Throughout his journey to Berlin, he worried she would change her mind, but a day later, the car drew into the city and Dolomeyer confirmed an uneventful ferry crossing.

With Blount still heavily drugged in the hotel room, he persuaded Annaliese to join him, in order to remove her thoughts from the nightmare of her husband's condition. They could walk around the newly reunited city for a glimpse of the future and he would probe her intentions. In London, she had refused to guarantee leaving her children, even though their plan was unlikely to work if she included them. *Blyat.* Their future somewhere else was his goal; London and Berlin would become their past, as would their names.

Reflecting on his first memory of Berlin, he remembered 27 October 1961, when he had been a ten-year-old youthful cadet with shiny boots and short hair, staying with a troop of military youth on the outskirts of the city. The training camp was his first trip away from home, and he revelled in all the activities. The leaders kept a radio blaring day and night as if to subdue their chattering with its decibels. Or to feed them with patriotic music. Or both. A hush spread throughout the camp when a broadcaster spoke about a standoff between Russia and USA at Checkpoint Charlie, barely ten miles away. The Americans, they said, were determined to break through to the Russian side. World War III was on its way. For a day, they oiled guns and pretended to shoot one another in a mock game of Russians versus Americans. They rushed to hear each news item, wondering when war would be declared. Not just any war – Nuclear war – and shivered in delight. Do not worry, said the newscaster, Russia has retaliated by sending ten M-48 tanks to the barrier. We are the mightier power. We will win.

'Stupid Americans!' cried one of the leaders. 'Who do they think they are! Those capitalist pigs – we'll blow their heads off!'

Everyone cheered. Too young to remember the last war, the boys considered a new war as good news. Maybe one of them would get to drive a tank or drop a bomb or shoot an American soldier for real. But much to their disappointment, the critical incident died, and they all moaned. They might not have been shaving, but they were ready for battle. He could look back and laugh. Sometimes. But he never forgot. Beneath a layer of peace, someone was always spoiling for a fight. And therein lay his talents: a loyal assassin for the Communist Party and Mother Russia.

But now, the trouble was glasnost. What next?

In a neat woollen coat and shiny black boots, she crossed the road to meet him, accepting his brief kiss on her cheek. The cold had pinched her face and her lipstick lay heavy on her sensual mouth.

'How is he? How are you?'

In response, she half closed her eyes, allowing him to take her arm and steer her towards the city centre. Winter had swept through early, dusting pre-Christmas paraphernalia with a fine lacework of frost. Wrapped in scarves and hats, people ambled, laughing and greeting one another in raised voices. The new Berlin was hip, according to Dolomeyer. They went past the S-Bahn at Warschauer Strasse and down to Potsdamer Platz. The former no-man's land was still a ruin. She looked around.

'All the cul-de-sacs have gone,' she said.

'It took two weeks to dismantle the wall.'

'My God.' Her breath rose in the air. 'But I can still see which side I'm on.' She pointed to the ornate nineteenth-century scrollwork that curled over a doorway, turning the windows into slices of iced grey cakes. 'West Berlin,' she said. 'Very nineteenth century, except for the bomb damage.' As they turned right, she gestured down a long, straight road that fed to the horizon. 'There! The GDR homes. I always thought they resembled giant Lego.'

Vronsky gave his customary huff of laughter; being at her side inflated him with happiness. 'Quick to build,' he observed. 'We never wanted the East Germans to feel like victors, so those big apartments were a kind of justice. Now the West Germans are giving them money as presents and welcoming them into capitalist businesses.' He puffed out his cheeks. 'The GDR is dead. Long live united Germany!'

'Why are they digging up all the roads?'

'They're uniting the infrastructure. Trickier than they thought.'

He lit two Marlboro cigarettes, handing her one, feeling nothing could dampen his spirits. Tomorrow former agent Alexei would die, and Annaliese would be free to run away with him. 'I always loved East Berlin,' he exhaled. 'I love the Ampelmann traffic lights, and the Trabant cars. And because Western capitalism is a market for nostalgia, I'm keeping mine in a friend's garage. It's in perfect condition, and one day it will be worth a fortune to collectors, or so I'm told.'

She rewarded him with a brief smile, slapping his arm, leather glove to padded coat. 'Come on, Comrade Millionaire. Let's go for a drink at our old haunt. I don't want to celebrate, but I don't want to cry. Not yet. Is the theatre bar still standing?'

'Yes but the new government is cutting chunks from certain buildings to exhibit in a museum about Berlin. They intend to catalogue the differences between East and West for the younger generation. *Blyat.*'

'Fuck,' she agreed. 'If they're so misty-eyed, they could have kept the two halves separate.'

He flicked ash. 'Tourist boards will replace the KGB and Stasi.'

She leaned against him, her scarf heavy with perfume, and all else vanished. Her beauty had never failed to bewitch him. He had to pull off this last stroke. Not Operation Rosewood, but Operation Anna. She had used one of the volumes to send him a note before they set off.

To my darling Vronsky,

See you at the usual spot.

Love from your Anna. x

The fact that she had secreted this in the book's spine was a hopeful sign. In the past year, he had located six of the volumes, leaving only two missing. His instructions were to destroy all copies to ensure their agents' identities remained hidden, and he wondered if she'd brought the remaining ones with her as requested. *Blyat,* but her husband's last outburst had thrown everyone into confusion.

His greatest niggle was would she agree to leave her children? She had rarely spoken of her daughter, and once, when he had questioned the possibility of his paternity, she had laughed and insisted the dates were wrong. 'Anna,' she had said, 'is my doppelgänger – not a brow or nose or mouth in likeness of any man.' It didn't worry him; he didn't want children. All he questioned was the strength of her attachment to her family. To start a new life with a new identity, it was safest done without a small identifiable child in tow. He sucked in a breath, allowing the cold air to rush into his lungs, confident in his powers of persuasion.

Tonight's plan was for them to take in the sights and return to his apartment, where they could make leisurely love. After, he would wipe her tears as he drove the logic of his argument. Pillow talk. That's how she had always referred to their post-sex conversations. Talk charged with emotion and passion while their bodies were entwined; brief moments when the rest of the world could go to hell. Pillow talk. The sweetest confidences of all.

FIVE

London

OCTOBER 2021

'THESE BOOKS,' said Anna, as she eased herself onto the petrol-blue sofa opposite Dolly. The antiseptic cream had turned her knees to fire. 'You said there was a character called Vronsky.'

Dolly flicked her plum fringe. 'Don't you know about Anna Karenina?'

A shrug was easier than beginning a game of one-upmanship. Anna tilted her chin as her sister-in-law pushed a plate of crustless salmon sandwiches across the glass coffee table.

'It's a bit like saying you've never heard of Dickens' Christmas Carol. Anna Karenina is a Russian classic. Pre-Communism and all that.' The coloured bangles jingled as she leaned over to nab a triangle and pop it in her mouth.

Anna parried. 'I know the title, but who reads Tolstoy today?'

'True. Rich people, trains, furs and samovars. That's

Anna Karenina,' continued Dolly with her mouth full. 'Kiera Knightly played Anna in a recent adaptation. Did you see it? No? Everyone loves the story because of the love triangle, and the decadence. A married woman – your namesake – begins an affair with a young, dashing soldier called Count Alexei Vronsky.' She ate another quarter, undeterred by Anna's silence. 'But it's very depressing, and very long. Nothing like a modern rom-com. Plus, your father's editions have tiny print. So, not much fun to read.'

'Are you going to show me or lecture me?'

'Of course.' Wiping her mouth, Dolly's eyes crinkled with a sly smile. 'But I thought you were here to talk about my toy-boy! Don't you want to know more?'

The sandwich suspended halfway to Anna's lips. 'You've begun an affair with a younger man? I thought...' She hated the way it sounded prudish.

'It's not what you think,' said Dolly. 'He approached me – not the other way around. He's such a gorgeous man-boy. Michel Vronskiy, half French, half Russian. A student. God, it's desperately romantic.'

'And you spell the name v-r-o-n-s-k-i-y?'

'Yes.' She raised an eyebrow at Anna. 'I'll admit to a certain fascination when we found the book.'

'The man who helped me at the station was called Vronskiy. Spelt with an iy.'

'Oh. So your knight-in-shining armour is a relative of my boy-wonder?'

'Possibly.'

'Must be!'

Anna gulped her cold coffee, making a face.

'I'm not stupid.' Her sister-in-law burst with sudden justification. 'A puppy is for life, but not a man-boy. A man-boy is for a season. I didn't cope well with lockdown because it was unbearably dull.' She flicked her fringe again. 'Dull is what you and Alex do, but not me. God! I've been itching to live it up a bit. So I'll admit to being flattered. Who wouldn't have been? He's gorgeous. All biceps and sexy eyes. He works behind the counter in the Deli and gets an hour between two and three, so I invited him home for lunch.'

Anna's mug sloshed, leaving a brown bobble on the glass, that she tried to wipe with a finger.

'Now I think about it, Michel said something about a brother coming to visit. Coincidence? Life's full of them, I suppose.' Dolly licked her lips.'Oh, but Anna. He's wonderful. Bouncy and mischievous. When I told him Stephen and I kept secrets from one another, he suggested we break into his study. Someone in Paris had taught him to pick old-fashioned locks. It was such a hoot! I felt like a teenager again. He told me that opening a lock was a magician's trick of smoke and mirrors – easily done! He wanted to show-off to me. And I was so impressed. I'd never felt so alive as when –'

'He's a thief!' Anna bridled. 'A common thief.' *Smoke and mirrors. Where is Frond Skis?*

'He's not a thief, for God's sake.' Dolly touched her beads like a rosary. 'He asked to borrow a book, not steal it. And I'm telling you this because I've nothing to hide. Your brother and I are modern. We may be fifteen years older than you, but you're the one who's old-fashioned. And right now, it's Stephen who's behaving oddly.'

'You've allowed a stranger into your home, and he's –'

'Michel's not a stranger.' Dolly brushed crumbs off her tailored trousers. 'And I thought his little act of anarchy was impressive. So we had a look around together – not that there was anything worth seeing – and,' she emphasised, 'there was no smoking gun.' She smirked and tossed back the remains of her coffee. 'But Michel found these three copies of Anna Karenina on the top shelf, and we examined them. They're clearly your father's, with some odd Russian scribblings inside. When he asked to borrow a copy to check if it was valuable, I couldn't see the harm, because I suspect they're worthless. They're in poor condition.'

Anna's hands tightened on her knees, unsure if stealing an old book classified as a heinous crime in Stephen's eyes. It was definitely a betrayal of trust. Her brother had never entrusted her with these books, and for a moment, she wondered which was the greater transgression. 'And you promise he'll return the book?'

'Of course. Anything else you want to know, my child detective?' She flicked a final crumb.

'Dolly, don't you understand? Stephen's worried, and I'm here because I care about him.'

'So do I! We've been married for donkey's years.' Dolly's face softened. 'It'll all blow over, little one, you'll see. I took the remaining two books out of his study and placed them on the top shelf in this room, and he hasn't even noticed they've moved, or if he has, he's said nothing.' She sighed. 'God! He's been so preoccupied this past year. Changed. You know what I mean? He doesn't talk to me anymore.'

'He's not a chatty person.' Anna scanned the bookshelves but saw nothing out of place.

'For God's sake, he's changed, I'm telling you.' Dolly slapped her hands on her thighs. 'Wouldn't you notice if Alex changed? But perhaps you wouldn't. When was the last time you had a good shag? I've only to look at you and your husband to know you have problems in that area. He never takes your hand or –'

'Stop.' Anna rose, returning to look over the autumnal garden. She didn't want Dolly to see how angry she was.

'You know what I think? I think those romantic novels you translate are nothing more than a substitute for actual sex.'

'Oh, for God's sake, stop Dolly.' She pressed palms to her ears.

But Dolly had not finished. 'You were so quiet as an adolescent. I was always hoping you'd party, break out with a bit of your own anarchy, but Stephen insisted on sending you abroad to those French families every summer, where they treated you as if you were five. Maybe that's why you don't know what I'm talking about. I'm telling you, in the past year Stephen's become withdrawn, and gone off sex, and I don't believe it's anything to do with Michel.'

'He told me how upset he is.'

Her sister-in-law carted the plates and mugs to the kitchen, before ripping a feathery scarf from its snake-like coil on a peg in the hall. She wound it several times around her neck. 'Tell you what,' she called to Anna. 'Forget the books: I'll show you later. Come to the Deli to meet this gorgeous young man.' She pulled a faux-fur jacket from the hallway cupboard. 'You'll see. It's all froth and fun.'

'Should I bother? You're going to ask for a divorce, aren't you?' Anna came to her side in rigid indignation.

Enveloped in a fluff of fake leopard, Dolly smiled, her eyes dancing in amusement. 'No, little one. And neither will Stephen.' She tucked a strand of Anna's black hair behind one ear. 'Come on. If we hurry, we'll catch him on his lunch break. You'll like him, and you'll see – it's nothing to worry about. Just a dalliance. It's the way we live.'

Pulling on her practical padded jacket, Anna followed silently, mulling over the conversation. Dolly had never flaunted her affairs in such an open fashion. If it was as transient as she suggested, why take Anna to meet him? *More smoke and mirrors?*

SIX

berlin

NOVEMBER 1991

'THESE BOOKS,' Vronsky said as they walked from Potsdamer Platz through the city to Alexanderplatz, arriving at the base of the Berlin Television Tower. 'Where might he have hidden them?'

But Annaliese ignored him, tilting her head upwards to gaze at the bulbous tip of the enormous metal spire. Someone had told him that the height surpassed the Eiffel Tower, and he knew the viewing platform acted as an East German landmark for both sides of the city. Although hoping for a serious discussion, he shelved it with a sigh. She was too distracted, and it was more important to raise her spirits.

In the run-up to Christmas, orbs of coloured lights dotted the streets, replacing the former greyness of a divided city, and he hoped it encouraged thoughts of future joys. For himself, the gush of commercial enterprises in former Soviet territories seemed gaudy, but the new buzz word was selfishness, and he intended to be very selfish indeed – once business was complete.

As the sun began its descent, they rose in the elevator,

surrounded by tourists speaking different languages. The group tumbled out, and he had a sudden vision of his reality. Soon he would no longer be an agent on a mission, but the same as all the other polyglots around him. He took a sideways glance, hoping to gauge her reaction, but her face was impassive.

The platform rotated, degree by degree, throwing Vronsky into disorientation. He gripped the guardrail, aware of Annaliese's silent and concentrated profile. What was she thinking? In this moment, she faced west, but as they moved, she looked out towards the old GDR. Below them, he could see the districts of Pankow and Marzahn with their rows of Soviet apartment buildings, punctuated by deserted warehouses and derelict blocks and roadworks. If she wanted to live here, she could rent an entire block for a couple of roubles. But he could not guarantee her safety in Berlin.

The turning platform took them to face the Napoleonic Brandenburg Gate, and far to the horizon, he could make out the decommissioned airport, now called the Tempelhofer Freiheit. The rotation continued, bringing them back to the western sector with its linden-lined roads and squares, and grander districts, a faded glory of stuccoed pre-war buildings.

Was it so hard for her to make a choice between life and death? Between pre-glasnost and post? From their height, the city showed the scars of the dismantled wall. His eyes traced along Bernauerstrasse on the eastern view. So many deaths in the no-man's-land, and all that remained was the pale earth, like the knee of a child with a freshly torn off plaster. How quickly the old guard had dismantled the border. Weeks to go up and weeks to go down. He had read they were intending to rebuild the

Reichstag dome to be energy efficient. *Blyat.* What did that even mean?

'Do you think they'll get rid of this tower?' she asked.

He hoped not, and had a sudden territorial urge to protect it. 'No,' he said.

'But the Eastern Bloc built it. They'll tear it down in their rush to spread Western values.'

He put a hand over hers as they rotated once more across the East-West scar. 'Some things will be kept, some will go on.'

'Neither capitalism nor communism?'

'Pragmatism and fast-food companies will be rapid, but the rest will change slowly. It will require committees.' He laughed at the thought of the Americans requesting the German capital change from Bonn to Berlin. Anything to de-Russify. 'My guess is Helmut Kohl will consider all options and work slowly.'

'And you, Vronsky? Quick or slow?'

Was she speaking of death? He dropped his voice to a murmur. 'My darling Annaliese. Put it from your mind. I've some money in Deutsche Bank, and some welcome payments from the Americans in Credit Suisse.' God bless the Yankees and Operation Rosewood, he thought; so lucrative for former KGB agents. 'And I've inherited a dacha with acres of land. I thought we might create a vineyard. What do you think?'

Her eyes widened, and the red lips curved into a sardonic smile. 'You capitalist pig.' She looked back to the horizon. 'Oh my God, Vronsky. We lost.'

He felt a frisson of irritation. 'I admit, the Bear is humbled, but it will rise.'

'Don't people realise America's creeping patronage isn't what it seems? Their government wants capitalism to control everything and everyone. The only thing that will matter is money and the poorest will lose.'

'The poorest always lose. And McDonald's always wins,' he said drily.

'But –'

Conscious of others listening, he gathered her close to him. 'Darling, with foreign money and my little dacha, we can step to one side with dignity.' Her reflections would lead to nothing, and he felt his patience slip. But he reminded himself she was mourning for her soon-to-die husband, and relented. He'd never experienced regret at the death of another. Regrets were an alien emotion.

The sun slanted across Friedrichstrasse. He could just make out the sandbanks surrounding the decommissioned Checkpoint Charlie, like tiny blocks of grey butter, and the people moving around them, scurrying here and there, no one to check papers or stop their journeys. They were all ants on an anthill, and the trick was to be the biggest ant in charge of the largest ant army. But failing that, line your bank account.

'What are all those lines criss-crossing the roads? They're tearing the city streets apart.'

'It's tubing. They're uniting the electricity grid,' he said and felt grateful that the scars across Berlin hid as the sun disappeared and the crescent moon rose to bathe everything in shadows. Perhaps then, she would concentrate on their future plans.

'Let me look after you.'

'I have children.'

'As I've said, the children will be safer without you. The intelligence services control operatives through their children and relatives. Instead, take a clean cut with me.'

'Reinvent myself?' The words held a tang of bitterness.

'Who will replace me as the driver of the Trabant for his last car ride? Who will tell the truth to Stephen and Anna?'

The truth? The notion was a bullet. What was she talking about? Nobody ever told the whole truth. The truth depended on the teller. The truth depended on the recipient. A lie or the truth – they were the same thing. She could choose to stay in London and look over her shoulder for the rest of her life, possibly facing coercion or a prison sentence for being a traitor. Or she could put her trust in him and his ability to play their games.

He gave her a quick hug, wishing she would stand firm and embrace his suggestions. How would he manage without the feel of her body next to his? The sudden vision of his neediness appalled him. He was Vronsky. He was a former assassin, although it might be argued assassins never retired. But in terms of his love for her, he would conquer, no matter what it took.

SEVEN

London

OCTOBER 2021

THE DELI SHOPFRONT shimmered under a grey cloud, its red and green striped sign lit by twinkling bulbs. On either side, the dull-fronted bank and the charity shop basked in its illuminations. Inside, miniature plastic skeletons danced on an electric circuit underneath the counter, winking orange and white lights, while felt spiders wafted on gauzy webs in the breezy opening and closing of the door.

Anna's nose twitched with the aroma of sugar-laced Danish pastries and choux buns. As a teenager, she remembered how the Station Cafe used to leave a greasy smell clinging to her clothes; this reincarnation was far more appetising. Exotic cheeses and salamis peppered the shelves, and a cornucopia of European salad options enticed customers towards the front counter.

'According to Michel, the guy who runs this place claims to be Portuguese, but really he's a Brazilian on some dodgy passport.' Dolly's mouth twisted in amusement. 'God knows how he found that out!'

They queued for coffees and Dolly told Anna to bag a seat. Shots of jet-black caffeine hissed like pistons as she manoeuvred between the counter and tables, heading for the back, until a shove almost knocked her over. Grabbing her bag, she turned to the young man who had opened the internal door, and was unapologetically striding to the counter. In a swift motion, he pulled up the dividing hatch, disappearing down a thin corridor towards the rear of the shop.

'Michel?' Dolly flung her arm as if hailing a taxi.

'He's on a break,' said the assistant.

Undeterred, Dolly followed, lifting the countertop and beckoning to Anna.

'I don't think –'

'I'll be two minutes.'

A sliver of light showed large boxes stacked against one wall and a half-open kitchen door. A second later, they were in a grey courtyard, part covered by a corrugated roof. At first, the man did not notice, frowning and fixated on his phone, but when Dolly touched his elbow, he smiled, enveloping her in an affectionate hug. Anna shuffled, looking above to the bird spatter on the plastic roof.

When they broke apart, Dolly waved a bangled hand in her direction. 'Meet my sister-in-law, Anna. She's curious about you.'

His lips curled in an arrogant smile. 'Hello Anna. I am Michel. *Quel plaisir.*' His accent was indefinable. Quasi-French with something rougher in the mix. He was clean-shaven with tousled dark hair and the deep brown eyes of a Latin lover. His white T-shirt sculpted his torso, and he wound an arm around her waist, showing a tattoo that read 'Mama' above the wrist.

She could see the appeal.

'Anna speaks perfect French. You could have an affair with her after me.' Dolly challenged him to disagree. 'Go on, say something in French.'

With a laugh, he waved a hand in dismissal and rotated his shoulders as if he had just released a heavy load. Picking up a packet of Gauloises and a Cricket lighter from an upended wooden box, he lit a cigarette, examining Anna through lidded eyes. With a puff of pungent smoke, he folded his arms across his chest, tucking both thumbs into his armpits. The word *poster-boy* came to her mind.

Dolly cleaved the lingering smoke with a hand. 'Don't tease, Michel. You're doing that sexy thing.'

'Dolly!' His mouth formed a kiss. 'She's naughty, but I tell her I am happy to meet the family.'

'Where do you live in France?'

She watched as Dolly's fingers twirled a short lock of his dark hair, and he stopped her wandering hand to kiss her knuckles. 'I am from Paris. This beautiful lady,' he kissed Dolly's hand once more, 'she has the chic of a Parisian woman.'

Her sister-in-law rumbled with the compliment and Anna was saved the need of a reply by the sound of footsteps descending an external iron staircase into the courtyard.

A taller man appeared on the bottom rung, and her heart turned over. 'You?' said Anna, forgetting his first name. 'Vronskiy!'

His smile bore none of the machismo of Michel's, and he dropped a light kiss on both her cheeks. 'Your knees are okay?'

'Ha!' Michel took up the cigarette like a sword. 'So, this Anna is the woman you saved, my comrade?' His fingers danced in the air.

'This is your comrade?' said Anna.

'My brother,' corrected Sasha, shoving him in the ribs. 'He was born in Ukraine. And you don't smoke, Michel. Is all fake!'

'You're brothers?' Dolly giggled. 'There's no family resemblance. Different colouring and –'

'Same father, but not mother,' said Sasha in amusement.

Anna could feel the blush rising on her face and pointed to the gauzy wrapping on his hand. 'Your injury was worse than mine. How are you?'

'Is nothing.'

'Oh yes, Sasha. Monsieur le Brave.' Michel infused his comment with more smoke and sarcasm. 'Or maybe a fool. You let a boy harm you? He wouldn't have touched me.'

Sasha flicked a good-natured V sign.

Dolly poked Anna's arm. 'Aren't you two meant to go to the police station to make a statement? You have your driving licence? Go. Michel and I can amuse ourselves.'

Sasha patted the outside breast pocket of his jacket. A piece of electrical tape covered the rip from the earlier stabbing, and Anna, magnetised, resisted the impulse to reach out and stroke him.

'I have documents,' he said.

'Go,' Dolly repeated. 'Get a crime number. It's your civic duty. We can have that coffee later, but too many people mug others, and nobody takes any action. Make a difference.'

Anna felt like flicking her own V sign and pointing out Dolly's civic action had never extended beyond haranguing traffic wardens, but Sasha was already three steps in front of her on the road. She put a hand to her cheek, thinking her colour must display her emotions, but he did not appear to notice. Instead, he was looking around and talking about how this was his first time in London, and that the visit was a combination of work and family demands.

'What do you do?' she asked.

'I am driver for BMW. Three-month contract.'

Avoiding the true reason for being in the city, she outlined her life on the Kent coast. 'I used to live here, but now I'm in Whitstable by the sea.' A travelogue wouldn't mean anything to him, she thought, and besides, she was far more curious about him. Where were he and Michel born? What was the age gap? Had they grown up together? Everything about them differed, from physique to accents. He answered a few of her questions, but chattered in broken English about the places he was hoping to visit – *Buck-ing-hum Place* – and the racing cars he was hoping to drive; and whether his money would extend far enough. His open enthusiasm touched her.

When they reached the top of the hill, they arrived at a row of shops, where queues of buses and cars waited at traffic lights. To one side of the busy road, the police station, a low, drab building, hid in an enclave behind overgrown fir trees. Outside was a ramp, and a small poster showing the site was due for closure. On a brick wall, someone had sprayed a slogan about Tories and cuts.

The station was empty, save for posters behind the glass of a notice board. They pressed the buzzer and a tired desk sergeant came into the protected cubicle. He took Anna's details first, recording her answers on the computer, and reading each question in a monotone voice, without hiding his disinterest. Then he turned his attention to Sasha.

'Name, sir?'

She listened, eager to find out more about him.

'Oleksandr Vronskiy.' He gave the spelling.

A large frown spread across the sergeant's face as he typed in Sasha's birthplace: Donetsk, Ukraine. Where was Donetsk, she thought? Her Eastern European geography was abysmal, seeing as so many countries had been sliced and diced. Prussia became Germany, then Germany became East and West, then the Balkans morphed and Yugoslavia broke up. The only way to keep track was to watch the Eurovision Song Contest, an event her husband loved when at home.

From his birthdate, she realised Vronskiy was five years her junior. She gleaned his visit to England was courtesy of a three-month visa organised by BMW, and his profession was listed as saloon car driver. For an address, he debated whether to record himself as staying in Surrey with a cousin, Betsy Vronskiy, or the staff accommodation booked for BMW, and opted for the latter.

She stared at his profile as he spoke, the scar mesmerising her. It looked as if the accident could have blinded him if a few millimetres to the left.

In answering more questions, he explained his lack of an official passport was because he was travelling on a group document with the team, and he slid his visa papers into the steel box under the bulletproof window.

'This work permit runs out in a matter of weeks. Are you about to leave?' The sergeant's frown continued to crease his brow.

'My bosses say they extend it for two months. Covid make delay. We race at Goodwood in February this next year, because we miss September. Lockdown. I am replacement driver for someone who has Covid.'

Faced with the humourless stare on the other side of the perspex, Sasha continued to smile. The man concentrated on the screens, tapping here and there, reiterating questions about the missing passport, and Anna could feel the heat of his suspicions. But Sasha appeared unconcerned, his good humour unwavering even when the sergeant insisted on taking every document for photocopying: driving licence, Ukrainian papers, work permit, details from Human Resources BMW.

'Wait here while I check.'

Enraged, Anna intervened. 'This man came to my aid when someone mugged me. He deserves a medal. What's this about?'

'So you think you won't be leaving in two weeks' time?' repeated the sergeant ignoring her.

'Usual driver is German, but he's sick. I am substitute. Many timetables change. Please, ring my boss. He explain.' His voice held a light tone, which did not appear to go in his favour with his interrogator.

'This is serious. A visa infringement. You may have entered the country with some Germans on a group ticket, but since we came out of the EU, they will also need the correct work-visas. I'm sending these details to the Home Office.'

Sasha shrugged, lifting a hand and letting it slap against his thigh. Pressed to the glass partition, Anna tried again to intervene, but the desk sergeant cut through her pleas.

'Madam. We get many muggings here. In the future, don't travel with a visible computer bag or wave your phone around. Put them in an unmarked canvas bag. Prevention is best.'

Normally reticent, Anna felt herself working up to an English rant, in true Dolly fashion, but she reminded herself her saviour was, after all, a stranger.

'Mr Vronskiy saved me from harm. Shouldn't you be recording that somewhere on your form?'

Without waiting for an answer, the sergeant left the cubicle clutching the papers.

'Is okay,' Sasha said, with good-humoured resignation. 'Russian police much worse in Donetsk.'

EIGHT

berlin

NOVEMBER 1991

THE BERLIN SHOP windows shimmered in the nighttime rows, enticing evening customers to sample their wares, but Annaliese walked in silence beside Vronsky, lost in thought. It was odd how one could be in a city, and not in a city, he thought. His life in intelligence had demanded sharp eyes, but now he saw the streets through a mist; his past and present in contradiction. He recalled the fear he used to inspire; the tap on the shoulder, the victim's pointless struggle to evade capture in the shadows, unattainable freedom but a few feet away. Only those who had inhabited the role of interrogator understood the intoxication, the absolute power of deciding another human's fate; a drug without parallel.

Yet here he was cajoling Annaliese with soft sentiments. Conflicting emotions squeezed inside him as he tried to decipher the reason behind her reticence. In their former lives, they had fallen into each other's arms at every available opportunity, using whatever bed was available. And in London, she had professed agreement with his plan; not happy, but willing to participate, and with an understanding of her limited options. But at this moment in Berlin, her distance made him nervous.

What were her unspoken fears as she bit the tips of her gloved fingers? The memories? They all had reminiscences. Or was it guilt? Given John's diagnosis of six months to a year at best, why stress? Vronsky had only to look at the man to see a walking cadaver, with all the signs of nearing death: confusion, anger; disinterest in food; the inability to dress himself; the loss of recognition of familiar people. The day someone told Vronsky he had this brain disease, he would put a gun in his mouth. At least the KGB training was useful for that beyond the Soviet collapse.

He took her arm, and they hopped on the U-Bahn to Bernauerstrasse. Without the Wall, traversing the city was simpler. When they reached their stop, he guided her towards the cafe, noting that now the sun had disappeared the stars shone in their millions, intransigent in the sky. He breathed in as if to inhale this alternative universe. Once, his superiors steered and directed him, but soon he would be free, and what would he do with so much freedom? He was aware that freedom for some meant abject poverty. But not for him. On the opposite side, large diggers stood motionless, casting monolithic shadows, resembling a miniature of the Soviet War Memorial at Tiergarten in northeast Berlin.

The Soviet Republic had always liked large structures; it signified power. Would his life's work, his footprint, remain in history, or would the new Russian Federation obliterate him as they obliterated so many others? As to the Wall's fate – it had disappeared, and what little remained, the government had protected belatedly from the never-ending march of tourist entrepreneurs, all eager to sell the broken graffiti'd pieces. It reminded him of the medieval practice of selling the bones of ancient saints and disciples. Currently, the black market flourished – and that was nothing new.

'Did you know they're making a memorial structure to show the faces of everyone killed crossing the Wall?' He tried to engage her from her silent introspection.

She nodded. 'Ridiculous. They died going from one side to the other, but what was it all for?'

'The greener grass?'

She bit the gloved fingertip once more. 'When I think of how many times John and I crossed to the GDR. We thought consumerism and big business were the evils; now everyone's celebrating them.'

'I understand.' He dropped a kiss on her head.

She gave a fleeting smile. 'I'm not much fun to be with tonight, am I? But I keep wondering whether our lives will be better with this new order or worse?'

'We're about to find out.' He spoke lightly before directing the re-conversation to his requirements. 'I need the Anna Karenina volumes. Are you sure you didn't pack them and bring them to Berlin? London was stressful. Perhaps you have forgotten?'

It was as if he hadn't spoken.

She clutched his arm. 'I believed in the cause. Communism was infinitely preferable to Thatcherism. In the North of England – the miners, the suffering. They threw them on a dirt heap. Whole towns ghosted. Rich university students bought their houses for pennies and trashed them, because the properties sold for less than paying for student digs. Families were forced out. My father –'

'– was a shop steward. Yes. I know.' He breathed in to hide his impatience.

'So where do my principles fit in now?' She spat. 'And for that matter, where do you fit in, Vronsky?'

He drew out his packet of cigarettes, wanting to claim they were experiencing the same sensation, but he wasn't sure. 'Did I tell you I was in Berlin the week the gates opened? I came to Checkpoint Charlie and watched an East German and a West German guard put their heads together, discussing how to police the crowd. It was like a board game where someone had ripped up the rules. And the only law was pragmatism.' He thought about his current instructions: find and destroy the books; close the cell. 'We will manage.'

She clutched his wrist as if it held a secret key. 'Have we lost all moral compass?'

'Yes. No. Maybe.' He put the packet away and patted her hand. 'I will protect you. Is that what worries you? Give me the remaining volumes and we'll burn the lot.' He hoped his request sound like an invitation to a party. 'Anna Karenina belongs to the past, but the future is ours, my dear Anna.'

'For God's sake, stop calling me Anna.' She pulled away, a heavy breath clouding in the cold air. 'My husband is dying. Too noisily, some would say, and all you're worried about is evidence and stray volumes. It's not as if I haven't searched. No, I haven't brought them to Berlin. John scribbled in them – God knows what – and hid them when I was out. I opened every cupboard, but we ran out of time.'

She marched ahead and he followed, keeping to her left beside the line of the speeding cars. This was getting him nowhere. He'd have to collect the books himself, which was annoying, but workable. He didn't want to lose sight of the prize: Annaliese. She was unique, even if she bore the traditional angst of all women. She reminded him of the Tolstoy character, but as a Soviet man, he was more straightforward. A gun solved everything.

When she stopped abruptly, he almost tripped over her, and she stared at him accusingly.

'You've never told me your real name. You know all about me. But who are you? Is our arrangement private or are you still working for the secret services?'

Young people pushed past with wild movements and wild eyes, and he gripped both of her hands as if to stop her being swept away. 'I'm with you. Soon this business finishes and I'll get the sign-off from my superior, Stepanov. Then we escape and I promise there will be no secrets in our new life.'

Her mouth hung open in surprise as if he had mentioned a new idea. But it was an empty promise, because he would never divulge his past to her. He kissed her. He was mad with desire, but at the same time made a mental note to return to the London flat for the lost volumes. If the deranged John Blount had written in them as Alexei, there might be sensitive admissions, and besides, Stepanov would insist on seeing them before shutting the files on the Anna Karenina cell.

Her body softened into his, and she made a mew of apology, returning the kiss. He felt her melt, but the chill of winter's arrival forced them to continue moving.

Without warning, she detoured, dragging him up a set of concrete stairs to an open balcony that offered a view over a section of the former Wall. She bit her glove, staring at the cordoned-off section of no-man's-land. An empty guards' watchtower protected the scrubland sheltering between the high walls where iron brackets sagged, devoid of their searchlights.

'Did I ever tell you I met with Stepanov?'

Vronsky hid his surprise. 'You met Stepanov?' Although

his senior, Stepanov was a younger man in post for the past three years. 'When?'

'Just before the end. He didn't tell you?'

'Oh yes. I forget.' But he hadn't. 'He's not a field operative. A desk man. So what did he want?'

'Everything happened so fast.' Her teeth marks set like an animal's into the leather glove. She forced a smile. 'I'm freezing. Let's get to that cafe and I'll tell you.'

NINE
London

OCTOBER 2021

BY THE TIME Anna and Sasha stepped out into the cold sun, she was in full apology mode. How dare they grill him! How dare they treat him like a criminal when he had sustained an injury assisting her. He made light of the incident, suggesting British Police Officers held no fear for him in comparison to Russian soldiers. His blue eyes softened and he suggested a coffee.

'Dolly will wonder ...'

'No,' he said, and she knew it was true. Dolly wasn't thinking about her, and she wasn't thinking about Dolly or Stephen.

'I think, Anna, we met in another life. You are like dream.'

His thought echoed hers, and she felt a skip of joy. Sunlight created a halo through his unruly blond hair, as if somewhere in a European castle, he had escaped from a medieval painting depicting his likeness; Saint Sebastian, injured with an arrow; an angel in black leather. Her heart raced as she led him towards a small green space that opened into a narrow strip of city park. On one side was a Victorian church, and beside it a village-styled tea shop, where cast-iron tables dotted along the decking.

'Let me get these,' she said, feeling on stronger moral ground if the purchase was hers. 'You'll need a new jacket.'

With a shrug, he picked at the electrical tape that frayed over the torn sleeve and accepted her offer. Was the bravado for her benefit, or did he hold little value for material things?

They sat facing one another, steam rising between them, and she found his intense gaze both unnerving and exhilarating. Alex had never looked at her like this.

'So, Anna. Why is your computer your life?'

She laughed, happiness bubbling inside her, and offered a brief outline of her work. They blew on the hot drinks, cupping them in their hands. He had done a stint in the Ukrainian army, he said, before becoming a professional driver. 'Things change. We must change.'

It sounded so profound she wanted to write it down.

She admitted failing to complete her university degree, and her sense of shame. 'Now I translate self-published books.'

'Famous books?' he asked.

'Un-famous,' she said, 'but entertaining stories.'

'So. You are un-famous translator and I am un-famous driver. We are good. Yes?'

They laughed, and as she sipped the coffee, she felt a glow of warmth that had nothing to do with the drink, but when he touched her wedding ring, she drew back in embarrassment. Her husband often worked abroad, she explained, and she was normally to be found at home with her ten-year-old son, Simon.

He professed surprise. 'You have a child? He is ten?'

She knew he meant it as a compliment, but she flushed in embarrassment.

'I have three brothers. Family is important,' he added, with a note of sadness.

'And you? Are you married?'

'No. I live with my father. Michel's mother divorced Papi.'

'In English we say he is a half-brother. Only one shared parent.'

'I want he comes back to Ukraine to see our father. Papi is sick and wishes to see Michel before he dies.'

Before she could express sympathy, her phone rang, and she slopped the coffee, fumbling to take a call from Alex. Without preamble, her husband asked why she wasn't with Simon at Halloween, and she reminded him that Halloween at the Faver Estate was an annual event she had attended many times. 'He doesn't mind that I'm not there; I told you – I'm staying with Stephen.'

Throughout the brief conversation, Sasha listened with open curiosity, and as she finished the call with a curt goodbye, and began mopping the coffee stain, he asked. 'Where is your husband?'

'In Brussels.'

'Why?'

'He's on some sort of EU business.'

Talk of Alex flustered her, and she gathered her things. 'I'm so glad we met again. I wanted to thank you for your kindness.'

He took her hand for a long moment, pressing her palm. An unfamiliar sensation stirred inside her, and she pulled away, but undeterred, he strode by her side as they set back.

'Michel sees your sister?' he asked.

'Sister-in-law.' She saw his confusion. 'That means she's married to my brother.'

'Ah, Michel.' He looked at the sky. 'He is a revolutionary.'

Her lips twitched. 'And can a French lover be both revolutionary and a cad at the same time? Might he ask Stephen how he feels about lending his wife?'

He did not understand her words or the sarcasm. 'In Ukraine, we are revolutionary and democratic. But I, too, worry about my brother.'

Explanations appeared too complex to translate, and she shifted the conversation to remark on the geese in the nearby pond. Once more he displayed a childlike enthusiasm as the birds created ripples that dispersed like foam. For as long as she could remember, she explained, the pond, the Victorian clock and the old Bank had existed, untouched by modernisation, and neither Blitz nor economic catastrophes had destroyed them. They were now walking along a row of semi-detached houses bordering the narrow road.

'Suburbia,' she said. 'This is suburbia, not real London.'

'Suburbia?'

He linked his arm in hers, and she was powerless to refuse. Her fingers longed to touch the silver-pin scar and trace the outline of his lips. He was fire, and she was a moth. The emotions forging through her were absurd and yet too strong to deny. It was as if she had waited for him a long time.

'I make Michel to leave London and he come with me. I am driver and must race at Goodwood in twelve weeks. You know Goodwood race track?'

'Not really.'

But if you're there, I shall visit, she thought.

His brow creased with worry. 'I'm sorry, but Michel is not –'

Her throat tightened. 'I realise that –'

'No. The situation with your sister is –'

'Sister-in-law –'

'– Is not simple.'

'In what way?' Anna searched his face for clarification.

'I find out more and tell you.'

Thank God, an excuse to keep in touch. She felt giddy with relief as they stopped, and he drew her to him. 'I think Michel is in trouble.'

'Because of the affair?'

'Maybe worse things.'

What could be worse? she thought. Perhaps her behaviour might qualify as worse. 'Sasha. I'm married, and marriage is –'

'You are not happy with this man. I hear you on phone, and feel this in my heart.'

A denial died on her lips. The Deli was fifty metres away, and they came into view of Dolly pressed against Michel's arm. Michel was leaning forward, talking to a small plump man with a ponytail, who reclined against a dirty Transit van parked on double yellow lines. Dolly's body language, chin on Michel's shoulder, reminded her of a love-struck teenager, and Anna caught her breath. What did that make her? She'd come to London to speak to her sister-in-law about the affair, and here she was – behaving like a foolish girl.

The men's conversation was raucous and sounded Russian. It ended with the rotund man snatching a padded envelope from Michel and waving a brief goodbye.

'Enough,' said Sasha, striding over to Michel. He spoke

in a harsh tone, then appeared to soften as the three men chatted.

'What took you so long?' Dolly twisted her lips into a sarcastic curl. 'Having fun? I was about to send out a hunting party, but parking is even more of a nightmare near the police station than here.'

The plump man sank into the van, firing up the engine and moving away.

'They almost arrested Sasha,' said Anna.

Michel growled something to his brother, and Sasha shook his head. Then Sasha kissed Anna on both cheeks, Michel kissed Dolly on the lips, and both men walked into the courtyard garden. Their expressions suggested war, and Dolly waved in disappointment.

'Shame. We were having such a good time.' She raised an eyebrow at Anna. 'Getting friendly with Michel's brother? They don't look alike, do they? But perhaps they act alike.'

'What was Michel doing? Dealing drugs?'

'Drugs? God no!' Dolly scoffed. 'He was sending parcels of tea and coffee to Warsaw and Lviv. Apparently, that guy's a delivery driver who shuttles between London and Ukraine on a monthly basis. He takes heavy goods. Cheaper than the post office, would you believe?'

'How would you know? They were talking in Russian.'

'Or Ukrainian. Haven't you noticed how the languages sound the same? I can't tell the difference. Can you?'

Anna admitted she couldn't, and Dolly smirked.

'But I know when a man fancies a girl. Perhaps you can kiss goodbye to your perfect marriage and indulge in a bit of Anna Karenina. It would do you good, and give Alex a wake-up call.' She cackled, rattling the beads at her neck. 'Although, spoiler alert; it doesn't end happily.'

TEN

London

OCTOBER 2021

DETERMINED to avoid Dolly's questions, Anna had plenty of her own. She remembered Stephen mentioning that her father specialised in nineteenth-century military history, and she had a slight recollection of her four-year-old self, running fingers along dark shelves, sniffing the leathery smells, and picking at the cracked bindings in his cluttered library.

Balancing in bare feet on the back of the sofa, Dolly plucked two thin volumes from the highest shelves. With their dull calfskin binding, the books were inconspicuous among the row of glossy hardbacks.

'Stephen and I haven't broached the subject. If he's noticed, he's avoiding an argument.' Without reverence, Dolly dropped them on the floor, and Anna picked them up to marvel at the faded gold lettering.

Anna Karenina,
by Leo Tolstoy.
trans. by Timothy Motts.

'Never heard of this translator,' she said. 'I'll start reading tonight.'

'You'll not read that edition. I told you, the print's too small.' Dolly chinked her rings with mischievous glee. Anna opened Volume I and read the pencilled inscription inside.

This book belongs to Professor John Blount

of Cambridge University.

And my other name.

The writing was uneven and spidery. Was this her father's hand? She had no memory of seeing his correspondence, but Stephen had mentioned their father had Alzheimer's. Many pages bore a mixture of Cyrillic and English scribbling in the margins, seemingly referring to people and places, and she turned her attention to Volume II, noting it bore the identical erratic handwriting, but with a different message.

This book is Vronsky's.

Where is he?

It was as if a stone had hit her stomach. *Where is Frond Skis?*

'Who's Vronsky?' she said. 'Do you know? A friend of my father's? And where's Volume III? Is that the one Michel took?' She placed Volume I and Volume II on the coffee table.

Jumping down from the sofa's back, Dolly fingered her beads in thought. 'Must be. I expect Vronsky is the equivalent of Smith or Jones in Russia.' She tossed her plum fringe. 'Anyway, it's clearly the property of your father, John Blount. So take one.'

Picking up Volume II once more, Anna spread the pages in the middle. After peering at a paragraph, she realised the translation was awful: jerky sentences, awkward phraseology and inconsistent verbs. She puzzled, before examining more annotations.

'Do you think my dad was ill when he wrote it? This writing is so unsteady.'

'Could be. As I recall, his behaviour was challenging, and your mother was a saint.' Dolly picked up Volume I, flicking through a few pages with scant interest. 'But I only met them the once. You'd have to ask Stephen about this. There must be a reason he kept them in the study instead of the living room.'

But asking about their parents always made her brother withdraw, as if the mere mention caused him pain. Stroking the calfskin, she wondered for the thousandth time if her mother and father had ever loved her; 'their little accident'. She had no memory of sitting on her mother's knee or her father reading to her; only the nightmares lingered. With a sense of confusion, she gathered both books and took them to her bedroom for further study.

Over dinner, her brother listened to her account of the mugging and her subsequent criticism of the police. From his swift kiss when he had arrived home, she could tell his mood was dark, and during supper, he and Dolly barely spoke, avoiding all mention of the connection between Michel and Sasha. It was a relief when she could clear the plates and they moved to the living room. The seven o'clock news flickered on the wall as a background to their silence and Stephen finished his third glass of wine. With uncharacteristic diplomacy, Dolly absented herself, throwing on a thick mohair jumper to walk to her office shed. Anna sighed. Perhaps now she could speak candidly, but her brother stopped her mid-sentence.

'Not tonight,' he said. 'Definitely not tonight. It's been a bad day at work.' He took her hand in a quick, brotherly squeeze. 'Thanks for coming. I really appreciate your support. But let's talk tomorrow.' Head bowed, he crossed the living room to pour himself a small vodka from an expensive-looking bottle with a Russian label. 'Sorry Anna, I must complete some emails.'

The blaze of light at the bottom of the garden showed Dolly's shadow behind the blind, and Anna had to concur: Stephen's behaviour was odd. Deep in thought, she picked up a magazine, flipping through the pages without reading. She ought to examine the Anna Karenina books further, but she rubbed tired eyes. The television continued to burble at low volume with news about troops amassing on the Russian/Ukrainian border, and she looked up. Maps followed satellite images as she tried to memorise the shape of the region. Compared to England, Ukraine was vast. Where was Donetsk? Were there castles and churches in Ukraine? Was the schooling the same as England? When the announcer made mention of the Crimea, she thought of Florence Nightingale and Mary Seacole who had once raised their lamps. Was the land Russian or Ukrainian? She knew so little about Eastern European geography. And she knew so little about Alex's job. Where was he in Belgium? She wasn't sure which city he was staying in. Brussels or Antwerp? No wonder she didn't know anything about Ukraine.

The television screen gleamed onto the glass coffee table. Marrying Alex had inevitably created comparisons between her and Stephen's lifestyle. Her mother-in-law, Nina, had once commented that Stephen's home had the opulence of a hotel, but the soul of a hotel lounge; as opposed to the Whitstable house, which was crammed with Victorian furniture and ceramic knick-knacks. What would Nina make of the Vronsky and Vronskiy puzzle? She had always claimed a Russian heritage, but then again, Anna had rarely listened. She gave herself a mental shake: she needed to pay more attention.

The following morning, hoping to catch Stephen in a better mood, she ran downstairs in her pyjamas, but the front door was closing and she caught his scurrying shape under an opal sky as he headed towards the Underground.

In the garden, she saw Dolly in her brightly lit office shed, the window open a crack, mobile clamped to her ear. Feeling unwanted, Anna poured herself a coffee to take back to bed, and opened her laptop. She searched for the unknown translator: *T. Motts.* A solitary page listing disappointed her. There was a small, grainy photograph of a man in a bowler hat, the brim obscuring his face. Long and lanky in a trench coat, the figure held a furled umbrella in a pastiche of a 1950s black and white film, and she wondered if it was fake. According to the brief biography, Timothy Motts, a Cambridge alumnus and friend of G. Burgess, was a recognised interpreter of Russian classics. He died in November 1978. But why would anyone commission him to translate, given his deficient skills?

A ping on her phone, and Sasha's name illuminated.

We meet. We talk about Michel.

A thrill of sweet and sour guilt and happiness ran through her. She had a husband and a son, but she longed to see Sasha again. Outside the window, two pigeons canoodled despite the wintry season and she knew she would not refuse his request. *I am married*, she thought. *But not happily*, he had said.

Alex was twenty years her senior. At first it had not mattered, but over a decade, the age gap seemed to widen. When first meeting him at one of Stephen's work events, she recalled his confidence, his kindness, and his expensive suits. She felt flattered at the way he listened attentively, rather than making fun of her like Dolly. Even when her mother-in-law insisted on a prenuptial contract, it could not dampen her love. She wasn't after his riches – just an escape from her brother's house. Nina Faver had paid for their wedding, with a full photographic album and a honeymoon in the Seychelles, and she had laughed at Stephen's evident relief and his comments about the expense of two boys at private school. Then came the birth of her own child, Simon, a boy to follow his father to Harrow. She loved him beyond words even if he had cut short her studies with his cherubic smile.

It was a fairy tale, despite the low point when Alex insisted on having a vasectomy. He was too old to have more children, he had said, and although they'd argued, she'd swallowed her disappointment. Alex was a good father, and he tolerated Anna's visible dislike of his mother. Why now did she feel their relationship was crumbling? Could one man in a ripped leather jacket change everything? Or had she been seeking him for a long time?

A fresh text from her son Simon showed three photographs of him with his best friend, Callum. The boy was the Head Gardener's son on Nina's estate, and he had become Simon's inseparable chum on weekends. She looked at the gaudy pirate gear and their childish grins under thick war paint. It was Halloween, and he was happy with Nina; she had to quell her jealousy.

Do you like our costumes? We'll be apple bobbing with Granny at the fete and there's a quad race. I'm sure to win. xx

Was she a terrible mother? For a decade, she had weathered Nina's cold eyes and perpetual judgments and tried to mould her views to family expectations, but she was weary of the demands. She texted back kisses and approval and encouragement to him, before texting Sasha.

I can meet you at the Deli. Noon? But she avoided signing with a kiss.

ELEVEN

berlin

NOVEMBER 1991

DETERMINED to avoid asking too many questions, Vronsky examined her quick anxious movements. Something about the streets was haunting her, and he wanted to know exactly what was said when she met Stepanov, but how to get her to talk? They hurried towards their old haunt to find the place derelict with newly boarded windows and fresh graffiti covering the front; one more casualty of regime change.

'Come on.' He pulled her back to the U-Bahn. 'I know a better place. It won't take long.'

He could say that with confidence. Compared to life in the GDR, travelling from Bernauerstrasse to Charlottenstrasse was now fast. He'd spent a decade manoeuvring agents, ferreting information to and from the Kremlin; delivering intelligence to and from the West; all with skill and precision. It had taken false papers and false names to get the Blounts in and out of East Berlin, but now any idiot could jog where once people had risked their lives. He watched her continue to nibble on her glove. *Blyat.* Whatever his boss had said, didn't change the situation. If she went back to England, she could potentially face a prison sentence, and in that scenario, she wouldn't have her children either.

They arrived at a large-fronted cafe that took up an entire building. Taking on the persona of a guide, he told her that the Rausch Schokoladenhaus had created beautiful chocolates for a century, and heaved open the door for her to go through. Condensation speckled the vast windows, and her reddened nose twitched with the aromas.

'You like? Their hot chocolate is the best.'

'I remember this place, but John and I never came in here, because he considered it decadent.' With a sad smile, she stopped to admire the wares. A skilled artisan had sculpted dark chocolate models of the Brandenburg Gate and the Eiffel Tower, eight feet high, displayed in a prominent position. Nearby a large bowl flowed with a liquid cocoa fountain surrounded by a selection of square samples in every hue from creamy white to mahogany brown.

'A family firm,' said Vronsky. 'Not political. The current owner is Jurgen, a very nice man. I've met him once or twice.' He couldn't resist the boast. 'The Nazis loved it.'

'You mean even Hitler had a sweet side?'

It was her first joke of the evening, and he huffed in approval.

In the upstairs cafe, they found an empty spot and slung their coats on the backs of the chairs.

'Is this the Last Supper?' she said.

His hand slid under the table to rest on her knee. 'You know how I feel about you. It won't be the last of anything if you let me help.'

She peeled off the abused gloves while a young waiter hovered for their order. Vronsky discussed the options and deciding she had lost weight, ordered two hot chocolates with extra cream.

'You were going to tell me about Stepanov?'

'Friedrichstrasse was my last drop.'

He gave an encouraging smile.

'I took over John's meeting. He was ill, stomach trouble. So I grabbed the Anna Karenina copy and went to the cafe in his place.'

'You never said.'

'Didn't I?' She pushed back a lock of dark hair. 'There was a tall, lean man sitting with his copy in full view on the table. I sat down opposite and we exchanged the correct words.' She bit her bottom lip. 'He ordered schnapps for us both and thumbed through the book like a librarian. He had long, thin fingers; it was hard to believe he was KGB.'

Vronsky frowned examining his own squat digits. 'I told you. A desk man.' The description of Stepanov was accurate, but it should have been his usual agent, Levin. Over her shoulder, a child's complaint distracted her and a momentary pain crossed her brow. He noticed but said nothing. Unlike Annaliese, his had been a solitary life, so he rarely responded to children's whines. He urged her to continue.

'He had Brezhnev eyebrows,' she said with a faint smile. 'A bit more plucked, perhaps, and I'd say he was in his thirties.'

'Yes, yes.' He leaned towards her. 'And ...'

'We talked. Nothing personal, you understand, but we stayed longer than intended.'

He saw her eyes flick to gauge his reaction.

'He told me his name was Stepanov, and he knew my real name, which unnerved me. So I said Alexei was ill –

making sure to use the codename, and he said that was fine and he trusted me and I should trust him.'

Vronsky stroked the packet of Marlboro in his breast pocket. He had read that cigarette smoking was bad for his health, but he reckoned he had done enough bad things in his life to counteract the effect. Unsettled, he waited for her to speak.

'He told me you had sent him. What do you make of that?' She twirled a strand of hair around her finger, checking his reaction.

He twirled a knife on the table through 360 degrees. He had never given Stepanov orders. That would be against protocol, but it occurred to Vronsky that even before the collapse, things were going awry.

They paused as a round of 'Happy Birthday' broke out behind him, while he thought things through. His young boss used women like taxis and he fought a momentary flash of jealousy. Had she slept with him? It was said his promotion was due to a relative in the Kremlin, a top bureaucrat, so he did as he wanted.

Her face flushed, and he thought she had never looked more desirable than when she trembled.

'We just talked,' she said as if reading his mind. 'I only saw him the once.'

The waiter set the hot chocolate in front of them, and he urged her to use the long-handled spoon to scoop the whipped cream, watching the foam dissolve on her lips. If only they were back at his hotel. In private. He crossed his legs to hide his erection and sipped.

'That's when it happened,' she said.

His throat dried.

'I'll admit, at first I thought it was a trap.' The whipped

cream melted on her spoon and she ladled it into her mouth.

'What was a trap?'

'The meeting.' She sipped the hot chocolate and her tongue poked out to lick the stain from her mouth. 'As I said, we chatted. I don't remember everything discussed.'

She's lying, he thought.

'Then, hell broke loose.'

'In the cafe?'

'No. Outside. People were running down the road, and everyone abandoned their seats to spill onto the pavement.' She sipped again. 'This hot chocolate is divine.'

'And?'

'And Chris Gueffroy.' Her eyes reddened. 'I found out the boy's name later. He was only twenty, and they shot him for trying to cross the divide. They were taking his body out of the no-man's-land. Someone shouted about them arresting his pal, Gaudian. He'd been taken to a certain jail and we all knew what that meant.'

Vronsky shrugged. What was her point? 'They shot quite a few. What did Stepanov say?'

'Nothing. He left.'A tear slinked down her face. 'But looking back, the wall came down eight months later. Eight months! The boy died in February. He was Stephen's age, and the wall came down in November. So young. And his death was pointless.'

'We can't bring them back.' Vronsky wasn't enjoying the hot chocolate as much as he'd hoped. 'So what was the point about your meeting with Stepanov?'

'I had the weirdest feeling.' She struggled to swallow.

'About what?'

'He kept giving hints that the end was coming.' She sipped again and rubbed her nose.

Was that it? The great confession? Two years ago, whispers ignited a storm about Gorbachev's direction. In the Kremlin, some people privately agreed with his strategies, and others wanted to arrest the President for treason. For a week, the army had tried the latter with no success. Throughout the world, the end of the twentieth century was being flattened by a tank of change. You couldn't stop it so you had to get out of the way, and who could predict the layout of the new landscape?

'And so?'

'What were we doing, Vronsky?' she said, hands gripping the half-full glass. 'I thought we were building a better world. Not this capitalist shit. Oh, I know, I know, people talk about personal freedom, but Thatcher did monstrous things to the coal miners in the name of the free market. I could give a speech about the injustices –'

He fought the overwhelming urge to kiss her to keep her quiet. Seeking the past was futile when the future was wide open. 'It's possible that one day the Russians will lead the world again, so let's wait and see. We will rise –'

'It's not about Russia, but communism.' She put a hand across the table, her mouth crooked in a half smile. 'Wait. You're thinking of resurrection? I thought you didn't believe in God.'

TWELVE

London

HALLOWEEN 2021

SHE PULLED A BATTERED velvet box from her wash-bag and placed it on the sink beside her toothbrush. Inside was the only piece of her mother's jewellery she possessed: a gold crescent moon on a thick gold chain. Fastening the links around her neck, she held the pendant between finger and thumb. Sasha had texted to cancel their lunchtime meeting, causing her an irrational depression.

All happy families are the same, but all unhappy families are unhappy in different ways.

She had read the opening to Volume I. Was she unhappy? Dolly had been correct about their sex life, and at that moment, she acknowledged that Sasha's hand in hers had fuelled a desire which was still churning through her body.

Where's Frond Skis? Where is he?

The familiar nightmare took on a new meaning. Perhaps her father had been jealous of the mysterious *Frond Skis*, and if so, might Alex feel the same way if he found out about Vronskiy? She stroked the golden moon, pondering, but a text brought her back to reality.

With two emojis of happiness, Stephen's message said he'd booked a table at the local Turkish restaurant. It was Halloween and he wanted to thank Anna for visiting, adding they'd have a proper talk later that night. Another oddity – Stephen never sent emojis, but at last, she might have some answers.

By seven o'clock, Dolly had changed into muted rust-coloured trousers and a silky top with a rope of thick amber beads setting off her plum hair. 'Do you like them?' She fingered the fat uneven droplets. 'It's Russian amber. Stephen gave it to me a couple of years ago; worth a fortune, or so he claimed. Not sure I believe him.'

'I believe him,' said Anna. 'They're beautiful. He loves you.' Upstairs, sounds of Stephen splashing in the shower filtered down, along with a weary groan. 'Will you be nice to him tonight? He's making an effort.'

Dolly threw a wink before rummaging through her handbag and pulling out *J'adore* – her latest favourite perfume. 'Michel loves this smell. Want some?'

Even though she protested, Dolly doused her, and for a moment, she remembered why Nina Faver disliked Anna's family. Her mother-in-law divided the world into people who were obsessed with sex and designer goods, and people who wanted to save the planet. As a devoted Greenpeace fan, Nina despised Dolly's consumerism, but then she despised a great many things. Sometimes, Anna wondered what had caused Nina to initially dislike her, but she knew she would never ask.

'Were you ever in love?' Dolly drummed one foot as

they waited cross-legged in the living room. 'Romeo and Juliet love? Sapphic love at your boarding school? I saw the way Michel's brother looked at you. It must be exhilarating to find someone who lights up when you come near.'

'Stop teasing.' Anna picked up her phone. 'By the way, I googled a summary of Anna Karenina, and you're right – the character's names are remarkably similar to ours. Stepan Oblonsky had a wife called Dolly, just as you said. Perhaps that's why you married Stephen.'

Dolly cackled. 'Good God, no! Nothing to do with it. Then or now – Russia is so out of vogue at the moment. Of course, if you'd read the novel you'd know it's the husband, Stepan, who has the affair, and his wife forgives him. So I don't see why it can't work the other way around. Subversion of genre and all that.'

'So how long will this – *thing* – last?' Anna gulped her words as her brother descended the stairs in boxer shorts, grey chest hair damp and curling.

'Dolly, where's my ironed shirt?'

Grumbling, the undutiful wife stomped upstairs, while he trailed behind, and Anna gazed at the elongated stripes of light stretching into the nighttime garden, indulging in a fantasy of running her fingers along Sasha's bare torso.

Near the station, a new Turkish restaurant had opened in the wake of a Covid bankruptcy. The servers welcomed them enthusiastically to their table. During the first course, Anna was relieved to see Dolly drinking and eating without comment, as Stephen rambled about past theatre visits, and their youngest son's successes at university. Anna answered in monosyllables, and he turned the topic to future holidays abroad.

'Now the world has opened up, a metropolitan jaunt might be affordable, don't you think, Dolly? We could go to Berlin. I've read it's one of the top destinations this year.'

Berlin? Why choose that city? Anna gulped her wine.

Dolly toyed with the Russian amber beads. 'Croatia, I think.' From the set of her jaw, she was determined to be awkward. A vibration alerted Anna to a text, but she ignored it. Stephen asked after Simon and his love of nature. 'A regular little David Attenborough, your boy! Or perhaps a Greta Thunberg in ten years' time.' Anna had never thought of her son in those terms, but realised her brother was attempting a clumsy compliment.

Scraping back her chair, Dolly rose. 'Sorry but I'm going out for a vape. Leave you two to chat.'

They shuffled their feet under the table, unsure where to begin or end.

'I have questions,' said Anna.

'Okay.'

'Do you see Alex at work?'

'I'm not at the Foreign Office.' He looked at her in surprise. 'Well. Sometimes.'

'Sometimes you see him or sometimes you work for –?'

'What's this about?'

'The man who saved me seems to have visa problems.'

He laughed. 'Oh God. I thought – Is that your main concern! All foreign nationals working here have visa problems. You need the Home Office and –'

But Dolly's return cut the conversation short as she moaned about the lack of smoking areas at the back of the restaurant. They struggled through the rest of the meal, finishing with Stephen ordering black coffees without dessert. Anna's cheeks ached from fake smiling, and she sensed Stephen felt the same as he sorted the bill with an uncharacteristically large cash tip. The warring couple had drunk too much to fill the awkward silences, and as Anna finished her glass, she imagined the three of them – like tiny figurines dancing around the rim; one step out of line and splash or crash.

Dolly lurched and steadied herself, high heels spiking the uneven pavement slabs outside. 'We said we'd take a taxi.'

'I'm going to walk back,' said Stephen. 'It's early, and it's not raining, and you could do with some cold air.'

'What's that s'posed to mean? I want a taxi. I'm too full.' Dolly growled at him and grabbed Anna's arm.

A group of youths burst out of the train station to disrupt their argument, and the young males rustled past in black and orange plastic costumes, arms flung in exuberant gestures. They knocked against Dolly, who erupted in alcoholic anger. Unwilling to intervene, Stephen turned his back as if he belonged elsewhere. The boys leered at her fury, putting up two fingers, and crossed the road heading for the strobed red lights of a new nightclub.

The sign pointed to the basement of the Deli, and all the young people seemed to be heading for the same destination. Girls in filmy white and gold organza dresses flashed tickets and goosebumps at the doormen, their faces strobing chalk and shadow grey as they descended into the venue. Behind them in a queue, monsters and punk fairies of every hue congregated, eager to enter the party.

Still seething, Dolly followed them across the road, weaving on high heels. Earlier in the day, neither she nor Anna had noticed the unassuming black door beside the Deli, but now with an unfurled awning and large bouncers outside, the entrance to hell was clear. Nearby, two men in

Dracula capes huddled in discussion, one facing the wall, talking into a phone, while the other listened.

'Michel!' Dolly waved, her anger evaporating into ecstasy. 'Hi. Fancy meeting you here.' She turned to Stephen with a cruel smile. 'Let's all go in.'

Anna saw her brother stiffen, nostrils flaring. 'Is this what you've arranged? Well, let me tell you, we're too old. Look around you. They're all kids, and you'd embarrass yourself.'

Her eyes narrowed. 'Well, if I'm too old, Anna isn't. Why can't she have some fun? You'll take her in, Michel, won't you?'

'I'm not dressed for Halloween,' pleaded Anna.

The other man turned, putting his phone in his pocket, and with a leap of relief, she recognised Sasha. He held a hand out to Stephen in greeting, a smile warming his face.

'Hallo. You are Anna's brother, Stephen Blount. I am Oleksandr Vronskiy.'

Fixated on Michel, at first he made no immediate response, but then he shook himself.

'Ah! I must thank you for helping my sister. It seems you were both injured.' In a flash, Stephen became the essence of polite Englishman as the strobed light bleached their faces, deepening the lines on her brother's tired face. From down below, the decibels increased, and Anna dodged some teenage ghouls fighting in the queue. A balaclava-hooded figure threw an egg onto a passing car's windscreen, and the onlookers erupted with laughter, delighted by the driver's gesticulations and swearing.

Michel plucked at Sasha's sleeve. 'I must go in now.'

'And we must go,' said Stephen. 'I don't want to be caught in this.'

From the underground station, two special constables

appeared, radios crackling, as the crowd jeered. Sasha took the opportunity to move nearer to Anna. 'Come with us,' he breathed into her ear. 'Later you can tell your brother we are respectable men.'

'And what if you're not?' said Stephen. His eyes had lost their bonhomie quality. 'Everyone here is high on something.'

Dolly hissed. 'Don't be stupid, Stephen. They're kids out to dance and have a good time after months of Covid restrictions. I don't see why Anna must sit at home with us. She's much younger. It's not as if Alex would take her to a club like this; he's older than we are.'

'Exactly,' said Stephen. 'Anna, you shouldn't go. Alex is expecting us to look after you while he's away.'

Inflamed, Anna tangled her fingers around the golden moon. 'I'm here for you, Stephen, not the other way round. And I don't need looking after. For God's sake, I'm a grown woman with a child.' She turned to Sasha. 'I'd love to, but I don't have a costume.' She held open her coat to reveal the plain black dress.

'No. Is okay,' he protested. 'Look at notice board.'

A star-shaped light illuminated a scrawled chalked notice.

Jeans forbidden: costume optional.

Stephen hesitated. The police ushered everyone to the side, straightening the straggling queue. From the two spots on her brother's cheeks, Anna knew she had to make a quick decision, especially with Dolly's complaints increasing in volume.

She moved closer to Sasha. 'I haven't been to a club in ages, but I'd love to go. Just for an hour. I'm much too tired to stay up late.'

With an irritated shrug, Stephen began walking toward

home, as Dolly gave Michel a public kiss before waving and crossing the road towards the taxi rank. They waited for her to slump into a taxi.

The music eked from the dark stairway, and Anna said a silent prayer for peace in her family, whilst berating herself for her decision. She should go back. What was she thinking? But her sensitivities melted when Sasha put an arm around her and said, 'I have extra ticket.'

From awkwardness to desire, her body shifted as she pressed into him. He spoke to the bouncer in another language, and the man waved them through. Behind them, three skeletons complained about queue jumping, but the bouncers were too wide and tall for anyone to mount a serious challenge, and they descended unchallenged down the narrow steps.

Into the bowels of hell, she thought, giddy with nerves. What she was doing was wrong, and yet she felt swept along on a tidal surge. 'Do you know the book Anna Karenina?' As soon as she spoke, she wanted to kick herself, for how could he understand the Vronsky connection. She hoped the music had masked the comment. Floor lights sparkled as they entered the low-ceilinged room, and the heat increased. He took her coat and checked it in the cloakroom, then turned, his eyes searching hers. 'You speak of Russian classic book? I say *Slava Ukraini*.' As he leaned towards her to place a soft kiss on her lips, she felt the floor tilt.

THIRTEEN

berlin

NOVEMBER 1991

HE PULLED a pristine velvet box from his coat pocket and placed it on the table. 'A gift.' He had spent the previous day in Berlin searching for the perfect present.

With a shy moue of gratitude, she bit her lip as she handled the elegant gold links, admiring the crescent-moon pendant. Having never given her a lover's token before, he felt the need to explain how the gold crescent represented what remained when one stripped the handle from the sickle of the Soviet emblem.

'No longer the way it was and yet it retains its beauty,' he said, noting the glisten in her eyes. He waited for her to say something. 'Put it on. Please.' They had been together for the best part of the decade, and he considered himself worthy of her trust. Yes, there were certain things he'd done that were best left in the shadows, but why would she now have doubts? Had she not come to Berlin in the full expectation of ending her husband's life – and perhaps her own? He marvelled at her courage. Then a thought occurred to him; she had never been responsible for someone's death before. Not directly. For him, it was routine, but for her she could not be blasé. He felt humbled by the thought.

She fastened the necklace around her throat and the moon gleamed in the electric shop light. He knew it would hang at her cleavage when she was naked.

'It's lovely,' she said. 'I'm touched. Really.'

His heart swelled. 'Good. Twenty-four carat gold. The best for you.' He smacked his lips. 'So let me tell you as an addendum to your story. Sven Hüber was the man who shot Chris Gueffroy.'

'Sven who?'

'Sven Hüber. And not only did he shoot Gueffroy, but he is currently the Chairman of the German Federal Police in this united Germany.'

A roar of jollity came from the nearby family and she blinked. 'How awful. Shouldn't he –'

'Anna,' he said, then corrected himself. 'Annaliese, please stop holding the problems of the world in your hands. We have done what we could. Now I have a little place, a dacha.'

'You said.'

'It's a hundred acres, not so far from the Crimea.'

'Crimea is no longer Russian.'

'Exactly. You've done your geography. Then you will know it's a no-man's-land in terms of culture. Neither East nor West. Exquisite beaches.'

'I see.'

It was obvious she did not understand. 'My dacha,' he continued, 'is near to a small city called Zhdanov.' He paused. 'It's renamed Mariupol, but my point is, we could be safe there, far from Moscow or London, and I have money enough for us both, and an idea for a little enterprise.'

A faint smile ghosted across her face. 'Gardening? Beach cafe? No! You said?'

He leaned back and splayed his hands. 'A vineyard. We can make trips to France and Italy and Switzerland. Even if the rouble dies, I have funds in Swiss banks. We'll get new identities. A better life. No secrets. What do you say?'

'But no children.'

Ah. The crux of the matter. It was not like him to put so much effort into persuading a woman, but he explained once more in a low voice, that the way to protect her children was to fake her death. If she stayed in England or moved anywhere in Europe with them, the newly created GRU or SVB would force her back into service by threatening members of her family. If they declared her dead, and Vronsky confirmed to Stepanov that the Anna Karenina books were burnt, then the Kremlin and the CIA and MI5 would scratch her off their list.

She nodded, and tinkled the spoon in the empty cup as he paid the waiter, counting out a tip. The idea of paying more than you had to was an unwelcome novelty, but Dolomeyer had told him about tips, and he knew such absurd fashions would creep in everywhere. He held out her coat and took her elbow as they returned to the cold outside. 'Everything is ready for this plan.'

She looked across the square at the soft haze of shop lights. 'Can you trust Dolomeyer?'

'*Blyat.* No. He's an American. But he likes money, and I've enough shit on him.'

'It's hard to leave my baby, Anna. Poor poppet. I've hardly been with her since she was born.'

He pulled her close, whispering in her ear. 'But you want the children to be safe?' Families, he thought, in exasperation. In the past, he had threatened a child or two to ensure the parent co-operated, and it always worked. He had no family, which he considered an advantage.

'Come to my hotel room. Dolomeyer is with your John. Later, you can go back and see him and –'

'Yes.' She put her gloved hand in his. 'But tomorrow, I want you to give me twenty-four hours before –'

'*Konechno*.' He smiled. 'We can go see the Candy Bomber plane that's on display. Clear your head.'

She pulled away. 'No. I meant – Sorry. I need to be on my own. Leaving my children is a hard decision.'

'*Konechno*.'

Angst! Soviet mothers fuelled their morning coffee with angst and propaganda, he mused. The famous Candy Bomber was an American warplane that had dropped sugary sweets over West Berlin. The pilot had wiggled its wings to let the children below recognise the descending parachutes were full of chocolate, not bombs, and the Americans hailed this initiative as a kindness to those trapped in the glitch of a West Berlin blockade. But as any Russian knew, the Kremlin was complicit. Their leaders pretended to be angry while the plane's flight path went unchallenged. Behind the performance, everyone understood the importance of trade entering and exiting West Berlin. Vronsky and his band smuggled secrets across the border, so, more than most, they needed the blockade to lift. And it did – with a whoosh of angst and propaganda. Angst, he thought, was part of life for some.

'Take twenty-four hours,' he said, adding he had to speak with his contacts in the *Leichenhalle für Tote*. 'I must visit the morgue to finalise things.'

She looked stricken, and he hurried to calm her.

'Certificates. The Ossis work there, the Wessis don't like

such work.' If she understood his reference to East and West Berliners, she didn't comment. 'Come now. Come back with me to the Mitte Hotel.'

They waited for the Ampelmann signs at the traffic lights to turn into the green figure walking, and she put her head on his shoulder.

'Anna Karenina threw herself under a train,' she said, her voice soft. 'I read the novel years ago in case anyone asked me about it.'

He groaned. 'I've read it too. Vronsky shot himself in the foot when he lost a horse race, the stupid man. But the Kremlin loves Tolstoy. The director, Bondarchuk, did a famous film about *War and Peace*. Did you know? Twelve hours long. *Blyat.* Luckily, I am not sentimental about this book. Are you?'

'No.' She smiled at him, then twisted her face into a grimace. 'But life is so unjust. Poor John. Nothing can be done for him, but I want to live.'

Kissing the top of her head, he silenced her with a hug. He badly wanted a Marlboro. 'So live, my darling. Forget *War and Peace*. Forget Tolstoy. We invent a happy ending. For you and for your children, even if you are not together.'

A thousand coloured lights lit a pleasure boat drifting down the River Spree. Under cover of glass, revellers drank and laughed. There, he thought, that is the crystal ball for the future, and it looks wonderful. In a week, he would be with *his Anna* and maybe she would be a little sad at first – but in time ... a new start in a new world. A new life with Annaliese by his side. Forget assassinations and torture: stretch out under the sun. Grow grapes. Get fat.

'So you don't need me to drive the Trabant?'

'No.' He squeezed her hand. They were at one end of

Kochstrasse, near to Friedrichstrasse. At some time or another, every member of his cell had walked here and crossed Checkpoint Charlie. They had slinked past the guards who were trained and itching to fire at anything irregular, and in some respects, Vronsky understood her lament: 'What had it all been for?' But he suspected this was a blip and soon, the gunman would retake control of the world. It was the way things went. He retained an arsenal of weapons tucked away and he wouldn't be selling them anytime soon.

He felt a bounce in his stride. 'Did I tell you I met one of my East Berlin friends the day after the wall came down. His parents went into shock; they believed the West would let them starve, and they were crying like babies, shouting about mass unemployment, and how they would have no health care. Even the payments promised to them by West Germany for joining the new unified country were bad. A cheap bribe, they said. Please, they said to their son, do not abandon us, because the West will kill us. Ah, propaganda, propaganda. In the end, it is up to each of us to choose what we believe.'

She shook her head. 'You don't understand, Vronsky. I'm a bad person. All I can think about is that I don't want to die.'

Was this her definition of bad? 'You're not a bad person,' he said with a frisson of impatience. He wondered if Stepanov had said anything about his history, but he doubted it. She wouldn't be by his side if she knew.

'Anyway, to finish my story. So, in the week the Wall came down, I walked all across the city and wound up at the Brandenburg Gate. The road was fuming with Wartburgs and Trabants driven by Ossie sightseers, and along the pavements, the Wessie youths chanted football songs, hunting in packs with beer cans and bottles of Sekt. If you got in the middle, they whacked you. Were they good or bad people? A bit of both. And as for fear. All I knew was I didn't want to die there, either. Certainly not with a knife in my ribs.' He hugged her again. 'So, my lovely lady. Come to my bed and I will show you how I can protect you forever.'

FOURTEEN
London

HALLOWEEN 2021

THE DJ'S music vibrated through her body. Unaccustomed to the frenetic throng, she clung to Sasha. Underneath the low ceiling, the costumed ghouls gyrated on the dance square, their awkward headgear and fake nails scraping the air. Every werewolf and gremlin had emerged to shed lockdown blues, the whites of their eyes gleaming under UV lights.

The bass voice energised the crowd with laughing menace. 'Express yourselves, people. Tonight, the graves are blown open. Covid is over and we've been waiting for this.'

Elbows continued to jostle Anna, and Sasha drew her around the edge of the room to the bar, coming to stand by a woman poured into a latex outfit leaning on Michel's shoulder. Her costume mask with little ears partially hid her face as she mouthed something. Michel nodded, turning in surprise as they arrived. Catwoman stared at Anna for a second, before launching herself at Sasha.

'Oleksandr,' she shrieked, gluing hands behind his neck. 'When are we going to get together? You promised.'

Michel smirked and extracted himself, pressing through the crowd, leaving Sasha pinned against the bar.

'Slow, slow, Kitty. What are you on?'

'Nothing.' She pressed against him. 'It's the effect you have on me. I know you feel the same.'

'I am here with someone.' He nodded towards Anna.

'Oh.' She bared her teeth in a brief smile, conceding with ill-grace to follow Michel into the dark recesses of the club.

He apologised and waved at the overworked bartender, but a second later, Michel returned, easing himself between them, pushing Anna further back as he murmured to his brother. In response, Sasha frowned but Michel had plunged into the blur of dancers again.

'What was that?'

But her question was lost in a nearby scuffle. Four bouncers in black shirts moved across the dance floor ejecting several boys in devil masks. A brief uproar cut through the music before a noisy peace continued.

'Drink?' shouted Sasha in her ear.

'No, I've had enough at dinner,' she shouted back, then felt foolish. What did it matter? All the rules were broken tonight. Someone had prised open Dante's Hell, and all the post-Covid revellers were running in the streets. Sweat trickled down her back. Was the heat oppressive, or was it her nerves?

Short spurts of artificial smoke emanated from valves in the ceiling. *Smoke and mirrors*, she thought, feeling a hysterical laugh rise inside her as Sasha propelled her to dance. Beneath their feet, colourful lights pulsed from glass circles, and he urged her to join the tempo. Hesitantly, she copied him, fascinated by his co-ordination. A hard elbow dug in her back, flinging her forwards and he caught her, spitting strong words at the couple behind them. The men in black capes laughed, unaware of the fake blood melting to their chins. Their eyes rolled in a drugged orbit, and Anna shrank back, noting Michel arriving with gyrating arms. He grabbed at the capes, and they turned to him in euphoria, snatching at his hands, intent on dragging him into the *danse macabre*, but Michel clenched one of their upper arms and yanked both men away. Immediately, more dancers occupied the vacated space, rolling into position like marbles on a slope.

'Was that –' she mouthed at Sasha as he encircled her waist, guiding her towards a darkened recess, but again her questions were drowned. Her hand wrapped around the bandage of his injured hand. She followed Sasha, who was trying to catch up with his brother and the two men. Too late – they disappeared behind a heavy fire escape door, blocked by a thickset man, sat with Catwoman on his knee. The pair were at a small circular table, and while one hand thrust out to stop Sasha and Anna opening the door, the other fondled the space between the latex thighs. The man licked his lips, showing cheese-white teeth. 'No further,' he said as the woman glowered at Anna.

'Oi! Don't you look at me like that!' Catwoman gave a sudden jerk, picking up the drink on the table and sluicing the ice and liquid down Anna's front.

'Fuck! Kitty!' Sasha pulled Anna behind him. 'She's with me.'

The man tipped the latex girl off his knee and stood with an angry leer. 'I own this fucking place. Do not forget,' he said in a heavy accent. 'This morning I tell you – no guests. You only stay for a few days. And this girl, she upset my Kitty. Get out.' His hand tightened on Kitty's waist. 'Poor Kitty. You lost your drink? Tell Vadim, we want another. Go.'

'Ta, Gonzales,' said the woman, poking her tongue at Sasha.

Furious, Sasha dragged Anna across the club to the stairs, retrieving her coat. Outside, his mood scalded her, but the wind sliced through her wet dress, and she shuddered.

'Sorry,' he said, taking a deep breath. 'Sorry. I dry you or your brother is angry. Come.'

'Dry? Where?' Despite her thick coat, her teeth began to chatter.

He drew her along the pavement, past more ghouls poised to enter the club. Near the courtyard entrance to the Deli, a couple necked with abandon, and Sasha shouted at them to leave, forcing them into the street. He muttered in Ukrainian while steering her up the metal staircase. Dirty and disenchanting by day, the stairs took on a menacing vista under the shadows of the thin crescent moon. Their feet clanged on every rung as he propelled her towards the front door, withdrawing a key from a coded box on the wall.

She felt a surge of panic, and leaned over the side of the railing, wondering how fast she could descend without breaking her neck. But as he swung open the door, warmth flooded out, and she saw a clean hallway with pine flooring and the same chalky walls as her brother's home. At the end of a short corridor, the arm of a leather sofa was just visible beside a white coffee table.

'This is Deli apartment. My brother stay here. The man in club, Gonzales; he own Deli building. He say I am allowed to stay for a week, but he can be nasty. Sorry. I get you dry.'

'I think I should go home,' she said.

But his eyes softened with concern. 'Please. We have hairdryer. I promise is okay.' He closed the front door, but didn't lock it, and she tried to relax. This was her good Samaritan.

There was a noticeable absence of clutter. On the living room walls, Union Jack plaques jostled with pictures of Buckingham Palace and Piccadilly Circus. In the adjoining kitchenette, a jar of instant coffee and a mug tree rested beside an artificial fruit bowl, as if actual food would corrupt the decor. She inched towards the bedroom, noting the double bed was smooth and wrinkle-free. In the corner, zipped and propped against what looked like an IKEA wardrobe, were two khaki rucksacks. Sasha was opening and closing drawers as she stepped into the pristine bathroom to splash water on her face, and check her mascara.

What were Sasha's intentions? Come to that, what were hers? A thought crossed her mind that he might have paid that girl to pour a drink over her, but she dismissed the idea. At least she had avoided more alcohol, so nobody could have spiked her drink.

'Anna!' He stood in the kitchenette with a boyish grin, holding the dryer, plugged and ready.

'Your brother is so tidy,' she said.

'Is me. I clean this morning.' He spoke with innocent charm. 'Army life. Michel spend too much time in Paris, spoiled student. He is slob.' He laughed.

She bit her lip. Had he cleaned to prepare for her visit, she wondered, but his face was so open and guileless. With finger and thumb, he snagged the material at her collarbone, easing it away from her skin to bend the dryer's jet downwards, gushing warm air between her breasts.

Her body tensed as she studied his face; the purple

beneath his eyes; the pin-like scar; the heat rising between them; and the desire smoking between her thighs. *Smoke and mirrors.*

'Why is your brother here? What is he doing with my sister-in-law?'

His irises were the deepest blue, the pale fringe of lashes so long as to be feminine.

He smiled. 'Someone in Paris tell him he has job with Gonzales for three months.'

'But why?'

He clicked off the drier and smoothed the hair from her eyes, before taking another strand from her lips.

'Sorry. I don't know. He won't say. I ask him to come home because Papi is sick.'

Running fingers along her dress, she tested for dampness. 'Michel has upset my brother.'

He stood close. 'He is bad.'

She felt magnetised, unable to put distance between them.

'But soon he finishes and then we go to Ukraine.'

'Finishes what? Stephen's marriage?'

'This hurts you, because you love your brother. I am sorry,' he repeated. The fingers on his bandaged hand stroked the slope of her cheek. 'You are kind. I see this in your face.'

His touch made the blood roar in her ears. She should walk out and put an end to this, but the temptation to stay was overwhelming. Desire made her lightheaded, as he leaned in to kiss her, and a primeval response made her wrap her hands around his neck. Somewhere at the back of her mind, she had known it would be like this all along; he was the longed-for final piece of her unfinished puzzle, and completed her.

Peeling off clothes, they moved to the bedroom to lie naked, marvelling at each other's bodies. Every touch was a gift, received and given; each scab and scar kissed from pain to joy. When they made love, she knew everything that had gone before was nothing more than a habitual matrimonial effort. This was passion; the strongest emotion she had ever experienced with a man, and she wondered if she could ever let it go.

Afterwards, in the double bed, no longer wrinkle-free, she propped herself on one elbow to gaze at his sleeping body, recumbent in *le petit mort*. Desperate to commit all to memory, she examined every molecule of his body as sensations raced along her skin and heart. She gazed at his face; the bandaged hand, the blond tangled hair around his brow, the curve of his ears, the line of stubble, the rugged bandage on his powerful left hand, the speckling of chest hair that went from pale to the dark brown at his groin, the small tattoo of a Ukrainian flag on one bicep, and another scar in the shape of a peach pit near his hip. Her hand tracked across the flesh toward his penis and returned to rest on his upper torso. If only she could box this moment in a velvet case like the one she used for her gold chain and moon, and take it out to examine when she needed. She inhaled his scent, knowing – here in this bed – here, she had become a different person – not Anna Faver, wife and mother – but a desirable woman with a lover. She burned with colours and a hunger too fierce to quell with sensible moralities. Where would it end?

His eyes opened and he kissed her. 'Are you real?' he said, and she laughed because he echoed her thoughts.

'Very real, but I must go. My brother.'

'And my brother.' He made a face of disappointment.

They dressed each other, fingers and thumbs skin to skin, reluctant to lose touch. He planted kisses in the crease of her neck, and she pulled his T-shirt over his head, putting her lips to his tattoo. She pointed to the circular peach pit flesh.

'That is soldier bullet. I am lucky to live.'

She wanted to tell him that the luck was hers; that she was lucky he'd come into her life. She kissed the scar by his eye.

'Is Russian tax. For freedom.'

She didn't understand. There had been no war with Russia that she knew about. 'Tell me everything.'

His finger went to her lips. 'Not now. Not tonight, because tonight is perfect. No Chechens. No Russian soldiers.'

Chechen rebels: the mention stirred a vague memory that surfaced and dived as his arms drew her to him.

'I've never done anything like this.' What a cliché – but she didn't know how else to explain. 'I've been a good –'

'When someone saves your life, they belong to you,' he murmured. 'Tonight you save my life.'

'No, it was you who were my saviour.'

He kissed her. 'I tell you truth. You belong to me and I belong to you. Maybe forever.' He smoothed the tangle of her hair before releasing her. 'I saw you and I thought –'

'And I thought the same.'

A thousand nights would not be enough to satiate this desire. With reluctance, she pulled on her coat. She wasn't Dolly. This couldn't be a one-night stand or an affair, yet the two knapsacks stood to attention in the corner, evidence of two men who would soon disappear to battle. The thought of never seeing him again pierced her heart.

'I'm married, Sasha, and in a few days, I must collect my son from his grandmother's house near Canterbury. So I will leave, and you will go back to Ukraine.' She had to force herself to say this without a sob.

His fingers touched the golden moon resting above her cleavage. 'My cousin, Betsy Vronskiy, lives near Canterbury. Amberley Hall. We meet there?'

'Amberley Hall?' It was five miles from Nina Faver's vineyard estate. 'Had you heard of my family when you helped me? Did you check me out?'

He frowned, pulling on his battered jacket. 'What does this mean? Check you?'

She shook her head, trying to dispel the kernel of doubt. 'Never mind.'

'Tomorrow Michel meet Dolly. And we meet after and I tell you more?'

Anna bit her lip; suspicion colliding with yearning. Their meeting was coincidental, wasn't it? And this act of madness was joy; an awakening; a rebirth. Her whole body buzzed. They had to see one another again.

FIFTEEN

berlin

NOVEMBER 1991

THE RADIO BEAT VIBRATED through his body as the van jittered across the night city, driven by Dolomeyer. At four in the morning, he had returned Annaliese to her hotel, relieving the sergeant from his babysitting duties, and although she disliked the American, she had not objected to the arrangements. After last night's pillow talk, he wanted to feel positive, but ...

Between tuneless mumbling to cheesy songs, Dolomeyer confirmed John Blount was stable and in a deep, injection-induced coma. Annaliese had told him she intended to sit with her dying husband until the fake paramedics arrived with their 'borrowed' ambulance. Then she'd spend some time alone preparing.

'So, you think she's on the level?' Dolomeyer chewed a stick of gum.

'Of course.' It went without saying that Vronsky trusted Annaliese more than the American. Agent Dolomeyer was too fond of Bourbon and cocaine, and indiscriminately dispatching inconvenient intruders. But he had his uses. The man loved old Western films, with a side order of prostitutes, and he combed an Elvis Presley quiff, claiming to be a Vietnam hero, which meant women adored him and would tell him anything – until he got kinky. He was neither a sergeant nor born with the name of Dolomeyer. That was his codename, and Vronsky often referred to him as Dolly to rile him. In reality, he was plain Corporal Henry Snooks, dishonourably discharged from the US military.

Exhausted but eager to complete the last leg, Vronsky assured the American that Annaliese was on board and everything would go smoothly. At Tiergarten, they changed the BMW for a pickup truck as arranged and continued towards the car graveyard in the eastern suburbs of Berlin. In the pre-dawn, the junkyard loomed as a black blot in the middle of desolate fields, under a descending half moon. He thought of the gold moon between Annaliese's breasts and regretted there was no time to indulge in fantasies.

On three hours' sleep, he rubbed sore eyes, still relishing the touch of Annaliese's flesh. He must not distract himself, he thought, oe hand folding over the Beretta in his coat pocket, as he repeated the plan in his head. They would position the junkyard car on the quiet backstreet near the old Olympic stadium. Vronsky would be the one to wait for his paid Ossie helpers to arrive with the ambulance, the body and the fake paperwork, while Dolomeyer would return the pickup truck and fetch Annaliese in the BMW. With Blount in the car and the Ossis departed, he would torch the scene and take photographs, adjusting the pictures later to include a female cadaver. He had made the plans some weeks ago and in the current climate of chaos, he was confident it would work.

. . .

A bald man in a thick padded coat greeted them, unlatching the junkyard gates. 'So Hans,' the man shook Vronsky's hand, 'one last time, heh?'

Dolomeyer turned off the pickup's engine.

'One last time, Siegfried,' he said, accepting his fake name and handing over the usual ten packets of Marlboros as a sweetener.

Siegfried opened one packet, flicking off the film, to sniff like a bulldog. 'Ja, ja, ja,' he said with evident appreciation.

Walking along the line of crumpled wrecks, Dolomeyer stopped to inspect an engine, allowing Vronsky to go on ahead and light two of his own cigarettes, handing one to Siegfried – the usual preamble of business. The Ossie knew Vronsky as a former Stasi. In the past, when they needed to extract something from a car before crushing, or crush something that didn't need finding, Siegfried had obliged. He delighted in his payment of contraband and a fistful of cash, and never attempted to squeeze more than his due from the transaction. Vronsky liked that about him: he was an honest criminal. He took out his wallet, counting German marks into the man's meaty hand.

Despite the hour, the German was cheerful and chatty. 'So, you guys disbanded? You got something new? You lucky bastards. The Wessis are rehiring on bigger salaries – so I'm told – but not for me.'

From the corner of his eye, Vronsky saw Dolomeyer lean over a car bonnet, and suspected he was taking a line of coke. Siegfried checked the notes, cigarette smoke dribbling from his lips, and with a nod, he thrust the wad inside his dungaree pocket.

'Ja, ja, ja. *Gut.* You, I trust, Hans, but nowadays you can't be too careful.' He rubbed his veinous nose. 'It used to be I could rely on the Stasi. Massive corruption – ja, ja, ja – but if Stasi hired you, then Stasi didn't arrest you. Now it's different. Tricky, tricky. These guys show up, ask me to do this and do that. But you never know! You take the pay, then maybe someone else comes to take you to the cells. Very tricky.'

'Ah, the good old days,' said Vronsky, unmoved by Siegfried's moaning. 'So, where's the car?'

'Ja, ja, ja.'

They crossed the yard to a filthy tarpaulin. Thrusting it aside, Siegfried paraded the wreckage of a Trabant. As ordered, the back wheels were perfect, but the nose had crumpled, as if it had hit a brick wall, which was most likely the case.

'Here is the Trabi,' he said. 'I took the radio out. You don't mind?'

'No.'

It was almost impossible to tell that it had once been white. They began the procedure of loading it on the trailer. Despite the chill, Dolomeyer and Siegfried sweated as they struggled to pull the chains tight before winching it onto the pickup, and then all shook hands like politicians.

'Ja, ja, ja. Good to do business with you, Hans. You want to hear a joke? How do you double the value of a Trabi?'

Dolomeyer raised irritable eyes to the glimmering dawn.

'You fill it up with gas.' Siegfried roared with laughter. 'Plenty more if you need it. No one wants the old cars, so ask anytime. I'll be here. Me. Poor Siegfried.'

'Enjoy a unified Germany,' said Vronsky.

'I'll enjoy this new money more. Heading somewhere nice with the wreck?'

'We're going to put it in a West German museum as an exhibit.'

Siegfried guffawed, spit arcing from his mouth. '*Sehr gut.* You know how to play the game, Hans, you clever devil.'

The American swung the wheel of the pickup right, then left, avoiding the worst of the potholes. 'Yeah, you clever devil,' he murmured, 'Ain't you just, Mac.'

'Shut up.'

'By the way, I reckon this whole mock-up cost you a fortune. Why bother?'

'Expenses. Your names are on the lists of agents given to American and English intelligence, and she'd prefer to show up as dead. It's her prerogative.'

Dolomeyer chortled. 'A bullet would have been easier.'

'A non-suspicious death.'

With cocaine-fuelled energy, Dolomeyer laughed so hard he almost plopped the front tyre into a viscous black ditch, fishtailing the trailer with a whoop of delight. It took every ounce of Vronsky's self-control not to shoot the man, take over the wheel and burn his corpse in the Trabant alongside John Blount's. But two male cadavers might cause complications – so maybe later. He sighed. He didn't trust Dolomeyer to keep his mouth shut long-term but an American counterpart would deal with that.

The gun was cold and comforting in his coat pocket. Don't get derailed, he told himself. Follow the plan.

SIXTEEN

London

NOVEMBER 2021

THE SWING of the front door revealed Stephen's silhouette, backlit by the art deco light. With one arm aloft, he twirled his glass in salute to her.

'It's been a riot here,' he said. 'What a way to start the November month.'

Anna dropped her coat, heart sinking, and when he offered her a drink, she refused, trying to savour the last few hours. She flung her boots, skittering, across the herringbone floor, and collapsed onto the sofa, rubbing her arches. It was impossible to ignore the broken vase on the polished fireplace, nor that Dolly appeared to have shredded the silk petals onto the Berber rug. She grimaced, remembering her childhood, and Dolly's sudden angry flares that left everyone skittering to other rooms.

Stephen waved a hand over the chaos and hiccuped, while Anna plucked a cream cushion and pressed it to her stomach, sensing he was at a critical stage of inebriation.

'I think Michel is on drugs. Is that Dolly's thing now?'

He smiled wanly, appearing to discount the idea. 'So that's your verdict?'

'I'm just saying. Maybe it's not an affair. Maybe she's giving him legal advice.' She counted five, six, seven silken petals around her feet, her mind on the odd relationship between the two Vronskiy brothers.

'This affair could destroy me,' he pronounced.

She waited for his explanation, but he meandered into the kitchen, where she heard the chink of ice in a glass. A yawn escaped her and she saw the glint of a text inside her open clutch purse.

Is everything alright? I texted my mother and

she says you haven't texted good night to Simon.

Oh God. Not now. Not this. Guilt surfaced with a sharp stab, followed by Sasha's text.

Goodnight my dearest Anna. I belong to you. X

How was it possible to feel ecstatic and downcast at the same time? She'd have to ask Dolly tomorrow. God knows her sister-in-law had put in the practice. She watched Stephen return to the vodka bottle on the sideboard, wondering what to say next.

Stumbling, he collided with a large spider plant, scattering the dirt across the floorboards. 'Too bad,' he muttered, pouring a generous three fingers and resettling himself in the leather armchair.

Holding her phone beneath a cushion, she texted two quick replies.

Dinner with Stephen went on. Simon must be asleep. X

And to Sasha, two kisses, before she buried the mobile in her bag.

Unaware, her brother spoke with a thickened voice. 'I hope it's the bloody menopause, because for God's sake, surely she can see the little brat isn't interested in her. Look at the age gap.'

'What! There's an age gap between Alex and me.' The comment needled. 'And what about our parents? Age isn't the issue.' She flipped a pink petal with her big toe. 'And another thing. Those volumes of Anna Karenina in your study. You never told me you had some of Daddy's books. I have nothing of his apart from a few photographs.'

Stephen's knuckles whitened on the crystal glass. 'When were you in my study? Has Alex suggested you snoop on me?'

'Alex?' Sometimes, her brother's thought processes were a mystery to her. 'You were the one who asked me to come and help you. No, it wasn't me, it was Dolly looking with –' She clamped a hand over her mouth.

'What the fuck?' Stephen flushed, striking his forehead with a fist. 'I knew it! I knew Michel had been in this house. I knew it. He's bloody well been in my study checking my bank accounts, hasn't he?' Stephen shook a finger at her, spitting with rage. 'But how? It's always locked.'

'I don't know,' she lied. 'Dolly wanted to show him some French classic literature.' Another lie slipped out like lubricant. 'You've an old copy of Maupassant, haven't you? He's half French.'

Stephen's fist struck the coffee table and the magazines jumped.

'He was only here for a chat,' she pleaded.

'Michel is a snake, and he's not French.'

She frowned. 'His mother is French, and his father is Ukrainian. Like Sasha, he was born in Donetsk.'

'Then they're fucking Russians. Don't you know anything?' He rose to pace the room, his face glistening with sweat. 'But what would he want with me? Why check up on me? Unless...'

'What's this about?'

For a moment, his eyelids fluttered, and she feared he was having a stroke. Rushing to his side, she urged him to sit, resting a hand on his shoulder and crouching beside him.

'Hey. You can tell me. I'm your sister.'

Head in his hands, he let out a long breath. 'They promoted me. Dolly doesn't know.'

'That's good, isn't it?' Anna's confusion increased. What was wrong with him? 'Are you still working in the Whitehall offices?'

He raised bloodshot eyes. 'I didn't earn it. Someone knew about our parents. There's a file.' His voice had dropped to a whisper. 'Our parents were what you might call champagne socialists. Educated people who thought Russian communism preferable to American fascism.'

'Really?' The evening was turning into a macabre Halloween-fest of secrets, and for a moment, she wanted to giggle.

'They were Cold War operatives. Both father and mother.'

Unable to contain herself, she gave a bellow of laughter. 'Who the hell have you been talking to? Daddy was a Professor of History at Cambridge. Mummy was a housewife.'

'I found out some years ago.' He put the glass to his mouth and drained it.

'Years ago?' With a scoff, Anna returned to the sofa. If they were going to have a ridiculous conversation, she needed to sit in comfort. She had a flash of recall: her father shouting – *Frond Skis. Where is Frond Skis? I'll kill him.* 'Is this to do with their car crash?'

He nodded. 'A suicide pact, except Dad was ill, and apparently she opted out.'

Her laughter died, replaced by a hard lump in her throat. Stephen had organised the return of their parents' ashes, and a memorial plot. He would know who was buried and who wasn't. 'Mum would never have done that. What evidence do you have for these awful lies?'

'Thirty years ago, the German authorities told me our parents had hired a Trabant. Those cars creased like a tin can, so I had no reason to disbelieve their documentation, although we couldn't explain why they were in Berlin. It was not long after the fall of the Wall. Anyway, years later a man stopped me and suggested Mum was alive.'

Her mind cartwheeled. 'When was this?'

He moaned and cradled the empty glass. 'Five years ago.'

'Five years ago?' Anna felt a fury sweep through her. 'If it's true, then where is she?'

'I don't know, but Michel will use the books to blackmail me. I became aware they had some significance.'

'How?'

'It doesn't matter.'

For a moment she fell silent, picking the strewn silken petals from the rug as she tried to clear the mental mist of anger. 'No,' she pronounced. 'Internet nonsense, no doubt. I'm absolutely certain if Mum were alive, she'd have contacted us. And as for the books, they're old and in poor condition. And Michel works in a sandwich shop, hardly an aficionado of literature.' Moving to the tiled fireplace, she tried to position two of the broken vase pieces to fit the sides together. 'Whoever spoke to you about our parents and the books was evil. They wanted to cause you pain, and if Michel's prank bothers you so much, why not talk to

Dolly?' Light from the art deco lamp glinted against the crystal glass. 'And why tell me about this now? You've not said a word for five years, so I assume you know it's not true. Otherwise you would have involved me. Wouldn't you?'

He let his head hang. 'I thought you could – I thought you might – But you're right. As you say, the Cold War is over. Abramovich owns Chelsea Football Club.' He drained the last drop with a wild-eyed laugh, and let the empty glass fall.

She stared at him. Was her brother having a nervous breakdown? Anxiety lines gouged around his eyes and mouth. Perhaps he had reached that time of life when a new promotion was too much. Or Dolly's credit card had become onerous, and the pressure of debt weighed him down. Would he benefit from counselling?

'Dad was a card-carrying member of the Communist Party, you know,' he said, his face twisted with derision. 'He encouraged student protests at Cambridge – He –'

She stopped his juggernaut of thoughts. 'It's a big stretch to say Michel is out to extort money because he's seen a copy of an old book, and it's an even bigger stretch to claim Dad was involved in something sinister. Lots of university staff were left-wing in the sixties and seventies. I'm sure I read that somewhere.' She returned to his side to rub his shoulders. 'I'm not such a baby anymore. I know about things, too.'

And yet, her nightmare rose afresh. *Frond Skis.*

'He had dementia.'

'Yes, but –' Her fingers continued to knead at the back of his neck.

Then the fight seemed to leave his body and he sagged. 'No, you're right.' He puffed his cheeks. 'I see how this looks.' Rising, he shrugged her off and staggered away. 'Sorry. Sorry to have worried you. I'm being ridiculous. But I must have the books back. Must. Must.'

'I've got both of them in my bedroom,' she said and tensed, waiting for another outburst at the missing third, but his head bobbed like a pigeon. 'Yes, yes. That's good. Good night, dear Anna. Sorry. So sorry.'

He wove his way to his study and she heard the key turn in the lock, followed by a high-pitched noise. Stephen was crying.

The smell of sex clung to her, but the thrill had dissipated.

All those years ago, the sudden deaths; the vanishing of her parents; and the raw childish pain emerged from her subconscious to swallow her in sadness. If she had grown up having nightmares, he must have suffered in his own way, but they'd never talked about it. Every familiar item of furniture, every bauble, every pummelled soft toy, every note and slip of paper had been his decision to save or destroy. They were inanimate points of reference, intrinsically worthless, but their absence represented an emotional loss, and thirty years later, she and Stephen still held a connection to that life. Old books, books with poor translations such as Anna Karenina, invoices, bills, library tickets, the gold moon necklace – like love letters – they floated together in a sea of memories.

Was Stephen crying because his wife had a younger lover or was he melting in the past? She tip-toed upstairs to throw herself on the bed, hands gripping chunks of the duvet. The cotton was rough-hewn, reminding her of Sasha's body. He was youth. He was the future, and she wished and wished ... but for what, she was not sure.

SEVENTEEN
London

NOVEMBER 2021

ENCASED in early morning mist and perfume, Dolly left the house the following day, claiming 'business', although a wink made clear her true mission. Knowing about the flat above the Deli, Anna texted Sasha, proposing an alternative cafe for them to meet at, and Sasha agreed. She and Dolly had avoided conversation about last night, except to comment on the fate of the many South Koreans crushed in the post-Covid Halloween celebrations. A news item from the other side of the world was safer territory than anything happening in London, and unused to subterfuge, she walked the half-mile to her meeting point alive with nerves.

As soon as they met, they linked hands, immersed in each other. Sitting side by side on a worn couch, they ordered coffees and spoke about Dolly and Michel, while their eyes held a different conversation. Michel was pretending to be a Russian spy, he claimed.

'Which makes no sense because Gonzales is Portuguese

running a European shop,' said Anna, happy to be pressed to his shoulder. 'Your brother must be joking.'

'I agree,' said Sasha returning the pressure, 'especially as he hates Putin.'

'And Dolly is disinterested in politics.'

'And Michel is stupid kid.'

And on and on: their agreements and linked hands unglued only when they sipped their coffee. Every absurdity was tossed like confetti, until she placed her fingertip on his silver streak. 'How did you get this?'

'It was car accident,' he said. 'I was with my older brother, Andrey, he is soldier.'

'I didn't know you had an older brother.'

'Andrey was killed.' His eyes clouded. 'We not speak about this now.'

She apologised and briefly explained she hated to talk about her parents' death. It was not the time for sadness, they agreed, but the pain was something they held in common.

They walked to Stephen's house, and finding the place empty, she guided him upstairs to her room, alight with desire. She would have made love to him on the Berber rug without the trappings of bed and Sanderson wallpaper, such was her hunger to tear off clothes and stand hip to hip and heart to heart with him. His touch brought her to life and his kisses melted her guilt as they tumbled into the sea-blue duvet. How could she bear to walk away and return to Whitstable without him?

When asked, Stephen was happy to have Anna stay longer, too wrapped in his own misery to recognise her true reasons. She texted false claims to Nina, contacting her son each day to allay maternal guilt, but the guilt was gossamer thin compared to her passion. Her heart and soul lived day by day in a perpetual madness, where she convinced herself this relationship was not a fling, but an indefinable emotion – sturdy, wide and deep; not a whirlwind romance, but a profound connection. And she was sure he felt the same as they rolled in their joyous duvet world, where after lovemaking, they talked of anything and everything, except the troubles of their errant siblings. After four days he told her he wanted to marry her, and she knew there was no obstacle so great that she would not tear it down to be with him.

Unusually Dolly did not tease her. They avoided each others' eyes, and when Stephen locked himself in the study each night, absorbed in his subterranean problems, she felt giddy with relief. Let him and Dolly take control of their emotions: she could not control her own.

In their daily meetings, they edged towards a greater understanding of each other's lives. She took the copy of Anna Karenina from the bedside drawer to show him the scribblings.

Sasha read it with interest but little comprehension. 'This is Russian and says he wants to kill Vronsky. Here he writes – but no. I am not sure.' He smiled. 'He is teacher, yes? This is about literature.'

'A commentary for students?'

'I think, yes.' He tossed the book onto the floor and kissed her. 'But we are real.' She returned the kiss with gratitude that his explanations were deliciously simple. Her father, an academic, a tutor at Cambridge, had used the books to illustrate a period in history in his lectures.

Stephen was wrong, and there were no conspiracies, and when Michel returned the borrowed copy, they would laugh, and talk openly about their parents, laying their ghosts to rest.

Sasha told her stories about his childhood; about eating huge cherries in Melitopol, and allowing the red juices to run down their chins; about how his grandmother smacked the back of their heads when they were naughty, and explained the tribulations she endured under Stalin. Her toughness knew no sympathy for cuts and grazes, always reminding them of what it felt like to be hungry, or beaten. He mentioned his grandmother's funeral, where the whole family went for a meal at a restaurant near Donetsk airport, so that Andrey could be there. He was a soldier, a Cyborg, he said proudly, and Anna laughed at the name. Sasha explained the unit had fought for over two hundred days to take back control of the airport from Russia, and because Sasha was then sixteen, it influenced him to join the army for a couple of years.

'How long did this war last?'

'Still war in Donetsk.' He shifted his body to gather her in his arms, and she sensed his sadness. In her head, she did the math between the fall of the Berlin Wall and her parents' car crash in Berlin, but for her the twentieth century would always be a rough sketch from history books.

He explained Andrey was six years older than him and his parents had separated when he was very young. His mother, a nurse, took an apartment nearby with other nurses, and although they lived with their father, the family remained close. One day, his Papi brought home a French woman, Astrid, to meet the family. They liked her; she was kind, and a year later, Michel was born. When Astrid almost died of complications, his mother nursed her in the local hospital, after which the two women were firm friends. 'Yes,' he said as if she had asked, his childhood was happy; he had been loved by two mothers.

She did not want to speak of her childhood. Her capacity for happy reflection was less than his, and he must have seen the wistful look in her eyes, because he gathered her into a kiss and then said, 'No more history. We will have good life together. Always.' He reached for his phone. 'We take selfie! Yes?'

Grinning and making faces like teenagers, they took photographs. Alex hated taking photographs of himself, but Sasha turned and preened, before positioning himself on the end of the bed to take a picture of Anna on her own. Embarrassed, she drew the sheet to cover all but her cleavage, positioning the gold moon pendant.

'Beautiful Anna,' he said. 'I make real photo to hold in hands and you be at my heart for when I go home.'

She couldn't bear the thought of his leaving. 'Are you going back to Donetsk?'

'No. Russians and Donetsk Liberation Army control it now.' He stashed the phone in his jeans' pocket. 'I live in Mariupol. After Russia invade Crimea, we must leave or they catch my brother. They hate the Cyborgs. So we lock door and I never see that house again.'

Anna had a vague recollection of leaving her bedroom, unaware she would never return. 'Is Mariupol far from Donetsk?'

In response, he removed the duvet with a flourish, pushing her gently to lie flat on the bed, so he could use his fingertips to draw a map on her naked body.

'Here is Donetsk, here is Melitopol, here is Kramatorsk, here is Bakhmut, here is Kyiv, here is Mariupol.' He touched her shoulders, left and right, then ran the line from the top of her torso to her hipbone. She shivered and laughed.

'See. My father's sister live in Mariupol, so we move from Donetsk to there.' He pressed on her hip with one finger. 'There is some fighting, but after 2014, it is Ukrainian. Hurrah! Mariupol is beautiful. Big parks, beautiful beaches, wonderful opera house. My mother love music. This is my home.'

'So when did Michel go to Paris and why is he now in London?'

The question was like throwing cold water, and his shoulders bunched, flexing the tattoo of the Ukrainian flag. 'Enough history.' He kissed her. 'Yesterday is sometimes bad, but today, you are my light. I belong to you, and you belong to me. Do not forget.'

Her hands wrapped around his chest. 'How can I forget? I love you,' she said. There was no other truth.

He clutched her hands. 'With you, there is hope. You make me live. *Ya lyublyu tebe.* We have future. We find a way to marry. I leave London for work, but it cannot end here.'

She did not know how to make this come true, but there had to be a way forward, and she would find it.

EIGHTEEN

berlin

NOVEMBER 1991

ENCASED in early morning mist and reeking of petrol, they arrived at the old Olympiastadion. Dawn struggled through the wintry sky as the two men heaved to release the chains and position the Trabant against a tree. Vronsky watched Dolomeyer take the canister and the blowtorch from the back of the pickup truck.

'Tip it into the front passenger seat. Not too much.'

The odour of the translucent liquid rose in the frosty air, and the American inhaled. 'Sheer napalm.'

You could almost believe he'd grown up on the stuff in Vietnam, instead of deserting and running home to Texas thought Vronsky sourly, looping the camera strap about his neck.

'Did that guy remember to siphon out the gas? Otherwise they'll be one helluva bang.'

'Siegfried will have taken every drop.'

'Shall I check?' Dolomeyer unscrewed the cap, sniffing like a bloodhound. 'Shucks. He's done a good job. Shouldn't wonder if he licked it clean.' He created a pool of petrol on the passenger side, and set the blowtorch on the ground.

'The Ossis are going to be here any minute.'

His agent stroked his Elvis quiff, buzzing with cocaine. 'Can I get my new passport and pay now?'

'Not before you return the pickup and collect Annaliese. I'll wait here for the others.'

Like a dog, Dolomeyer turned circles in the grass, arched his back, looked about to argue, then shrugged and got in the van. Crunching gears, he drove away, trailer swinging behind. Relieved to be on his own, Vronsky shook the penultimate cigarette out of his packet. *Blyat.* He no longer had a spare packet. Regretful of his generosity to Siegfried, he strolled along the grassy verge towards the stadium, enjoying each lungful of smoke.

He wanted it over now, and kicked his feet in the grass as he waited for the ambulance. His nerves jangled. He was more confident of the loyalty of his driver, Gunther, a former GDR runner, than Annaliese, and the thought pained him. Currently, Gunther was in the employ of the German Police, but on standby for Vronsky. Annaliese had said the right things last night, but he had been in the business long enough to smell problems, and he knew any change, no matter how slight, brought increased risk to a plan as complex as theirs.

Checking his watch for the tenth time, he followed the path around the relic of Hitler's pride to avoid appearing suspicious loitering near the crushed wreck. But the place remained deserted, and he'd chosen the venue for that reason, aware the U-Bahn no longer went this far, after they shut it in 1980. The nearby S-Bahn's stop to Olympiastadion was intermittent, so he expected few problems from early commuters.

The old stadium was small by 1984 Los Angeles Olympic standards, and held an air of neglected greenery.

He recalled reading about Jesse Owens' treatment, the winning runner, denied a handshake from Hitler on account of being black. Franklin Roosevelt had also refused to meet the runner, he had noted, but few Americans chose to remember that. But, thought Vronsky, spitting into the grass, he ought to stop his criticisms: supposedly they were all friends now.

The sound of an engine rumbled through the early morning birdsong, and with relief, he saw the ambulance come into view.

'*Blyat.* What kept you?'

'The paperwork had to dry. I don't like rush jobs,' complained Gunther.

The two Ossis drew out the covered body on a wheeled stretcher, and Vronsky lifted the white sheet. John Blount looked more peaceful than dead. 'Is he still alive?'

'Can you feel a pulse?'

Vronsky checked the man's neck to find it cool and lifeless. 'Okay. Put him in the passenger seat.'

Gunther and his junior assistant pushed the dead man into position behind the crushed Trabant's wheel, cramming his limbs into place, and cracking cartilage. Thank God the rigor had not yet set in. With a last shove, the Ossis stepped back. The younger man had a green tinge in his cheeks and rushed to return the empty stretcher to the ambulance.

'Is he trustworthy?'

'Sure. He's my cousin,' said Gunther, handing a thick brown envelope to Vronsky. 'Three copies of death certificates, three passports, two driving licences, three fake police reports and coroner verdicts. An official record showing two people killed in the crash.' His narrowed eyes flicked to the solitary body in the ruined Trabant. 'Someone missing? For an extra fee, I could have fetched another corpse from the morgue. We've had two unknowns this past week.'

'All's good,' said Vronsky, as he sifted through the false paperwork. 'I'm doing the photos, and we'll make adjustments. I'm glad to see this is good quality stuff,' he added.

'For you, the best,' said Gunther, waiting for his money.

In his head, Vronsky ticked each item on his list. One complete copy would go to Moscow, another to the CIA in Washington who would pass it to MI5. Then, the intelligence agencies would close the file on the Blounts. The third set of paperwork was to convince Annaliese's eldest son, Stephen, of the demise of both parents. He had to admire the handiwork: the documents looked authentic, especially the report from the German Police confirming the site at the scene. An additional letter, ostensibly from a local police station, gave more information, the details drafted with the help of a comely and compliant police secretary, who, for the price of a meal and a night with him in a hotel room, had agreed to obtain authorised paper and stamp. This was the ultimate piece of faux evidence. He would present the documents to Stepanov in a week, but he doubted his boss would scrutinise them. The former KGB superior was now working for the SVB and trusted Vronsky to oversee the closure of the Anna Karenina cell as it was in everyone's interest.

A closed book? He inhaled the smell of grass and petrol, offering a silent prayer. He wasn't a believer, but it didn't hurt to cover all bases. He was determined to make his dream come true – if that didn't sound too Disney.

NINETEEN

whitstable

WINTER 2022

HER LIFE REVOLVED around the affair, and she rose each day to gaze across the harbour, but through his eyes, she saw mountain ranges, the Carpathians, wreathed in autumnal glory, and an unknown narrative of pre and post-Soviet ideology. Her world had been so small before she met Sasha.

He belonged to her and she belonged to him. Their refrain replaced her nightmares about *Frond Skis* and *smoke and mirrors*, and because she loved her son, she invented scenarios that included Simon and Sasha. They developed a routine whereby he drove three hours from Goodwood to lie in her bed, and on school days, she took the train to London to ferret out budget hotels and welcome him into her arms. Their joy compressed into managed units of time.

The radio threw out rumblings from a distant shore, but when she was in his arms, world leaders' pronouncements were no more than seagulls squawking, or traffic honking.

Christmas blurred to January, and Sasha told her he had news: Michel had agreed to return to Ukraine to see their father, and while she welcomed his words for Stephen's sake, her heart dipped.

'When do you go?'

'In a month.'

Desperate to offer a solution, his kisses suggested he felt the same. As soon as she went home, she investigated his two-thousand-mile journey. The plane to Kyiv took four hours, and then there was a train. He would arrive into a different time zone; a different climate; a different alphabet and customs, to an unknown place. Mariupol. But how to join him? Maybe he could collect his father and join her? Two thousand miles. It was like going to the moon, and she clutched her gold moon pendant, willing herself to come up with a workable plan.

When she kissed Simon's cheek as he ran to play on Nina's estate, she wrestled with maternal guilt, arguing if Alex could be an absentee father, she could be an absentee mother. But could she do such a thing? Could she rush to Ukraine and abandon her child? Or might she take him with her? Perhaps she could stamp her feet at Alex; threaten lawyers. Insist she had custody. She needed both and could not give up either.

When Alex rang mid-week to inform her that from now on, he would spend the weekends at his London flat, she felt her throat dry. There was a crisis in Europe, he said, but she didn't believe him. She was *too happy*, that was the true problem and her behaviour had made him suspicious. Why couldn't they talk about this? But the distance between them only served to highlight the extinguishing of the marriage.

. . .

The first weekend in February, she drove Simon to his grandmother's as usual, arriving on the wintry estate. Empty staked grape vines stood like soldiers in rows along the hillside, and wisteria, twisted in naked poses, clung to the gables. The Georgian mansion was a brick skeleton without florals in these months, and the severity of the landscape matched Nina's gaze at the door. As Simon disappeared to find Callum, Nina insisted Anna stop for a tea.

Head down, Anna followed her into the kitchen, counting the large red flagstone tiles under her feet rather than raising her eyes. Fifteen across and thirty deep to the back of the house. She sat in a Carver chair and placed hands in her lap, staring at the worn pine table. Her mother-in-law began the obligatory process of brewing: warming the pot, pouring the milk, fetching the silver strainer and the tea canister, and Anna struggled for a bland topic of conversation, mentioning her father's volumes of Anna Karenina. 'I should have brought one to show you. You'd be interested.'

'My grandmother was a second cousin to the Tsar.' Nina wiped a damp hand down her cashmere sweater as if stroking a cat.

'You told me.'

Every year at Christmas Nina mentioned her connection to the Russian nobility. Alex had called it her 'getting out the family jewels' moment, and they used to laugh behind his mother's back. On her own, she failed to muster a silent laugh.

'She fled when the Bolsheviks came. I hear Dolly is obsessed with a man who's Russian?'

Anna clutched her knees. Who had told her this? 'He's part French, part Ukrainian, I think.'

A sly smile flicked at the corner of Nina's mouth. 'Ukrainians are Russians. Perhaps you didn't realise.'

'I don't think they see –'

'My grandmother left Russia by travelling through the territory known as Ukraine,' she spoke over Anna. 'She sailed on a British ship docked in the Crimea. Ukraine was part of Russia in the First World War and also after the Second World War. Perhaps no one taught that at your school.' She passed the crockery across the table.

The tea set was of the thinnest china. One day, Anna thought, she would bite a chunk out of one of those cups in frustration. She stared at the wisps of smoke escaping from the old Aga's door.

'They had about thirty years of independence, but then Russia took back Crimea in 2014.' Placing a pan of hot scones on the table, she began pouring the tea. 'Lenin's men killed most of my grandmother's family. Sadly, history has a way of repeating itself.' She pushed food towards Anna like an advancing army. Anna refused.

'I know what Dolly is doing seems wrong,' said Anna, 'but I don't think Michel is working with Lenin's army.'

Nina sipped and replaced her cup onto the saucer, turning the handle so the flowers and the stems aligned. 'Did you know Alex studied Russian at Cambridge?'

'He told me he'd studied politics.' The tea burned her throat.

'Russian and politics.' Another sly smile. 'So you weren't aware he'd studied both? How long have you been married? It's the reason he works at the Foreign Office. I wanted him to work with me on the estate, but –'

Nina had often aired her displeasure at Alex's lack of interest in the land.

'What's your point?'

The older woman raised an eyebrow and ran her index finger over a rivulet in the wooden table. 'My grandmother was an unhappy person,' she said. 'She arrived in England with nothing but a suitcase and a few photographs. My grandfather was smitten by her beauty.' Nina rose and tugged at a drawer in the oak dresser, extracting a silver frame. Three sepia women stood in stiff Edwardian dresses. 'She's the one on the left. Wasn't she beautiful? Black hair and black eyes. You remind me a little of her.'

'You've shown this to me before,' said Anna, 'and I'm nothing like her.'

'Your colouring is the same.' Nina held the frame against the light. 'And so's your attitude. You see, she was unhappy, and you're unhappy, my dear. I'm old enough to know some people are incapable of happiness. My grandfather provided my grandmother with this beautiful land, but it wasn't sufficient. Her family had a palace in St. Petersburg, so the Faver Estate didn't compare.'

'That's not me.' Anna bit her cheek in annoyance.

'But just like my grandmother, you have never warmed to the Faver legacy. In Russia, she was a princess, but in England she was Mrs Faver, the wife of a country squire. And you –'

Finding herself unable to listen to more of Nina's platitudes, Anna gathered her coat and purse from the back of the chair. 'I signed the prenup you asked for. What more do you want from me?'

Simon's entrance saved the situation from further escalation. He flew into the room, flapping a pamphlet. 'Look. It came in the post, Granny. Look, Mummy.' He thrust the paper under Anna's face. 'When I'm older, I'm going to university to study oenology.' He pronounced the word as if he had spent a week practising. 'That's about vineyards. Granny says she'll help me.'

Anna bent to give her son a kiss. 'It's a big decision to make when you're ten. See what you think when you're sixteen.'

'Oh, I won't change my mind,' he declared, and Nina gathered him in a hug.

She drove down the long driveway, blasting her car radio. It was clear Alex and Nina suspected her relationship with Sasha, so why hadn't they come right out with it? But then, why hadn't she? A gardener stooped over one of the outer fences and gave a wave of recognition, but she was too flustered to acknowledge it. If only life were as simple as mending a fence with a nail and hammer and a new plank of wood.

The radio newsreader burst through her thoughts.

Russia is amassing troops on the Ukrainian border.

Her body stiffened in the car seat.

Ukraine has asked to join NATO to avoid bloodshed, but NATO has refused, afraid to inflame the situation with Putin.

Oh God! Pebbles scattered as she shot out of the drive onto the country lane.

Putin claims he has no plans to invade Ukraine, but American intelligence suggests otherwise.

When exactly was Sasha leaving? The plan was for her to take the train to St. Pancras to meet him today. Matching her thoughts, his voice text came through the car intercom.

Michel is away doing work for Gonzales, so we stay in his flat tonight.

Tomorrow he come with me to Goodwood. xxx.

She answered and put her foot down, racing to the station. This was the moment of decision.

'Are you worried about returning to Ukraine?' she said as they hugged.

They ran through wet snowflakes to the Deli flat.

'No. I am like Vitali Klitschko. You know him?' He rolled his eyes in mock despair as she professed ignorance. 'C'mon, Anna! He's hero. Mayor of Kyiv and big man. Big, big man. He was world champion boxer. Famous! Big fight in America. Nobody beats Vitali Klitschko.' He silenced her worries with kisses and drew her into the bedroom.

It was as tidy as before; the two knapsacks stood on guard as if they had never left, and for a time, the world ceased to exist beyond the confines of the bed. The heat of their passion filled her with courage; she would tell the world about their love, and damn the Favers.

'I wanted to go with you, but –'

'I am here for big race in two weeks. I do not go until it is done.'

'But when you return won't you be in danger?'

'Ukraine is big country. You can travel for hours with wheat fields and blue skies and rivers. I read this from travel blogger! So, I will be safe. Look, I've made your photo.' He held the two celluloid photographs between finger and thumb. She blushed when she saw her naked shoulders and the half-moon pendant slotted into her cleavage, and he laughed, placing them back into his wallet.

'But Sasha, will there be war?'

He flexed the Ukrainian flag bicep like a child imitating a heavy weight boxer. 'I am soldier.'

'You're a driver.'

'But no difference! I drive a tank!' He teased her with a mime, and she had to smile. Compared to Alex's constant cautions, his optimism was glorious.

The phone chirped with a newsflash.

Breaking. USA intelligence insist Putin has amassed 130,000 troops on the Ukrainian border.

'Oh God. Read this.' She thrust it in his hand and he tapped and read.

'We're used to such things. Ukraine has been fighting Russia since 2014. You know Minsk Agreement? Russia broke this. And Minsk Agreement number two? Russia broke this, too. They are scum. They tell lies.' A sudden invective replaced his good humour. 'If Russian soldiers come to my family, Michel and I will grab gun and kill them.' He sat up, thrusting aside the duvet. 'I swear I kill every one of them.'

She ran a hand down his bare back, watching the tattoo flex.

'Better still, let's get your father a visa and we can all live here. I'll find a good solicitor.'

He sighed and pressed a light kiss to her lips. 'Ukraine is my land. Sometimes, Anna, we must fight.'

She pressed her body to his back, tightening arms around his chest. 'I can't lose you. Is it so important where we live?'

They remained entwined and silent. Anna put her face to his collar bone, inhaling his unique scent. Wherever he was, she would be there.

He sighed. 'Like England, we are old country. First there was Kievan Rus, then there was Russia. Kievan Rus was centre, when Moscow was huts. They take name, Rus, but we have castles –one thousand years old – and we will always fight for our country. So please, you understand, I must go back to Papi. His heart is there. Although the Soviets force him to speak Russian, he is Ukrainian and he bury my mother in Mariupol.'

She felt his shoulders tighten and she struggled to find a way through this puzzle. 'At least, wait a few months.'

'But I must take Michel to Papi, and this is good for your brother's marriage. Also good to get Michel away from terrible people in Deli.'

'Terrible people? Who?' She released him from her grasp, and he slipped a T-shirt over his torso, covering the peach bullet hole.

'Gonzales is Russian, and every rich Russian in Europe has blood on their hands.'

Bemused, she allowed Sasha to put the folds of her T-shirt over her head. 'But why would a Russian be running a sandwich shop in East London? My mother-in-law believes anyone from Donetsk is Russian, so do you mean the owner is of Russian extraction?'

He made no reply, walking from the bedroom into the living room window to check the street below. Anna followed, pressing into his broad back and glancing over his shoulder. In front of the neon tube sign, she saw the outline of someone in a dark coat. A man crossed the car park, briefly lifting his head to look up at their light, before disappearing under the Club's awning.

With a jolt, she retreated. 'My God, that's my brother. What's he doing here at this hour? Is the Deli still open?' In answer they heard the jangle of the shop door.

Sasha took her face between his hands and kissed her. 'This end soon, and we go. Please, Anna, come with me to Ukraine. Don't stay here.'

She put her head to his chest. 'I want to, but I have to think of Simon.'

His arms held her close. 'He also come. We go to Mariupol. It's beautiful. And remember: you belong to me, and I belong to you.'

'Yes, yes,' she murmured, but in her heart she was unsure how to fit the pieces of her life together.

TWENTY

whitstable

FEBRUARY 2022

> *Despite building military hospitals on the shared northern border, Putin says he has no plans to invade Ukraine. But the Biden administration suggests this is a lie.*

ANNA BEGGED him to extend his visa. With each news bulletin, her thoughts went to the impossible. How to keep them together if Sasha was determined to return to Mariupol? She had said nothing to Nina or Alex, unwilling to broach the subject until she had a firmer idea of her movements.

On Sasha's next visit, she insisted they went to the beach promenade, determined to discuss other possibilities. Wrapped in scarves against the buffeting breezes, they held hands, walking the length of the grassy Tankerton slopes, passing the brightly coloured beach huts, shuttered, and in need of a varnish. The retreating tide shrank from the pebbled shore as they stepped over the exposed stones that wove a path into the North Sea. They strode out on the shingle until water surrounded them on three sides, and they gazed at the old army forts, eight miles out, rust-red under a sudden flare of angry sun. He appeared sad as he tracked the line of wind turbines on the horizon, and she suspected he was seeing another sea and another horizon. A terrible premonition hit her: was he about to admit to some other reason for needing to leave? Had his declarations of love been thin? The harsh cry of the seagulls echoed her anxieties.

'Do you want us to separate? Is this affair to end?' She could not keep the tremor from her voice.

He gripped her hand, his gaze remaining on the horizon. 'Is complicated.'

'That's not an answer,' she said, feeling as if her feet would turn to shingle with the cold.

He kissed her hand with a fierceness she did not understand and began to talk to the sea. She leaned against him to listen.

'Many people fought on different sides,' he said, adding it was important she understood his teenage life. The Ukrainian eastern borders comprised Chechens, Cossacks, Russians, and Ukrainians, as well as those of mixed heritage and allegiances. He listed the armies: the Donetsk Liberation Army, the Luhansk Liberation Army, the Russian Army, the Ukrainian Army with units under the control of Kyiv. He remembered peaceful times, but he also recollected skirmishes and fighting where soldiers with guns shot others on little provocation.

He was so proud of his eldest brother, Andrey, who had been part of the Ukrainian Army, the Cyborgs, defending the Donetsk airport. But once the Russians took over, that put Andrey at risk of capture and torture. Everyone knew Russians tortured prisoners of war as a matter of policy, and both of his mothers insisted the family relocate to a relative in Mariupol, now under Ukrainian control.

So they piled into the car, taking what possessions they could. Their dog sat in the back with him and Michel and Andrey. The two mothers squashed in the front, and they set off, aware they would pass many army checkpoints on the long drive. The plan was that whenever they faced a security check, they would cover Andrey with a blanket and sit on him, making him invisible under the clutter. Since the Russians had confiscated their Ukrainian passports, everyone had Russian documents except for Astrid. Each time they stopped, his father showed Astrid's French passport, claiming they were heading to Paris, and this seemed to work.

But when they came to the last checkpoint, the Russian soldiers were nervous, jumping like crickets. In a previous skirmish, the razor wire and barriers had taken a battering, offering clear passage to the long straight road ahead. Without the usual blockades, the guards stopped every car, forcing out the occupants to search the vehicles. Nobody knew what they were looking for, and the queue mounted. When they were ten cars from the front, they watched as the Russians seized a man, pointed a gun at his head, and forced him into their army jeep. Panic rippled down the line. Some men got out of their cars to huddle, whisper, plot and wait. It was dusk, and the soldiers had become irritable waiting for a relief unit, as the line stretched to over a hundred cars.

When his father arrived at the gate, the guards instructed him to switch off, but he crashed through the flimsy pole blocking the way, and five other vehicles of differing sizes roared behind him in their pre-arranged flight. Glass flew everywhere as bullets shattered windows. People screamed; some shot back, but the element of surprise gave them an advantage. The last car to cross took a hit to the petrol tank and burst into flames, killing everyone in their vehicle, but assisting the getaway of those in front. With so many others waiting at the checkpoint, the border guards had no option but to defend their barrier, so they didn't give chase. Sasha remembered how a bullet had grazed his father's neck, and from behind, he watched the blood seep across his old man's shoulders. He felt damp around his hips but did not register that he had been hit.

Then Michel began to scream in a high-pitched girl's voice. The dog lay dead at his feet, and Astrid twisted in her seat, trying to soothe her son as they raced towards the next checkpoint. The four cars braked in a cloud of dust as the Ukrainian soldiers attempted to block their entrance, but a woman jumped out and ran to them, waving Ukrainian documentation, speaking to the main guard until they signalled them through.

Sasha remembered how his mother had groaned and closed her eyes and his father had pulled over, clambering out of the car, soaked in blood and trembling. He and Astrid eased Sasha's mother out of the car to lie her on the ground and check her wounds. One of the Ukrainian guards came over to ask if they needed help and called the paramedics. Too shocked to feel pain, Sasha's wounded hip went unnoticed until much later. He leaned over his mother, who was asking for Andrey, and it was only then they realised he hadn't emerged. His father lifted the blanket. A bullet had pierced the rear window, travelled through the passenger seat, and lodged in his head. He had half a face.

Sasha spoke without emotion, and except for the tightness of his grip on her hand, he might have been recounting someone else's escape. She shivered as the sea began to invade, the tide turning, dampening their feet while the seagulls screamed overhead.

'Come,' she said, pulling him towards the shore, but he wouldn't move.

'My mother die in hospital, and we bury her with Andrey at Mariupol.' His voice retained the same monotone. 'Astrid take Michel to France. So, you see, I lose two mothers and two brothers that week. This is why Papi won't leave their graves.'

She held onto his hand, tugging.

'Michel came here and stay with Russians. Pah! But he says all done now.'

'I see,' she said, but she had no idea what he was talking about, and again tried to pull him out of the advancing waves. The shingle was disappearing as they made their way back towards the concrete promenade.

'Come, please. I'm getting wet. You are alive and I love you.' She put a hand to his cheek, to draw him from the past to the present. 'Please.'

With a sudden shiver, his picked his feet out of the water and followed her to the shore, where he wrapped his arms around her as if she might disappear.

'I'm sorry.' And for the first time, she began to see that the laughter and bravado hid something too large for her to take away. All she could do was love him.

'I can't lose you, Anna,' he said, burying his face in her shoulder. 'When Papi dies, you are all I have. I love you. If you cannot come to Ukraine, you must promise to wait for me if he is in hospital. Do not forget me. I belong to you and you belong to me.'

She promised, kissing him wildly as if to banish his sorrow, assuring him he must not doubt her, because she understood he had no choice but to leave. Ben Wallace had spoken of *a whiff of Munich in the air*, and she felt crazy with fear for his safety, but he had to take Michel to say goodbye. There was no other choice.

A few days after Valentine's Day, Alex returned to the house. There had been no flowers and his grim expression told her he was ready to discuss battle lines. He seemed older and greyer; his shoulders stooped as if he had sat too long in front of a computer. They struggled through family time, waiting until Simon was in bed to perch on opposite sides of the kitchen table and negotiate.

He began. 'Of course I know.'

She said nothing, steadying herself for the confrontation.

'How often have you met with that man?'

'You mean Sasha.'

Alex snapped his fingers in irritation. 'Alex Vronskiy, the Russian who deliberately inveigled his way into your life.'

Inveigled? It seemed an old-fashioned word, but Alex tended towards pedantry. 'Let's call him by his correct name, Oleksandr Vronskiy.'

He closed his eyes, a deep frown line creasing his brows. 'Have you really no suspicion of what's going on?'

'I know Sasha came to my aid when I was mugged. And he offered to prise Michel away from Dolly – which he has done. I can't vouch for his brother, but Sasha is a good man.'

Alex leaned across the counter, grabbing her arm, and she cried out in surprise. 'Listen to me, Anna. These men are only interested in you and Dolly because they're seeking leverage against me and your brother.'

'Leverage?' That was another curious word. Anna pulled from his grasp to tuck both hands under her thighs. 'Is that what Stephen's saying? Because if this is to do with my father's old books, it's nonsense. I think my brother is having some kind of breakdown.'

'I'm not getting my information from your brother,' he spat. 'This man – this Vronskiy – speaks Russian and works for the Russians. His brother has been living in a Russian safe house and has approached us for payment with some intelligence he's unearthed. Michel Vronskiy wants to betray them – unlike your lover-boy.'

She recalled Stephen's words about Michel, but hesitated to amplify the narrative. It had to be nonsense. Nothing more than rumour. *Smoke and mirrors.*

'You're listening to crazy conspiracy theories. Stephen is a boring civil servant. He has nothing to hide, and Dolly has always had flings. As for you – your work involves the Official Secrets Act – so why would anyone hang around me for intelligence? I don't know anything except information about the latest French romance. Or perhaps they want Dolly to do some conveyancing for them?'

His fist banged on the table, and she flinched, appalled that his anger might escalate to physical violence. As if to quell his fury, Alex rose and went to the back door, pressing his cheek against the cold glass. 'Sorry,' he said. 'You're such an innocent.'

'And whose fault is that?' she raged. 'You've never treated me as an equal. I'm the mother of your son. I'm your wife, but you tell me nothing. If anyone's Russian, it's you with your mother's pride in her noble lineage. If you'd ever spoken to Sasha or Michel, you'd know their father is dying.'

'Russia and Ukraine are on the edge of war.' He put his two hands together in a semblance of prayer. 'For God's sake, Anna – believe me – this isn't about you or Dolly or an affair that I couldn't care less about. I'm sorry but that's the truth. I don't care. What I care about is the leaking of sensitive information. Espionage.'

The turn of conversation was so bizarre, she burst into laughter. For all her years with Alex, the closest they had come to talking about spying was watching James Bond on Netflix. 'It must be contagious,' she said, spitting with scorn. 'First Stephen, now you!' She laughed again as he continued to look out to sea. 'All Michel did was borrow an old book, a copy of Anna Karenina – a book that belonged to my father. Next you'll be telling me my father was a spy.'

'Ah, the book.' The information did not surprise him as she thought it would. 'During the Cold War, that book had its uses.'

Anna blinked. 'The Cold War? Last century?'

He put his hands in the pocket of his jeans. 'People used microfiche to pass information to an enemy – dots in books.' He dismissed her potential interruption. 'One thing that hasn't changed is the law pertaining to treason. When you are a traitor to the realm, you're not treated like a common criminal. When they arrest you for spying, you're no longer *entitled to a phone call*.'

She swallowed. 'So who's the traitor? Why must you talk in riddles?'

He ran a weary hand over his eyes, and she bit her lip in anger. Nothing bad had ever happened to Alex. He was a man who came from a wealthy family and had lived with a proverbial silver spoon in his mouth. He didn't understand the pain of loss.

'Here's a theory for you.' She rose and advanced on him. 'Maybe you're jealous because another man expresses interest in *me*. Though God knows, we haven't had sex in ages. Maybe you pretend your secrets are official because you're the one having affairs. What do you think of that?'

He pushed her away, his voice rising in frustration. 'I've let this arrangement of yours go on without murmur, but it has to stop! Do you hear me!'

'I hear you, and I'm leaving you.'

From the top of the stairs, Simon's call of confusion sounded and Alex hissed in suppressed anger. 'You want this Russian guy? Fine. I've bought tickets to the Goodwood charity car race on the 20th, the one where he's driving for BMW. We're all going to go, and then we'll see –'

'Daddy, why are you cross?'

Simon entered the kitchen, rubbing his eyes, and Alex deflated.

'Ask your mother.'

'Did you say car race? I want to see a car race.' His childish plea cut through their argument, and Anna curled protective arms around her son.

'You can go if your mother wants to go. I'm attending with a Russian delegation. They've given me free tickets because they have business interests in one of the car manufacturers. Your grandmother will be there, too.'

Simon's face lit up. 'Please, Mum, please?'

'Of course, my darling.' She smoothed a cowlick of his hair. 'We were talking about Uncle Stephen and Aunty Dolly.'

'Are they getting a divorce?'

Alex pushed past them to retreat to the study, and Anna sighed.

Nausea assailed her, and she swallowed the burning reflux. Returning to her role as a mother, she settled her son in his bedroom, fielding his questions. A gust of freezing night air rushed up the stairs as Alex called from the front door.

'It'll be cold at Goodwood, so put on your furs.' A slam, and the car slid off the driveway.

Tears brimmed and Simon continued to demand answers. Why furs? Why was Daddy gone? Why was everyone angry?

'Don't worry, darling. All adults argue,' she soothed, knowing she possessed neither furs nor answers. Sitting with him until he slept, she went into the bathroom to vomit as doubts sidled into her brain. First Stephen, now Alex. Even Sasha had said something about Michel finishing what he came for.

We have no plans to invade Ukraine. It's just army manoeuvres.

TWENTY-ONE

goodwood, sussex

FEBRUARY 2022

SHE COULD NOT BANISH a sense of foreboding. Checking on Google, she researched the Goodwood Charity Race finding it involved competition between certain top of the range electric cars. BMW, Lotus, Renault, Peugeot and Lamborghini were taking part, with money raised from ticket sales going to a veterans' charity. Sasha's last text said Michel was helping as a go-fer, but on the lead up to the event, his communication ceased, and she felt tangled in vague, amorphous fears.

'What's he playing at?' said Dolly, who rang the morning before the race. 'Why would Alex give us tickets to this event? Doesn't he know Michel will be there? And even more weird is Stephen's agreed to go. Something about keeping in with Alex.'

They discussed plausible explanations, each feeding to the other's fears. Nothing made sense, and they thought about boycotting the whole thing, but both wanted to say goodbyes. And Anna wanted to share news.

• • •

The day of the event, the weather demanded furs; or at least, stout coats and scarves. An icy wind cut across the south of England, and Anna suspected there would be no fashion models in fancy hats, or girls in skimpy shorts as was the norm for PR occasions. Alex drove them to the venue in oppressive silence, while Simon sat in the back, immersed in war games on his tablet. The clouds intensified as he swung his Saab into a field, passing under a bridge with a Dunlop logo. People stepped from their cars, gathering their coats, waiting for golf buggies to ferry them across the muddy terrain to the hospitality suites.

Along the row of grey buildings, Anna saw the shuttered shop hubs, reminding her of Covid's recent past. To one side, a London double-decker bus stood on a large concrete plinth with the insignia of BMW. Despite Simon's entreaties, Alex ushered them away from the bus and towards the suite, where they walked under a huge corporate banner to climb a flight of stairs. Spotting Nina at the back of the room, Alex left Anna, while he and Simon surged forward. She pretended to examine the sepia race prints dotting the walls, trying not to imagine what a confrontation between Alex and Sasha might look like. She told herself that Sasha was on the other side of the track in the pits and unlikely to come into the visitors' zone.

'I must go. There's this meeting with foreign investors. We're discussing their financing,' said Alex, loud enough for her to hear.

He brushed his mother's cheek and ruffled Simon's hair, then left a few moments later, joining a group of five men in expensive-looking black jackets. They formed a huddle of conversation. Nodding to her mother-in-law, Anna wandered over to the external viewing terrace to watch the marshals in high-vis vests on the track. The weather was not auspicious for an enjoyable race; naked trees cupped the pit area, and beyond, the fields were muted green against thick cloud.

Two cars glided into view, the mechanics trotting alongside like coach dogs. Simon came to her side, trying to prise open the viewing doors, but his grandmother held him back. 'It's too cold,' she said. 'You can go outside with your father later.'

'He's working,' said Anna.

'He works too hard,' said Nina, as if it were her fault.

The delegation reminded Anna of a murder of crows; all dressed in dark suits with polished shoes. She felt relieved when Alex led the men down the stairs into one of the conference rooms below. Chattering to his grandmother, Simon spread leaflets along the trestle table. The glossy pamphlets extolled the virtues of English wine: *New English wines from an Old English family*, the printed logos said, with descriptions of the Faver Estate and vineyard visits.

A curvaceous woman in a purple suit headed her way with a label that said, Betsy Vronskiy, BMW Marketing. There was no mistaking the surname, but the painted dark lips and brassy blonde hair did not remind Anna of either Michel or Sasha. She bore a retro-1950s look, her bun swept like whipped cream and a pinched-waist dress with high heels. Anna felt dowdy in her sensible trousers and flat shoes, chosen for standing in a field and possibly running across the track to speak to Sasha.

'Good to meet you, Anna.' Betsy smiled and turned towards Nina. 'You must be proud of your mother. Such a talent to run a vineyard on her own!'

Unusually, Nina didn't correct the woman, instead

accepting the compliment without hesitation. Betsy sidled around the bar, steering Anna away from the trestle table towards a large circuit map on the wall.

'If you can bear the cold, go to the Paddock grandstands,' she whispered. 'Nearest to the pits.'

Anna stared at her.

'I've lived in Surrey for twenty years, so when Sasha stopped by, we discussed a good meeting place for the two of you.' She gave a small laugh. 'Did he tell you, if he wins the race, he will receive ten thousand pounds?' She tapped Anna's wrist. 'But don't get too hopeful. He's driver number three. Not allowed to win! All fixed, you know. Just for show.'

Anna hadn't known, but felt lightheaded with relief, sensing an ally. Before she could ask more, Dolly arrived, shouting a greeting as she entered the large room. Swathed in a large Barbour coat with a fur hat, her sister-in-law clumped in wearing fashionable Hunter pink wellingtons, as if awaiting a Horse and Hounds photoshoot. Stephen followed in more sober attire, matching the Russian delegation's garb.

Simon ran to his uncle's side. 'Have you brought my cousins?'

'Sorry,' said Stephen. 'They're busy at university.' He patted the boy's shoulder, but his eyes searched the room, and Anna felt a twinge of guilt. From the thinness of his face, she could see the strain the last few months had taken on her brother's health.

'Bad visibility for this race,' said Dolly, massaging the beads at her neck. 'But I understand they're doing it to catch up on the Covid backlog.' In a covert gesture that would not have been out of place in a magician's show, she withdrew a small book-shaped package and slid it inside

Anna's coat. 'Put it somewhere safe,' she muttered, with a sideways twist of her mouth. 'I'm sick of arguing with Stephen about this. He's crazy. He even took away my Russian amber necklace.'

Anna darted a look at Stephen, who was retracing his steps towards the stairs, and threw the copy of Anna Karenina in her bag, firmly closing the clasp.

'Is he still suffering?'

'Not on my account. Michel has gone, but he's still behaving oddly.'

Returning to them, his lips set in a peevish curve, Stephen grimaced. 'Why did I agree to this, Dolly?'

'No idea, darling.' Dolly took out a vape.

Anna squeezed his coat sleeve to gain his attention. 'How are you? We haven't spoken for the past month.'

He grunted as Betsy came to their side.

'Sorry, you can't vape or smoke in here. You'll have to go on the double-decker bus for that.'

Several people looked around and headed off. Dolly pushed her plum fringe out of her eyes. 'What a great idea! Can I walk over to the pits while I'm outside?' She shot Stephen an ugly look.

'Off limits, I'm afraid,' said Betsy, red lips drawn wide.

'I want to go to the bus, Aunty,' Simon interjected. 'Can I drive?'

'Also off limits, I expect,' said Dolly, waving her vape in mock film star style. 'But let's see what I can do, young man. I can be very persuasive.'

Simon bowled down the stairs, and Anna wondered if she should follow. Perhaps Dolly's plan was to drive the bus away and create a diversion in order to find Michel. She wouldn't put any extremes past her.

'It's been a nightmare,' muttered Stephen in her ear.

Anna leaned against him. She wanted to give him a hug, but wasn't sure he'd welcome such a display. 'Would it help to see a counsellor?'

'What the hell are you talking about?' He pulled away.

'Now Dolly's affair is over, I thought things might be better.'

'Keep your nose out, Anna.'

She protested. 'You asked for my involvement.'

'Things have moved on. I thought you of all people would have been aware.'

The package in her bag felt like an unexploded bomb. 'Aware of what?' A sudden queasiness struck her, and she wondered whether to give him the Anna Karenina copy as a peace offering, but he left in a huff, following the others downstairs.

Her stomach fluttering, she stood alone beside a group chatting about the weather.

'Will it rain?'

'It's bound to rain.'

'But it might not.'

An argument arose about the conditions for the race. Dry tyres or wet to start? An inside viewing platform or an outside one? Who would win the race? Italian? German? French?

'Or Russian,' someone said. 'I hear they're heavily invested in Renault.'

'This is the BMW suite,' protested another. 'Germany!'

'They'll start on dry,' said a tall man in an authoritative voice. He wore a tie with BMW colours and insignia. 'Even if it's dangerous, it's so much faster.'

At the mention of danger, Anna's nausea redoubled. She tried texting Sasha from the external viewing gallery doors, but the text didn't go through. A fair-haired man in padded overalls arrived, parting the room to shake hands with the tall man. They spoke in German before retreating down the stairs to emerge jogging toward the pits.

Betsy arrived at her side with a tray of champagne glasses. 'That's the top driver for BMW. Heinrich Brewer. Have you heard of him? And the other man is the CEO. I've heard they're worried about the competition. Oh my God, the rivalry!' The red lips pulled wide. 'We missed so many dates last year, so now they're squeezing the events in every week but at least it keeps me busy.'

A clap of hands and someone urged them to take up a viewing position. Betsy insisted Anna take a glass, with a small whisper, 'Now go,' and before Anna could react, she moved away, skirt sashaying like a flag. Some retreated to the double-decker bus, but others went through the opened glass doors onto the external viewing platform.

Placing her glass on one of the small round tables, Anna hurried to the stairs, running down to hear a ribbon of heated foreign conversation behind the door near the exit. Was that Alex speaking? But she was in too much of a hurry to eavesdrop and rushed across the thatch of lawn where a thin path shadowed the building. At the corner, she spotted a figure waving; Sasha in padded overalls. She dashed to him, and he took her hands, pulling her behind a large advertising screen, where rain-soaked moss swallowed her feet.

'No CCTV here,' he said, kissing her. Behind them, she saw the grey mouth of an underpass leading to the pits.

'Sasha, you haven't answered your phone for days.'

'Is because I was arrested.'

'What for?' Her stomach jolted.

'I have special interview with Home Office.' His face darkened. 'They mention your name and your husband.

They take my phone. Is why I cannot answer you. And they arrest Michel and ask for our Russian passports. BMW boss help, but we must leave with team or they arrest us again for visa problem.'

'Arrest you? For overstaying your visa? That's crazy. And Michel has a French passport.'

'This is Michel's fault.'

'How?'

His hands tightened on her. 'What is Alex's job?'

Confusion washed over her. She had important news and could not fathom why her husband's work was relevant. 'He works in the Foreign Office.'

'He is visa person?'

'No. That's the Home Office.' She put a finger to his lips, shushing his anger. 'Please. It's terrible this happened but my news is important.' Her hand searched his cheek as she tried to choose the words to make their circumstances easier. Her socks soaked up the damp, spongey earth, and she gathered her thoughts. Perhaps there was no easy way to say it. 'I'm pregnant. I found out only this week.'

His expression changed in a confluence of emotions. From anxiety to surprise to joy, and then he crushed her to him, breath catching in his throat. 'Is wonderful.'

His kisses melted her worries and they laughed together.

'You're okay with this?'

'Is wonderful, but you must come with me to Ukraine. You cannot stay here.' He pressed her hands between his. 'Does your husband know?'

'I would hardly tell him before you,' she said, revelling in his joy. 'It's not Alex's. He had a vasectomy.'

Sasha nodded in wonderment, a light of determination

in his eyes. He squeezed her hands harder. 'You must not stay with your husband. He is bad for us.'

She kissed the bristles of his throat. 'I don't think he'll make problems. Our marriage has been dead for a while.'

From across the track, she heard mechanics calling for him.

'I love you,' he repeated, and touched her coat as if to feel the baby through the wool. 'You and baby come with me. Yes?'

'Yes. But I have to arrange things. My son, Simon, and other family. I'll follow.' Tears pricked at the thought of her fantasy becoming a reality. 'I love you, too.'

'But your husband –' Again, someone screamed Sasha's name. 'Please, for me, find more about his job. Michel say things. You come meet me at train station. St. Pancras. Noon. I go in two days with team on Eurostar. I get new phone.'

'I'll try,' she said, kissing him again. 'But –' The shouts grew louder and she forced herself to slacken her grip.

Another angry shout; Sasha kissed her palms. 'You give me this special gift and I will protect you and baby. I promise. A boy?'

'Or a girl.'

They kissed again. Another shout. She did not want to let him go.

'I find money for us! You see! I am happiest man in whole world.' He held her at arm's length, staring at her abdomen as if to see the child inside, then pulled her into another hug. His exuberant joy touched her, and when she could bear to part, she watched as he jogged through the underpass. He turned. 'Remember, Anna,' he said. 'Your husband. Be safe.'

She waved as he disappeared, a shiver of concern

running through her as water trickled into her shoes. Had he asked her to snoop on her husband? Returning to the path, she looked up at the dark clouds, ripe with impending rain. Wet or dry tyres? No, she thought, people are trying to part us, and I will not believe them. The clouds gathered. He had spoken of an arrest where Alex's name was mentioned, and she could not shake her dark thoughts.

TWENTY-TWO

berlin

NOVEMBER 1991

HE COULD NOT BANISH a sense of foreboding. Annaliese had withheld something from him, her dark eyes giving veiled clues, but when he asked, she insisted it was nerves. Eager to have her by his side, he rifled through the documents.

The Ossi ambulance driver stood at attention, waiting for Vronsky's approval, and when each document passed inspection, he held out his hand for the expected two thick envelopes.

'*Danke*. Shall we notify anyone?' Gunther was keen to encourage more business, unaware of Vronsky's impending departure.

Vronsky shook his head. His aim was to set fire to the wreck, photograph it, and alter the evidence in a laboratory; then call the German fire brigade and police as he drove away. He had confidence the *polizei* would record an accidental death of an unknown person with little or no real investigation. They didn't have the manpower, and recent political upheaval meant the government system was overloaded, left and right sides out of sync.

As the ambulance pulled away, he lit his last cigarette and threw the match onto the petrol pooled interior. A crackle of orange and blue spurts tore through the vehicle, incinerating the body with the sweet smell of burning flesh rising in the thick smoke. Black stripes marked the tree's trunk, and the dampness limited the flames, leaving smoke to curl into the sky. The birds had taken flight, and in their absence he could detect no sound of fire engines, so he paced around the wreck, taking photographs from various angles.

As he completed his task, the rumble of the S-Bahn indicated the first morning train had left for the city centre. He walked down the lane and turned a corner to find his BMW approaching. Dolomeyer was in the driver's seat, but the passenger seat was empty, and Vronsky felt a spurt of adrenalin.

'Where's Agent Anna?'

Dolomeyer stepped out of the car, leaving the keys dangling. 'She wasn't there.' He scratched his head, swiping a thick thatch of hair from his brow. 'Not my fault. I did everything you asked and now I want my passport and my money.'

Vronsky swore, one hand curling on the gun in his pocket. 'Am I the Deutsche Bank?' A burning sensation arose within him. He swore again, in Russian and in German and in English. 'You'd better tell me what's going on, or–' He patted the envelope inside his large black coat.

'Hey, don't get sore with me, Mac. She wasn't there. The place was empty, so I thought she'd hitched a ride with the ambulance.' His eyes were pinpricks, and he swayed, holding onto the BMW's open door.

Vronsky inhaled like an asthmatic on oxygen. 'No. The Ossis have been and gone.'

'Maybe she went to a bar around the corner; shall we look?'

He lunged at Dolomeyer's leather jacket. 'Talk, you shit. What the fuck's going on? Tell me or I'll put a bullet in you now.'

'Cool it, man.' He giggled, staggering backwards. 'Last night, she said something about returning to England to find the missing books. I thought she'd told you. Ya think she's headed over there?'

Vronsky pulled Dolomeyer to his chest, eyeball to drugged eyeball. 'Impossible. I've got her new passport. She wouldn't use her old one. It would destroy the plan.'

'Dunno, then.' The American shrugged him away, weaving a few steps. 'You ordered me not to kill her or I'd have sorted it. S'not my fault.'

In a red mist, Vronsky charged him in the gut, pushing him to the ground. Scrabbling in the dirt, Dolomeyer whipped out a knife and Vronsky produced his gun.

'Tell me how she could leave the country without her new passport?'

'You want the truth, Mac?' He wiped his dribbling nose. 'She had another passport. I saw her tuck it in her handbag.'

'What?' A roar erupted from his chest. 'Why didn't you say? Who the fuck gave her another passport?'

Giggling, the American rolled on the cold road, picking up black specks of asphalt as he turned himself over, scrambling to his feet. The knife glinted in his hand. 'I dunno, but I thought you'd given it to her. Don't get mad at me. You said sort the husband, not the wife.'

'Have you taken another line of coke at the hotel?'

'Maybe. But, hey, I've done my bit, and you owe me, 'cos

I'm heading back to sweet ol' Mom and apple pie. Got me a little farm in Texas.'

'You hate America.'

'Yup. You can take the boy out of the Texas, but you can't –'

'Enough. Enough shit. Fine. Go be Henry Snooks. I don't care. But where's our agent?' Was Dolomeyer telling the truth?

'Look, you can shoot me, but that won't get you info.' He squared his shoulders. 'I've told you all I know, so whaddabout we part company and you go look for her.'

Vronsky threw the brown envelope onto the road, and the man dived for it. 'I never want to see you again, but if I find out you've lied to me ...'

The man giggled and snorted. 'Yeah, yeah. I'll even give you a forwarding address. Y'know, if at some day in the future, you spot her and want me to finish the job ...'

'Go to hell.'

'We might all meet there. Who knows?'

Vronsky spat a large gob of phlegm into the gutter. The stench of smoke and petrol lay heavy in his nostrils. 'You're going to hell sooner than me. A farm in Texas? Growing peanuts?' He spat his scorn once more.

'That was Jimmy Carter.' Dolomeyer laughed, his elbow against the BMW.

With a right hook, Vronsky struck him across the face and the knife skittered to the ground. 'Tell me what you know or I'll –'

'Fuck you, Mac.' He wiped the blood from his mouth. 'You crazy Ruskie. I'm on your side.'

'There are no more sides. And you never had a side.'

'Sure I did.' The American hawked blood. 'I was on the side of the highest bidder and the best coke.'

'You know what we say: the only free cheese is in the mousetrap.'

He watched Dolomeyer search his pockets and wipe his nose again, eyeing up the fallen knife. 'Look, if this is about Anna or Annaliese or whatever she's called, she's not worth it. She's a two-timer and you know it.'

A flash of madness shot through him. One half refused to believe such a thing, and the other half leered at his own foolishness. He wanted to kill Dolomeyer, eviscerate him with his own knife, gouge out his eyes, and chop off his fingers, one by one. He wanted to hear him scream. But he needed to get out of the country, and Stepanov might not be so happy to extricate him from a brawl in a Berlin suburb. In the distance, he could hear the S-Bahn disgorging passengers and the sound of a fire engine. Someone had seen the smoke and made the call.

Had he ever understood Annaliese? Her ridiculous marriage; her passion for communism. Last night she had given him assurances, and he had wanted to trust her, because he loved her. But did she love him?

He ground his teeth. 'I'm warning you. You'd better not be fucking with me. If you've arranged something – some American deal, I'll find you and rip your tongue out. Slowly.'

'Good luck with that, Mac. When I'm stateside, I'm invincible.'

'Except to the FBI. You'll never be free. Even in Texas. There's no glasnost for traitors like you, and if you've double-crossed me, I'll fucking well find you and extract your brain through your nose while you're tied to a chair.' He stepped into the car and slammed the door.

Dolomeyer went to the passenger side, but Vronsky

pushed down the lock. 'Walk,' he shouted through the glass.

In the rear mirror, he saw the American cursing and stamping his feet as he drove away. What was he going to say to Stepanov? All that effort; all that paperwork and one missing agent, and three missing books. He'd have to go to England to search her apartment. But what would he do if he found her there?

TWENTY-THREE

goodwood, sussex

FEBRUARY 2022

IN TORMENT, she returned to the hospitality suite. The wet rim of her trousers chilled against her ankles, and her feet squelched with every step as she pushed into the curious crowd on the viewing platform. A mist of impatient breath puffed from the spectators awaiting the starter's klaxon. For those who leant over the railings, gripping the metal in expectation, an accident would give spice to the race, and she bit a fingernail before pulling on gloves. The cars were in position on the grid with the mechanics shouting their last checks. Her breath came in short pants.

'Electric cars don't have that marvellous roar.' A nudge at her side, and Betsy dimpled, now wearing a thick leopard print coat. 'Do you think it's going well? It's my first time managing an event at this venue. Usually everything takes place at Silverstone or Brands Hatch.'

A server glided forward with a tray of champagne, his frozen nipples raised under his thin white shirt. Anna refused the glass, but Betsy grabbed a flute and took a gulp.

'See? Look down there. He's in third position at the back of the track.' She gave Anna a kindly squeeze. 'Hey. Don't be so worried, it's not a championship race. It's PR. They're here to showcase new electric vehicle technology. Look, there's Heinrich at the front of the grid along with the others. The second and third drivers have to outmanoeuvre the competitors, so Sasha's job is to block the Lamborghini to make sure Heinrich wins.'

Anna searched amongst the mechanics, trying to identify Michel, but she couldn't see him.

'It's not the Grand Prix,' laughed Betsy, 'but the drivers will fight for the purse. Ten thousand is a good incentive. Poor Aleks. I know he would like the money, but he has a job to do.'

'What did you call him?'

'Oh yes.' Betsy dimpled. 'Sasha. Oleks. Different members of the family call him different nicknames.' She peered over the barrier. 'And there he is with OV.'

Anna followed her line of vision to see a driver levering himself into a car with the initials OV on his helmet. 'But he's Sasha.'

'Yes, but everyone has old Soviet ties. Bad memories for some, like Aleks' father. Many change to Ukrainian names when we became free. And his mother – God bless her – she always spoke in Ukrainian and called him Oleksandr, but his father calls him Sasha. For the sake of this job, he is Oleksandr on visa papers, but Alexandr on Russian papers.' She waved her glass. 'But not important. He is my lovely cousin, and it is good to see him after so many years.'

Anna's mind absorbed the contradictions: Aleks, Oleks, Sasha. The Ukrainian soldiers were Cyborgs, a news item had said they called the Russians orcs. Alex's and Stephen's comments. Sasha's news about his arrest. The pieces stubbornly refused to coagulate into a comprehensible picture.

'Will Sasha rejoin the army when he returns to Ukraine?' she said.

Betsy pulled a face, but before she could answer, a horn blasted and the mechanics withdrew. The race marshal held a flag upright, swinging it downwards like a sword at the second squawk. The cars shot forward, sleek, silent hunters, creating a whine and a whoosh of displaced air along with the sound of tyres on tarmac.

Within seconds, they disappeared and Anna felt a surge of nausea. Human decibels rose along the terrace, combined with wild shouts from the competitors in each hospitality suite. Icy winds bit cheeks and hands, forcing some to retreat inside to watch the vehicles' progress from the warmth of the giant screen. They jumped on the balls of their feet as cars leapt from camera to camera. Anna followed them, desperate to track the OV and BMW insignia painted on Sasha's car roof.

After two laps, the BMW director radiated anger, shouting instructions into his phone to a hidden minion. 'We can't be beaten by Renault. *Gott.*' He cursed in German.

Another circuit. And another. Positions changed. BMW was through to the front. The director wiped the spittle from his mouth.

'The cars are on dry tyres, but look at those clouds.' An older woman in a red coat nudged the tall CEO, who barked again into his phone. Anna watched as a rolling mass of black unfolded across the sky, covering the land like a dark fleece. Within seconds, fat drops fell, and the remaining crowd on the terrace hurried inside. One by one, the cars pulled into the pit area. In and out, they went. In and out, in lightning time, from dry to wet tyres, emerging to shoot away and regain places in the race. The sky crackled with lightning, and the enormous screen flickered, catching each jostle, each overtake and undertake. Two further circuits, and the rain descended in sheets, the track changing from light to dark grey to water-slicked black.

'Look at that idiot. He's refused the marshal's flag. He needs to pull in or any minute now, he'll slide like a bloody Olympic skater.'

'That's our number three. What's he doing?'

The group hungered for an accident; she felt it instinctively, and the thought crushed the breath from her lungs. Sasha's car zipped past the viewing area in pole position. Everyone had been into the pits, except him.

'Idiot.' The CEO growled, cursing in German and shouting into his mobile.

On camera, the OV car slid. There was a gasp as it regained the line.

'We don't crash cars for a race like this. If he so much as scratches it, he's sacked.'

Two more circuits, and still Sasha clung onto pole position. A few cars had come close to bouncing off the haystacks lining the bends, but Sasha was sliding, correcting and increasing speed in a charmed existence. The stem of the BMW man's glass broke, and he swore as a dark stain slashed down his trouser leg. The number one driver, Heinrich, was now in third position for BMW, with Renault just in front, and Sasha leading the pack. Visibility lowered as the rain intensified. Even Nina was squinting and tutting at the race conditions.

'Someone must stop the race,' said Anna to no one in particular.

Betsy gulped more champagne.

On the straight, Sasha zig-zagged in a move to block the

Renault. Both cars fishtailed, and one of the saloon cars behind them veered off the track, bouncing against the haystacks to become smothered. In the split second of confusion, Heinrich overtook the Renault. Hay bales flew, muddy projectiles bounced off the cars at the back. Anna pushed her fist into her mouth to stop herself from screaming. The speed was dizzying. Next to her, someone jumped up and down, laughing, and it was all she could do to stop from slapping his face.

Another circuit done, and in frustration, Lamborghini made a sudden charge to overtake on a bend. Ousted, the Renault fell back further, but Heinrich held his second place. As they rounded the corner, the Lamborghini touched Heinrich's back wheel. By the laws of physics, both cars should have gone flying, but Heinrich drove straight on, while the Lamborghini careened off in a spin. The room erupted in excited swearing. Renault came to challenge from behind, but Sasha drove on, his defiance creating further consternation among the spectators in the suite.

'Aleks has to ease back and let Heinrich overtake,' said Betsy in Anna's ear. 'What's the matter with him?'

A penultimate circuit and they neared the end of the race as the BMW CEO bellowed at the screen, neck tendons bursting with frustration.

In the middle of a collective gasp, Anna's husband appeared with three heavy-set men, wafting in a faint aroma of something acrid. She turned to see Alex with a drink in one hand, whispering with one of the delegation, and watching the screen. The second Renault made a daring charge overtaking on a tight bend. The spectators roared. They were coming up to the final lap.

But the accident took a split second.

With no tread, Sasha's car fishtailed on the penultimate bend to glide across the circuit, spinning left to right in a skiing motion, he spun, winding up nose to the oncoming cars. With expert manoeuvres, Heinrich powered past, but the Renault, desperate to overtake, nudged too close and clipped Sasha's car, causing both cars to swivel, spin and crumple through a barrier, fifty metres from the track. With a sudden crack, the BMW burst into flames.

The CEO stopped mid-swear, and for a moment, the room went ghostly quiet watching flames shoot into the sky. Smoke billowed as the Renault driver squeezed out through his window, running towards the BMW door, but the fire was too intense. Within seconds, the on-site fire brigade arrived with paramedics as viewers screamed. Unable to take a breath, Anna ignored Heinrich's BMW crossing the line to victory and huge applause. Then she heaved in air and shrieked as the BMW number three car became consumed by fire.

'Sabotage,' thundered the CEO. 'Electric cars don't catch fire. Fucking sabotage. I'll kill whoever did this.'

In a frenzy, she ran down the stairs, along the narrow pathway and towards the track underpass. Her wet trousers and shoes weighed her down, with each stride becoming more laborious, but she pushed on, ignoring the thud of footsteps behind her until someone grabbed her arm.

'What the hell do you think you're doing?' Soaked and furious, Alex grappled with her.

'He might be hurt,' she shrieked at him. 'I must go to him. I love him, don't you understand? I love him and I'm pregnant.'

Alex took hold of both her shoulders and shook her hard enough to make her teeth chatter. 'Stop it, Anna. This isn't the time or the place.'

She spat, forcing him to recoil, and ran to the mouth of the tunnel.

Then stopped.

Behind her, Alex skidded to a halt in the mud. 'Shit.'

They both stared. Slumped on the floor of the underpass, a man lay, chin on chest, blood soaking his overalls from a gash at the throat. Alex pushed Anna to one side and kneeled over him, placing two fingers behind one ear. He swore again and took out a handkerchief to wipe his bloody hand.

'Michel Vronskiy,' he said. 'What the fuck were you doing here?'

The rain slammed at either end of the tunnel, curtaining them off from the rest of the group.

'Get out, Anna. Now. Immediately. I don't want your name dragged into this.'

But her body would not obey, her feet magnetised to the dirt path. 'I must go to Sasha,' she repeated.

Striding to her side, he gripped her upper arms. 'Anna! Listen to me! Go back to the hospitality suite! Now.'

A buzzing sounded in her ears, and her eyes clouded. 'I don't understand. All he did was borrow a copy of my father's Anna Karenina.'

She saw Alex's mouth move, but heard nothing, feeling his hands restrain her like an animal.

'Wake up, Anna,' he shouted, manhandling her to the end of the underpass.

She struggled free to land a vicious slap on his face. 'I want Sasha.'

A red weal rose on his cheek. 'Are you completely out of your mind? Michel's dead, and as for your lover boy, let the paramedics treat him. For fuck's sake, go back to Simon. Or have you forgotten you have a son?'

She fought for air, stumbling as he gave her a hard shove towards the red BMW bus. Rain sluiced between her coat and neck, and her feet slipped. She brushed wet hair away from her eyes, listening to the echo of Alex's words behind her. 'For God's sake, fuck off Anna.'

She walked several paces on unsteady feet and turned to see him clamp a mobile to his ear, speaking with an icy calmness. 'It's me. Lock on just three words. Containment situation. Urgent.'

He had never sworn at her, and she had never hit him. They had had a civilised relationship, and she rubbed her tingling hand in disbelief. This was a war zone, and she had witnessed death for the first time But Alex appeared frighteningly familiar with the situation.

TWENTY-FOUR

berlin to london

JANUARY 1992

IN TORMENT, Vronsky returned to Berlin's city centre to finish his assignments. Doubling his daily ration of cigarettes, he sent the required information to the relevant offices, paying close attention to all incoming communications. A telegram confirmed the arrival of Henry Snooks in Texas, and his other cell members notified him with agreed codes. But nothing from Annaliese.

When he could delay no longer, he organised the appointed meeting with Stepanov at the Russian Embassy. His immediate superior flew over from Moscow, an ambitious man embracing change and eyeing new territories. Vronsky wondered how much to tell him, deciding to avoid mention of the loss of the books, and blame Dolomeyer's incompetence for his agent's disappearance.

'So. You can account for everyone except the agent, Anna?'

'Yes,' said Vronsky, hiding his surprise when Stepanov chuckled.

'Are your powers waning? You, the architect of the Anna Karenina cell! I know all about your plans with that beauty, but you can't trust women.' He leaned back in his leather chair and took out a cigar.

Just like a Yankee to muddy the story, thought Vronsky, with a sour twist of his lips.

'They say Gorbachev's love for his wife has been the USSR's undoing.' Stepanov spoke a homily between puffs, and Vronsky listened with scepticism. He had heard subtle criticisms of their president, but always in a back room with a bottle of vodka, and never in a daytime meeting, so he avoided comment.

'What do you want me to do?'

'Nothing. Leave it. Take my advice – forget the woman. She's not the only one to flee. Leave their governments to unearth traitors, and let someone else pay for the trial, and the prison, because frankly, they're a minor threat, so why should we bother? After all, this is the new age of peace and love.'

'You're sure? Cell closed?' He squashed his cigarette into the schnapps glass.

'*Opredelleno.* But you? You still intend to live in a dacha? Retirement? You're too young.'

'It's a change of career, not a retirement.'

Stepanov purred and puffed. 'But –'

Vronsky's hand crushed the cigarette packet. There was always a but.

'But for a man of your experience, we can find uses. I'll contact you. Where exactly are you heading?'

'Zhdanov.'

'Where the hell is that?'

'The Ukrainians call it Mariupol, a day's drive from Crimea.'

'*Blyat*! What a choice. Rather you than me. There's

nothing there but old Cossacks, farms and beaches. Beautiful beaches, so I've heard, but even so – you'll get bored.'

'I own hundreds of acres and I'm thinking of creating a vineyard.'

'How very bourgeois. I had no idea you had these aspirations. Wine!' Stepanov chuckled again. 'Not vodka?'

With increasing irritation, Vronsky wondered why everything he said provided the man with humour. He looked at his superior, hoping that his face did not reveal his thoughts, because he would not admit to the black hollow where Anna should have been.

'Wine,' he confirmed. 'The traitor who handed me the deeds –'

'As a favour under interrogation?'

Vronsky inclined his head. 'This man had begun creating a vineyard. A little private enterprise, and I thought I could improve on it. I know quite a few owners of French and Italian vineyards.'

'You are a man of many talents,' said Stepanov. 'All the people you've met while dining with KGB connections. Well,' he puffed, 'the KGB is finished, and the SVR replaces it for foreign intelligence, and seeing as I'm up for promotion with them, come on! Give me your new address, and I'll pay you a visit. We'll discuss what advantages I can bring to you.'

Dismay settled in Vronsky's stomach. This meeting was proving to be more indigestible than bratwurst. Stepanov's monitoring would mean once a Chekist, always a Chekist, and there would be no escape. Should he forego his ideas, seeing as Annaliese was unlikely to be involved? Should he give in and go to Moscow? The thought plummeted him to a dark space.

Certain ex-colleagues had told him of the Moscow afterlife, a mix of absolute poverty and wild gangland excesses. Owning his own land in Ukraine sounded better. Maybe he should renew efforts to locate *his Anna* but what if Stepanov intervened? Might this ambitious man with the thick eyebrows and cruel smile organise her death – tie loose ends? Vronsky had never been troubled by a conscience, but he didn't want that. He loved the woman; every curve, every delicate touch, the sound of her voice, the smell of her Chanel No. 5, her passion. Yes, love trapped him in its breast. He was a murderer by trade, but he wasn't a monster.

With mixed emotions, he flew to London on his new passport, barging into the second floor Kensington flat only to find her eldest, Stephen, clearing their effects. *Blyat.* He had hoped to get there sooner. Everywhere there were packing cases sealed with brown tape, and the few that were open showed items of clothing and bric-a-brac. With quiet frustration, he scanned the empty bookshelves.

'Can I help you, sir?'

The boy was so typical of the English – hair flopping over his collar and his milky soft hands – even when confronted with an angry Russian, he chose to be polite.

'I'm a friend of your father's,' said Vronsky gruffly. 'I wish to give my condolences to your mother.'

The young man's knees sagged. 'You haven't heard the full story?' He pulled out a crumpled tissue. 'They died together in a car crash, although I can't tell you why they were in Berlin. I'm sorry. Did you know them well? Did you see them in Berlin?'

It struck Vronsky as odd that the son did not express greater surprise at the sudden arrival of a foreigner in the flat. Had Agent Alexei said something? But the only way to get further information would be to rough the boy. From the look of him, it wouldn't take more than a few punches, and he weighed the advantages, choosing to ask more questions. Stephen explained he had seen shocking photographic evidence of their death, and both the police report and the coroner's report laid blame on the faulty brakes of a hired Trabant. The German Police were sending him the paperwork later, but they insisted it was a tragic accident.

The young man spoke between grieving sobs, the tissue moving from eyes to nose, while Vronsky scrutinised every twitch and finger movement. His analysis was that the paperwork had stood up to scrutiny and the son was telling the truth. So where was Annaliese? If she was intending to fake her death and disappear without him, wouldn't she have returned to her children to say goodbye? It was possible she had returned and frightened them into lying, but if so, the son's performance was stellar. Stephen said he'd last seen his mother when she dropped Anna at his door, promising to return in a week, and he blew his nose, apologising as he fished in his pocket for paper and pen to write details about the times and dates of the funeral.

Vronsky thanked him, explaining he wouldn't attend as he had business pressures in Europe. It didn't pay to hang around. He offered his condolences once again, annoyed that he could find no reason to request a search of the sealed boxes.

To the world, the cell door had closed, even if three copies of Anna Karenina were missing. He was positive she had taken one copy from his hotel bedroom, but there had to be two somewhere in those packing cases. He walked along the pavement, smoking and thinking. If Stephen didn't know the significance of the editions, then the books did not warrant a night-time break-in so soon after John Blount's death, for that might raise suspicions in the wrong places. Best to let them lie forgotten on a shelf until a later time.

He leaned on the black railings that overlooked the secluded gardens with a bittersweet remembrance of the past. Leave it, he said to himself. Loose ends had a habit of working their way to the surface, like seeds heading for the light, and there was nothing she could say to harm him. If she was alive – He stopped. The thought of her death was like a stab wound. But if she was alive, she could not speak without incriminating herself, so he had to live hoping one day their paths would cross and then ...

Deep in thought, he returned to his former landlady's residence, hanging his coat on the usual peg, unlacing his shoes in the usual manner. But the world was different. He would never return here. He made a promise to himself: if he ever heard of some rogue agent leaving *his Anna* dead in a ditch, he would find that person and inflict the worst of agonies. That was the least he could do.

He spent his last night in London ringing every contact in his book: English, French, Russian. Like Stepanov, they all denied knowledge of her whereabouts, and none claimed to know her real name. Many continued to encourage him to join the realms of the former KGB, pushing paper in The Central Bank of Russia, but to hell with them.

A few expressed their anger at the loss of power the Soviet Union had undergone, but most were taking the American line that money was the salve, so steal what you could.

'*Tovarich*, the Cold War is over,' one colleague joked. 'Transfer your money into private accounts and buy an island. We're all doing it. As for the proles, let them eat bread. I've heard people are starving in the streets, but seeing as it's Gorbachev's policies causing a recession, let them blame him. Each man for himself, heh?'

Blyat. Of course he knew about the lie of the land, but how could he explain he was in no mood for a celebration? After smoking an entire packet and drinking a bottle of vodka, he still felt riled. What was the sum total of his life? He was a Chekist without someone to interrogate, a former big cat lacking a mouse, a torturer who was being tortured. Yes, he had a Swiss bank account, but he craved answers. Had Annaliese betrayed and lied to him for years? To him! She was the only woman he had loved and hadn't he promised to protect her? He did not know which hurt more: his pride or his heart.

With a flash of anger, he contemplated smashing his glass and jabbing a jagged edge into his carotid artery. But would she even receive news of his death? *Blyat.* Where the hell was the satisfaction in that?

TWENTY-FIVE

goodwood, sussex

FEBRUARY 2022

SHE PEERED around the edge of the building, her heart hammering. The corporate sponsors and mechanics huddled in the rain, stamping their feet like racehorses, while firefighters stood over the wreck, now buried under foam. Two paramedics were dragging a blackened and unconscious Sasha to a nearby stretcher. A second ambulance arrived with a brief flash of blue light struggling towards the tarmac.

Her coat dripped and she retreated inside to hear the BMW CEO reassuring a crowd of his driver's good health. 'Excellent fireproof overalls. Singed eyebrows. Nothing too terrible.'

Her brain fogged as Betsy slotted by her side.

'There is no fuel on these cars. What happened?' Betsy held a hand to her mouth. 'I think sabotage. But who would do this to dear Aleks?'

Anna's mouth opened but no words came out.

'And where's Michel? He will be so worried.'

The crowd's ignorance was offensive, and the world undulated beneath Anna's wet feet: her pregnancy, her future in Ukraine, her love for Sasha, the death of his brother – everything was drowning.

Simon bowled over, eyes shining. She looked at his innocent enthusiasm with disbelief.

'Did you see that, Mum? Wasn't it great?'

Mute, she shook her head as people flooded in and out of the hospitality suite. Simon squinted up at her before saying he would find his grandmother. Arms pushed through the crowd, and Dolly arrived, breathless.

'Chin up. They'll treat him for burns. He'll be right as rain.'

Still, Anna could not speak. She heard people express opinions through a gauzy haze.

'What terrible safety. These cars shouldn't catch fire.'

'I heard the battery was faulty.'

'The driver was careless.'

'The driver was fearless.'

'Did you see that overtake?'

'BMW will be pissed at the damage costs.'

'I hope the fireproof balaclava protects the eyes.'

'Worth a pic if it doesn't.'

There was the whine of zips and a clatter of people placing down their glasses and closing their padded jackets. Some grumbled about the slow progress of the security guards who had materialised at the bottom of the stairs, insisting everyone leave, but also checking names before they could climb into the golf carts. No one mentioned Michel. He did not exist.

Alex arrived, wet through, and brushing off the mark on his cheek as a bruise where he had slipped and fallen. He pointed to the mud on his trousers.

'Where's Michel?' Dolly whispered to her. 'I wanted to say goodbye before he leaves.'

She stared at her sister-in-law, who returned the look with a frown of incomprehension.

'We suspect arson,' said Alex, 'so we've instructed all hospitality guests to leave. Even Mother has to leave without clearing her stock.'

'And I'm not happy about it,' said Nina, ushering Simon to descend the stairs. 'If my stock goes missing ...'

At the bottom, Stephen stepped out of the toilets, tucking the back of his shirt into his trousers. 'God, what a thing. Made me quite queasy.' He looked upwards. 'What's happened to you, Alex? You're covered in mud?'

'So's Anna. Some of us got caught in the rain.' Alex took Anna's hand preventing her from following the others. 'We'll be off in a minute. You lot go on ahead.'

At Alex's request, Simon went with Nina, and Dolly joined Stephen, and then he propelled her into a side room, telling her to wait while various officers conglomerated outside the building. He left and she saw the window overlooked the track. Moving with shaky limbs, her mind replayed finding Michel and his blood-soaked neck. She pressed her brow to the cold pane while Alex spoke to the paramedics.

Nothing was real. Everything she had seen or heard in the past hour was fake. The bright red torrent running like paint down Michel's overalls had to be some sick pantomime.

When Alex returned, he plunked a polystyrene cup of hot tea at her elbow. 'Sugared, good for shock,' he said, and despite her best efforts, she burst into tears. He placed a supportive arm around her, while she buried her face in his side. With a few pats to her back, he eased away and offered a clean white handkerchief. It was so typical of Alex to use a cotton square instead of a tissue that she suppressed a hysterical laugh before blowing her nose, desperate to appear in control. From his pocket he withdrew a two-bar packet of shortbread.

'Eat. Drink. Keep your blood sugar up.'

'Stop being so fucking calm,' she said, sniffing, but biting into the biscuit.

It tasted of cotton, and she forced it down with a sip of tea. He insisted she finish before talking, crossing his arms at the window. The rain fell in a steady drizzle, while those outside could be heard shouting over the wind.

'To business,' said Alex. 'I'll share some details with you because I don't want you to do anything stupid.'

She swallowed the insult with the remains of the shortbread.

'Months ago, there was a tip about someone coming from Paris to join the Deli group, so Michel's been under surveillance for some time. Last month, he surprised us by approaching British intelligence.'

'Is that where you actually work? Not the Foreign Office?' She twisted the handkerchief in her hands.

'Forget about me. I'm –' He shook his head. 'Just listen. Apparently, Michel had been pretending to assist the Russian spy ring, but was in fact intent on breaking them.' Alex's eyes were on the tarmac as he kept speaking. 'It seems he was more stupid than we thought. According to the interviews, his brother tried to dissuade Michel against betraying the Russian group, because he considered it dangerous. As a result, we weren't sure if his brother was loyal to the Russian cause or unaware of the full extent of their operation.' He turned back to her. 'Are you following this?'

Anna blinked. 'The Russians shot and killed their mother and brother.'

'In my line of work, you learn not to take people at face value.' He gave a puff of exasperation. 'Remember that to a terrorist, a pregnant woman is collateral damage.'

'He's not –' she struggled to find convincing words. 'He asked me to go to Ukraine with him.'

'There's going to be a war between Russia and Ukraine.' Alex continued scanning the track. 'Trust me, this will happen. You want to have a baby in a war zone? It's idiotic, but go ahead. But you're definitely not taking Simon.'

'It will be a cold war, like the one our parents survived.'

'Is that what YouTube is claiming?' His fingertips tapped on the windowsill.

Through the half-open door, she could hear voices issuing orders for the removal of the burnt-out car.

'I always felt it wasn't necessary for you to know anything about my work, but today I want you to believe me when I say you know nothing about the way the world works.'

A ripple of irritation shot through her. 'But I trust Sasha,' she said. 'I've shared more with him in three months than I have with you in our entire marriage. His older brother was a soldier in Donetsk, and Sasha did military service. He now lives in Mariupol, and his father is sick. He has lived the reality of army life. You're just a desk in an office.'

Alex narrowed his eyes.

'If I go to Ukraine,' she continued, 'Simon can visit during his school holidays. What would be wrong with that?'

His fist slammed onto the windowsill. 'You're not listening, Anna. There's going to be a war. No ifs or buts.

Why do you think thousands of Russian soldiers have amassed on the Ukrainian border? Your man is either joining them, or going to be massacred by them. Take your pick.' He pulled out the second handkerchief streaked with Michel's blood, and folded it to a clean portion before wiping his face. 'How long have you known him? What makes you so trusting?'

She bit her lip and thought of her last conversation with Sasha. 'I know he's telling me the truth.'

He scoffed. 'You have a conviction he's telling you the truth, but that doesn't make it a fact. Some people believe the world is flat.' Alex pulled a heavy chair into position so he could sit opposite her. 'Let me explain. Intelligence departments get thousands of pieces of information every month. Thousands. Not hundreds. Thousands. Every month.' He thrust his face near hers. 'They have to decide which trails to follow and which to put on hold. They can't follow them all because there's limited personnel, so they prioritise those they regard as an immediate threat. Some agents come and go so fast, actions can only be assessed in hindsight. Like the men who poisoned Litvinenko and the Skripals. But increasingly, that style of espionage has gone. Today, we're experiencing an influx of disruptors. Young people working the gig economy, who sign onto Telegram, contacted by hostile networks sited in Russia or Iran or a host of other countries. These young applicants have few loyalties. They bomb, maim or kill for a fee, and what links them to foreign powers are the overseas payments into their bank accounts. When caught, these kids will go to prison, but the instigators don't care.'

She blinked, burnt by his intensity. 'What does this have to do with Sasha and –'

'As I said, the Deli Cafe has been under surveillance for

a year. Bugged. Ostensibly run by the Portuguese, but they're Russian. Gonzales is an organiser. If you listen to both languages, the accents use similar consonants and vowel sounds. So here's the problem.' He pressed his hands together. 'You and Dolly wanted a little fun? Right? Well, congratulations, your fun was on camera.'

Her stomach gave a seismic shift, and she gagged.

'Exactly,' he said. 'How do you think I've felt sharing my wife's love life with an intel team?'

'Oh God. No.'

'Oh God. Yes,' he mocked. 'But our marriage isn't the central issue here. They'd already placed an agent to work undercover at the Deli club, and there's been a delay while they gathered sufficient evidence to make arrests. Hence, they couldn't rock the boat by saying anything to you or Dolly, so they said nothing.'

'They spoke to you.' She fought the desire to vomit. 'Sasha would never –' But the last conversation with Sasha ran through her mind.

'They spoke to me so I was in the loop. Both guys have Russian passports, and forensics have just told me there were remnants of an explosive device in his BMW car. Amateurish but effective. Could be a double bluff to convince us he's not here on terrorist-related issues – seeing as he survived – but it's more likely he pissed off the wrong people, and it's a warning. Life is cheap in Russia.'

She rose to avoid the blackness in his eyes, and pressed her head once more to the windowpane.

'The point is, you can pretend I'm lying, but what is certain is that you and Dolly are at risk. Suppose these foreign agencies believe the Vronskiy boys told you their plans? There's been one murder, so why not another? This is why Simon must stay with my mother on the Faver

Estate, where I will provide protection. Whether you want to stay with them in Canterbury or go to Whitstable is your choice, but there'll be no one guarding our house.'

'Why didn't you tell me this back in November? You could have trusted me –'

'If you don't believe me now, you wouldn't have believed me then.' He sighed. 'But if it makes it any easier, they didn't inform me until January. We're spread across different offices, and nobody trusts anybody.'

Anna held back tears, unwilling to appear unstable in the face of Alex's businesslike demeanour. 'Regardless, Alex, I want a divorce, and I want to speak to Sasha. I'm going to find him in hospital.'

'Divorce isn't the problem: you signed a pre-nup.' His face tightened. 'Sorry to sound cold, but there you have it. And you can't see him in hospital because he's under arrest until they clarify a few things to do with his brother's death. Let me remind you that you're pregnant, and we both know the baby's not mine. Plus, you're living in a Faver property. So before you decide anything, you ought to prepare yourself for the possibility that if they release Vronskiy without espionage or murder charges, he might disappear.'

Shouts of denial welled inside her, but her thought processes were like sponge.

Alex checked his watch. 'I've still a lot of work to finish. There's a car that can take you wherever you want to go, but you'll leave me to explain things to Simon.'

'You'll lie to him. You'll frighten him.'

'I'll certainly lie to him, but the truth would frighten him more.' He crooked a finger for her to follow. 'Let's at least work together where our son is concerned.'

The thought of others viewing her sexual encounters

made her stomach contract again: men in a dark room examining hers and Sasha's lovemaking – leering, laughing. Her legs could barely propel her to follow Alex as he directed her towards the golf carts. The rain lightened to leave a layer of damp mist that made the sodden grass in the field resemble a forgotten cemetery. Her soaking feet were numb with the cold.

She remembered how she and Sasha had walked, hand in hand, along the Tankerton slopes while he described the death of his brother and mother. In her head, she could hear every syllable, and feel the sincerity of his grief. But who would kill Michel, a kid in a sandwich shop? Or sabotage Sasha's car, number three driver for BMW?

TWENTY-SIX

ukraine

WINTER 1992

HE PEERED around the edge of the building, his heart hammering, as the emergency services extracted a woman from a car accident. It was Annaliese! Her shoes, her bag! The shape of her calves! But a second glance revealed a dark-haired stranger, and he recoiled, disgusted by his panic. What was happening to him? Such sightings had tortured him for several days as he crossed roads, ran through crowded streets, and dodged between traffic, often tapping the shoulder of some unsuspecting traveller, before being forced to apologise. He cracked his knuckles and breathed. Mother Russia might pat him on the back for continuing his vigil, but if he stayed in Berlin, this new Germany would arrest him for pestering women.

With a sullen acceptance, he packed, gave back the keys of his rented accommodation and booked a flight to Kyiv. He would enquire about trains and distances to Zhdanov or 'Mariupol' when he arrived.

For a few days, he lingered in a good hotel in the capital city, adjusting to the change of environment. The Ukrainian economy had collapsed, with a mix of people sinking in nostalgia or swimming with the new tide. He heard the muttered conversations around him. They hated the Soviet government and were glad they'd gone, but they had no blueprint for the future and unlike Germany, there was no affluent sidekick to bail them out. Along with joy, poverty paraded in the streets.

One junior clerk pushed a map labelled with Russian names across the counter. 'Have it for free. We're getting new ones printed. See. Zhadanov.'

Studying the route, he drank several bottles of wine while sitting alone in the hotel foyer, and then set off for his daily stroll. The wine was remarkably good, better than some he had tasted in Berlin, and his mood lifted. After all, he was a survivor, and he had money, and this was an opportunity. He had loved Annaliese, he told himself. *His Anna.* He had loved her beyond reason, and coveted every molecule of her body, so her sudden disappearance jabbed his heart and pride. But that was in the past: he had lived thus far without attachment, and he would not allow sentimentality to destroy him.

Around the square, the churches and domes began reverberating with pealing bells, and three young women skipped with their young men to a unknown tune – a future population eager to cast off their Soviet heritage. He lit a cigarette and listened until the sonorous chimes died away. A girl with long, rich brown hair sat on a stool and struck a melody on a multi-stringed instrument that he recognised as the Ukrainian bandora. The Soviet regime had banned it, and he watched as in minutes, a crowd assembled, some sitting, some singing to the tune. Gone were the balalaikas and the obligatory Russian patriotic verses. The youths cast off shirts of red to put on blues and yellows. The street signs were in Russian, but all around him, the young were determined to celebrate their freedom from oppression.

He felt a certain bitterness. Once, he had been a part of something powerful and important, and now he was a nobody, but if he wanted to continue with plans for his vineyard, he would have to adapt. In his career, he had dodged bullets, assassinated people and gone undercover many times; a true chameleon, so this was no different. In mimicry of those around him, he fell into the easy, clapping rhythm of the crowd, and returned their smiles with forced cheerful nods. One day, he would hold power again, but a power of a different kind. And one day he would find Annaliese. But not today. This moment was about establishing a new Vronsky with a new name, and he gave some thought to what that identity might look like.

After another stop and another drink, he meandered back to his room, where he made some phone calls to various French and Italian vineyard owners. It was ironic that he had forged these acquaintances when paying to use the dungeons in large chateaux and palazzos. Keen to take his coin, the owners never asked questions. It wasn't their concern, they said, what happened in basements of old castles nestled conveniently on large estates. Few heard the shrieks muffled by thick stone walls, and there was always an anonymous Swiss limousine to remove bodies.

In his traipses across Europe, he had caught up with many foolish men and women; amateur espionage dolts, easy to break, and in the aftermath, he always made a point of enjoying a glass or two with the local landowners. Money was a leveller. Approaching his European contacts from the other side of the Iron Curtain's history, he had wondered if they might turn him away, but they were ecstatic to take his Swiss francs in return for plants and advice. Within a few days, he had laid the groundwork for everything he needed and still had change left over.

'Monsieur! Welcome to the European business hub,' said one of the French viticulturists. 'Glasnost works for everyone. You make wine in Ukraine? How interesting. I hear it is the perfect climate on the coast of the Azov Sea, and we are happy to send you advisers for a reasonable fee.'

Such enthusiasms took the sting from Anna's betrayal. Fuck her. Well – he had, many times – but it was helpful to feed his ire, and he began to recall how he and Annaliese had not always shared a mindset. She craved a sympathetic communism for all, but he was pragmatic. From now on his refrain would be: Long live McDonald's and have a glass of my wine.

Through his hotel window, he spied a running figure below. Annaliese! The woman moved with her customary grace, the court shoes tapping on the pavement, dark hair whipping behind her as she jumped onto a bus. He rose from the hotel desk in panic.

part two

the tyranny of hope

'Not knowing is the hardest thing.
The tyranny of hope.'

Lyndsey Hilsum
Speaking about the wives of the POWs held in Russian jails.
Channel 4 news

TWENTY-SEVEN
whitstable

FEBRUARY 2022

HER SCREAM FOLLOWED the invading field mouse who jumped from the cupboard and scuttled into the frozen grasses. She watched it disappear with a twinge of conscience. It was the only other living being in the Whitstable house, and like her, it was seeking refuge against the cold.

Without the normal flow of activities, her home was icy, and she could not stop shivering. Intent on finding Sasha, she and Betsy had phoned every hospital to ask if someone was treating him for burns, but he had vanished. There was a cold war between her and Alex, with neither mentioning the events at Goodwood, and the media had only posted the results of the charity race. There was no mention of murder. It was as if the world had sent her to a bunker, and she stood at her bedroom window overlooking the mist-swathed sea, listening to the waves whisper at the radio wondering: what next?

. . .

February 24. Breaking news.
Russia has invaded Ukraine.

There it was: confirmation of Alex's statement, and she felt her muscles sag with despair. A seagull landed on the back fence taunting her with orange eyes, as she began texting. But no one answered. Nothing from Stephen, nothing from Simon. No reply from Dolly? That was unheard of.

Jittery with anxiety, her two current commissions lay neglected on her laptop as she dressed and strode out to the high road, desperate to wander among ordinary people with ordinary lives. The narrow pavements were empty, lacking the summer crush of shoppers with their boutique purchases; the only inhabitants at this hour being mothers chivvying children to primary schools. She bought cut flowers to brighten the home, but when she returned Zelenskyy was on the television installing martial law in Ukraine. The words skinned her heart.

Alex had suggested Sasha would be deported straight from hospital, but he had not confirmed the departure. Days ago, she and Sasha had agreed to meet at St. Pancras station, but since the accident, she had heard nothing, and her husband's caveats ricocheted in her brain.

Suppose these foreign agencies believe the Vronskiy boys told you their plans?

There's been one murder, so why not another?

It was easy to hate her husband. She wanted to blame him every time she heard details about the war. Her former YouTube channels no longer interested her as she searched for serious news reports and tried to imagine where Sasha might be. If he had left, he would be pulled into the military, and sent to the battlefield. The thought terrified her;

for how would she survive if he died? How did anyone survive the death of their loved ones on a battlefield?

A ping and she saw a text from Alex. Sasha had been neither arrested nor charged, he said, but the authorities had taken him from the hospital to the airport and put him on a flight to Warsaw voluntarily. Ukraine had installed a no-fly zone, so it was anybody's guess as to his final destination.

I'll text you if I have further news.

A second text from Simon gave cheerful assurances that he was having fun and doing well at school.

Get better soon, Mummy, and you can come to Granny's to see me next weekend.

Guilt washed through her. She was torn between two loves. Opting to text the story of the mouse, she sent him all her love and kisses.

Another sudden ping delivered a brief text from her sister-in-law.

I'll contact you when I can, but please don't text me for the moment. xx

Why? she thought. Why, why why? She wanted immediate action, not subterfuge.

In the absence of personal information, the television news consumed her days and nights, filling her head with soundbites and analysis. She watched everything: British early evening news, late night news, BBC Newsnight, Channel 4, CNN, Fox News, Euronews. In between, she searched Instagram, Twitter and TikTok, swiping away the inane or humorous to seek out more video clips from politicians. Image after image flew before her eyes. At certain points, she pressed pause on the screen, searched amongst the frozen faces of a Ukrainian crowd, and ran the item again. Pause. Search. Pause. Search. Where was Sasha? If only she could glimpse his face and know he was alive. Had he stopped in Poland? Had he gone to Russia? Was he in Kyiv? Her thoughts shifted between absolute loyalty and a hollow mistrust of her own judgement.

With every passing day, the images became more horrific: people cowering under bridges, cats in baskets, dogs on rope leads, buildings reduced to rubble, crying children clutching a small soft toy, adults with grey faces; bombs ripping through walls and floors; tanks obliterating obstacles; those who had lost everything, weeping to camera; each explosion taking her further and further from sanity.

There had been other wars: she understood that. All over the planet there was always a war somewhere, but she had never felt so close to the terror, and she wondered how her parents had felt, growing up in the shadow of the Cold War. Were their sympathies founded on fears? She stroked the crescent moon, willing herself to get answers from her dead mother, wanting her advice, but the surrounding air remained cold.

With a sudden thought, she retrieved the additional copy of Anna Karenina from her bag, and placed it next to the one she had taken from Stephen's. She had taken Volume I and Dolly had given her Volume II. What had happened to the Volume III borrowed by Michel? According to Dolly, the books had caused arguments, but why would Stephen fester over old books? He'd mentioned their parents' political leanings, but why would anyone argue about it now? It was history.

She opened Volume I which bore the familiar inscription:

And my other name.

She opened the second volume.

This book belongs to Professor John Blount of Cambridge University.

Where is Vronsky?

She held the covers aloft like the wings of a bird, hoping a letter might fall out to explain the strange inscriptions, but instead, she stared at the semicircular hollow created by the arc of stitched pages and realised something lay inside: a thin, yellow paper. Fetching a small cheese knife, she snagged the material and eased it from its hiding place. The tissue was so fine as to resemble cigarette paper. Careful to avoid tearing, she smoothed the rectangle to reveal a tiny, penned message.

To my darling Vronsky,

See you at the usual spot.

Love from your Anna x

It sounded like a lover's tryst, and she checked the other volume, hoping for more, but the space was empty. Sasha had suggested the scribbles in the margins were academic notes. She wondered. A tutor had once taught her Occam's Razor: the simplest solution was often the correct one. But she could find no simple explanation for the note as her mother had always been known as Annaliese, and to the best of her knowledge, no one had ever shortened her name to Anna or Annie. She mewed in frustration, placing palms on her abdomen. If she couldn't decipher this simple conundrum, how could she expect to find Sasha, the man with two names, two passports and different paperwork? Aleksandr and Oleksandr.

Determined to keep probing, she phoned Betsy to set up a meeting in London.

TWENTY-EIGHT

London

MARCH TO APRIL 2022

THEY EMBRACED each other with tears. Walking along St, Pancras shopping arcade, Betsy was hollow eyed with grief, her mascara blotched with crying. She insisted that Sasha would not have gone to Ukraine under his Russian name of Alexandr Vronskiy. Once more, Anna asked Betsy to clarify his name, and the cousin gave a sad trill. 'Most names translate,' she said. 'John in English is Giovanni in Italian. But now, there is a greater importance in rejecting everything Russian.'

They had coffee in one of the cafes by a piano, listening to an old man play a Scott Joplin rag. Betsy wore muted jeans and a cashmere jumper. Her dark red lipstick accentuated the downturn of her mouth, and she clasped her hands in grief.

'Translation is not sinister,' she insisted.

'But I ask because I don't know how we can find him,' said Anna. 'If he's gone to Ukraine, I want to follow. He's had to buy a new phone, and I'm four months pregnant. I can't bear the torture of not knowing where he is.'

Betsy extended a hand across the circular table. 'Last month, many fled – except for the journalists, and even for them, it's risky,' she said. 'It used to take four hours to Ukraine, but now it takes twenty-four because they have no-fly zones. Someone in your condition shouldn't be heading there. And Kyiv is under threat, because the Russians are trying to kill Zelenskyy.'

'Do you think Sasha might have gone to Russia?'

Another trill. 'No,' she slapped the table. 'What your husband is saying is nonsense, although I understand why he might believe that. Years of occupation followed by corruption have left its trace, but Sasha will go to his father in Mariupol, just as he told you. As soon as I met him again, I saw he had grown into an honest man, for whom family is important. Poor Michel.' Her face creased and her knuckle swiped at the mascara line beneath her eyes. 'I feel so terrible for those boys. They had to leave their home and then their mother was –'

'I understand, because ...' Anna briefly mentioned her parents.

Betsy put hands to her heart. 'Poor Anna. The best we can do is hope he stayed in Poland. Maybe he contacts a friend to collect his father.'

They parted determined to keep in touch, and Anna felt reassured by Betsy's narrative. To Alex, Sasha was a piece of paper, but to her and the child, he was now a part of her family. She had grown up without a father and she could not bear the idea of her baby living in a repetition of history.

• • •

Back home, she dithered over what to pack, while the radio burbled. Despite Betsy's warning, she was determined to head to Poland and take a train to Kyiv. It would be easier to find him in Ukraine than in England.

Bucha.

The name bled through her consciousness. The radio announced that Ukrainians had driven out the first wave of the Russian army, re-entering the city to find a scene of horrors. Reporters interviewed witnesses of drunken Russian soldiers murdering Ukrainian civilians. 'This is the Russian playbook,' they said, as if describing a game. 'They shoot the husband, rape the wife, torture the teenagers, drink vodka in their gardens and then the soldiers move on.'

A renewed terror energised her. Flipping open her computer, she checked Bucha's location, scanning pages. In various accounts it was described as a dormitory town to Kyiv for wealthy middle-class commuters, and her imagination exploded with new terrors. What if he had stayed with friends in Bucha on the way to Mariupol? What if he had become caught in the butchery? What if he'd been randomly shot? Or tortured? A thousand violent images fled across her brain, and she struggled to pull herself back to the immediate issues confronting her. He had never mentioned a specific route, and when she moved the cursor around the map of Ukraine, she saw the vastness of the land from western to eastern borders, realising he could be anywhere.

In a car.

Or hitching a lift.

Or on a train.

Or in a ditch.

Gulping back tears, she remembered his descriptions of

fields of wheat, blue skies, and beaches, cherries and rivers, but every recent video showed an apocalypse.

Stashing her bag in the hallway, she checked her phone, wondering why Stephen hadn't returned her calls. What was left for them to argue about?

But that was a separate puzzle, and she put it aside.

Completing her research, she made a few travel notes before flinging open the kitchen door and taking in lungfuls of cold air to steady her nerves. She could do this. For too long she had been a passive woman, accepting the Faver family restrictions, filling her time watching amusing but bland items on screens, translating happy-ever-after romances. It was time to join the wider world. The tide edged from the beach, exposing the long shingle bank where two people wandered to throw stones at the restless water. A month ago, she and Sasha had trod that path, wetting their feet in the North Sea while he admitted to his family's tragedies. Below, the peaceful scene was at odds with past and present news; a shoreline of denial of everything happening one and a half thousand miles away. A couple tripped and stumble over the pebbles, and in a flash, she realised how impractical her suitcase would be on an unpredictable journey. Another delay: she had to buy a lightweight backpack.

In search of the local camping shop, she trudged up the high street only to find her way blocked by an older neighbour – Jean Stanley lived two doors down, a keen sea swimmer with a weathered face. She and Anna had never shared more than a few good mornings, but now the woman launched forward. 'I've been meaning to speak to you.' Her words gushed. 'My husband and I have taken in a pregnant mother and her eighteen-year-old stepdaughter. Homes for Ukraine. Maybe you've noticed?'

Anna hadn't, but blustered congratulations, unsure if that was the appropriate response.

Jean dismissed her comment. 'We've got the space, but here's the thing. The stepdaughter doesn't get along with the mother. They have shouting matches. Not that we understand a word, of course.'

Anna offered a diluted apology, but the neighbour had not finished.

'The point is – and we have discussed this – we wondered if you would take in the girl.' A flush of colour rose in the woman's leathery cheeks. 'Seeing as it's just you.'

Anna could feel her own colour rising. 'You've heard we're separated.'

Jean gave a vague apology.

'But I'm not allowed a lodger unless Nina agrees. She owns the house.'

Another apology. 'I hope you don't mind, but we've already contacted Nina Faver. We've known her for years. Same generation and all that, and she says it's fine if you agree. She rather thought you would, seeing as you had Ukrainian sympathies.' By this time, Jean was standing so close, Anna could smell her breath. 'Of course you can say no, but it would be so convenient. She speaks remarkably good English so no trouble communicating. It would be wonderful if we had more room for the babies. They're due in a few months.'

Was it Anna's imagination or did Jean's eyes drop a fraction, inviting baby confidences? Unable to explain her travel plans for fear they would shoot back to Nina and Alex, she could find no reason to refuse, and watched Jean's shoulders dip in relief.

'Marvellous. If you're sure. Of course, we don't want to trouble you, but –'

To which Anna found herself replying that it was no trouble at all, and it was the least she could do to help people fleeing a war-torn country. A sudden thought kindled her interest. 'Where do these Ukrainians come from?'

Jean looked perplexed.

'I mean, which part of Ukraine? Kyiv? Bucha?'

'Oh my dear, not Bucha. Can you imagine? They'd be in bits. No, they're from a city further east. Kharkiv. Or at least I think that's what they said. Is that important?'

'How did they get here?' persisted Anna.

'They flew into Stansted.' Jean's puzzled brow creased further. 'I'm sorry, I don't know. We haven't really got to the stage where we're chatting; it's more a case of adjustments to meals, use of the kitchen, and bathroom routines. That sort of thing. You'll see.'

Anna felt unable to ask more without raising family suspicions and facing more obstacles, so she confirmed her agreement. Perhaps she could settle the girl into the house, elicit useful information about Ukraine, and then leave quietly in a couple of weeks. She returned home to shove the suitcase under her bed. Just a couple of weeks delay and she could set off.

A morose stringy teenager, Olena arrived at the house with a Homes for Ukraine council official who walked around, tick sheet in one hand and pen in the other.

'Your landlord, Ms Nina Faver, has organised a fast-tracked police verification for you – a DBS.' The man wafted the paperwork in her face, asking for a signature. 'Next. I'll sort a gas certificate, and sign here for assurances about a six-month minimum term.'

A carbon monoxide alarm went above the kitchen door and after fiddling with bathroom locks, the man advised certain adjustments. All the while, the disinterested Olena hunched on the sofa, rubbing the purple slashes of fatigue under her eyes, and yawning theatrically in between scrolls of her phone.

After half an hour, the official declared himself satisfied. 'Is the room ready, Anna? Have you got your things, Olena?'

Her initial resentment turned to curiosity before flipping back to resentment. Olena might be able to advise her about the journey, but the girl wasn't talking. Asking for travel information was futile. All Olena wanted was to put the Wi-Fi code into her phone, and shut herself into the spare room. She became a ghost teenager, exiting on alternate days to attend a college in Canterbury. For a week, Anna tiptoed around the house, listening to Olena's strident voice on the phone arguing with someone – presumably her stepmother.

While they settled in together, Anna doubled up on Betsy's efforts to find out where Sasha had gone. She hesitated to contact the Foreign Office as Alex worked there, although after recent conversations, she wondered if that was the truth. She doubted she would ever know everything about Alex, but tried to push those concerns away and stay focussed.

Betsy tried the National Crime Agency, but was told the British Police and Interpol did not investigate foreign nationals who had gone abroad of their own volition. Anna phoned The Lucie Blackman Trust who were supportive but not hopeful, given the situation in Ukraine. Other phone calls went to automated replies, and when on the odd occasion they returned the call, the answers were dispiriting. The Ukrainian Embassy wanted to know his patronymic, his middle name, and date of birth, something that distinguished him from *all the other Vronskiys* missing or held prisoner or dead. When she rang Betsy, the cousin admitted she couldn't remember his exact date of birth.

'I'm sorry but I have many cousins and I don't know them so well. I've lived in England for ages.'

In frustration, Anna insisted she would go to speak to someone and thrust a photograph under their nose. 'Listen, they'll have to talk to me. I carry his baby, his DNA.'

With soothing words, Betsy reminded her that she was one of many and they were swamped. 'Look after yourself and the baby,' she said. 'It's what Sasha would want.' And Anna could hear her crying on the other end of the phone.

Along with visions of Michel's bloodied body in the tunnel, and imaginings of Sasha in distress, the despair of idleness was not something she could suffer, so she tried to thaw Olena, finding herself rebuffed at each attempt. The girl spoke English, but made it clear she wanted no conversation. At night, the teenager sat cross-legged on the garden bench, wrapped in a blanket, her face turned towards the red blinking of the wind turbines on the horizon, as she smoked roll-ups in the breeze. If Anna approached, Olena's black eyes repelled company.

Food disappeared. The shower ran at odd times, and Anna felt increasingly frustrated at her inability to open channels of communication. If she chose to leave Olena and set out to Ukraine, she would be abandoning a young, angry mortal alone in the house. Might she return to find the house burnt down or the place turned into a drugs den? She delayed her departure, her temper fraying with inaction.

Towards the end of the second week, Anna rose at first light to find Olena nursing a thick black coffee, her attention absorbed by an English magazine. Tentatively, she asked if Olena could read both the Latin alphabet and Cyrillic script, and if so, might she translate the scribblings in the margins of her copy of Anna Karenina? She waited, expecting the usual rebuttal.

TWENTY-NINE

ukraine

THE END OF THE TWENTIETH CENTURY

HE DREAMT of embracing her with tears, but doubted she used the name of Annaliese Blount. Irritated by the way she haunted him, he put out another set of feelers in Berlin and Moscow before heading to the coast. Giving different reasons, he asked colleagues and contacts if they had come across her, but no one knew anything. How he hated himself for the wretchedness that engulfed his heart. To rid himself of this human weakness, he explored building materials in Ukraine.

There was no industry or West German banker to bail out the population after Russia's withdrawal, and having fought his way across a vast expanse of country, he arrived at his property near Mariupol to find a ruin. It would be a large project, but the scale of the task helped sharpen his mind. He called a meeting of locals with farm experience, and fabricated a story of how he had inherited the land from his Ukrainian grandfather. He sensed their disbelief, but knew his money would buy co-operation without questions. They were hungry and desperate. His priority was the restoration of the main building, and to improve and expand on the existing vineyard, he said. He would also maintain the outlying farm and animals. Within twenty-four hours, he had found a nearby hotel, basic but suitable for his short-term comfort, and hired thirty able-bodied men and a manager, reaching out to his Muscovite colleagues for investment. Pleased with himself, he represented his move as a good business deal, and as agreed, Stepanov motivated others to invest, mentioning Vronsky's Swiss bank account.

Dressed in his best suit, Vronsky flew back to Kyiv, with the help of a newly independent firm of small aircraft. *Blyat*, but there were thousands of acres of wheat fields and old castles and tiny villages and churches to cover, all criss-crossed with railway tracks and uneven roads. The Soviets had put in little infrastructure, but in the capital, potential Russian investors arrived to meet him. Not the emerging oligarchs – he wasn't in their league. But many aspirational middle managers came, who had heard of Vronsky's KGB reputation to deliver what he promised, regardless of laws or other inconveniences.

They greeted him effusively, their mouths full of recent stories of Americans, economics and new battles. Star Wars and Starbucks. Tales of hands-in-the-till and roubles gushing like broken dams from the old National Bank. With feigned interest, he listened to their reasons for investing and discussed how best to use his Credit Suisse account; Ukrainian currency was irrelevant.

After two days of feasting and drinking, they signed contracts and left with smiles. Sat in a corner of the hotel's lounge, Stepanov remained, indulging in strong coffee with liqueur and eating Belgian buns. He cast an eye over the photographs of the rough-hewn house in Mariupol while Vronsky tugged at the collar of his new shirt.

'As you know, I'm not one for pen and paper. Look at these hands.' Vronsky splayed thick fingers. 'But we have the beginnings of a simple accounting method.'

Stepanov lit a gold filtered cigarette. 'I'm glad the meetings went well.' He blew smoke. 'Is it too late to say you ought to return to Moscow?'

Vronsky gave a rumble of laughter. 'You're younger than I am. For me, this is perfect.'

'There's a position in the new GRU, a unit known as 29155.' Stepanov puffed. 'We don't use names anymore. Anna Karenina has died! But this unit – they specialise in tracking defectors abroad, and doling out ...' One finger mimed slitting his neck, and the cigarette smoke undulated into the air. 'You'd be ideal.'

'You want me to disappoint my new business friends?'

'No.' Stepanov took a long drag on the cigarette and sighed. 'No. I'll have to find someone else. I suppose it's too much to expect you to do both. But I'd hate to think the reason behind your exile is a woman.' He chose another sugary bun and eyed it like prey.

'It's nothing to do with her.' Vronsky made a show of bridling offence.

'Good. Because no woman is worth it.' Abandoning his cigarette in the marble ashtray in favour of the bun, he chewed while Vronsky waited for him to finish. 'In any case, you're probably wise to move on. A new breed of spies use the internet. An army invention.'

'Internet.' Vronsky had learned about this from a keen young man in Mariupol, who explained how it created a layer of anonymity to correspondence.

'We are preparing to offer a one-off payment straight into their banks, and in return they'll do anything. Bomb a factory, set fire to a house, deliver a bottle of something fatal.'

'Childish disruption?' Vronsky scoffed. 'What's the point? The Cold War is over.'

'You don't believe that, and neither do I.' Stepanov wiped sugar dust from his mouth. 'There's a future plan to divide the Europeans, and keep Russia strong. Many are unhappy that we've given away the empire.'

'So you're going to do a little bomb here and there, somewhere in Europe, and blame another European faction?'

'Small but beautiful concept, eh? Like persuading a woman to fall into your lap.'

Vronsky knew Stepanov's reputation, and for a moment, he deliberated as to whether that Berlin meeting with Annaliese had been random or planned. The thought brought the familiar stab of anger. 'It sounds petty. Count me out.'

'Ah but consider,' said Stepanov, picking up the smouldering cigarette, 'you can wear down a stone with dripping water.'

Vronsky took a linen napkin and wiped his hands. 'Give me a gun any day. A good, clean kill. Or a sharp knife. But frankly, if I'm not in my former profession, I'd rather make wine. Some bottles last for hundreds of years.'

Stepanov smirked. 'Oh, you want legacy. I get it. But there are those who resent Gorbachev's legacy and I predict it will prove a mistake.' He puffed smoke towards the skyline of Kyiv's golden domes. 'Russia will rise.'

'Ask me again in a few years,' he said, humouring the man. 'For now I've told the locals my grandfather was Ukrainian.'

'You're pretending to be part colonial?' Stepanov raised his thick eyebrows in mockery.

'Don't forget, this wider enterprise is your suggestion. I create the superb wine, you pay double the worth of each bottle, and I return the excess to you in Swiss francs.'

The scheme was so transparent, Vronsky had wondered if it would work, but Stepanov insisted he'd already floated it with the two new FSB bureau's up-and-coming ex-apparatchik: Sergei Stepashin and Vladimir Putin; and both approved.

With a final kiss to the cheeks, they said goodbye.

'To keep you in the loop,' said Stepanov, lowering his voice. 'Russia is in negotiations with the Americans to make Ukraine give up its military and nuclear weapons in return for our protection. If Mother Russia ever wants to take back her former colony, it will be easy. A military walk in the park. So stay with us. Loyalty is always rewarded.'

Vronsky nodded. He wanted to ask one last time if Stepanov had any information about Annaliese's whereabouts, but held back. Best not to dampen this new camaraderie.

In bleak moments, it occurred to him she might have joined Dolomeyer in the States. His bones pointed to her fleeing to America, but seeing as the Russians were pretending to be friends with the Yankees, he had no authority to fly the ocean and deal with it. Success in business would have to fill the hole of his failure in love.

For years, the European vines grew, their roots thrusting deep into the Ukrainian soil, as both he and the plants acclimatised to the new Eastern European vibe. Local Ukrainian families accepted him as a familiar figure in the region, and although on hot nights, his mind wandered to thoughts of Annaliese, daylight saw the dreams dissolve. She no longer appeared in bus queues or running into shops, or turning corners, and he was able to relegate her to evening shadows, when he'd drunk his fill.

As the bottles rolled into the cellars, Stepanov arrived on annual visits to check the accounts. On one such visit, as the new century bedded in, he dragged along a woman with rough cut hair and blunt features.

'This is Katerina. She'll look after you.'

Vronsky kissed him on either cheek and suggested the man take back his whore. They both chuckled, ignoring her.

'You're pining, comrade,' Stepanov teased. 'No wife, no mistress! You're missing the hand of a good woman kneading your cock. And that isn't good. You need to throw the memory of that Anna woman under a train. She was English. This Katerina is Russian. Much better.'

Vronsky grimaced, refusing to look in her direction. He found it embarrassing that Stepanov knew of his celibate existence.

'You're a landowner,' his friend continued, 'living a farm life where every animal fucks another. It's not right you go to bed alone. You'll get cancer or go blind.'

The girl in the corner gazed at the everlasting horizon, and Vronsky assessed her solid nose and down-turned lips. She reminded him of a hen trapped in a cage.

'Take Katerina. I'm reliably told she's a good cook.'

'I have a cook,' said Vronsky.

Stepanov's face lit with humour under heavy eyebrows. 'Yeah, but she'll be loyal. Not like your other one. Katerina was in an orphanage. Not well educated, I grant you, but she won't give you any trouble. She married a man who beat her.'

Katerina dropped her gaze to her scuffed boots.

'It's a tale I've heard before,' said Vronsky, unimpressed. 'But I employ local families. It's important they see me as supportive of their way of life.'

'Nonsense. Half the people here speak Russian. Of course they're loyal. Anyway, we arrested her husband for drug dealing, and he went to jail, so she's on her own. But when he gets out ...' Stepanov made a slicing gesture. 'He's one of the new drug lords working within organised groups for our President, Vladimir Putin. Have you heard about them? Apparently, this guy made the mistake of venturing out on his own, but he's learned his lesson as far as drugs are concerned. Not that he'll turn over a new leaf where women are concerned – he'll still beat her like a dog, so I thought of you – as a friend.'

Vronsky raised his eyes to the ceiling in mock horror, and poured wine. They set to drinking and talking. In his peripheral vision, he saw the girl leave the room, but neither man asked where she was going. Stepanov's visits always involved a little business and much smoking and drinking and hashing of news about old colleagues, especially those who had fallen foul of the new system. Vronsky enjoyed the gossip.

'Putin is a powerful leader, unlike the guy leading Ukraine. President Kuchma is forced to be pro-Russia, but he wobbles. Putin told him, we expect Ukraine and Georgia to toe the line. Former colonies should be grateful for Russian patronage, not behaving like a dog with it's tongue up an American's arse.'

'I've noticed,' said Vronsky drily. He recalled one of his managers requesting he negotiate for the return of some icons looted by the Red Army. The man cited a trend for Western European countries to give back valuable stolen artworks to the country of origin. Most of the stolen Ukrainian icons were in Russia, sold to the highest bidders around the globe. Vronsky knew the request was pointless. Russia took and did not give back. That's just how it was.

Interrupting their chat, his cook, an elderly woman with a thatch of long greying hair, brought in fresh borscht with thick slabs of pork and bread. Her hands trembled. She had never felt comfortable in front of Russian power, and he dismissed her from the room. After a few bottles and a good meal, Stepanov accepted a cigar and shared more thoughts. 'There is unrest, or so I've heard, but if these Ukrainians think they can snub Mother Russia, they're crazzzy.' His words slurred. 'We'll never let go. The only cheese is in the mousetrap as far as they're concerned, and it's a good thing you're here to be our ears and eyes and...' He fell asleep in the large leather chair, emitting fruity snores, and Vronsky dozed to wake and stumble through the house. He needed to explain to the girl that she had to leave in the morning, but he couldn't find her. Perhaps she had curled up in Stepanov's Mercedes. Fatigue overcame him, and he fell asleep on his bed.

The next morning, he woke with a dry mouth to hear shouting outside his window: a worker was yelling about a strange woman in the garage.

'*Blyat.*' Vronsky rubbed his grizzled hair and tucked in his shirt, crossing the courtyard in bare feet. 'Enough. Enough. She's with my friend.' They backed away. 'Ho!' he yelled at Katerina, although she was metres from him. 'Come and take a bed in the house. You're not a dog to sleep in the back of our delivery van.'

Without a word, she brushed dirt from her dress and

followed him. He shrugged at his manager to convey apologies.

'Bathe and then breakfast,' he ordered. He meant as a guest, but an hour later, when he'd showered and had his daily talk with the estate workers, he entered the kitchen to find her frying bacon and potatoes. The smell was delicious.

'I have a cook,' he grunted, unwilling to thank her.

'It's her day off,' said Katerina, wiping hands on her sleeves, leaving greasy imprints. 'Your friend has already eaten.' She dished the food in silence and stood to one side. He took a reluctant mouthful, allowing the creamy sauce to burst on his tongue, and swallowed with pleasure.

'Don't think you can stay,' he said. 'I don't know what Stepanov has told you, but I have a woman. I'm waiting for my Anna to return.'

THIRTY

whitstable

APRIL 2022

ANNA SAT NEXT TO OLENA, pasting on an eager smile as she slid one volume of Anna Karenina across the kitchen table. The girl's shoulder moved, which might have been an agreement or a refusal, so Anna pointed to the scribblings in the margin.

The other shoulder twitched. 'Is English but book of Russian classic.'

'Look at the handwritten notes?'

'I never read this, but of course – Tolstoy.' Olena sipped her coffee and allowed one painted nail to rest over the Cyrillic scribblings, while she wrinkled her nose. 'It makes no sense. It says Anna going to a cafe with Sibylle.' She looked up. 'A note for you? You are Anna, but it is in Russian, not Ukrainian.'

'It's not a note for me.' Anna stared in surprise at the scrawl. 'How can you tell it's in Russian? Don't Ukraine and Russia have the same alphabet?'

Olena slid the book back to Anna, a painted fingernail underlining one word. 'Look. This means Anna in Russian.' She pointed to: Анна. Then taking a pen from a pot above the fridge, she wrote on the back of an empty envelope. 'Here, I write for you 'Anna' both ways.'

She wrote Анна and then wrote Ганна.

'We have our own language – similar but different to Russian – our own culture, our own history. I am Ukrainian, not Russian.' Her nose tipped upwards in a disdainful gesture.

'I see, like Spanish and Italian are similar but different.'

The shoulder twitched. 'I don't know this. I know that Soviets forced everyone to speak Russian and learn Russian history, so my parents speak both languages. But I am free Ukrainian.' The girl shuffled the pages. 'Look. Here and here, it says they meet at Cathedral near the same person called Sibylle.' She flipped several pages and pointed again. 'Here and here, someone is called Alexei, and he meets Levin at the usual University.' She pointed again. 'And here are details about another meeting, but no date.'

Anna put the words and decades into Google to make a search. After a few moments scrolling while Olena returned to her magazine, she finally opened a page of what looked promising. 'Sibylle was an East German fashion magazine and a cafe in the GDR,' she said. 'But Alexei, Anna, and Levin are characters in the books. Can you find a mention of Sasha?'

The girl leant her head to one side, shooting a curious look at Anna. 'Sasha is a Russian name for Alexandr. The Ukrainian is Oleksandr, or Oleks.'

'But Sasha came from Donetsk.'

'Okay, in the Donbas, many speak Russian.' An irritated

look came into Olena's eyes. 'But there are castles a thousand years old in Ukraine. Not Russian castles, Ukrainian, but Russia say the castles are theirs.' She ran a hand through her hair, before wiping both palms on her yellow T-shirt with a logo that said Limewax, beneath a photo of drums. Olena seemed to identify with Europe so Anna determined to ask more, hoping to find the secrets in these copies of Anna Karenina.

But Olena was shifting in disinterest. 'Maybe you do me favour? I can have some friends here?'

'Of course,' said Anna, pleased they were communicating. 'I meant to ask: where is your father now?'

The girl stiffened. 'In military, Zaporizhzhia. Near the power plant.'

'Is that near Mariupol?'

She scoffed, her lips twisting in exaggerated disdain. 'Ukraine is very big: much, much bigger than England. Do I ask you if we are near to Scotland?' With an air of superiority, she picked up her bag and slung the straps over her head. 'I go now to college.'

Anna watched the girl stride to the front gate, and disappear towards the bus stop. She texted Dolly, desperate to tell someone about Olena's translations.

Come stay with me. More info about the books. Please.

I know about you-know-what, came the reply.

Oh God, Dolly, I'm so sorry. What else could she say? Did Dolly know everything about Michel's death, or had someone sanitised his bloody end?

My boys are spending the weekend at home before going to Australia for a year. University placements. All arranged last minute.

She replied with the only thing she could think of to say. *You'll miss them.*

But the text went unanswered, and a thousand questions rose in her mind. What prevented Dolly from speaking to her? Why were her sons going to the other side of the world on short notice? And why would old scribbles about meetings that took place over thirty years ago have caused Stephen pain?

She sighed and thought about her next move. Olena could manage in the house on her own, she decided, and as if in agreement, the baby made its first small kick. Yes, it said. Don't just sit there. Do something. You have already delayed longer than intended. Her hand rippled over her abdomen, just as the radio news broke through her consciousness.

Mariupol.

With a gulp, she switched on the television to watch journalists report on the Russian advance which had left four hundred thousand people without electricity or water. More photographs popped onto the screen.

An opera house with the words 'children' spelt in stones outside. Russian army bombed and killed them regardless.

A baby with her mother and grandmother bombed in the kitchen of their home.

Two men shot in a car trying to flee. Just like Sasha's brother and mother, she thought.

The names and crimes multiplied like a virus, and she felt paralysed, unable to switch off in case Sasha's face came into view. Please, she prayed, do not let them imprison him in the Azov steelworks.

Do not forget us in the darkness. Rescue us.

Unwilling to block out the news in case Sasha's face came into view, she absorbed every detail over the next few days, desperate to find the outcome for his hometown. She had to procure sufficient information to formulate the correct questions when she arrived in Kyiv. She texted Alex for information and he rang her late at night.

'I have some news,' he said, his voice heavy with fatigue.

She sat up in bed, her knuckles whitening around the phone.

'The Red Cross and the Ukrainian military have posted lists. If he's in Mariupol, the situation's not good. I'm sure you know this already. There's someone with a similar name on the list of the POWs, although it might not be him.' Alex cleared his throat. 'Without a military number, it's unclear.'

'Can't you find out for sure?'

He gave an irritated sigh. 'This is war, Anna. The spelling of the name listed is slightly different, so if he's Russian, it's not him, but if he's Ukrainian, it could be him.' His voice mellowed. 'I'm glad you've taken in Olena. It was decent of you to help the Stanleys.'

There was a moment's silence, in which she felt unworthy of the praise.

'I've sent a message to the girl via Jean,' continued Alex. 'The nuclear power plant at Zaporizhzhia has fallen, and it's not clear if her father is alive, dead or a POW, so please be aware, she must be feeling wretched.'

If he was trying to make her feel selfish, he'd succeeded. Finishing the call, Anna wrapped hands around her stomach, wondering how to share her terror with Olena. Despite the hour, the girl was out.

She woke, hearing her return in the early hours as a storm swept in across the waters. Unable to sleep, Anna listened to the thunder and lightning creating its own war over the North Sea. High winds thrashed the beach, rattling every moving part in the cottage. Anna swung her feet out of the bed, tiptoeing to the bathroom, and felt a tremendous gust smack the hallway glass. In wretched contemplation, she walked across the landing to place her forehead on the window, connecting to the vibrating pane. From outside, a ghostly scream echoed, and she drew back in alarm, flicking the catch to open the window and spreading her arms into the buffeting wind.

Anna. Don't forget me.

Rain splattered against her. Was the voice in her head? 'I'm coming. I'm coming to find you.'

Another crack of thunder and the door opened behind her.

'Anna?' Olena's pale face resembled a ghost.

'Did you hear him? Did you hear him cry out?'

She stared at Anna, before giving her customary shoulder twitch. 'I hear the voices every night,' she said. 'Close window. It's cold.' The bedroom door shut firmly, and Anna heard a muffled groan. It took a moment for her to realise the sound came from her own lips.

If she continued to stay in Whitstable doing nothing, she would go mad, she thought.

At first light, she rose to pack her small rucksack, then made a strong coffee while checking train timetables. No more delays. With a thump of the metal letterbox, she went into the hall to find a solitary envelope on the mat without a postmark. Wrenching open the door, she ran to the gate to see a dirty white van pulling away. She tried to flag it, but it was gone.

But the letter remained. The address was in an unfamiliar script and there was no sign of postage. Inside was one dirty sheet of paper.

Anna, my love, if your husband say I am Russian, he lie. The men say this to me and it's wrong, but they take my phone. I arrive at Mariupol. Bad fighting.

Her heart raced as she scanned for the signature. *Sasha.* Followed by kisses. She had never seen his writing as they had always communicated by text, and it took her a moment before she could read on, staring at the strange scrawl.

I try to help get people to safety. You see Dmytrov? I pray he is alive. I get another phone and find my father, but phone stolen. Russian army is close. Old man say he will put letter on post train if they catch me. I belong to you and you belong to me. We will be strong for baby. I love you. Sasha xx

The paper rippled between her fingers. The van belonged to the man chatting to Michel outside the Deli – she was sure of it – but how had they found her? The only date was the month. April. And she wanted to wave this letter like a flag under Alex's nose, remembering the ghostly scream. He was alive. He was alive. She was sure he was alive. But where?

And then she thought if they had captured him, what could she offer for his life? What was valuable to Russia? How much money would buy a life? She thought about the Anna Karenina volumes with their odd messages of meetings. If someone in the Russian delegation had murdered Michel for this book, might another volume serve as a bribe to release Sasha? She would give any amount of money for him, but her money belonged to the Faver Estate and was not hers to give. She could beg. She could plead. But first she had to find him. In a frenzy, she hid one volume in a secure place in the house, and slid the other into her toiletries bag in her rucksack, putting on her gold moon for luck. She would start her search by locating the van men in London. They would know where Sasha might be.

THIRTY-ONE

London

APRIL 2022

'DON'T SPEAK. Things are bad here.' Dolly's words bled through the mobile like gunfire. 'Stephen's gone. A training course. Bullshit. Men in Black. Sunglasses! In the house! Fuck! Took apart his study. Boxes and boxes. White gloves. Fuck! I feel dirty. Cameras in the Deli. Did you know? Fuck! England's a fascist state.'

Despite the shorthand, Anna recognised the reason for Dolly's text silence. Her sister-in-law cut the call, but Anna was not to be deterred.

In the background, there were radio soundbites from Mariupol.

Just bake them a pie, my father said, and I said Papi, it's not like that.

All Russians live in dictatorship. We're European and we want freedom.

No one is oppressing me in Mariupol. Why are the Russians attacking?

They've taken my children to a camp and now I can't contact them.

People were disappearing. Sasha, Stephen, her nephews ...

Next on. How to protect your mental health in troubled times. Is it best to switch off and look at the blue sky?

She switched off and stared at the seagulls crying a harsh fugue. What if you couldn't look away? What about all the families flooding out of Ukraine or trapped under Russian attack? How did they protect their mental health?

On the horizon, the English sky was a gunmetal grey; the clouds hanging low over the rows of wooden groynes protecting the beach from erosion. What protected her soul from erosion? The baby kicked, and with renewed determination, she grabbed her rucksack, and scribbled a brief note for Olena.

Walking in her most sensible trainers, she texted Simon to say she was going to switch off her phone because she was changing to a new one. Paranoia was her buzzword. If she wanted to travel without Alex's interference, she would have to turn off her mobile so he could not track her.

She had chosen a loose, anonymous grey tracksuit and a stretchy T-shirt, winding her hair under a white baseball cap. Alex's office might have connections at airports, so her car would show up on vehicle number recognition cameras, but no one would look for her in a nondescript van going through a ferry terminal, and once in Europe, she could fly to Poland and take a train, moving beyond Alex's remit.

I'll find you, Sasha. This baby will have a father.

She arrived at Dolly's at lunchtime, unprepared for the person who opened the door. With creased clothes and plum hair ceded to grey, an alternative Dolly pulled Anna into the house, glancing down the road. Devoid of her usual bangles, beads or makeup, she spoke in a whisper. 'What are you doing here? I told you not to contact me.' Without waiting for an answer, she gathered Anna into a fierce hug. 'Stephen hasn't been home in weeks. The men in black told me he'd been arrested, and I was to stay in the house and speak to nobody.'

'What reason did they give?'

Without her usual makeup, Dolly's eyes were small and puffy. 'My phone went missing at Goodwood. S'pose I was a bit pissed, but then I found it before I left, so didn't think anything, but when I got home, I saw someone had texted Michel – told him to meet me in the underpass. Alex said I'm lucky they didn't accuse me.'

'You've spoken to Alex?' That seemed the most bizarre news.

'He claims he stopped them arresting me.' Dolly's nose reddened as she pointed to Anna's swelling stomach. 'God! While I was being Mrs Robinson, you were enacting a full-on Anna Karenina. How was any of this going to end well?' Two tears rolled down to her chin. 'What a mess.' She opened the fridge and uncorked a half bottle of white wine, pouring a large glass. 'Anaesthetic.'

'Concentrate Dolly,' said Anna. 'Listen to me. Did Michel ever translate the scribblings in the Anna Karenina books and explain them to you?'

The bloodshot eyes filled with more tears. 'Not to me.'

Her voice wavered. 'No matter what, he didn't deserve ...' She took a gulp of wine. 'Poor sweet Michel. He was just a kid. What did he do?' She blew her nose. 'How many weeks?'

'Twenty-eight, I think.'

'So you haven't been to a doctor? God, what a mess. If you had any sense, you'd have had a termination. Or pretend it was Alex's, although that video ...' Her sister-in-law gripped the sink. 'I'm falling apart. How are you so together?'

'I have the baby to think about.' Anna tried to keep the irritation from her voice.

'Well, they can't arrest me for drinking in my own home.' Another gulp. 'The van men came. They wanted your address.'

'I know.' Impatiently, Anna demanded their phone number, and Dolly pulled a leaflet from the kitchen drawer. She hiccuped and explained the man with the ponytail had knocked at the door to commiserate about Michel's death.

'God knows how they found me. I didn't ask.'

The leaflet showed the postal business had changed into a charity run, with a request for nappies, clothes, bedding and donations of money. At the bottom of the page, there was a phone number and a venue.

Although Anna would have loved to share her thoughts, she didn't trust this version of Dolly. Her sister-in-law was already uncorking a second bottle as she went to leave.

'Promise you won't go out in a drunken haze on the streets, shouting conspiracy theories.'

'I'm not that stupid. I'm just the mad woman in the attic.' Dolly drained a glass. 'You're the one who's crazy. How can you still trust Sasha? Neither of them were who they said they were.'

THIRTY-TWO
London

APRIL 2022

UP CLOSE, the van driver reminded her of a Toby jug with a hairless crown and ponytail. He cracked his tattooed knuckles, speaking in accented English to explain he and his co-driver only took parcels, and they never went further into Ukraine than Lviv. Most likely, they had collected the letter in a batch delivered to Warsaw. Anna planted her feet in the North London community hall and continued to haggle. Opening her bag, she took out one roll of banknotes, covered it with her palm and pressed it into his. He looked dubious, so she took out another, urging him to place it in his jacket pocket as a donation. His eyes softened, and she took out another roll, asking if they had an understanding. Behind him, a thin man with a beaked nose spoke in a rapid exchange.

'Not me, Mykhel,' the driver said with wide eyes. 'Money for charity. Money for petrol. This is good for us. Maybe? You think?'

Standing close, Anna passed another two rolls into the thin man's hands.

He snorted, then nodded. 'Okay lady. This is not a bribe. We need the donations, but Vovo is in charge, and no trouble, hey?'

She smiled, aware her timing was auspicious as they were preparing to leave in an hour. Jumping into the cab, she wedged between Mykhel's beak and Vovo's stomach. Vovo was driving the first leg, and the thinner man settled himself, dipping into a large bag of onion and beef crisps, releasing a greasy meat stink.

With a frenzied chewing of gum, Vovo squashed his belly behind the wheel and turned up the van radio to pump out rap. She tried to ignore the smells and noise, nausea spreading through her as the air coolant pumped in exhaust fumes.

'The air con doesn't work,' said Vovo cheerfully. 'Very sticky when we get to Poland. Very hot! We drop you at Warsaw. With passport, you find someone to help get train to Kyiv.'

Anna nodded, desperate to breathe in fresh air. If the nausea continued, she would get out at Belgium and fly to Warsaw. Presumably Alex wouldn't be looking for her in every European airport.

'We gonna feed people and then we gonna kill some Russians.' The beak spoke as if the whole expedition was a computer game.

'*Tak.* You hear what they do in Bucha?'

She commiserated.

'Those pigs don't have toilets; they thought the toilet was a fountain. They steal it right from the floor!' Vovo's stomach heaved in laughter.

'A fountain!' laughed Mykhel. 'A fountain. Imagine! Those Russian soldiers. Slobs.'

'*Tak*, it's true. They stole my uncle's toilet. Put it in their tank. Stupid *svoloki*!'

'If we find them, we spear them like pigs,' the beak flourished a crisp in one hand, 'cook their kidneys and stick their heads down the toilet. *Pomsta*!'

'*Tak*. Revenge!'

They laughed, switching between Ukrainian and English, until she noticed a single tear track down the driver's face and wedge in his bristles.

'If we don't laugh, we cry,' Vovo said to her, wiping his face and sniffing.

She listened to their double act humour, the guffaws and the anger, the switching of language and mournful pauses, until they petered into silence. Mykhel had finished his crisps, and with an enormous yawn of yellow teeth, he fell asleep. Unperturbed, Vovo switched to English and chatted to Anna. His wife was from Sheffield, which explained his presence in England, but he had left behind a large family in Donetsk, and in the fifteen years since they married, the situation for his family had deteriorated. He outlined his fight to get some of his relatives to England.

'Not everyone wants to come. Some move to the west to Lviv and I see them there.' He sighed. 'Beautiful country. My wife never learn a word of Ukrainian, and my English is still terrible, but she love me.'

As they neared the port, Anna worried about her switched-off phone, and felt a stab of guilt in case someone was trying to reach her. Suppose Simon had had an accident at school? Was it responsible to be out of contact? Packed in the bottom of her rucksack, she felt the pull to turn it on, like an itch waiting to be scratched. What if

Sasha were trying to contact her? What if Stephen needed her help? What if her phone didn't work in Poland and her family panicked at her disappearance?

She had to have one last dip into the network. Reaching forward, she retrieved the mobile and pressed. Immediately, it trilled, then nothing. A message lit the screen and then went black. She poked it and there was a resounding ping from an unknown number. Her heart raced.

It's me, Sasha. I use a friend's phone. Things are bad here. Can you send money to my friend. I love you. x

Oh my God. She fumbled to reply. *Where are you? xx*

Two ticks. Three wavering dots. Someone was writing. She held her breath.

Vovo glanced in her direction. 'I thought you said no phone?' He pushed a fresh stick of gum in his mouth as the van halted in traffic. 'You said best no one knows you go.'

'I'll turn it off in a minute. I have to find out ... I think ...' Any minute now, she expected a text from Alex demanding to know what she was doing and why she was in Dover.

Three dots wavered on the screen. And wavered and wavered.

The van joined a marathon queue to enter the port.

'Crazy, man!' Vovo added a few swear words in Ukrainian. 'This is what happen when we leave the European Union. Bang.' He slammed his fist on the wheel. In previous years, they would have left the country in one smooth operation, he claimed as he stretched arms above his head, baring a hairy stomach.

The three dots wavered.

She ought to turn off the phone.

Vovo switched off the engine.

Leaving Mykhel to sleep, the driver stepped out of the cab and waved to a friend in an adjacent lane.

The three dots wavered.

Anna cursed under her breath. Mykhel woke up, his large nose sniffing like a dog's. He yawned and joined Vovo with a gaggle of other van drivers waiting and chatting. Someone was offering food and handing around a communal bottle from which they all took a swig. The driver looked over his shoulder, motioning to Anna, but she shook her head. They ate and laughed.

The three dots wavered on the phone.

She had to turn off, but any minute now ...

Outside, the men rolled on the balls of their feet, shouting and cursing, laughing and joking. The words Lviv and Kraków surfaced, but she couldn't translate their humour.

The mobile had been silent for minutes; the three dots wavering.

And then a ping.

I give you my bank details. Send it here. I really need help. I love you. xx

Although the message ended with kisses, she hesitated. How could she know this was Sasha?

Can you send me a photo to show you're safe? Where are you? xx

She stared at the screen.

The three dots wavered.

Vovo climbed back in, pastry flakes clinging to his cotton shirt. His mate pushed in beside her with an uneaten pie leaking grey insides. Steak and onion, the label declared, but the flaccid crust oozed nondescript juice over his shirt.

The phone pinged.

Too dark to take photo. I am in bad trouble. Send money, help me. Please I beg you. Or they kill me. Here are the details. I love you. Please help me. xx

She bit her fingertip, breaking the skin. It was ten in the morning. Where in the world would it be dark? Or was he locked up somewhere? She drank from her water bottle to ease the tightness in her throat.

'You still have your phone on?' The driver looked uneasy. 'You said –'

'I'm sorry. I'm switching off now.'

The queue began to move. 'Finally,' Vovo groaned, pumping the clutch.

With huge reluctance, she buried the mobile in her rucksack. There was something wrong about the texts, and she tried to formulate the reasons. Wouldn't he mention the baby? He had crashed a car attempting to win ten thousand pounds for this baby. Surely he would say something about her pregnancy?

'Best kids in the world,' said Vovo, opening a picture on his phone while edging the vehicle forward. His half-smile tipped with sorrow. 'Ukraine is beautiful, but Putin is a winker.' He winked, and spoke to his mate in Ukrainian, and the thin man laughed, showering pastry down his chin.

'Your Boris Johnson – very good,' said Mykhel, and the pair set off on another comedic, aggressive rant. Inch by inch, they neared the top of the border office.

Officials in high-vis jackets walked alongside the vehicles, ordering people to switch off and use the facilities. No one needed to be asked twice. Most made an eager pilgrimage to the Portakabins. Holding her nose, Anna went, returning to find an older van driver in the centre of a cluster of men. His tousled white hair framed a long face. Those nearest slapped him on the back in enthusiastic greeting. After a spirited debate, the group stared at her, and the old man approached, shaking a finger. She shrank into the cab under his flint eyes.

'Why are you going to Ukraine? Are you nurse or doctor? Are you journalist?'

She explained her desperation to find the father of her baby, who might or might not be in Mariupol, or in a Russian prison, and held her stomach tightly.

'Say again,' he demanded.

She repeated herself and watched him rear back, raising his head like a horse.

'How crazy are you, lady? You can't go. This is war, not action movie. We supply nappies to mothers in Kyiv who have left their homes in Kharkiv and Bucha. They have only clothes they stand in, and must live in train stations. What use are you to them? Another person to feed? Another baby born on the street?'

Angrily, she pulled out her phone and switched it on to show the texts. He read, then spat.

'Fucking Russians steal phones. They either smash them or check them for pictures and phone numbers to run fraud. Vile *svolochi*. Bastards!' He spat a large blancmange gob on the pavement. 'It's a scam. Go home, lady. Someone has taken his phone. He could be dead or in Russian prison and then he's dead anyway.'

Vovo edged up to him. 'C'mon, Bogdan. Is problem? We drop her at Warsaw.'

The old man turned on his compatriot, shouting first in Ukrainian and then switching to English. 'We need aid, not pregnant women. Send her home. Did you see that girl in the news? *Svolochi* even bomb maternity hospitals. They're not human.'

Around them, the men gave a nervous titter.

'But Bogdan, she want to come. She pay. It pay petrol.'

Swearing, he stomped back to his vehicle as the signal

turned green for go. 'She's useless, as useless as you are, you fucking idiot,' he called over his shoulder.

Anna clenched her hands, determined not to cry. She clutched the phone to her stomach, determined to do this for Sasha. No matter what people said to her; no matter the insults; she would not rest until she had found out what happened to him.

Mykhel touched her shoulder. 'Get in van, lady. Here comes real trouble.'

THIRTY-THREE

dover

APRIL 2022

EYES SHARP, the border officials patrolled the queues. Mykhel ate salted peanuts, while he and Vovo exchanged a few words. Beyond the first barrier, a second queue formed for French border control.

Vovo clicked his tongue. 'Maybe someone escape from prison.'

'Is that you?' said Mykhel to Anna, with a jocular flourish of the peanut bag.

But the conversation died as one of the uniformed men approached his open window, and peered in. 'What gives?' said Vovo with forced laughter. 'You don't check us when we leave, you let French do that.'

'Can I see in the back, Sir?'

'Certainly.' With a sigh, Vovo slipped out of the cab. 'You want nappies? We have nappies.'

Mykhel stashed the remains of his peanuts into the glove compartment and continued chewing. 'You, lady, you know people in opera house die? Mariupol. In the Azov steelworks – bad situation. Russians surround them. They die if those *svolochi* get inside. Bogdan has bad temper, but is true. This is war. You should go home and look after baby.'

Sweat trickled down her sides. 'I have to go to Kyiv,' she said. 'No one knows anything here. Maybe in Ukraine.'

'Listen, lady, those going to Kyiv want to meet Zelenskyy, but –'

'Sasha went to fetch his sick father. I don't know what happened after that.'

The beak sighed. 'We all fight for our families. Our families, our land, our lives. Russia says the land is theirs, but it is ours. You are English. You are an island. You not understand.'

A second Border Force official approached the window. 'Passport.' He directed this at Anna.

She handed him the purple book and he flicked through the pages, nodding as the van vibrated with the slam of the back door.

'Get out please, Madam. We need to have a word with you.'

The first uniformed border official arrived to join his side. 'It's her?'

'Yes.'

'Me?' A surge of adrenaline powered her body. 'Why me? I'm allowed to go to Europe.'

'Is problem?' asked Mykhel.

'Not you,' said the official. 'You two going to Poland?'

'And Lviv, if we don't get shot.' Vovo eased his backside into the driving seat, tittering with nerves.

The official didn't smile. 'Careful on your way back. At least, I'm assuming you're coming back. We've had reports of migrants jumping on board at Calais. You know the thing, holding the tailpipe to get to England. We'll search you.'

Vovo relaxed. 'Oh yes, search away. I am used to strip search.' He tittered again. 'Should I wait for my passenger?'

'You taking supplies? Food and the like?'

'Yes. Nappies. Baby food. You've seen everything.'

'Take your place on the ferry, please, Sir. The supplies are needed, and she will delay you.'

'What have I done?' said Anna. She wanted to run or argue.

'If you would be so kind, madam. We don't wish to arrest you in front of everyone if we can avoid it.'

She saw the look of relief on Vovo's face, and her mind buzzed. A conspiracy had caught her in its net. But even as she formulated this idea, she refuted it. She wasn't interested in politics, nor did she have a job in journalism. She was an interpreter of romantic fiction, and she loved a man, who loved her in return. Why should she be arrested? Weren't there enough criminals trying to escape from justice? But the border guards brooked no conversation and she cringed at the stares from other cars as she walked between them, her rucksack banging against her back.

Locked into a small Portakabin, her feet swelled with the heat, and she kicked off her trainers. Through a small window of stippled glass, she could hear the slow wheezing screech of lorry brakes and an occasional shouted instruction. She sat on one of the two hard blue plastic chairs, elbow on the cheap black desk. Someone had taken her bag, promising to return it, and she longed for her phone.

When the door opened, a woman in a blue uniform brought in a pre-packed ham and salad sandwich, a KitKat and tea in a polystyrene cup.

Anna rose to her feet, indignant. 'This is unlawful. Why

am I being detained? At the very least, they must allow me a phone call.'

'It's not up to me.' The woman placed the refreshments on the desk. 'But in your condition, I thought you needed something.'

'Please.' She hated herself for pleading. 'My husband is in the Foreign Office. Call him.'

'They've called him. So relax Mrs Faver. I'm sure someone will arrive to speak to you shortly.' She cracked open the top pane of the reinforced window and left with a smile.

If they'd called Alex, this had to be his doing, she thought as she sat simmering. A moment later, she opted to force down some food and tea for the sake of the baby, but the stale exhaust fumes washing through the room made her feel sick. Perhaps she could fake pregnancy pains, but she felt too strung out to put on a convincing performance. When she was free, she promised herself, the first thing she would do was take up self-defence classes. And nursing. Never again would anyone tell her she was useless in a crisis. But God, first, she needed a pee.

Standing on tiptoe, she squinted out of the window, and saw a dirty sign with an arrow pointing to the staff toilets.

'Hello,' she called. 'Hello. Can someone help?' She rattled the knob.

A moment later, the door unlocked.

'Thank God, I need the loo,' she said expecting the woman, then stopped. Before her, stood a slim, grey-suited man. His thick black hair was sleekly combed showing a high, smooth forehead, and his deep brown face broke into a smile of recognition, despite him being a stranger. She stared back, conscious of her perspiration-riddled track suit.

'I'm here on behalf of your husband, Mrs Faver,' he said in an accent that suggested an English public school. 'He's not able to come in person. Let me introduce myself. I'm John Farquhar.'

The name was at odds with his Asian ethnicity, but her bladder didn't care. 'I need the ladies room. Now.'

He stepped aside to let her through, and followed her out, with a nod to the woman in blue uniform who was waiting outside. Scooping her rucksack from him, she ran in the pointed direction. Her legs ached, but her only thought as she completed her ablutions was how to escape. But they were keeping close watch.

'There must be some mistake. It can't be legal to detain me like this.'

He cut into her words, taking her elbow and steering her like a trolley towards a row of cars. 'I understand you're distressed, Anna. I hope I may call you Anna. I'm Alex's colleague, and we're aware you're trying to leave the country. Alex thinks you're probably heading for Ukraine, and that would be very foolish.' Farquhar smiled again. 'I agree.'

She bit back a swear word, unsure if antagonism was her best defence. 'Am I under arrest? Because you have no right to do this. Or is this about the death of that man at Goodwood? Because I had nothing to do with that. Ask Alex.'

Mr Farquhar showed no surprise. 'Thank you for switching on your phone. It made things easier. But we were checking every port once we realised you'd shown up at your brother's house. All bases covered, and that sort of thing.'

He unlocked a black BMW, and she held in tears of frustration.

'Now, to the matter at hand,' continued John Farquhar. 'We're heading to your mother-in-law's in Canterbury. Your son, Simon, is expecting you, and I understand he's quite excited. He hasn't seen you for some time.'

'The subtle art of blackmail?' she growled.

He laughed.

The seats emitted a strong, but not unpleasant, leathery smell. After hours in the van, her body relaxed into the soft upholstery. She watched him wipe a tiny mark of dust from his shoulder, before turning to examine her. His grin showed bright white teeth. 'Mrs Faver, I'm not usually sent out for such mundane activities as collecting other men's wives. I have more pressing things to do. But I volunteered to fetch you because I care about Alex's wellbeing and this is important. Do you understand?'

'*This* is important? What is *this*?' said Anna.

He didn't answer, but eased the car gently around the periphery roads, packed with vehicles. When they were further from the port, he spoke. 'I can see you are brave, but you lack information. The situation is important. National security. And you are an inconvenience we'd like to remove.' The even teeth flashed once more. 'Would it help if I said please?'

No, she thought, irritated by his mild disdain. 'Promise we're going to Nina's?'

'Oh dear,' he sighed with a twinkle. 'Never ask people to promise things. If they want your co-operation, they'll say yes whether or not they mean it. Promises are best left behind in the schoolyard, don't you think? Alex made all sorts of promises when we were at school together. It was like he was always in training for the service. And I imagine your Vronskiy man promised all sorts of things. Promises he couldn't possibly keep.'

She crossed her arms in silence.

He placed sunshades over his mocking eyes. 'You don't have to talk to me, but I'm taking you to meet someone who knew both the Vronskiy boys rather well. I think you'll find what they have to say is very illuminating.'

THIRTY-FOUR

ukraine

THE NOUGHTIES

EYES SHARP, he patrolled his estate. Katerina stood at the barn door, watching the farm hands move around. The girl's face lacked the finesse to be desirable, but it was pointless arguing with Stepanov, so he had found her a temporary bedroom on the ground floor. Never voicing an opinion, Katerina ambled around, eating peanuts, until Vronsky spoke to his cook, and she went to work in the kitchen. In a subsequent phone call, having cursed Stepanov for lumbering him with this woman, the man laughed, wishing him a cell in a Siberian Gulag.

'Do me a favour in return. Cast your eye over a few of these Telegram applications,' said Stepanov. 'Just a few of the trickier ones. Advise our team on which little shits to avoid and which ones will set fires and move weapons without giving us grief. You've lived in Europe long enough to understand the mentality of these people. Some of my PR people have never left Russia.'

'*Blyat*,' said Vronsky. 'Do I look like a man who sits in front of a screen all day. I'm too old and I don't like the SVB telling kids to do an adult's job.'

'Stop!' said Stepanov. 'You're only slightly older than Putin, and this is his brainchild.'

'Go fuck yourself.' He could afford to be rude, as their friendship was richly oiled with money.

'I might,' chuckled the friend, 'but I have several willing to do that for me back in Moscow, and I was hoping that Katerina would do that for you.'

In the end, he found himself enjoying the girl's cooking, and he was reluctant to admit that after a month and a few drunken nights of reflection, he had turned up at her bedside. She neither objected nor seemed startled, and they fell into an informal relationship. It wasn't his fault. She was there, and he was a man with bodily needs, but if he couldn't offer her love, he at least tried to make her life comfortable.

'Katerina stays or goes,' he would say feigning disinterest, when Stepanov ribbed him.

Given the fomenting situation in the Crimea, he was astonished to find that his workers accepted her as one of them, until he noticed she chattered to everyone in Ukrainian. She spoke to him in Russian, as did all the workforce, but his manager informed him that her Russian father had killed her Ukrainian mother. That explained the orphanage, he thought.

The money rolled in and out of his Credit Suisse bank account, and with Russian investment, he extended his luxurious home, creating a place fit for the glitterati of Moscow and St Petersburg. Locals dug the land and constructed the outbuildings. Here and there he heard grumbles from older staff about certain Russian visitors – but many were flexible and happy to be in his employ. He paid well and the gun remained in his drawer.

As always, the black market flourished, although Vronsky avoided this. He was making enough profit not to need such complications, and he preferred to keep the gangs at arms' length. His Kremlin chums arrived for holidays, buying cases of wine before driving over to the Crimea and frolicking on their beaches. They feted him with trinkets from their gains, playing poker till late at night. One by one, they sat in his study to do business, swelling their riches and waistbands. Some of the local girls vied to catch their eyes, because rich men were in short supply in this region. But as the years went by, many preferred to leave to study at foreign universities. More were learning English rather than Russian, watching Hollywood films, and everyone was on the internet. Archie and Lycos became Yahoo and Google. The world was changing, and he made a point of keeping in step with recent developments.

His wine improved year on year as he applied himself to the new science of viticulture. With the assistance of foreign experts, he created a community of Ukrainian vineyard owners. First, he travelled to Bakhmut to get ideas from Artwinery, which was on track to be the largest Ukrainian producer of sparkling wines. The following year, he met the family running Chateau Kurin in Kherson, who had a warehouse in Kyiv that was booming. Then, he went to meet the founder of Olbio Nubo's winery, Pavlo Magalias. Pavlo had been in the Armed Forces and saw Vronsky as an ex-military fellow enthusiast. Together, they compared many species of vines and subsequent blends. Pavlo's land looked out over the River Buh, not far from Krivyi Rih, and when the two exchanged visits – Vronsky's land straddled a tributary of the Dnipro – they marvelled at the beauty of Ukrainian rivers and the hot summers that warmed the soil.

Their existential conversations gave Vronsky an understanding of the Ukrainian love for their land. His hands had once held a gun, but now revelled in swilling glasses, watching the wine rotate and the alcohol legs slide down the goblets. Only Stepanov's visits brought him back to the reality that he was a Russian laundry facility. He washed their stolen roubles and their illicit money through his Swiss bank account, and they would never let him stop.

The sun beat his skin to a wooden hue, and his face crinkled. Vronsky boasted of his newly developed sparkling wine, and Stepanov alone received his confession: 'Anna Karenina inspired this wine.'

His former colleague made a wry face. 'Don't tell me you're still looking back. You've got Katerina, what more do you want? One arse is much like another.'

'I'd like to know where Annaliese went,' he admitted. He was getting old and it was hard not to look back.

'Leave well alone.'

Vronsky mulled. 'But you know something? Tell me, you bastard.'

Stepanov laughed. 'Psht. She's not coming back, *tovarich.* Abramovich bought an English football club – far more absorbing than growing grapes. If you're bored, I can find you more work.'

'You can lose in the game of football. Everyone always wants a drink.' Vronsky refilled their glasses.

Stepanov sniffed and drank. 'Very true, and besides, we

should not deprive the world of this excellent vintage. But remind me next time I come, I may have news of a former Anna Karenina agent. So wait for my visit!'

'Bastard,' he spat, but it never paid to look too keen when you wanted information.

THIRTY-FIVE

canterbury

APRIL 2022

THE RADIO PRESENTER moved spoke about the Azov steelworks. Farquhar switched off as the blacked-out saloon eased its way out of Dover. He manoeuvred through the one-way systems with an adept familiarity, and upon reaching the M20, broke into high speed. Anna gripped the rucksack between her legs, glancing at his profile. Attached to the mirror, a plastic label swung with the name 'Zelenskyy: Best in Class'.

Noticing her gaze, he gave a small laugh. 'It's an office joke.'

'Is it?'

'The art of satire and the hero. You're into literature.'

Anna eased the seatbelt from her stomach. 'Am I?'

He ignored her belligerence. 'In my opinion, any media guy who gets standing ovations in every country's parliament leads a charmed existence. Obama was similar. That man's brilliant.'

'Zelenskyy?'

'His speech writers.' He dodged lanes. 'No. Zelenskyy. Of course. Zelenskyy.'

They raced off the motorway onto a dual carriageway. 'It half made me wish we'd elected an actor. Peter Capaldi, perhaps.' A fraction of a glance in her direction. 'You know. The actor who was in the political skit, *The Thick of It*? Or am I showing my age?'

Refusing to engage, she unzipped the rucksack and pulled out the phone. It was still switched on. She flicked through fresh texts. Farquhar remained silent as she read more pleas for money, each one more desperate than the last.

He swerved between lanes and sped up. 'Demands for dosh?' Farquhar flicked a wrist in irritation. 'We looked at your texts – all scams. Phishing.'

He was parroting much the same line as the van men. 'Yes, I know.'

'Do you? Alex said you were naive, but if you ask me, it's an understatement. What you were about to do shows a complete lack of understanding.'

A tang of blood flooded her throat where she had bitten her tongue. 'Maybe I know more than you think.'

He swerved to avoid a lumbering lorry. 'Interesting,' he said, raising an eyebrow. 'So has Alex mentioned me?'

'No.'

'Then you don't know.' He tutted. 'Everyone calls me Jogi, by the way. I thought he might have said.'

'Seeing as he never repeated office gossip, he wouldn't have mentioned you. But anyway, Alex hasn't lived properly with me and Simon for four years. He spent every week in London in the family flat, and now he's there all the time.' She took in a deep breath of frustration.

'I know.' They bounced down a potholed road.

Lapsing into silence, Farquhar focussed on navigating without the need for satnav. The Kentish fields gave way to new housing, old housing, signs to small villages and larger towns, all vanishing as the car sped towards Canterbury.

'Torture doesn't give reliable information and the Russians rely on it completely. So we don't know where your lover is at the moment.'

She gripped her phone.

'Sometimes, the enemy claims Prisoner X is alive but then we receive a body. You can imagine how upsetting that is for the family.' He outlined the statistics of fraudulent emails and texts. 'So if we appear evasive, it's for your own good.'

Her eyes blurred.

'And naturally, we receive a lot of fake news. Propaganda. When you work in my line, you come to understand that most people are dishonest. On a scale of one to ten, mass murderers are ten in the dishonesty stakes. Fraudsters are six depending on the amount of money, and an affair is right at the bottom. Not even one. More like a half. So, for the record, I'm not interested in your affairs and I'm not judgemental. Most of us lie to avoid conflict.'

Farquhar manoeuvred through a petrol station and out onto another dual carriageway, accelerating fast. He was exceeding the speed limit but they passed a police car without a hint of a blue light. Beneath the seat belt, the baby kicked.

'Is this an unmarked police car? Has Alex sanctioned you collecting me or –?'

'You think I'm abducting you?' His eyes crinkled. 'Sorry. You're not my type, darling.'

'Are you MI5?'

The giggle turned into full-blown laughter. 'You're thinking Bond films. My department doesn't gather information; we sift it, but this car has a certain plate. You didn't notice? Dear me. You wouldn't make a good witness.'

'So why am I being sifted?' she said, attempting to match his sarcasm. 'Are pregnant women a threat now?' From her vantage point, she could see the needle exceed one hundred miles an hour as they flashed past slow-moving lorries. Up ahead, the sign showed Canterbury and she breathed out in relief.

'This guy you think is so wonderful – you don't really know him, do you? You've accepted everything he says, ignoring the fact that sometimes people swop papers or passports and change identities.' One wrist flicked. 'In times of war, it's very difficult to trace people unless we have fingerprints and DNA or dental records. Now, Oleksandr Vronskiy or Alexandr Vronsky, with an A and without the letter I – both appear on the papers we examined before he was arrested and left the country. So at least we have him on record, but until we triangulate Ukrainian and Russian information, he could be anybody. He could be someone who puts ricin in your food. How would you feel if he wanted to poison your nearest and dearest?'

Her fingers knotted and she focussed on her memory of Sasha and the way he spoke about his family, and his arms around her. 'You expect me to believe you, but I don't see how anyone in your line of work trusts each other.'

'Touché.' A smile flitted across Farquhar's thin lips.

The saloon car veered off the dual carriageway, and her phone pinged again.

'More money? Block that number. If he's asking you for money, then he's not the man you thought he was. But to put your mind at rest, I'll check those texts when we get to the Faver Estate.'

Anna saw the familiar roads and houses, the lines of trees and woodland. Over the brow of the hill, the vines flourished in the late spring heat.

'Has Alex had me arrested because he's jealous?'

Farquhar's eyebrows rose in a comical arch and he guffawed. 'You don't know Alex at all.' He puffed out his cheeks, his dark eyes dancing with amusement. 'He's not jealous, but oh my goodness, he hates to upset his mother.'

Another text pinged from another different, unfamiliar number.

I write for Sasha. His father died and the situation here was bad, but I escaped. Dmytrov.

The words punched a hole in her chest. 'I'm sure this is a friend of Sasha's.'

'What does it say?'

She read it out and texted back. *Where are you? Where is Sasha now?*

Three dots wavered as they passed the signs for Mystole and the Kent Downs. Farquhar waited at traffic lights, flicking a glance at her screen.

Sorry, came the reply. *Delay. I get phone and have to find you. I escape to swim from Mariupol to Melekyne and almost die. But Sasha not go.*

She texted back, her fingers fumbling in alarm. *Where were you both? Mariupol? Inside the Azov steelworks? Where is he now?* The phone took on a life of its own, pregnant with wavering dots. She held it tightly. 'This is genuine, I'm sure.'

Farquhar sighed. 'He's not jealous, you know – Alex. He and I have lived in his London flat for the past seven years.'

Her sole focus was on Dmytrov's response and the three wavering dots.

'Did you hear me, Anna?'

'You're a flatmate. So what?'

The three dots wavered. They passed the sign for the Faver Estate.

Farquhar hissed. 'I'm his partner and at work.'

The three dots wavered. Where was Sasha? 'I don't give a fuck who he works with.'

The wrist flicked. 'For heaven's sake.' He jerked the car to the right, and stones spat as he drove past the Faver Estate gates.

She felt a rush of anger. 'This is important.'

Farquhar puffed in irritation. 'I thought he might have told you. Wake up, Anna.'

In response, she thrust the phone into his hand as they came to a halt in front of the Faver Grange oak door. He yanked on the handbrake and examined it with narrowed eyes.

'It's possible this Dmytrov is genuine,' he pronounced before scrolling through her other texts. 'But he's not with Sasha and the rest are definitely scammers. So switch off and concentrate on this meeting.' He opened the car door. 'We've gone to a great deal of trouble to find the one person who might talk sense into you.' Pressing the off button, he pocketed her phone.

Any minute, her son would appear, and she needed to be in control. She took a deep breath and climbed out of the car. Around them, cherry blossom trees painted the driveway with a carpet of rich pink petals. She was in middle England, under a mantle of peace, but far away, Sasha needed her: she was sure of it.

In a blaze of excitement, Simon rushed out of the front door, crushing her in a hug. With tears, she hugged him in return, reminding herself that she had one beautiful son, and she loved him.

In smart trousers and a clean blouse, Nina circumvented Anna to greet Farquhar with a small kiss to one cheek. 'Dear boy,' she said, 'it's been too long. When did we last meet?'

Farquhar returned the kiss on the other cheek. 'At Harrow's alumni day?'

'The one before Covid? Oh yes. So good to see you. I still have the photo of you and Alex together on that geography trip. Amazing that you're working together now. I always thought you'd go into the sciences.'

'Ah, but you can't separate a good team, Mrs F.'

Anna had never seen her mother-in-law display such fondness. Grateful to be bombarded by Simon's chatter, she allowed herself to be led over the threshold and down the red flagstone hallway to the kitchen.

'Gosh, aren't you getting fat? Is it a brother or a sister? Have you and Dad decided on a name? When will the baby be born? Is it twins? I'd love it if it were twins; they could help me manage the estate when they're older.' Simon leaned across the table for a large homemade biscuit, oblivious to the crowd settled in the room.

Hesitating to sit down, Anna looked around. Her visits usually entailed eating cake with the Head Gardener and his son, Callum. This audience confused her. Three strangers sat in the Carver chairs, drinking tea with the ease of old friends. In front of them lay a selection of quiches, salmon sandwiches and an untouched raspberry Pavlova. Turning to Simon with a large plate of sandwiches, Nina suggested he might want to share it in the garden room with his friend, and sensing he was being dismissed, Simon gave his mother a wan smile of acceptance and left. She wanted to grab her son's hand and insist he stay, but Farquhar put gentle pressure on her shoulder and she sat, aware she was the focus of attention.

'So where is Alex?' she asked. 'And what is this about?'

THIRTY-SIX

ukraine

SPRING 2014

THE RADIO PRESENTER spoke about Dolomeyer. The news reached Vronsky before Stepanov's text. He listened, cup halfway to his lips as he heard how Henry Snooks, a disaffected Vietnam veteran, had tried his hand at a political assassination. The FBI had liquidated him. With a sigh, he finished his coffee. He had often thought about pursuing that particular avenue to gain information about Annaliese, but it was now a dead end. He scanned the internet for any further references, such as a mention of a female partner, but Snooks was considered a loner. A few strands on Twitter – (a platform Vronsky detested but used at Stepanov's insistence) – suggested Snooks was an inept Russian agent, although others claimed it was fake news. Vronsky muttered and lit a cigarette.

Later in a phone call, Stepanov was in full humour. 'Here's the joke everyone speaks in the office. What do you call an American with a gun and no cause? A dick. How does this translate?' Vronsky gave the Russian approximation and his friend guffawed. From this, he inferred the Kremlin had had a hand in Dolomeyer's fate, which did not surprise him. From his part-time work perusing Telegram channel applicants, he knew Russia had embedded into the West, particularly in the USA.

But Snooks was soon forgotten. The Ukrainian headlines were full of the downing of the Malaysia Airlines Flight 17, which had become a hot topic of discussion in bars and on the streets. Everyone had an accusation and counter-accusation.

On a visit, Stepanov insisted the blame lay with the Ukrainian army, and said it was typical of the Ukrainian Government that they pointed the finger at the Russians. Or if not the actual Russians, then the Russian-backed separatists: the Donetsk People's Republic and the Luhansk People's Republic, both of whom were declaring independent states under the Donbas People's Militia.

'Can you blame us for supporting them?' Stepanov was tucking into one of Katerina's traditional Russian dishes. 'Those who speak Russian should live under Russian protection.'

Vronsky was aware some Russian journalists blamed pilot malfunction, or at a push, the Chechens acting on their own, which gave no comfort to the relatives of the two hundred and ninety-eight people who died, one of whom lived on his extended farm. He sighed. Try as he might to avoid the political arena, Vronsky found international relations creeping closer to his vineyard.

He had heard of skirmishes breaking out in Mariupol between Russian and Ukrainian factions and knew each side would force his hand.

Are you Ukrainian or Russian?

Many were of mixed parentage, but he saw the quick eye flicks of distrust among the locals when he passed. He was regarded as a pure blood Soviet. What would Annaliese have made of these choices? Would her English presence have altered their views? Once she had been pro-Russia, or at least pro-communism, but where were the communists now? Vronsky thought they were all in Italy enjoying fine wines.

Like the old days, a fart in public became political, so when he did the rounds on his estate, he spoke with caution. He explained to Stepanov that the Ukrainian army was composed of men who had had a taste of freedom, and were not ready to give it up, but his friend dismissed his qualms. In the event of military intervention, Russia would always win.

What about the Minsk Protocol, he insisted?

Stepanov waved a hand. The man's hair had greyed with age and his formerly lean figure filled, but his position in the Kremlin was more powerful than ever. Was Vronsky of sufficient use to keep his vineyard safe? The fighting had gone on for months, leaving dead on both sides, and still, the Ukrainians were unwavering: they wanted their Ukrainian passports, their Ukrainian language, and to lean towards Europe.

Are you Russian or Ukrainian?

'You know the way it is,' said Stepanov, settling to a cigar. 'Give people food and water and let them get on with things, and they'll vote for anyone who doesn't shoot them. The people here want to be with Russia, because Russia is strong, and I hear the Crimea is settling down nicely.'

The problems in the Donbas, thought Vronsky, whose mind ran along different lines, was an inability for one group to take control. He disagreed with his friend, remembering that the battle for Donetsk International Airport had gone on for months and inconvenienced his travelling plans. Even local Russians had nicknamed the Ukrainian army 'Cyborgs' because they were so resilient in their defence, and although Russia had won by supporting the paramilitaries, nobody could claim control over the Chechens. That morning, Vronsky had had an email from a vineyard owner bemoaning the damage done to their land with landmines. What could he say? The Russian army cared little for farms and livestock, and even less for humans.

Are you Russian or Ukrainian? Ukrainian or Russian? Pick a side.

They ate their dinner, while Vronsky steered the conversation to useful areas, hoping for insight into the future. In some towns, you could get shot purchasing a packet of cigarettes if a young soldier didn't like your face. And then there were the Muslims, practising a faith he did not understand. With as much diplomacy as he could manage, he probed, but every question was met with a retort that showed Stepanov had little understanding of the Ukrainian people.

'Who gave these groups their guns? Russia. So we expect some loyalty.'

'But,' said Vronsky, 'the Ukrainians are hardheaded, and determined to retake their land.'

A puff of the cigar, and smoke thickened in the room. 'Their land? It's our land! Ukrainians, the DPR, the LPR and the Chechens. They're too splintered and if China dropped a regiment into the mix, it wouldn't surprise me. We'll crush dissent.'

Vronsky kept silent. He was keen to protect his vineyard. Pragmatism. That was his chosen route, then and now and always. A hero was a dead man.

'All these Minsky nonsenses. I tell you, Putin doesn't give a vodka burp for them. He wants Ukraine to be like

Belarus and Georgia. Why should our neighbours, our former lands, look to Europe or America? They were Russian and they will remain Russian.' He stopped his rant to eat some truffled chocolates, while Vronsky opened a fresh bottle, turning the conversation to his latest white wine blends.

Holding the glass to the light, his friend leaned back in satisfaction. 'I must say when you first started this vineyard, I thought you were mad, but you've made a good industry out of empty land. And of course, you've helped move money. We'll not forget you when the time comes.'

But when was that time? Vronsky longed for specifics. If only he could wrestle an itinerary from his former boss. When he had controlled the Anna Karenina cell, he always made a point of precision and timing. Sloppiness meant capture.

'I'm concerned that Russian soldiers will mine my land. They've done it elsewhere.'

Stepanov poked out his tongue, pinching a speck of cork and throwing it to the floor. 'Pah! We'll help. You'll see. If it makes you feel any better, I'm travelling through the Donbas and the Crimea to collate information first-hand and send it back to Moscow.' Outside were two large bulletproof Range Rovers and a collection of armed henchmen. Vronsky nodded.

'Don't worry, old man,' he teased. 'We need to gauge the pliability of people and the state of the army, but if we have to arrest and kill half the population, that's what we'll do. You'll be fine.' The wine encouraged his friend to expound further, and unable to do anything but listen, Vronsky paid attention. Information was currency.

Draining his glass, his friend wiped his mouth with the back of his sleeve. 'Also, the Kremlin is altering the terms of giving gas and oil to Ukraine, so the Donbas will have a preferential rate. Hit the businesses. It always works. And we have more up our sleeves. As for the old president, Yanukovych, he was pro-Russia, insisting Ukraine shouldn't join the EU, but when he lost the election, we removed him and put another candidate in place.'

'But,' protested Vronsky, 'that candidate dealt poorly with the Euromaidan riots, and failed to convince people to change their minds. How will the next one –?'

The conversation was going nowhere, and he was glad when Stepanov slipped into an alcoholic doze.

The Revolution of Dignity had taken place last year, and Vronsky recalled seeing footage of the Ukrainian people in Kyiv, waving Ukrainian flags and banners against corruption. They'd frightened Yanukovych into firing on the crowd, before fleeing to Moscow, which, in Vronsky's opinion, could not be defined as Russia removing him from office. To every Ukrainian, it spoke of corruption, and when they'd opened the presidential palace, everyone had spat on his gold bathroom taps, and his cellars stocked with luxuries and other mementoes from his abuse of power. Another Russian PR disaster, thought Vronsky. It was so much simpler forty years ago, when you persuaded people with a gun and to hell with morality. The trouble was Russia still expected things to work this way. How to make them see the internet changed things?

'In my opinion, freedom is overrated.' Stepanov waved his hand like a king, half asleep, continuing a conversation from his dream. 'The only true freedom is money. Most people need to be told what to do.' His head slumped to his chest and then raised again with a snigger. 'I suppose you're going to ask me for machine guns and a tank.' His mouth fell open, emitting a snore and Vronsky caught the half-full glass before it hit the carpet.

Blyat, he hoped none of his staff were listening. Guns would be good, he thought, because Ukraine's current president, Poroshenko, was a committed Europhile. Despite being a millionaire, the man had refused to align with the oligarchs, and when he'd gone on a state visit to the Donbas, the Russians had fired on his car. If the Ukrainians couldn't protect their president, how were they going to protect his precious vineyard and land?

Despite a life of cynicism, he'd become attached to the vineyards. His plants were strong and resilient to the temperature changes, and the business thrived. It was true; none of his workers accepted him because he was a Muscovite, but Katerina mediated, and proved surprisingly useful. When the fighting was over, he might even take a holiday to search for Annaliese, leaving her in charge of the house.

As if sensing his inner thoughts, Stepanov woke with a start. 'But you're okay! How's the girl?' He wiped his mouth, looking for his glass. 'Not so young now. Hey? Did I tell you her husband is out of jail? Conscripted into the military. He'll probably arrive in your neck of the woods with a submachine gun.' His laughter spattered red mist. 'Don't worry, I won't say anything. But it's genius, don't you think? Send the murderers to do what they do best. There's this guy, Prigozhin –'

'Very effective,' said Vronsky, with a pretence of mild amusement. 'But not a word to Katerina or she'll bugger off somewhere else and then who will cook those delicious meals?'

'Another disappearing Anna Karennn?' Stepanov slurred his words in merriment. 'We can't have that!'

THIRTY-SEVEN

canterbury

APRIL 2022

THE STRANGE GATHERING sat in Nina's kitchen court, and Anna positioned herself, hands in her lap, deliberating her next move.

'Cup of tea?' said Nina to Farquhar. World War III might break out, but Nina would begin negotiations with tea. Farquhar slung his jacket over the chair, commenting on how the old farmhouse had not changed.

'I'm afraid Alex rang ten minutes ago. He can't make it.'

'Pity.' Farquhar accepted the cup with thanks.

'Dear boy, you see him more than I do.'

Ferociously thirsty, Anna drank, wondering why no one had introduced her or themselves. The assembled crowd chattered about Nina's lost wine, all aware of the real events at Goodwood. The two burly men attributed the blame for the missing crates to the Russian delegation, but the blonde-haired woman suspected rogue police. Sympathy was offered in return for cake, and after five minutes, with a nod from Farquhar, the two men in black suits stood and whistled for an Alsatian, discretely concealed under the table.

'We'll be just outside, sir,' said one. 'Thanks for the tea and lovely spread, Mrs F.'

The unknown woman remained, legs crossed in leather trousers tapering to a pair of high heels. There was something familiar about her thin, lanky build. She leaned forward with a friendly smile. 'Hi Anna. Let's go in the other room to talk.' Her accent matched Farquhar's. 'Do you need to be making tracks, Jogi? I've got my car here, so no need to wait.'

Nina's cup chinked in the saucer. 'Honestly Anna, the trouble you cause. Poor Jogi having to run after you.'

'She's in the dark, Mrs F.' Jogi smoothed his trousers, a smile playing on his face as he ran a palm along his thigh. 'By the way,' he tapped Anna's elbow. 'I'm John Farquhar in meetings but I'm Jogi to friends. Father's English, mother's Indian.' He leaned back, cradling her mobile in his hands. 'Here's your phone. I've sent the numbers for checking.'

'Well now we've explained the simple stuff,' said the woman, rising. 'Come on.'

Anna was ushered out of the kitchen, and led through the corridors towards the small snug in the eastern wing. The woman shut the door firmly. The fire was unlit in the grate, but the sun shone through, coating the worn brocade sofas with a warm glow. She extended a hand for Anna to settle.

'I met you as Kitty, but it's not my real name.' There was a hint of pity in her eyes. 'Do you remember?'

Anna thought back to Halloween, and the girl in the spandex cat suit, lolling on Gonzales' lap.

Without waiting for an answer, she continued. 'I recognised you from Alex's work files. For operational reasons, I knew about his extended family. So, I was undercover at the Deli, and when you showed, I thought it best to remove you quickly. As far as I was aware, you weren't involved.'

A crushing thought came to Anna. Had this woman seen her and Sasha on video in the flat? She couldn't ask, but Kitty seemed to read her thoughts.

'I work in British intelligence. Not Alex's office. There are many departments.'

Anna felt her body sag in defeat. 'I used to eat chips in that cafe after college.'

'Things change,' said Kitty briskly. 'I suppose you think Russian safe houses have a sign over the door saying: Watch out, here are the spies?' She uncrossed and recrossed her legs. 'This shop came to our attention before Covid when it changed management, and we noticed a pattern of young kids coming into the country, staying there for a few weeks, committing political sabotage and skipping out again.' She examined Anna for a response, before continuing. 'We arrested one of them for torching an MP's house. Simple arson. And found he'd received payment from a Russian account. He claimed Gonzales gave the orders. The news reports ran it as an example of mindless thuggery.' Kitty paused again, but Anna said nothing. 'Anyway. Halloween at the Deli club and things were happening, so that's why I threw the drink over you.'

Lacing her fingers, Anna absorbed the information. 'But I might have gone to the toilets and continued dancing.'

'It was a judgement call, and I was pretty sure the other Vronskiy would take you upstairs to the flat, or walk you home. I could see he had the hots for you.'

Sunlight striped Anna's eyes, and she put her head in her hands. 'Did you have Michel killed?' She half expected a scornful response, but Kitty leaned forward with an earnest expression. 'I wasn't at Goodwood, but that was a shock for us all. A very brazen act, considering he was a minor player, so we had to ask ourselves who knew the boy had offered us intelligence.'

'Who?' Anna looked into the woman's unblinking blue eyes.

'I'm not at liberty to say. But potentially your Vronskiy was far more useful to the Russians than his brother because he knew how to use a gun.'

'He wouldn't ...' The words died in her throat and she struggled to breathe. 'I've had a letter –' Bile rose in her throat as she thought of Dolly leaning against the young man's shoulder, absorbing the smoke from his smouldering Gauloise. 'Russian soldiers killed his family at a checkpoint.'

Kitty narrowed her eyes. 'There's two sides to that. The Russians will reverse it and claim it was the Ukrainians who killed his family at a checkpoint. We've looked into it.'

'But Sasha wants me to go to Ukraine with him and I'm carrying his baby. We don't have anything to do with this. We're ordinary people.'

'Just because his story is plausible doesn't make it true. This is why I'm here. You're connected to Alex, who's connected to us. That means you are at risk of being kidnapped and used as a hostage if you go to Ukraine. The country is full of Russian spies, and if they know you're coming ...'

In a frenzy, Anna opened and thrust her phone at the woman. 'Look! Look at these texts.'

Kitty read in silence before pulling out her own phone, taking screen shots and forwarding each picture. 'We'll trace this. One is definitely a scam. Not very expert, but good enough for someone like you. Dmytrov might be a genuine friend. I'll check. For the moment, we've arrested Gonzales and his gang, but he's got links to another safe house in Manchester, so we're keeping things quiet. You're not safe if you go wandering until we've got them all.' Her eyes pooled with sympathy. 'I'm here talking to you as a favour to Alex, because your husband's a good guy. He doesn't deserve to lose his job over your doings. And plenty have. Rumours can kill.' She returned the phone. 'You won't see me again. I'm going to be deployed elsewhere, but please believe me: Michel was involved with a Russian cell, and in the current geopolitical climate, your actions have consequences. Those people don't care if you're pregnant or if you have a babe in arms. They'll harm your child right in front of you to get your co-operation. Our enemies don't play by Geneva rules, so if you remember nothing else, remember the world is larger than your affair.'

Anna swallowed. 'I know that. I'm not the same Anna I was a few months ago.'

'Good.'

Kitty opened the door indicating the meeting was at an end. They began retracing their steps to the kitchen. Her high heels clattered along the wooden flooring. 'By the way, have you looked into your parents' history?'

Anna frowned. 'Why? Stephen told me Dad was a card-carrying member of the Communist Party.'

Kitty stopped. 'Do you have the rest of the Anna Karenina books?'

Anna blinked. 'Why?'

'So you do have them. I'll tell Alex.' She smiled. 'It might be unconnected, but I think you ought to see if you have anything else hanging around your house that belonged to them.' She went into the kitchen, extending a hand to Nina. 'Thank you for your hospitality. You have an interesting family history, Mrs F.,' she said. 'A Russian princess! We'll tease Alex about that one, won't we Jogi?' She twinkled at Farquhar, who had already put on his jacket.

'So where's your grandmother now?' he asked Nina.

'Buried in the Faver plot along with my parents, of course. Where we all end up.' Nina gathered the plates. 'Dust to dust. The land is the only thing worth saving.'

Anna had heard this sentiment expressed many times, and picked up her rucksack, feeling weary. 'I'd like to go home.'

'We thought you would, and my orders are to drop you off,' said Farquhar.

She put arms around her stomach. 'Can you give me a minute with Nina?'

As soon as they had shut the front door, she turned on her mother-in-law. 'Has Alex said anything about my brother? Does he know where he is?'

Unperturbed by the harshness in Anna's voice, Nina swept crumbs into her hand. 'Why should I know anything about your brother? His wife is –,' she paused, one finger rotating the debris in her palms, '– a perfect horror.'

Anna felt herself flush, and the baby kicked. 'Why must you always be so rude about my family?'

'Why must you always be so naive? You're a foolish girl, Anna, and Simon isn't safe with you. Now say goodbye to him and leave.'

Pressing her palms on the table, she leaned forward, the conversations of the past hour ringing in her ears. 'I know things about Alex you don't know,' she spat, before hitching the rucksack onto her shoulder. The comment made no dent in Nina's upright demeanour.

part three

search & find

'If I had a hundred lives, I'd love you in every one of them. And I'd search for you among millions. Just like now: I love you. I'm searching for you, and I'm waiting.'

Iryna's story as told by UNITED24.media
on Threads

'Well, I was hoping to go home,' Yurko muttered.

'Real friends don't abandon you in their hour of need,' Ryabtsev announced to nobody in particular.

'You're not my friend,' Yurko shot back.

Jimmy Hendrix Live in Lviv (Quercus 2023)
by Andrey Kurkov. Translated. R. Woolley

THIRTY-EIGHT
whitstable

MAY 2022

EASTER WAS A TORMENT. Trapped in her home, and lacking information about Sasha, Anna pretended to Simon that all was well. Her scant consolation was that her son appeared happy with his living arrangements, but for Anna, the annual pilgrimage of holidaymakers strolling past her back fence made her feel irrationally resentful. How could they ignore the world news?

Yellows and blues stroked the slopes; purple and pink weeds pushed upwards amongst cracked pots and benches. Her garden spiralled out of control. From her upstairs balcony, she saw cyclists and Park Run competitors pounding the concrete promenade against a glittering tidal flow, absorbing their cheerfulness for mockery. How could they smile knowing one and a half thousand miles away, people suffered?

Sometimes she returned to examine John Farquhar's oblique insinuations. What was behind the old school ties? It was true, she found Alex's offhand manner to their marital failings both a relief and a puzzle, having little stomach for a fight. But mostly, her thoughts focussed on Simon and the baby and Sasha and their future and how to draw these disparate elements together.

Social media circulated the shocking abuses perpetrated by Russian soldiers against Ukrainian civilians and prisoners. Each fresh story tortured all those with loved ones caught in their snare. Why could no one stop Russia, and why were Russian soldiers so keen to grab weapons and torture and kill?

In a weekly phone conversation with Betsy, Anna explained she was learning Ukrainian. Unable to share Kitty's information, she hoped to travel when the arrests were complete.

'Do a first aid course,' suggested Betsy. 'Then when someone near you is injured, you can be useful.'

Useful. That was a good word. Since Bogdan's tirade, she was determined to be useful. Hoping to practice her language skills, she sought to speak to Olena's friends when they came into the house. They clustered like starlings in black T-shirts, cross-legged on blankets in the garden, but as soon as she set foot outside, the teenagers veered to the side gate, leaving behind bottles and stub ends. Don't go, she wanted to say. She had so many questions about their homeland.

One Saturday afternoon, they congregated in her living room, and she fully expected them to vacate when she walked in, but they stayed.

'You have big screen,' said Olena. 'We want to watch Eurovision Song Contest. Ukraine has Kalush Band.'

There was an eruption of blue and yellow flags, and the three girls squashing together on the sofa insisted she join them. In embarrassment, she accepted the invitation, offering drinks and snacks before pressing herself into the suggested space. After a few moments, she began to feel a sense of camaraderie as they watched Mica introduce the event in English and Italian. Live from Turin, he said, and she thought gloomily of how she could not even travel to Italy under the current threat level dictated by Alex. But as each song was presented, her gloom lifted and she celebrated with the Ukrainian teenagers.

They provided a nonstop fragmented commentary combined with various gestures of thumbs up and down, bottles and cans rising and falling to their lips. She wondered why they had insisted she stay, but by late evening she had her answer. They were expecting her to vote on their behalf. In good humour, she placed ten votes for Ukraine, each one receiving a cheer in the room. And when the Kalush Orchestra won, the kids whooped and cried, and Anna wiped tears. What were they all hoping for? That a song could save their country? If so, she hoped with them.

In that brief moment, everything seemed possible, as they hugged and sang Stefania over and over. At midnight, the kids began to trickle out, and exhausted, Anna sank back on the sofa to find herself weeping, although she didn't know why. Olena crept into the room, and put an arm around her.

'I'm being silly, Olena. Ignore me. You've lost your father. You should be crying. But today I read about that woman, Margherita, who tried to leave Bucha with her three children, and she put a sign 'children' in the back of her car, but the Russian soldiers shot them and set them on fire. And now my baby grows, and I don't know where Sasha is.' She sobbed, not caring that her witness was a nineteen-year-old girl.

'Is hard,' said Olena, her voice unusually soft. 'Hard for all of us.'

'How do you bear it?'

'We sing as loudly as we can,' she said and began to sing the Ukrainian national anthem in a high sweet voice, and afterwards they sat together, huddled on the floor amongst the party debris. After a few moments of silence, Olena stood up. 'Tea?' she said. 'You see, I understand English now. Always tea make you better.'

With the window wide open, they listened to the soporific sounds of waves slinking up and down the empty beach, as they sipped tea, each with their own thoughts. Olena fell asleep, her head on Anna's thighs. Would the girl stay here long enough to teach her baby Ukrainian? But that would mean the war lasting for years and years, and where would Sasha be?

On 17 May, Zelenskyy told the Azov soldiers to surrender at Mariupol's steel works. It was clear the Russians were intending to starve them to death. Anna held her breath, searching photographs as each uniformed man was led into captivity. Those incarcerated were pallid and frail, their faces telling the fears of future tortures in Russian captivity. Anna wanted to reach into the ether and pull each one to safety. She rang Betsy, desperate to believe that Sasha had escaped such a fate. Betsy shared her fears but admitted she had heard nothing. According to cousins in Ukraine, they thought he was somewhere in that region, but it was too vast for accuracy.

Scrolling back to find the text from Dmytrov, she sent him a message. He replied to say he had no further news about Sasha, but confirmed he had a German visa and was in Berlin, where she was welcome to visit. He could only pray that by some miracle Sasha had escaped. In their short exchange, they avoided mention of the terrible accounts of POWs, castrated, branded, sliced and shocked with electrodes.

That was the torture for those who loved them and who were free: the knowledge and the narratives that smashed their lives. Even those who had escaped to nearby peaceful countries, knew no peace of mind as the war raged.

THIRTY-NINE

whitstable

MAY 2022

A VISIT to the midwife told her the baby was breech, its head knocking against her ribs. She received the news with acceptance. Her frustration at being grounded in Whitstable was melting as her body filled with hormones, and she sat on her balcony, staring at the sea, wondering about a land she could not see. Was her relationship with Sasha real or imagined? They had had a short yet intense time together. Had her marriage always been a sham? She and Alex had had a long time to remain strangers. It was the contradictions that puzzled her. She wanted to investigate her mother and father, and their secrets held in the Anna Karenina volumes, but the past was a confusion. Despite combing old letters and papers, and re-reading the scribbles in the two books, she felt none the wiser. Who were the people called Alexei, Lenin and Dolly scribbled into the margins? What had her parents been doing in Berlin?

Perhaps it did not matter, she thought. Ukraine was dropping from the headlines, seeping like rainwater into the gulleys of less important news, and she felt her momentum dripping away as her stomach enlarged. All she knew was she would never give up her search for Sasha, but it would have to wait until after the baby's birth.

In the afternoon, a car rolled onto her drive, and she looked out to see Dolly's Polo. Excited at the thought of seeing her, she stumbled to open the door, finding Stephen staring at her. The gauntness of his face shocked. 'What are you doing here?'

'Anna.' He held her hands, his eyes full of warmth. 'I'm here to see you.' He pulled her down the side of the house into the garden, and she covered her eyes against the sunlight to look up at him. He gave the impression of being taller and thinner, an alien silhouetted against the sky.

'Where have you been? Why didn't you ring and warn me you were coming?'

'Because I'm here to say goodbye, Anna.'

'Goodbye?'

He hugged her, a gesture that was out of kilter for both of them. Beneath his cotton shirt, she felt his ribs.

'What's been going on?'

Stubble skimmed his grey pallor. Yet another oddity; Stephen hated to be unshaven. Without answering her questions, he insisted they sit on the garden bench, refusing her offer of tea or coffee.

'My God. Look at you.' He showed no surprise upon learning the baby was Sasha's, and kissed her knuckles. 'I'll tell you what I can.' And he began to recount his hidden story.

. . .

On his way home several years ago before Covid, a man approached Stephen and claimed to have a message from his mother.

'Our mother?' she said, but Stephen insisted she listened without questions.

Rebutting the stranger with a curt explanation of his parents' death, he tried to walk on, but the man insisted he could prove his statement, asking Stephen to join him the following day for lunch at an exclusive Mayfair restaurant. To entice him further, the man offered five thousand pounds if he agreed. That month, Dolly had run up huge credit card debts refurbishing the house, and so he was tempted.

At the back of his mind, he wondered if it would all be a prank, but when he arrived at the restaurant, it was so high-end that he had to knock on an old oak door and have an identity check before they would admit him. While ordering the most expensive items on the menu, the sharp-suited man, whose name was Marsalek, expressed superficial opinions about geopolitics, all the while appearing to enjoy Stephen's discomfort. Towards the end of the meal, when both had drunk a considerable amount, he leaned across the table and said he understood why Stephen did not trust him, but as a sign of faith, he would double the five thousand to ten, provided he invest the money in a company called Wirecard. When Stephen went to refuse, the man insisted that his mother was the source of the deal, but she could not give him the cash directly.

If his mother was alive, Stephen pointed out, why

didn't she contact him? But according to Marsalek, it wasn't that simple. Interpol had an arrest warrant out for Annaliese, because she had worked as a double agent during the Cold War. To back this up, he presented convincing details about the Anna Karenina books.

Anna mewed in distress, and Stephen held her hand and continued.

The champagne blunted his thinking processes, he said, and he could not figure out how this stranger, a man younger than he, knew about the books hidden in his study. He had never told Dolly, nor breathed a word about the Russian man who had arrived at his parents' flat in the aftermath of their death in Berlin. But Marsalek insisted he was a friend acting as an intermediary, and once Stephen accepted the money and realised a good return, his mother would feel she could rely on his discretion and would contact him. It was that simple, he said. He finished their meal by saying he would wait forty-eight hours for Stephen to consider the offer, but after that the offer would be null and void, and he would deny ever having the conversation. Marsalek paid the sizeable bill and left, and although Stephen wondered if accepting the meal was akin to accepting a bribe, he could not figure out what was behind the offer.

It didn't take long for him to research Wirecard and note it was a German payments firm that facilitated credit card payments. The entire company was buoyant on the stock market and worth billions. Based in Berlin, it operated throughout Europe. Stephen reasoned that if he used the ten thousand pounds to buy stock and made a profit, he could pay back the initial sum, and be free of any further obligations. So he phoned Marsalek and accepted the offer. Having done as requested, Stephen pestered for a time frame, eager to question his mother as to why she had abandoned them.

Marsalek insisted he wait until the opportune moment to withdraw his investment. Within months, the amount had doubled, and Stephen itched to sell and pay off his credit card debt, but Marsalek kept delaying. During that time, Stephen invested more of his own money and suggested to certain colleagues that they should do the same, without mentioning his source. Everyone watched the stock market climb.

Then Covid hit, and Stephen contacted Marsalek again. Was now the time to realise his profit? Again, the man told him to wait, but some months later he phoned Stephen on a different phone, specifying a particular date to sell, reminding him that because of lockdown, they had to delay any meeting with his mother.

Stephen did as he was told, and rejoiced in a huge profit, larger than anything he'd anticipated. He didn't tell his colleagues because he didn't want them to realise he was acting on the advice of a third party, and so it was with horror, he saw the company go bankrupt a week later. Wirecard became the largest financial scandal of the century.

Panicked and desperate for information about his mother, Stephen phoned Marsalek to find both numbers disconnected. The man had disappeared, and an anonymous text told him Marsalek had gone to join his team in Moscow and was beyond reach.

. . .

'But you'd done nothing wrong,' said Anna, interrupting again, and again Stephen insisted on silence although his voice wavered as he struggled to finish.

He realised others would interpret his actions as either a bribe from a foreign agent or insider trading. Some of his friends had lost thousands, so he pretended he'd increased his mortgage to make up for his losses. With the little information he had, he debated searching for his mother, when another stranger approached him, who knew all about Marsalek and the Wirecard dealings.

This man refused to give a name, but he also insisted his mother was alive and went so far as to suggest she'd had his father killed. If Stephen wanted to see her, he said, he had to accept a promotion to a specific government office and wait for further contact. He claimed Annaliese Blount's life was in danger from the authorities, which was why subterfuge was necessary.

Aware he was compromised, Stephen accepted the promotion with a large salary increase. But the first request came within weeks of him bedding into the new office. He was to gain the computer password of a certain person at a nearby desk, after which, his mother would contact him.

Stephen fell silent and Anna saw a tear crawl down his cheek.

She squeezed his arm. 'You were being blackmailed. Why didn't you go to the police?'

Their eyes met, and she saw the depth of horror.

'But,' she insisted, 'Mum –'

'He showed me a photograph of her in New York, and

it's definitely her.' A faint smile came and went. 'You look just like her.'

'It's a fake,' Anna said with emphasis, as a rush of indignation swept through her. Behind them, a group of seagulls squawked as if to agree, and the wind rushed angrily across the beach. 'Alex would say you were too trusting.'

'I doubt it.' He put his head in his hands and she leaned towards him, rubbing his thin shoulder blades. 'Once you've crossed a line, you can never go back,' he said. 'I've been helping pass information to Russia for the past two years. Michel saw me speak to Gonzales at the Deli, and then came snooping. I warned my contacts he was working for French intelligence, but I couldn't stop him from using Dolly, and I think they killed him.' He took a deep, steadying breath. 'After Goodwood, I was arrested, and thought I would go to prison.'

'But you're here?'

He wiped his face with a moist hand. 'Some Russian agent organised my release on a prisoner exchange. Me for a minor American journalist. I don't know if I'm lucky or doomed, but I've got a one-way ticket to Moscow.' He spread his hands. 'I thought if you came to stay in the house, we might shake off Michel.'

'Does this involve Sasha, too?' She felt a lump in her throat.

He shook his head, 'Not that I'm aware,' and touched her sleeve. 'Say goodbye to Dolly for me. She'll take it better than you think. I never told you: we only got married to give you a stable home. We made an agreement to have an open marriage because we were so young, but it hasn't really worked out for either of us.' He put an arm around her shoulder.

'But your boys? What do we tell them?'

'That's up to you now, Anna.' His lips twisted. 'My best advice is to hide the books, and say nothing. Tell my kids I love them, although love won't clear this mess. Maybe love will clear yours.'

Snaking her arms around his waist, she pressed her girth to him. Like her mother and father, he would disappear from her life. Would the people she loved always disappear? Was this to be her fate – their trickling away like the tides? From the other side of her boundary fence, laughter and conversation floated from the pathway as families went to and from the beach and the shops. Normality was but a few strides away and months ago, she had felt part of that society.

Once you've crossed a line he had said, in an echo of all that Alex warned.

'Don't judge me too harshly, Anna.' He spoke in a low voice as they waited on the pavement for the booked airport car. 'Most believe society abides by the rules, and those that don't are criminals. But beneath our feet, there's a seam that no one sees of the rich and corrupt who walk about in the daylight, operating with their own agendas. Mum and Dad broke the rules and no one knew. And as for governments – we see their parallel universe in glimpses.' He scoffed. 'Even then, we tend to believe what we want.'

He gave her a last kiss, wishing her a safe life and she waved at the taxi, wondering if his wishes would be granted. After he had gone, alone in the house, she wept bitterly. If her own mother had failed to keep her children safe, then how was she to manage with hers?

FORTY

ukraine

WINTER 2022

A VISIT from the veterinarian told him the baby was breech. The winter calf was an anomaly, and the man had rolled up his sleeves to pull at the calf's legs. With a slippery skid, it came out and the veterinarian lay it in the amniotic sac on the barn floor for the mother's large tongue to set to work. The calf lowed and the onlookers thumped the man's back, while Vronsky watched with a paternal pride. He had never before witnessed birth. Only death. And he found himself changing from the KGB man into someone he could not recognise, as he brushed away the moistness in his eyes.

The staked and fertile vines grew for miles under ice blue skies and snowdrifts. Speckled spotted flycatcher birds congregating in groups under the barn eaves to keep warm. Fights and wars broke out here and there, but so far they were surviving, and the older he became the more he wondered what Annaliese would have made of this hybrid life.

After thirty years, he had never come to terms with her unexplained betrayal, but recently he had made himself a fresh promise. If the army invaded his land, he would set off on a trip to find her; he would not die without answers.

Unlike Stepanov.

Because unexpectedly, his friend and one-time superior officer died. As the younger man, Vronsky had not anticipated Stepanov's demise through cancer. It was as if the finger of fate laid on his shoulder. The last time they'd met, they'd done their usual reminiscing, while giving his classic, swimming-pool blue Trabant a spin around the block.

Both had mooted a possible future meeting in the Crimea and his friend had expressed pleasure at the continuation of Katerina in his household, repeating his usual themes about Russia being invincible in this new world. Stepanov had always liked the sound of his own voice.

At one point he'd mentioned Annaliese, and Vronsky had waited, experiencing, as ever, a stab of pain. But then Stepanov had pulled out a small object from his breast pocket, and handed over what looked like a coin with a whisper-thin metal tail.

'It's a new wire. Surveillance. Tiny, heh? What these young Russian inventors are doing. You hide it in your jacket, and it sends the audio to a computer. I'll show you the program, because it will make you marvel at the quality of the recording. It's a world away from the clumsy old packs we used to wear. If you ever wish to send out someone to look for that woman, this is the surveillance tool you need.'

'Do you torture them before or after you use the wire?' he recalled saying.

But now the man who had taken an interest in new technology was dead, replaced by his son, Grigory. The son had written to Vronsky from the main SVB office, eulogising the father's work, and mentioning the medal his father had received for uncovering the double agent, Oleg Gordievsky, code named Hetman. Gordievsky, he reminded Vronsky – who needed no reminder – had helped Margaret Thatcher to format a peace deal with Gorbachev, back in the eighties. When the traitor had escaped to Britain, his father's efforts had ensured a Russian prosecution and an order for the death penalty in absentia.

Vronsky read the note, remembering how the British Queen had given Gordievsky a medal in a fancy ceremony. Such were the bizarre scatterings from the end of the Cold War. It all seemed longer than thirty years ago. But Grigory wished to see Vronsky, and he could not refuse, even though the population around him waited and watched, antagonistic to Russian visitors. He wrote back to welcome the son as a token of his admiration for the father.

In March, Grigory arrived to hand over some bequests. The special military operation had given Grigory a promotion, and like his father, he had risen through the ranks by outing those disloyal to President Putin.

'Why are you still here?' asked the young man, who seemed older than his age. 'This country is full of Nazis.'

It was a miserable spring, and the fields remained cloaked in deep snow, punctuated by the sleeping vines. Smoke rose from the occasional dwelling, melting the icicles that adorned various barns and storage areas, where his workers packaged the orders, checked the wine vats and tended to the cattle.

'You should sell up and come back to civilisation,' said

Grigory. 'Take it easy, old man. The lifestyle of a peasant can't be easy.'

His face bore his father's good looks, but with greater arrogance. Vronsky spread his thick hands. It didn't matter whether or not he agreed with Grigory, it was a foregone conclusion that a true Russian always toed the party line.

'What can I do for you?' He inclined his head. 'As you say, I am an old man. For your father's memory. Cases of wine? How many?'

Grigory grinned. 'It is what I can do for you,' he said, 'also in memory of my father,' and he pulled out a large A4 envelope from his briefcase. 'These are up-to-date papers. If our soldiers come this way, use it as proof of your connections with the current Kremlin. My father would have wanted this. Consider it a thank you for the work you did for him. He trusted you.'

'*Opredelleno.*' Vronsky put on his spectacles and urged his guest to help himself to the food and drink on the table. He read the document with care, noting the embossed, authentic official stamp. His eyes flicked over the half-moon lenses. 'Very kind. Am I to presuppose that trouble is coming our way?'

'Take it as advance knowledge. The timing depends on how hard the Ukrainians fight. If they're sensible, we'll roll into Kyiv and all will be done with a minimum of fuss.'

What would his workers make of such an assertion, thought Vronsky, but said nothing.

'Zelenskyy's a third-rate comedian who's unlikely to cause trouble; we'll take him to Moscow for trial. As for the Ukrainians with their Nazi cafe culture, they'll fall into line. They always did.'

'And if they fight?'

Grigory shrugged. 'No match for us. The documents are

there for you to wave at the most senior man who drives through.' He ate a mouthful of prime pork with enjoyment, although, unlike his father, he drank sparingly. The fire in the grate burnt high with the sweet smell of apple logs, and from along the corridor, in the kitchen, Katerina prepared a good dinner, while playing something loud and modern on the radio.

'I must warn you.' Grigory smacked his lips. 'These new recruits can be unreliable. They're mostly convicts or the dross from Siberia, ill-educated and ill-trained, and they never get paid, because the higher brass steal their wages. So the kids wind up pilfering. Petrol. Food. Trinkets. And they only drink vodka, so they're permanently mashed, morning, noon and night. That's why they've no fear. They'll rape the women, kill the old men, shoot the dogs, torture the prisoners, and put the photos on their cell phones to send home to Mama. What it is to be young!' Grigory clearly did not regard himself in the same category, for he made a face of amused disdain.

'But they instil fear,' said Vronsky diplomatically.

'*Konechco*! And let's not forget, they die like flies without complaints from their mothers, because most of them were layabouts kicking their heels at home. Dead, they're heroes. So they have their uses. But my point is that many of them can't read well. Bear that in mind when you're showing documents. Find someone who's literate.'

Vronsky knotted hands above his ample stomach and deliberated. 'So you're saying I should leave?' He sucked his teeth. 'But the vineyard is very successful. Would my Kremlin customers be happy?'

'It's your choice, but I would say that the scheme has run its course. You're not the only one caught in the crosshairs. His excellency Vladimir Putin has set his heart on rebuilding the old empire, and you have to crack a few heads. You know how it is.'

Vronsky nodded. He had a decade on Putin, which meant the president was young enough to enjoy orchestrating a battle, and old enough to remember the glory days of the USSR. Vronsky merely felt old.

'You said you would show me the new apparatus?' He poured a grappa, a lethal distilled liquor that would loosen Grigory's shoulders.

Within half an hour, Grigory had outlined initiatives for cybercrime, such as the use of drones and military computers. As the alcohol ran through his veins, he relaxed and bled secrets, and Vronsky became a suitable depository, wearing the wire and knowing his computer programme was running in the next room. Information was power.

After a third grappa, Vronsky remained clearheaded, and listened intently to the names and places and prospective dates. This information was more valuable than cryptocurrency.

'I nearly forgot. Here's a letter.' Unused to the strong blend, Grigory's hands betrayed a lack of co-ordination when he handed over a battered cream envelope with the watermark of Basildon Bond.

Blyat.

'A bizarre story. The letter writer was in New York and sent to our Parisian embassy, through the diplomatic pouch. Who writes letters today?' he mused. 'Anyway, my father kept it; some woman asking for you, you old goat.' He smiled with alcohol-reddened eyes and touched his nose. 'I don't think the others need to know.' His lower lip jutted as he refused another glass. 'Are you trying to get me drunk?' he laughed. 'From the perspective of my generation, old man, you lost a glorious empire, but we intend to reclaim it.'

Vronsky did not need to read the letter to know the writer. His heart sped up and he knotted his hands more tightly to prevent himself from snatching. It would have to wait until his visitor left.

'I have one request of you, if you would be so kind.'

'Anything.' Grigory chortled and belched. 'Well, when I say anything –'

Levering to his feet, Vronsky padded to his desk in the corner of the room, pulling out pen and paper. 'Can you tell me if this person is dead or alive?' He handed over the details. 'It's not for me, you understand, but I might take your advice and go to Moscow, so I need to know.'

FORTY-ONE
whitstable

JUNE 2022

'MY *LITTLE RUSSIAN* *Warship go Fuck Yourself* T-shirt has arrived,' said Dolly, who had shown up a few days earlier, suitcase in hand. 'This is how I put the finger to my husband.' Her two-day weeping marathon had come to an end and she stood, waving the white short-sleeved T-shirt in the air like a banner. She blinked seeing Anna's reaction. 'Sorry. I know he's your brother.'

'He's also the father of your children.'

Although Anna understood the sentiment, she did not feel like participating. Outrage was everywhere on social media, yet achieved little. If Dolly wanted a T-shirt commemorating bravery, that was fine, but action was needed. Anna had viewed the videos circulating about the dangers of bombing nuclear sites, with scientists pointing to the unstable ownership of the Zaporizhzhia nuclear plant, and she found it hard to muster anything but compassion, especially when she saw Olena cry.

Words. Words. Words. That was all the media had to offer.

Since Stephen had gone, she had searched again for information about Sasha, ringing and emailing the usual agencies with no success. Online accounts told of the Russian soldiers who, under orders, had dug trenches in Chernobyl, only to find months on, they fell sick with radiation poisoning.

'If they don't even care about their own troops, the captured Azov soldiers haven't got a chance,' said Dolly to no one in particular.

After a week, Anna wanted to scream at her to shut up, grateful Olena was out of the house, because news about Russian brutality had the girl slamming doors as if to break the walls. It seemed wrong that the sun shone when Russia might blow the world to smithereens.

Please help, said Zelenskyy on video links to various governments. *We are grateful, but we need more. Please.*

Why was the world hesitating? Her head ached, especially when her sister-in-law complained about people dawdling on conveyancing cases. Where were her priorities? The agencies had frozen their joint marital account, forcing Dolly to keep working, but still she threw up hands every afternoon and opened a bottle of vodka. What use was that, thought Anna?

'Is Russian, you know,' said Olena making a rare appearance in the living room.

Dolly examined the half-empty bottle and with a dramatic flourish threw it into the bin. 'Okay.' She raised her glass to the girl. 'So tell me where I can buy Ukrainian vodka and I'll buy it.'

The girl wrote the name of a store in Canterbury. 'Go in and say is for Olena. He have plenty delivery from Lviv.'

'Is that the van of Vovo and Mykhel?' asked Anna.

'Hey! You know?' And for the second time since she had come to stay, Olena hugged Anna, attempting to encircle the extended bump.

With puffed feet and an aching back, Anna rose early each day. She was in the middle of ordering baby items online when the vultures appeared. The bell rang, and despite her exposed belly, she opened the door looking for a postman.

'How do you feel about your brother's arrest? Did you know he was a traitor?' Two men in casual jeans and plain T-shirts stood inches from the door, shielding their eyes from the low morning sun.

She blinked. Her fleeting talk with Stephen had been four weeks ago, but it felt like a year.

'You're Anna Blount, Stephen Blount's sister? Is his wife staying with you? C'mon tell us how long this has been happening.'

One thrust a mobile to her face, and she heard the click of a camera shot. There were more questions, and outstretched arms held phones. 'Have the police told you what the charges are? Why did he do it? C'mon, Anna. People have a right to know. It's a matter of national security.'

'How much money have the Russians paid you?' said another.

With both hands on the door, she pushed hard. The foot that had stepped over the threshold disappeared at the last second, and the slam reverberated through the house.

'Anna. Did you know about it? Did you play a part in trading secrets to Russia? Give us a comment from your perspective.' A mouth moved at the letterbox.

She retreated to the cool of the living room where the drawn curtains helped her heart rate to slacken. Dolly tumbled down the stairs, and they looked at each other in horror as the shouts continued. Olena popped her head out of her bedroom door and then retreated, swearing in Ukrainian.

'What the fuck?'

'Who did you tell, Dolly?'

'No one. Just you. Who did you tell?'

'No one.'

They sat in a huddle.

'How are we going to handle this?' said Anna.

'You shouldn't have to fucking handle anything in your condition.'

'Be honest. Do you know more than you told me?'

'No. I've told you every shitty thing they told me.'

A moment of silence as the questions continued through the letterbox.

'WikiLeaks!' Dolly snorted, then she looked at Anna with wide eyes. 'What if they're monitoring our computers?'

'Who's they?'

'You know. Men-in-black.'

Anna rubbed her belly. The child was fighting, thrusting tiny fists into her bladder. 'We can't hide in here forever.'

'They'll get bored.'

'Or send reinforcements.'

Upstairs, Anna's mobile began to trill.

'Don't,' said Dolly, but Anna was already lumbering upwards.

It was an unknown number and could be someone with news of Sasha, so she pressed.

'Hello. Mrs Faver, I'm ringing from The Mirror. We

believe Stephen Blount's wife is staying with you. If you'd grant us exclusive rights, we could make the next few weeks much easier for you both.' The female voice spoke at breakneck speed, fitting in the maximum number of syllables.

Anna's tongue glued to the roof of her mouth.

'Mrs Faver, are you there? Please let me help. It must be such a difficult time for you. We know your husband works in Whitehall and doesn't stay with you in the week.'

She cut the call and gulped in air as Dolly appeared at the door.

'Are you alright? Bloody Stephen. How could he do this to us?' Dolly wailed, pacing around the room and swearing.

Anna swallowed. She needed coffee. And carbohydrates. And sugar. She needed to raise her blood sugar in order to think straight, because she could see Dolly was crumbling, tears lining her face.

'God! Trial by fucking media. Is there any possibility that he's innocent?' Snot ran down Dolly's face. 'What if it's all a big mistake? Maybe we should ask them. Michel never spoke about Stephen.' Her chest heaved with a sob. 'I thought ...'

'Stop.' Anna held up her hands. 'Sasha faces bombs and landmines and maybe brutal torture in a prison. Every day.' She knotted her hands in a warlike prayer. 'I refuse to believe he's dead. So look at it this way: this is our war. If he can survive that, we can survive this. This is our war, and those journalists are our bombs.'

'But I didn't ask for this.'

'Neither did the Ukrainians.' She pulled out her maternity jeans and a loose top. The sun winked through the fluttering curtains as Anna urged Dolly to get dressed.

'No,' squealed Dolly. 'I can't go out there. We must stay in here.'

'No,' said Anna, brushing her tangled hair. 'It's not fair on Olena. She's dealing with enough, so let's draw their fire. When you're under attack, you don't sit in a hole. That way leads to the siege of the Azov steelworks. We are going out to fight.'

'You've never fought for anything in your life!'

Anna bent with difficulty to find her shoes. 'Stephen caused Michel's death and, by association, Sasha's problems. But I have nothing to be ashamed of.'

Dolly's head sank into her folded arms. 'Oh God. Oh God. He used my phone to lure Michel into the underpass. Alex –'

'Bugger Alex.' She wielded the hairbrush like a sword. 'Bugger them all. Are you coming?'

'Why? What will we say? They won't stop until we say something.'

'No comment, no comment.' She slammed the hairbrush onto her dresser. 'No comment. And if they get in my way, I'll shove them. They wouldn't dare hit a pregnant woman on camera.'

In a white fury, Anna dragged Dolly through the crush of phone lights and heavy cameras held aloft by determined hacks with sweaty armpits. In her head, she and Dolly were carving through a line of tanks, fighting on an ethical battlefield, refusing to give way. Her child needed answers, not accusations. Whatever her brother had done, he'd been trapped, but she knew they wouldn't see it that way. Marching to the high street, she entered the Grain and Hearth bread shop with the procession behind her. Customers sipped tea in bemusement, croissants flaking onto their plates, while Dolly hid behind sunglasses, hunching her shoulders. With the bread in her bag, Anna led the procession out again and further along to the grocers. Without a word to those pestering at her side, she kept walking, buying goods, and moving on, until only a straggle remained, and even they realised there would be no soundbites for entertainment.

Over the next two days, the morning assaults continued. Olena evacuated to the Stanley's, and Anna waited for news about spies in the civil service to fade from the world's attention. She felt a bleak gratitude to Boris Johnson for causing the lockdown scandals, which provided meatier pickings than Stephen's defection to Moscow. In tiny back page articles, smaller paragraphs persisted. *It was alleged* that someone provided important information about the movement of munitions in the lead-up to Russia's invasion of Ukraine, and the word *alleged* resurfaced in multiple forms: *allégué*; *presunto*; *angeblich.*

The principal casualty of the morality war was Dolly's conveyancing business. When she'd tied up the last few house moves, she found her inbox empty, leaving her to curse and drink with self-pity. Anna handed her a paint-brush, insisting she help paint the smallest room pink for a nursery. Afraid to turn on the radio, they worked in the silence, save for the boom of the Shoeburyness military testing site. Somewhere far away, wars coated the planet with smoke, cruelty and destruction, but tucked in her womb, the baby grew. *I am coming. I am new life and hope. Will the world love me or hate me? Will the world let me live or destroy me?*

'I will love you,' she said to the unborn child. A fierce-ness she had not possessed before took hold of her. 'Your mother will always love and protect you. And I will do whatever is necessary to see your big brother, Simon, safe and happy.' Unlike her own mother, she thought.

And she would always love Sasha. It was not a dream or a mistake or a misconception; she would wade into the worst storm to help him, if only she knew where he was.

Unexpectedly, a letter arrived with a Polish stamp.

My dearest Anna, do not forget me, I love you. I belong to you and you belong to me. My only wish to see you again. Someone here says he will get this to you.

With love forever. Sasha xx

Scrawled on soiled paper, the anonymous sender had kept his promise, but the uneven handwriting whispered suffering and she pressed the note to her face. Soon the baby would be born, and she could go to Ukraine to demand his release, and to hell with Alex.

On Sundays, Nina and Simon arrived. Nina cooked while mother and son sat to play games in hearty pretence: Monopoly, Cluedo, Risk. Outside, a car parked with a solitary driver scanned the road, but inside, her son spoke with enthusiasm for all he had done in the week, while Anna forced herself to listen and offer love. Once they had gone, in the bleakness of the night, she felt breathless with anxiety, propping herself against pillows, unable to sleep, fighting a sense of doom. How to provide for both children? Wiggling swollen feet, her head filled with a jumble of thoughts: her affair with Sasha, her brother's crimes; her mother's mysterious life; her father's death; her son clambering around on his grandmother's estate. How could she fit the pieces of the puzzle together to make one solid, coherent life.

. . .

On waking, she heard news that Putin was comparing himself to Peter the Great, and she opened her laptop to find an email from a journalist requesting her participation in an article about *the enemy within.* Oh God, she thought, struggling to sit up. After a local search, she booked herself onto a four-week first aid course, starting the next day, hearing once more the ringing accusations of Bogdan that she was useless.

With waddling steps, she trundled to the local church hall where the instructor looked at her with a facetious smirk. 'Planning a home birth?' she said.

FORTY-TWO

whitstable

JUNE 2022

EACH MORNING, the seagulls painted the windows in streaks of yellow and white shit, and with sudden energy Anna slapped soap and water on the panes, dribbling the spray down her arms and across her belly. A Saab blocked her driveway, and Alex stepped out, which did not surprise her. Nothing surprised her in this final month of her pregnancy.

He had lost weight, and his grey hair was set with youthful blond highlights, but his eyes bore tired stress lines. The breeze caught at the collar of his half-buttoned shirt, and he pushed wrinkled, loose sleeves from his wrists.

'Is the baby still breech?' he asked, moving awkwardly into the hallway. 'Nina told me.'

'Of course she did.' Anna greeted him with caution.

'It's not a social visit. It's about Stephen.'

'Dolly,' she called up the stairs.

'Not Dolly. The books he gave you.'

There was a groan and muttering as Dolly descended, hair tangled around her face. 'For God's sake, Alex. This is fucking early. Have you finally come to give me Stephen's address?'

'Dolly,' Alex checked a bookcase in the living room, 'it's out of my hands.'

'You bastard.'

'Official Secrets Act.' His fingers walked along a line of novels on a middle shelf.

'Stop this.' Anna planted her girth at his side. 'I won't give you the books, no matter how much you beg. They were my fathers, so they're mine.' She couldn't give away her bargaining power. After the birth, she would use them to barter for Sasha's life.

Sidestepping her, Alex lifted the magazines on the coffee table and let them fall. 'They're important.'

'And they're important to me.' She felt the baby shift.

Irritation crossed his face. 'If you want to know more about your Oleksandr Vronskiy, then give me the books. We have a possible deal developing.'

'I'm not playing that game,' she spat. 'That's what trapped Stephen.'

'We can't trust you,' said Dolly, fumbling in her bag for a vape.

With a sigh, Alex sank onto the sofa. 'A member of the Russian delegation killed Michel at Goodwood, and that man is currently in Moscow. We've no hope of getting him into court, but you want to blame me, Dolly? Go ahead. I think you'll find Michel betrayed your husband. So how will you tell that to your sons?'

With a shriek, Dolly stood over him, quivering like a madwoman. Then she whirled around, slapped her hand on the wall and ran upstairs. 'You bastard!' she shouted before slamming her bedroom door.

'You didn't have to tell her that.' Anna could feel her own anger surging.

'You criticise me for withholding the truth and you criticise me for giving information. Make your mind up.'

With a deep breath, she put a hand under her belly and went into the kitchen to switch on the kettle. Tea, as Olena had discovered, tea was the only antidote to violence.

Alex followed, leaning in the doorway, hands in pockets. 'How are the scam messages? Recently the Russians have sent gloating photographs of corpses to relatives. It gives both evidence of their death and their torture, but some pictures are so gory, we can't identify the victims. There's one with Vronskiy's name on it, although we can't be sure. There are other Vronskiys so we'd need DNA.'

'You want DNA from my baby?' Anna steadied herself, gripping the counter's edge.

'Not yet, but we believe some of the people named in the Anna Karenina volumes are alive and working in advisory roles in our government, undermining our attempts to help Ukraine.'

'The books are old.' She pulled her face from the kettle's steam.

'If someone was thirty in 1990, they'd only be in their sixties.'

She shook her head, determined to play devil's advocate, even as a hopeful plan surged inside her. 'Photographs can lie and so can old scribbles.' She pulled out teabags. 'I've received another letter.'

'We know. Jogi intercepted it. It's not that recent.'

'Pah,' she spat, pulling mugs from the cupboard. 'I don't trust him either.'

Alex sat, while she made the drinks. ‘Do you know about me and Jogi?’ he ventured.

‘He’s your flatmate. Yeah.’

‘I thought he might have said –’

As she heard the words, a fresh piece of the puzzle slotted into her brain and she stirred the milk into the drink. ‘Oh my God. You bastard! I’ve only just –’

He took the drink, beginning a methodical search of her cookery books on a shelf. She sat at the kitchen table, forcing herself to breathe. The Braxton Hicks contractions were a welcome pain to all her preconceptions about her married life. Tiptoeing around her, he opened drawers. Rubber bands, screw drivers, knives, forks, glasses, plates, vinegar, oil, salt, dishwasher tablets.

‘You’re gay.’ She simmered with rage. ‘Why marry me? I can’t believe I didn’t –’

There was a fraction of a pause before he continued the search, sliding open the drawer of pans and saucepans, inspecting each one before placing it on the tiled floor.

‘No,’ she shouted and felt her stomach muscles tighten protectively around the baby as he reached down to the base and lifted a tea towel to reveal the two books.

Lurching forwards, her fists beat on his back. ‘You can’t have them.’

In surprise, he half turned, hunching his shoulders.

‘They’re mine.’ She kicked at his ankles and snatched one of the books from his hand, holding it to her swollen breasts. ‘They were my father’s and you’re not stealing them. Our entire marriage was a lie.’ The baby kicked out against the emotional storm, punching into Anna’s lungs, the skull against her ribs.

‘Be reasonable, Anna. This is my job and they’re just old

books to you. You're being difficult.' He adopted a paternal tone. 'Don't be naive.'

That word again. How she hated them all with their secretive smiles and knowing glances. Jogi with his wrist flicks, Alex with his golden highlights, Kitty with her smugness. They excluded her from essential information and then laughed at her behind her back. But she wasn't the nineteen-year-old Anna they'd duped all those years ago.

'Your behaviour makes you look complicit,' he said.

'Complicit?' Anna flapped the book at him. 'This makes me complicit?'

Alex rose to snatch the volume, and without thinking, Anna grabbed a knife from the countertop, hurling it at his face. Surprise delayed his reactions, and the blade hit the side of his eye, ripping through the eyebrow to slice a flap of skin. Blood gushed and he cried out.

'Christ, Anna. You're absolutely crazy.' He backed away, cupping his hand to the wound.

'You've done nothing but lie to me,' she raged. 'Our whole marriage was a lie, and how dare you try to tell me Sasha is dead. It's not true! I know it's not true.' She rushed at him, but he sidestepped, blood spurting across his cheek.

'I want a divorce from you and your fucking Faver family.' She sobbed, shoving his shoulder. Dolly tumbled into the doorway as Alex pulled a handkerchief from his trouser pocket to stem the bleeding.

'You'll get your divorce,' he said, 'but I'll get custody of Simon.'

Chest heaving, Anna emitted a wolf howl of fury, raising her fists. But before Dolly could reach her, a seismic shift in her belly forced her to double over, and a hot puddle hit the tiles, soaking her thighs and ankles. She sank to her knees.

'Calm down, you've wet yourself!' Dolly attempted to place arms around Anna's shoulders.

'My waters have broken, you stupid woman,' said Anna, shrugging her away. 'Fuck off!'

With the handkerchief clamped to his face, Alex pulled out his phone. 'If that baby is breech, we need to get her to hospital.'

'I'll decide whether to go to the hospital or not. If you treat me like a child, I'll fucking rip your tongue out.' Anna tried and failed to get off the floor.

Unfazed by the wound or the barrage, Alex barked instructions to the emergency services. Again, Dolly urged Anna to remain calm as Alex swore and slammed the mobile on the kitchen table.

'There's no ambulance available. They suggested it would be quicker to take you directly to the maternity hospital.' The blood continued to trickle down his face.

Dolly moaned. 'Look at her swollen ankles. What do they mean there's no ambulance?'

'Apparently, birth isn't imminent when the waters break.' He pressed the handkerchief to his wound. 'Where's her things? I'll drive you both to maternity. I probably need medical help even if you don't.'

'Containment situation, is it?' Anna spat. She could feel her body tensing with another contraction. 'I don't want you anywhere near me or this baby.'

'I'll drive,' soothed Dolly.

'You were drinking last night,' retorted Alex. 'And you stink of alcohol.'

'Fuck off, Alex.'

Olena poked her head into the kitchen, took one look at Alex's blood and the two women crouching, and retreated without a word.

As the contraction hit, Anna doubled over holding her belly, biting back a scream. 'I want Sasha.' Two more contractions came in swift succession, and the others scurried to collect things. In no position to refuse, Anna was manhandled into the back of Alex's car, while Dolly sat in the front, blotting the blood trickling down his face. He manoeuvred through the narrow Whitstable streets, racing from the Harbour to Thanet Way and shooting towards the maternity unit at Ashford Hospital.

Another contraction hit and she buried her face in her arms. She lifted her head, fingers scrambling across her distended stomach. 'The baby's not moving. What's wrong? I can't let this baby die. Please God, don't let this baby die.'

No one spoke, and no one bothered about the speed limit.

FORTY-THREE

ukraine

MAY 2022

THE DULL THUD in the distance reminded everyone of the approach of the full-scale military invasion. It annoyed Vronsky that they didn't call it a war. He'd lived through a cold war and knew a hot war when it came. But across the farm, the steady roar of machinery continued as Yakov and his staff struggled to keep the business going. Diesel was in short supply, and his manager approached him with a sideways look. Despite having worked the land for nearly twenty years, Yakov avoided eye contact with his employer. What should they do if the tanks broke the vines? Or salted the land with mines? Would Vronsky guarantee their safety, or would there be another Bucha?

The sprawling village of vines and animals and humans did not equate to the middle-class dormitory town of Kyiv, but it was in a direct pathway. Vronsky scratched his chin. The workforce needed him to make his position clear.

Are you Russian or Ukrainian?

He knew what they thought. Once a KGB, always a KGB. At the start of glasnost, he had sold himself as a wealthy Russian with Ukrainian ancestry, and because the land was so impoverished, they had accepted his money, willing to communicate with him in Russian. But increasingly, they spoke Ukrainian in front of him – almost as a jibe.

His manager wiped sweating palms down the sides of his jeans and asked for an update.

'Will the Russians arrive on our land soon?'

Tales of rape and carnage in Bucha had scared them, and since the Ukrainian army's retreat from Mariupol, they followed the daily terror of those trapped in the Azov steel-works with increasing anger. Anecdotes abounded of snatched Ukrainian children, shipped a thousand miles into Russia, their mothers' frenzied weeping echoing through the nightly social media.

'Are our families safe?' Yakov demanded.

'When I know something, I promise to tell you,' he said, aware of the insufficiency of his words. Cursing his need for a walking stick, he stumped inside. Although a product of the Soviet era, he felt their pain, because he had cherished this land as his only child. And then there had been a letter and that chilling phone call abroad. Not a reunion, but a request for retribution, placing metaphysical chains around his neck, threatening to drag him to hell. How could he undo the past? Putin eulogised the past. But Vronsky found himself unable to go that route. For the first time in his life he felt regret, and it made him bad tempered.

Without asking for his permission, Katerina gathered a committee in the house. Vronsky had not told Grigory that the woman supplied by his father had refused to have him in her bed for the past five years. In some ways, he was grateful to her. His hip bothered him and as each ache and pain took hold of his body, dreams of Annaliese had intensified. He could almost smell her perfume.

In front of the twenty people crushed into the room, Katerina prodded him. 'We can't wait here to be slaughtered. We must prepare.'

'Perhaps they will leave us alone if I speak to them,' said Vronsky, sitting heavily on his sofa, clutching the brass top of his cane.

'You're an old man.' One young labourer pointed out the obvious.

'From what I hear, Russia only wants to retake the territory from the Sea of Azov to the mouth of the Danube.' Vronsky regarded the man with disdain. 'We'll be safe.'

'Retake? It's ours.'

There followed an angry outburst; a fire of furious words.

'Mariupol, Melitopol. My cousins are there.'

'As far as Zaporizhzhia? My sister lives there.'

'Mykolaiv? Kherson? My grandfathers are buried there. Died from the famine.'

'Odesa is our port. My wife's family fishes there.'

'This is our land.' The cry ripped around the room as fear and anger for their friends and families struck like a hammer. Outside, the farm dogs began to yowl, sensing the alarm.

'What do you want from me?' said Vronsky. 'Maybe Katerina and I will leave and go to the Crimea. There I can plead for our safety.'

'What's the guarantee you will return? Perhaps you will leave us to suffer?'

And there it was. The historic mistrust; the remembrance of past sins; the Holodomor; the violence and censorship of the Secret Police, and all the deeds that summed his existence. He had interrogated in Berlin, assassinated in France, stabbed in Italy, shot double agents in Poland, grabbed people off the streets in Ukraine and Latvia. These were his sins in the name of the Soviet Republic. And afterwards he had changed careers to launder money for the minor oligarchs. What could he say to the crowd in front of him?

Dissent and confusion melted their questions into hot debates as they argued among themselves about the best way forward. Were they safer with him or without him? Should they stay or travel to another oblast? He listened to the timbre of their voices, recognising old systems flaring to the fore.

As they argued and ate and drank, Katerina moved around the room, filling up glasses, offering more food, joining each small conversation. Feeling superfluous, he sat on the leather sofa, where the richest backsides had once sat to discuss economic negotiations. The sky darkened and a stiff wind blew across the land, and still they came to no conclusions. Katerina nudged him, perching at his side.

'I'm not leaving with you,' she said. 'I know you intend to take me with you, but I'm staying.'

'Is this to do with your man in Moscow? Because he's dead. I got Grigory to check. Your husband died in prison. In fact, he had a son by another woman, who was also in prison, but Prigozhin co-opted him into the army. And he's dead too.' He took her hand. 'So it's safe to return.'

Her round jaw set tight. 'I will stay here. I am getting married.' Her nose flared with pride.

He withheld a laugh. 'And who are you marrying? Who will take you?'

It was then he saw the naked flash of dislike, the black

flint in the eyes, a flexing of her neck in wrath, and he leaned away.

'Someone like me? I'm going to marry Yakov. You didn't know?'

'My manager?' He could not hide his disbelief. 'He's offered? You're sure?'

'As if you care.' She spat a shiny gob into her hand and smeared it on his knee. 'And you don't care about Yakov either. To you he's just a *huis'gory*.'

He gripped his walking stick, anger flaring. It was true, behind his manager's back, he had sometimes called the man 'a dick from the mountains', but he thought she agreed with him. After all, his manager was a provincial Ukrainian.

'I've been good to you,' he grunted. 'I've been good to him as well.'

'You're good to your dogs. And the farmhands. But we all know you're only interested in yourself. You remember Dostoevsky's story of the old woman and the onion?'

'What onion?' *Blyat.* It was the wrong time for Katerina to become mulish and recount old Russian fables. 'What nonsense is this?'

'There was a man –'

'You said a woman –'

'– who did nothing bad, but neither did he do good. So they sent him to hell. But, undecided, heaven lowered him an onion on a string. Take it and we'll pull you up, the angels said. But when he gripped it, all the hell folk ran to grab it too, and he shouted at them, saying it's my onion, not yours. And at that, the string broke, and he stayed in hell forever. Which is where you belong.'

He puffed his cheeks. 'I saved you. Have you forgotten? I've saved all these people from poverty. Don't forget I created this vineyard from dust.'

'No. You stole the land. Your money bought the plants, the machinery, fertiliser and expertise, but the local men dug the land. It's their hard physical work that turned a profit for you with minimal returns. They planted the vines. They knew how to use the machines and how to tend the fruit and turn it to wine, and you took the money. You –' she spat again. 'You are the onion grabber. That's why they neither like you nor trust you.'

Unable to swallow his anger, he clenched one hand. He had often hit women, but not recently. 'Absurd. I've taken these *zasranets*, these little shits, and made something of them.'

Privately he thought onion grabber was a better term than assassin, but she was unaware of his previous life.

'Don't you think they deserve your respect?' Colour rose in her round face. 'Remember Yakov's wife died five years ago?'

A vague recollection of his manager taking some time off work filtered through his brain. He shrugged. 'So?' It wasn't his job to provide succour to the masses. A part of him wondered how he had ever slept with this solid woman, with her greying hair and heavy sun-stained cheeks. 'I'm sure I allowed him to bury her.'

'But no sympathies.'

'People die all the time.' And some under interrogation, he thought.

'Is that the best you can say? That's what the police said to me when they investigated my Ukrainian mother's death at my Russian father's hand.'

He thumped the carpet with the walking stick. 'You're a fool, Katerina. Ukraine won't survive a Russian onslaught. Nothing stops the Russian army. If you don't side with me, prepare to be crushed. The bear will always win.'

'This is your truth, not mine.' Her lips drew into a shark's smile. 'You have no love for anyone here, but don't worry, they don't love you either. Yakov and I will marry, and if we die, we die together in a free country. Because of what my husband did to me, I can never have children, but every child here is under my care. And in return for my years of service to you, I expect you to leave us with the means to protect ourselves, or I will find you in the night and put a knife into your fat, black heart.'

'You'll have to be quick to kill me. I used to be –' The walking stick clattered at his feet. What had he done to deserve this? Betrayal after betrayal. He had spent a month reading and re-reading the letter that Grigory had pressed into his hand. He had fought the pain of that final phone call. And now this. To find Katerina so disloyal. The weight of the chains intensified, and an abyss opened before him.

He could hear the men arguing in the room, and knew if any of them died, the community would wail and scream. But not for him. If he caught a bullet, there would be no wake. If he was lucky, the dogs might whine a fugue. Sweat formed on his wrinkled skin.

'Marry the bastard,' he growled. 'Take charge of the land, for all the good it will do you.'

'Do not underestimate us, you old fool. Love of our country and each other gives us the strength for your so-called *military operation*.'

She swept her skirt to one side as she stood, moving from him with a curl of her lips. His heart hammered. He had never loved her, but unlike Annaliese, he had never doubted her. In an effort to gain control of his limbs, he conjured that last night with Annaliese in a Berlin bed, when he had been fit and strong. Stretching his aching joints, he grabbed the stick from the floor, and levered himself to stand as tall as he could.

'I have come to a decision,' he rumbled.

Doubt hung in the air like the odour of sour wine. 'You want to protect yourselves from the Russian army?' He outlined the actions needed to save the vineyard from land-mines, explaining where to hide additional produce from the locust troops, and where to send their children to keep them safe. 'They want the cities, the energy sites, and to gain control of the Azov Sea and shipping to Europe. In that respect, you are safer than most.'

'And you?' Yakov insisted. 'Where will you be?'

Vronsky smiled, although he suspected it looked more like a grimace. 'Gone. You don't want me? Take charge and see how far you survive.'

A few mutters rolled around the room about the words of a Russian being worthless, before they spilled into the damp darkness.

Alone, he nursed his grievances, finishing his most expensive bottle of wine. *Blyat.* He was a man in his eighties about to lose the second love of his life: the vineyard. But he had his new task, and although there was no one left to enforce it, he had to complete this last mission. It was all that was left of his withered soul. He phoned an old contact in Berlin to enquire about his safety deposit box, finding confirmation that the books remained hidden. Now all he had to do was determine the best escape routes. Should he go to the Crimea and ask for safe passage? Or drive to the nearest border and take his chances with the missiles?

FORTY-FOUR

maternity hospital, kent

JUNE 2022

IN A PARALLEL UNIVERSE, a baby with no name arrived into a country without bombings. A thin, agitated wail cut through the mist, and drowsily, Anna felt a flood of love and relief: the child lived; after all the months of waiting, she was here and alive. But Sasha's absence cut into her heart and she wanted to cry.

'Considering she's three weeks early, she's a perfect little girl,' reassured the nurse. 'But we have to take her while we stitch you up.' Another nurse took the white blanketed bundle to the far side of the room.

'God knows how you had a normal birth,' said Dolly. Her hair stood on end and she pulled at her sleeve seeking invisible beads. 'She was breech and the cord was round her neck. You must have a guardian angel.'

The doctor stitched with surgical thread and Anna closed her eyes. 'I dreamt of my mother last night,' she said. 'She was me and I was her in some mirror existence. She was telling me things about the baby, but I can't remember.

Perhaps she's my guardian angel?' People fussed around her, moving equipment, clearing and chatting.

'Whatever.' Dolly yawned. 'At least the little one is safe.'

'I won't let anyone take my baby from me, but they can have the books. Priorities.'

'A book?' said the nurse, turning quizzically. 'That's a first. Maybe you can read later after we've monitored you and you're on the ward. We thought we were going to lose you when your blood pressure dipped. A midwife should have flagged you as high risk, but you don't seem to have seen one recently.'

'We were besieged,' said Dolly as she went to examine the child's weight. 'She's got black hair, just like you.'

By the time a porter had wheeled Anna to her room, a different nurse arrived, adjusting charts and pillows, handing over remote controls for the television, checking the plastic wristbands on mother and baby. 'Your husband sorted a private room for you. Such a pity he tripped on the way in. He's having a few stitches in A&E.'

'Alex the saint!' Dolly hooted. 'But Christ, Anna, his wound was deep. I thought you were doing First Aid, but it looks like you were taking lessons in knife throwing. I reckon he lost more blood from his face than you've lost from the womb.'

'I'm sorry,' Anna murmured as the nurse handed her the baby to feed.

She slept and woke to find herself alone, the baby sleeping in the cot beside her. Someone had put the television on low, leaving daytime television faces to beam. Next to her, she saw a glass of water and a jug, but was unable to prop herself upright to take a drink. Her brain struggled to attach to her body, and she tried to reach the call button, aware of snatches of conversation coming from the corridor. A news flash interrupted the programme, switching to a journalist in Ukraine.

'There's nothing visually distressing about this footage, but I must warn you, it's terribly sad,' said the correspondent, standing in front of a bombed hospital with an exposed, crumbling staircase. 'A direct hit on this maternity hospital caused many fatalities. One mother had just given birth when the shell exploded and the baby died.' On screen, people scurried and shouted.

It was beyond sad, Anna thought. It was unthinkable that anyone would harm small children, or that anyone wanted to murder or injure or harm another. Why had she thrown a knife at Alex? Because of her father's books? They were paper and calfskin and ink, but the sleeping baby was the only important thing in the world. The baby and Sasha, she thought, as tears brimmed.

'Baby blues? We don't want that,' said a familiar voice. Nina stood in the doorway with Simon.

With a shy smile, he kissed his mother on the cheek and stared at the bundle in the cot. Anna tried to lean over, but her muscles failed, and she asked Nina to pick up the baby and let Simon hold his sister. Switching off the television, her mother-in-law's expression softened as she guided Simon to sit down, instructing him how to cradle the child's head. He hunched, shoulders high, while the baby mewled, then settled.

'What's her name?'

Anna wiped her tears. 'I wanted her father to decide.'

'Daddy will be here soon.'

There was a pause.

'Alex and I have discussed things,' said Nina. 'You must

stay in the Whitstable house, while Simon remains in Canterbury. We'll visit.'

'Or you could stay with us at the Faver Estate, Mummy.' The baby curled a tiny hand around his finger. 'Isn't she lovely? Granny says I'm going to run the vineyard one day. So don't forget, baby girl, I'll be in charge.' He dipped his head to check if the baby was listening. 'I've learnt about cultivation and plants and lots of things. Can she sleep in my bedroom, Granny, when she visits?'

Anna smiled with a rush of guilt and love. How to sort the future? She wanted a life with Sasha and the baby, but she wanted her son as well. She wanted to live in Ukraine, but also to live somewhere without fear of bombs and drones; somewhere in a house far away from arrogant men plotting war. Perhaps they had already decided Sasha's fate, and more tears threatened at the thought.

'By the way, those volumes of Anna Karenina,' said Nina, sensing a maternal deluge, 'for goodness' sake, they're not worth fighting over. Old Russian classics, scribbled and annotated. Alex took them.'

Simon looked from one adult to the other. 'Is the baby going to be called Anna Karen?'

'No.' Both women spoke in unison, and then they laughed.

'Will you love her more than me?' Her son quavered.

'No. I love you both equally. Just like you love Granny and me equally.'

Nina raised an eyebrow as a nurse entered to check Anna's blood pressure. Scooping the baby from Simon, Nina gave it a swift hug before returning her to the cot. 'Why don't you go find Daddy? I'm sure the doctors have finished with him, and he could do with a hug. If you text him, you'll find him in the cafe on the ground floor.'

'Isn't he coming to see the baby?'

To cover the awkwardness, Nina opened her purse, pressing a five-pound note into Simon's hands and suggesting he buy some chocolate.

The nurse laughed. 'Did I hear chocolate? I'm about to go off shift; shall I take this young man to his father?'

As they left, Nina closed the door and tapped one shoe on the clean linoleum. 'Alex didn't deserve to be stabbed.' She gazed out of the window. 'And there are things you ought to know.'

Anna sighed. Nina's lectures were unstoppable.

'My husband was the youngest son of a respectable family. He'd had a good education but little money, and we both accepted it wasn't love. There may have been the Ban the Bomb and Burn your Bra brigade in the sixties, but my father was traditional, and I was determined to learn from my grandmother's behaviour. She lived with a complaint on her lips, whereas my father and mother wanted to be happy, and for me, happiness was looking after the estate lands. So I compromised.' Nina paused.

'You've told me this.'

'But I've never mentioned my husband was a man who had little interest in women.'

There was another pause while Anna thought about Jogi.

'We had one son, and I knew we wouldn't have more. But Alex was a delightful child, so I was happy. However, as he grew up, it became clear he wasn't interested in taking on the Faver legacy. I understand you regard those books as your father's legacy, so I feel a sense of sympathy. You want to keep possession of the Anna Karenina volumes, just as I didn't want to be parted from the estate and the vineyard.' She sighed. 'Anyway, Alex wound up working in Westminster, as did many of the old

Harrovians, and I pestered him to marry because I couldn't bear the idea of the land being sold off in parcels for some pepperbox housing estate. I wanted my legacy to go further.'

'And he did what you asked.'

Nina smiled sadly. 'I had wished he would find a woman who was interested in the vineyard. But you were little more than a child yourself, and it was soon apparent you held even less interest in the estate and farmland than he did. However, you gave birth to Simon, and it is my greatest joy that he wants to take over the legacy.'

Anna struggled to sit upright. 'You've brainwashed him.' She looked towards the cot, wanting to gather her child to her and blot out Nina's rigid form.

Nina put gentle hands to Anna's back, helping her to sit upright. Then she retreated. 'I know that's what you think, but he is genuinely interested in growing things. He loves gardening and everything to do with the land. Is that so difficult to believe?' She studied Anna's face. 'Happiness is where you find it, Anna. Love the land, my father said, and it will bring you joy. And for me and Simon, he was right.'

Anna wondered if Alex had spoken to his mother about his personal life, and as if reading her mind, Nina continued.

'You told me there were things that I didn't know about Alex. I accept that. There are things about my husband, that Alex doesn't know. He was a homosexual and I was rather good at turning a blind eye, because he was a kind man, and we both deserved some happiness. I tended the vineyard and our farm, and he stayed in London whenever he wanted.' She hesitated. 'He died of Aids.'

Anna twisted in shock. 'Alex never said.'

'Because I didn't tell him. Perhaps he knows now, but

we've never discussed it. We say his father died of leukaemia.'

The two women stared at each other.

Nina's face was drawn in pain. 'Of course, I mourned my husband, but the lesson I learnt is that what you cannot change, you must accept, and there's always a way around a problem if you're flexible.'

'You're saying, if my baby's father is dead ...'

'I'm saying, search for the truth. But be prepared to accept what you find. Alex has told me how war zones distort information. Be diligent, but don't become an Anna Karenina and throw yourself under a train.'

'You've read it?'

'With a grandmother like mine? Of course. And *War and Peace*.'

'Sasha wasn't spying for Russia. I'm positive he went back to Mariupol for his father. I've received two letters that seem to confirm that, so I have to try to find him.'

'Then do that safely – for your children's sake. I understand Ukraine's fight for its land and its culture. There is nothing worse than being unable to visit your homeland. My grandmother's sorrow was she could never return to the place where she was born.'

'But will Alex let me leave England?'

'He has told me that they've finalised all the arrests now, and the men protecting the Faver Estate have been reassigned elsewhere.' Nina smoothed back her hair and walked to the door, looking down the corridor. 'Ultimately, the earth will reclaim its abundance once humanity ends. Odd that we fight for glory, but in the end, we all push up worms. *Ozymandias*.' She waved to the arriving party. 'I promise to give you my support in every way I can, but please don't take Simon from me. If Sasha and this baby is your future, my grandson is mine.'

Bouncing with enthusiasm, the boy ran into the room and pushed his face to the sleeping baby's. 'Daddy! Mum might call her Karen!'

They both gave an awkward laugh, and Alex pretended to choke, placing a hand to the butterfly stitches on his brow. Then he smiled and commented on the baby's abundant black hair swirling around the crown.

Tentatively, he kissed Anna's cheek. 'I'm glad you're out of danger and the baby's safe.'

'You can have the books,' she murmured, sensing a return of tears. 'I'm sorry about...'

'We have to examine them, but we'll return them,' said Alex, putting an arm around Simon. 'Mother has given me a lecture on legacy.' With practised ease, he scooped the baby from the cot and handed her to Anna. Bending to her ear, he murmured, 'There is news coming through. Give me a few weeks and I think we'll finally get a fix on Sasha's position.'

'Will it be good news?' she said, holding in the threatened tears.

'It will be accurate news,' he said. 'That's the best I can do. I know you will be strong for your children.' He fingered his wound. 'I'm not as worried about you as I used to be.'

FORTY-FIVE

mariupol, ukraine

MAY 2022

MAXIM KONSTANTINOVICH POPOV drove south on the parallel road to the coast, sniffing the influx of acrid gunpowder. The distant thuds of approaching warfare reverberated along the ground. Mariupol was in the early stages of a likely Russian victory and therefore a seething pot of gun-happy troops. His aim was to circumvent both soldiers and roadblocks and take the lesser-known pathways to reach Melitopol. From there, he hoped to connect with his contact, who had promised him safe passage out of Ukraine. Too old to fight, he considered himself too young to die, but having spent days prevaricating about what to bring, and the most suitable route, he'd set off later than intended.

At first he wanted to head north towards the Dnipro, but didn't fancy his chances in Donetsk, let alone Luhansk. You couldn't trust the entrenched Chechens in those districts. Then he'd thought about the Crimea, but in a phone call, they said they'd rather meet him in Melitopol.

Next, he had dithered about which car to use for this leg of his journey. Age came with indecision. His beloved

Trabant, now a valuable classic, remained in the garage at home. For decades, he had kept the auto in perfect condition, but this was war – far more vicious than 'a special military operation'. And he knew no one would look favourably on an old man traipsing about in a boxy swimming-pool-blue East German car, even if it was ostensibly valuable. He'd discarded the idea of taking the Tesla because power plants had come under heavy fire, forcing some areas to manage without running water or fuel. He had even gone so far as to investigate the trains to Moldova or Romania, eventually discounting that route because he'd heard uncomfortable tales about the locust-thieves. Besides, how many suitcases could an old man carry?

In the end, after a vicious argument with the locals, his temper cracked, and he tossed a few things into the back of his Range Rover. To hell with them all. He hated the thought of his latest gleaming black purchase sustaining damage, but 635 horsepower would weather potholes and, if his contact failed to arrive, it could deliver him all the way to Berlin. Paperwork in his breast pocket, he placed a loaded gun in the glove compartment and a semi-automatic under the passenger seat, with two grenades in a holdall. If he sustained a hit, he'd blow himself to Valhalla, which wasn't a bad way to go. But he did have one last mission to complete, so he hoped it wouldn't come to that.

Attempting to circumvent the front line, he noted vehicles shooting in the opposite direction. One jeep, window down, veered towards him, the driver shouting in Ukrainian. 'Turn around, you idiot.'

He ignored the man. Since he was Russian, he wasn't afraid of meeting Russian authorities, but he was a little wary of meeting bombs. The sky rent with a crack and he saw the plumes of smoke gathering ominously in front of him. On the other side of the road, an old Volkswagen lay, nose into a ditch, with a young man waving, blood tracking down his face and arms. Reluctantly, Maxim stopped.

'Please help. Papi needs medical attention.' The man was somewhere in his twenties, grubby but determined. He motioned to a grey-haired man splayed across the rear seat.

'Wait.' Maxim sighed, easing out of his car to fetch the first aid kit.

With a pronounced creak, the back door of the Volkswagen opened, and two legs poked out. 'I'm okay,' the passenger wheezed. 'But I need my medicine.'

'Hello. I'm Maxim. I'm a gardener, not a medic, but I have a first aid kit.'

'He's not okay.' The young man buzzed with nerves, running hands through his dirty blond hair. 'They bombed the hospital. You'll give us a lift?'

'Where? Into Mariupol? I'm hoping to drive in a loop around the city.'

'It was chaos, but we'll to go back to the hospital. We need to find the medicine in amongst the rubble'

The young man introduced his father as Borys Vronskiy and jerked a thumb toward the smoke. 'Unless there's another medical centre?'

The name, Vronsky, spooked Maxim, but he concentrated on assessing the man's condition. Borys' hands bore none of the raised veins of the very elderly, but his pallor and purple lips showed the hallmarks of cardiac illness.

Maxim handed over the Range Rover medical kit. 'There's one fifty kilometres from this front, but I'm not making a detour.'

'Then help us return to Mariupol,' insisted the son.

'I've told my boy, don't go back. It's like Donetsk all over again. I told him: go west, not south.'

The son opened the Red Cross case. 'But he needs medical attention now.' He swore. 'There's nothing in here but bandages.'

'Come on,' said Maxim. 'You car's going nowhere. Get your father into my car. Wipe the blood off you while you're at it. I don't want my leather seats stained.'

The young man used his T-shirt to wipe his face and wrist and bent down to put an arm around his father.

'What about if I can take you to Melitopol?'

'We understand it's fallen. It's under Russian command.' He looked sideways at Maxim with obvious mistrust.

'Well, if it's under Russian control, then maybe the hospital is working. Anyway, what's your alternative?'

A thunderous blast shook the clouds as more smoke spread from east to west along the horizon. The line of vehicles speeding in the opposite direction increased.

'Find me a car I can borrow, and I'll drive us to the nearest hospital even if that's Mariupol.'

Maxim tutted. Privately, he thought Borys was nearer a grave than a hospital. 'They'll shoot you.'

The old man wheezed. 'You're Russian?'

'Russian speaking. You know how it is.'

'Yes. I left Donetsk in 2014. I know how it is.' The father gazed at his son with a mixture of pity and love. 'Leave me, Sasha, I beg you. Let this man take me to a hospital – anywhere. Melitopol is fine. It doesn't matter. You must get to safety and return to your English woman. She's expecting your child, so save yourself.'

'I won't leave you until you've got help, even if I have to fight the whole damn lot of Russian scum on my own.' His eyes flickered towards Maxim. 'Once you have your medication –'

‘No.’

‘*Blyat.* It’s dangerous to hang around,’ said Maxim. ‘Look, I’ll take you to the nearest dwelling where we see a vehicle but then I’m off to Melitopol.’

The son nodded his thanks, easing his father into the front of the Range Rover. ‘I’m sure there will be an abandoned car I can use.’

‘Get in behind your father,’ said Maxim. ‘Move the suitcases.’

‘We’re very grateful.’ The man wheezed.

Maxim sighed. He didn’t want gratitude; he wanted to keep going and avoid the carnage which was bound to spread. ‘So who’s this English woman?’ he said, hoping to keep everyone calm.

The father gasped for breath. ‘His Anna. Very beautiful. Show your photos, Sasha.’

First Vronsky, then Anna. Maxim fumbled as he started the engine, his heart racing.

The young man balked, but Borys insisted. ‘This helpful person needs to understand you have an English girlfriend from a rich family, and they might pay for your safety.’ The father moistened his purple lips, taking two photos from his son and holding them for Maxim to see.

Despite his impatience, Maxim could not resist slowing down to examine them. Two people were in a selfie, which had been transferred from phone onto glossy paper. The young man looked at a woman who returned his gaze. From the bare shoulders in the shot, Maxim recognised they were in bed. The second showed the same woman on her own, a sheet drawn over her breasts, and a gold chain dangling a crescent moon into her cleavage. His mouth went dry. With one shaking hand, he pushed the photographs away and set his eyes on the road.

'She is the love of my life,' the son mumbled. 'Our first child this summer.'

Maxim made a curt comment about the woman's beauty, steadying his fingers on the steering wheel as he put his foot down hard on the accelerator. The car surged. Those lips. Those eyes. The crescent moon. It wasn't possible.

Several more explosions reverberated and more plumes spread along the horizon. The sun disappeared, leaving the grey sky punctuated by orange and red fires. No one was behind them heading for the city, but coming towards them, several cars were attempting to outrun the destruction, engines labouring under loaded suitcases. *Blyat.* He needed to find a side road, and turn off this highway. It was becoming too dangerous.

Another explosion rocked the entire area, and Borys groaned, clutching his chest and arm. To his right, Maxim saw an object arcing across the sky and hurtling towards them. Instinctively, he snaked the Range Rover in evasive manoeuvres, yanking it left, then right, then left, just as a hunk of metal dug into the asphalt a hundred metres before them. He jammed on the brakes, throwing everyone tight against their seatbelts, and the Range Rover stopped within spitting distance of the smoking debris.

'*Blyat,*' said Maxim. 'That was close. You alright?'

The father's cheeks had gone from the high red of a diseased heart to the grey of death, but he nodded.

His son jumped out. 'Fuck. It's part of a jet, and it's blocking the whole road.' Dense shrubbery burnt fiercely on both sides, and a second gigantic explosion threw fireballs across the fields, making escape impossible. 'We have to clear the road to get to the hospital.'

The debris's innards smoked, dust swirled in a frenzy of

heat, and an evil-smelling liquid oozed. They coughed, raising their hands to their mouths.

'We can't do anything until it cools,' said Maxim. 'I'll have to turn around.'

'No. My father needs his medication.'

Maxim felt no compunction to obey, seeing as the way forward was hellward bound. His whole life had demanded pragmatic action, and the flurry of cars speeding towards them confirmed his opinion. It was crazy to keep to his original plan, but perhaps his black beast could plough through the charred and churned fields to escape.

The smoking wreck forced the oncoming vehicles into a disorderly queue. Anxious drivers leapt out, and a van at the rear careened across the carriageway, overtaking the line to nose closer to the obstruction. The driver jumped out and shouted. 'I've got a winch with a metal tow rope on the back. Help me attach it, and we can pull this thing clear.'

Wild-eyed, half a dozen men scrambled to assist, their arms pulsing with frenzied energy. The heat seared their attempts while on the wrong side of the road, Borys' son flailed, jumping on the balls of his feet in frustration.

Maxim watched with a critical eye. On its own, a solitary van possessed neither the weight nor the horsepower to move a hunk of jet, and being on the opposite side, the Range Rover could not assist. The situation for escaping Ukrainians was hopeless.

The grey man placed a chilly hand on Maxim's arm. 'Promise me, please.' White spittle formed at the corners of his lips. 'Promise me you'll help my boy. I know you are Russian. I see this expensive car. Your army killed all my sons except for Sasha. He is all I have left. Spare him. From the bottom of my heart, spare him for the sake of my grandchild. I beg you.'

'I'm not Russian,' said Maxim with an irritated grunt.

The breath gargled in Borys' throat. 'You go to Melitopol. It's under Russian command. You –'

'Shut up. This black beast of a car is built for off road.'

'I'm dying. You know this. He is a sweet boy. He is an innocent who loves this English Anna. They are both innocents – peacetime babies. They understand nothing of old grudges or the old ways. She grows my grandchild whom I will never see, but my boy deserves a chance.'

'Calm down.' Like a tumour, a knot formed in Maxim's stomach. If only he hadn't seen the photograph. If only he hadn't had that long phone call, forcing the chains of his past sins around his soul. He was old but the fear of death grabbed him by the throat.

They listened to the groans of those attempting to shift the heavy debris.

Droplets of sweat formed on the man's brow as he struggled to produce words. 'His Anna. She has a brother. Stephen. He works for Russia. For you. He will give a big reward for his sister's happiness. Plenty of money. Please get my boy to safety. Grant a dying man's wish.'

Irritation and regret coursed through Maxim's veins. Couldn't they see, at best he was an onion grabber, and at worst, an assassin? There was no point in appealing to his sense of compassion; he had none. Yet he was afraid. Was that how his victims had felt in their last moments of life? She'd talked to him about his profession. *His Anna.* And fool that he was, he'd accepted her last assignment, a form of atonement. But he had not expected to fulfil it. You could promise anything to someone who was dying – you didn't have to deliver.

The image of the black-haired woman with the golden sickle moon between her breasts burnt his retinas, as sour vomit came into his mouth. He swallowed.

In the distance, the familiar shapes of Russian army jeeps popped up on the horizon. If he squinted, he could see the Z. In front of him, the men clustered around the broken debris, shouting in desperation, but they were too late. The whole damn lot of them were too late to escape. Even Maxim was in danger from an aerial attack. How many were heading towards them? Two armoured jeeps? Three? Four? A hundred? Would the Russian soldiers be rounding people up, asking questions, and taking prisoners? Or would they shoot them on sight? Hard to tell. They might make everyone dig their own graves and then shoot them. More efficient. If so, then he would have a chance.

'Okay. I promise. I will get your son back to his Anna in England. Now calm down.' He kneaded the tension in his neck wondering if either of them were unlikely to see the end of the day.

The old man closed his eyes. 'Borys Vronskiy thanks you, Maxim. With all my heart. Get my son back to his Anna.' His lips fluttered as if he were sucking on an oxygen cylinder, and then he exhaled for a long, long breath, and his head slumped forward.

'*Blyat.*' said Maxim. Why were his hands shaking like a child's? With the number of people he'd killed and tortured, his reaction was absurd. Stop it, he told himself. Now was the time for cool, rational thought.

And a gun.

FORTY-SIX

whitstable

SUMMER 2022

DMYTROV CONTACTED her from Berlin where he was living with his wife and daughter, and she cried. Betsy sent a card and gift, and she cried. The Stanleys and Olena gave her a large bouquet, and she cried. Overwhelmed by hormones and tears, Anna felt grateful for Dolly's help, that allowed her the luxury of crying at every act of kindness. For a month, Anna mended, sobbing, and holding the baby with Sasha in her thoughts.

She mourned that the baby's father would never know the smell of his newborn child, or see her slate grey eyes, or the milk freckles along her nose, or the ragged fingernails. It was a time they could not recreate, a time that war had snatched from them, as it had done from so many mothers in other countries throughout the ages. She thought back to the early months of Simon's life, realising the insubstantial nature of her former self's insecurities and fears. This birth was different. Minor inconveniences held no fear. Beyond the baby's needs, her sole priority was to find Sasha.

The timbre of the house altered. Dolly declared her disinterest in all men, helping with chores. Even though she swore, vaped, and drank, she washed and cleaned, disappearing at odd moments, when Anna would find her gazing out to sea, lost in thought.

'I loved Stephen,' she said, as if to convince herself. 'And I think he loved me, but we were young and messed it up.'

Olena remained in the house, but spent most of her time at college or with her twin siblings. When she popped in to fetch things, she cooed over Anna's baby, taking a turn in holding the child and speaking endearments in Ukrainian.

Even Anna's divorce had gone through the courts smoothly, with Alex expediting paperwork, and sorting a passport for Anna and the baby in her maiden name.

Peace, she thought. That was what everyone wanted, and yet, despite Alex's reassurances that the threat level was lowered, she could not shake the sensation of someone watching the house. Would this be her personal Cold War? Was this to do with Stephen? She avoided mention to Dolly, because since his flight to Moscow, they'd heard nothing. But each morning when she pulled back the curtain, she noted the same black car parked near her gate, and a man sitting at the wheel, nose in his phone. The nearby Whitstable Castle had its own visitors' car park, so he did not appear to be driving tourists to and from the local venue. All she could do was remain vigilant, securing the house every night.

When Alex arrived unexpectedly, Anna gave a swift glance down the road, disappointed that the car had gone. She had taken no photographs, so didn't want to feed a paranoid vision to her ex-husband. They were in a phase of being ultra-considerate with one another, and she invited him in for coffee with a smile. Complimenting him on his new jeans and a Tommy Hilfiger T-shirt under his casual blazer, she told him the black briefcase in his right hand spoilt the affectation of cool. He laughed.

'So?' she said. 'You have news about Stephen or Sasha?' There seemed no other reason for him to be in Whitstable holding a prop fit for the Chancellor of the Exchequer.

Following her into the kitchen, he smiled wistfully at the sailboats clustering beyond the harbour. 'Just following up on things.' The baby slept in her pram by the back door, and he put a finger on the child's cheek. 'How is she? Has she got a name yet?'

'She's Baby until Sasha or one of his family members in Ukraine names her.' Placing mugs of tea and biscuits on the pine table, they seated themselves on opposite sides and she looked at his familiar face. Once she had thought she loved him. Now she knew she cared for him, but they had married before she'd understood the fullness of love, and only a desire for friendship remained.

Alex dunked a biscuit. 'According to records we've unearthed, Sasha had a Ukrainian passport, confiscated by the Russians in the Donbas about eight years ago, which is why he only had Russian identity papers.'

'That's old news. It's what I told you months ago.' She sipped, watching the sunshine highlight his furrowed brow.

Alex rumbled an apology. 'Data checking takes time. French intelligence recruited Michel. He applied to the Russians on the Telegram channel under orders from the French. The French have confirmed this.'

Dolly slid into the room, a pale apparition of her vibrant former self. 'Hi Alex.'

Alex beckoned her to join them at the table, and Anna

poured more tea. She wondered if she was turning into Nina.

'Russian money motivates most of their overseas agents, but Michel was acting for ideological reasons.' He dolloped milk into his cup. 'CCTV traced him as the person setting fire to some cars targeted against left-wing organisations. Obviously he was following orders from Gonzales at the Deli. But his final act of vandalism was against a Russian oligarch in the capital. He threw a firebomb into the cellar of one of their houses. It was his act of switching sides after he'd found his target and contacted British intelligence.'

Dolly swore. 'He found Stephen. And I led him right there.'

For a brief moment, Alex put a hand over hers. 'I understand this is hard to hear. No one wants to believe their loved ones are caught up in the underbelly of espionage.'

Retracting her fingers, Dolly stirred sugar in her tea. 'I would have sworn he wasn't capable of deceit.'

'Debt makes people easy to exploit. The Anna Karenina book mentioned the name of a young agent known as Oblonsky, but we couldn't find out who it was until we had the whole set. Since the fall of the Berlin Wall, this man has become influential in the civil service and it was he who organised Stephen's placement. We formally charged him last week, although you won't hear about it in the news for a while. We're still in the process of disentangling his network. What Stephen did was to hand passwords and memory sticks to Gonzales, who fed the information to a man in Moscow called Stepanov. So Stephen never saw the full chain.'

Anna wondered whether to say anything about Wirecard, but kept silent. Every door opened a trapdoor and she refused to follow Stephen into the tunnels.

'Oddly, Stephen kept a covert log of his actions on a tiny memory stick secreted in the spine of the Anna Karenina Volume III.'

'That was the one Michel took.' Dolly closed her eyes in pain.

Alex nodded.

'How did Michel know what it contained?' asked Dolly.

'He didn't.' Alex sipped, and gave a weary smile. 'He had seen Stephen in the Deli's backrooms, and when he went through the study, he was intelligent enough to spot the tiny device and realise its potential, which is why he asked to borrow the volume.'

Dolly swore, and pulled out her vape. 'But he didn't realise the danger he was in. He wasn't a master spy, just a kid out for revenge.' She fingered the vape and swallowed while Anna blew her nose.

'And you're saying the books prove my parents were spies working against the government?' added Anna.

A musty smell of leather eased across the table as Alex opened the briefcase and withdrew an Anna Karenina Volume from his briefcase, placing it on the table. 'I'm sorry, Anna. They were technically traitors to the British realm. Couriers,' he said. 'Like the people heading the Deli, they didn't obtain the information; they took classified information to East Berlin, using false papers to cross the border, arranged by their contact.'

Anna bit her lip. 'Olena translated some of the messages and they involved Sybille and Vronsky.'

'Sybille was a famous cafe in East Germany, and Vronsky was a code name. We know who he was.'

She felt the prickle of tears and he handed her one of his

white handkerchiefs. She gave a strangled laugh, checking for non-existent blood.

'There's a file at HQ – heavily redacted – detailing their roles. I've only located it recently. They were rumbled by British intelligence eight months before the fall of the Berlin Wall, but it was all hushed up when they were declared dead.'

'But why did they do it?' Anna tried to imagine her mother and father in such a role.

'They considered communism preferable to capitalism, and they weren't alone. Many in society thought like that at that time. And far as we knew, they died within eighteen months of the Soviet regime collapsing. Thought to be suicide.'

Dolly's eyes narrowed. 'Stephen told me his father had Alzheimer's and I met him once. That's not something you fake.' She clicked and clicked on the vape.

Anna hissed in exasperation. 'But someone persuaded Stephen to spy for Russia on the basis my mother was alive. At least, that's what he told me.'

'He said the same thing to us when they arrested him,' said Alex. 'We're investigating.'

'And Sasha?'

A flush spread across Alex's face. 'The dead man on the Russian list is a different Vronskiy. I can confirm Sasha is a Russian prisoner.'

All thoughts of her parents fled her mind. 'Is Sasha still alive?' She leaned across the table wanting to yank the information out of him.

'It's more complicated than that. We've had a couple of people defect from the Russian side, and they are helping us negotiate prisoner exchanges. Until that is completed, we won't know for sure.'

She crumpled, unable to stifle a groan. Pulling the crescent moon pendant from under her T-shirt, she rubbed the golden talisman. 'Will Sasha be on the list? How do you begin to choose one person over another?'

His brow's furrow deepened as he sought to explain the impossible. 'Leverage or sickness. You need a reason for putting someone on the list. Health, family, aligned interests.'

'What greater leverage than a baby?' said Dolly.

'Most of the soldiers have family, but I think you have more leverage than you know in terms of your family. Sorry. I can't expand on that till the negotiations are completed.'

'Alex!' Anna snapped, and then apologised. 'Don't do this to me again. Don't keep me in the dark.'

'Too right,' chimed Dolly. 'We're in this mud right up to our eyeballs!'

'I've told you both more than I should have,' said Alex. 'Keep in mind, you are one of thousands of people searching for their loved ones. Some families had their children snatched when they agreed to let Russians bus their kids to safety. Then they found them taken hundreds of miles across the border and brainwashed.'

He drained his mug of tea, and Anna tried to calm herself, looking out to sea. It was a timeless scene, she thought. The bushes swayed in the wind and clouds raced across a horizon dotted with wind turbines. But the landscape no longer held peace for her. She was desperate for accurate information about Sasha.

'I can't bear not knowing.'

Dolly fled to the kitchen door and stepped out into the cold air, vape in hand. 'And I can't find the words to tell the boys and they're beginning to demand answers.'

Anna watched her shut the kitchen door, enveloping herself in the vape's gaseous cloud.

'You said leverage. Do you know where all the volumes are?'

He nodded. 'The remaining five volumes are the goldmine.'

She stroked the book on the table. 'Good. I want to feel appalled that my parents were traitors, but I can only focus on one thing at a time. I must find Sasha for the sake of the baby. You were there for Simon, even though you're ...' She stopped, and their eyes met.

'Even though I'm gay?'

He had finally said it, and she smiled.

'I wish you'd been honest with me at the start.'

'If I had, we wouldn't have made Simon.'

'And you wouldn't have needed a vasectomy.'

'I tried to be a good husband and father.' Alex twisted one hand around the briefcase. 'Jogi and I were at Harrow together. It was easy to slip back into a relationship with him when he joined my department.'

'Did you ever love me?' She gave a light jab to his chest.

'I still love you, Anna. You've grown up, but I remember you as a lost teenager.'

'I was not lost,' she scoffed. 'My parents died when I was young, and I was immature. But you were nearly forty. Old enough to lead an honest life.'

The baby woke and squealed, and she gathered her into her arms, thrusting her nose in the child's warm, damp neck. Alex stroked the black whorl of hair.

'I'm sorry,' he said. 'It's not enough, but –'

'Tell Nina. She'll be more sympathetic than you think. All your mother ever wanted was an heir to take over her legacy, and we've given her that.'

He rubbed the blue streaks under his eyes. 'I'll try, but after my father's death, I didn't think –'

But Anna didn't want to go down the Faver family history path. She was ready to move forwards. 'If you don't give me concrete news in the next month, I'm going to Berlin to meet his best friend, Dmytrov. He'll help me knock on embassy doors and also contact some of his cousins. We must find him.'

She expected him to argue, but he agreed, claiming her new passport offered her a measure of anonymity from his department.

He gave a wry smile. 'I'll see if I can get the file on your parents de-classified, so you can find out more.'

The lump in her throat prevented her from answering.

'You're still determined to go to Ukraine?'

His anxious face made her smile. 'Ukraine is Sasha's country. This baby is half Ukrainian and I have to go there at some point. It's a big country, full of brave people. There seems no end in sight to this war, but I know some areas are safer than others, so I'll be sensible.'

'Our brave Anna,' he said and she placed a kiss on his cheek, feeling released from the Faver family boundaries.

'Anyway, even if I look like my mother, I'm not my mother. I'm not into politics,' said Anna, 'but if anyone threatens my baby, I will shoot them.'

Alex clutched the briefcase. 'You've bought a gun?'

FORTY-SEVEN

berlin

AUTUMN 2022

DMYTROV WAS A STOCKY MAN; a swimmer's physique, she thought, made stouter by his puffed jacket. He waved to her as she crossed the customs hall at Berlin Brandenburg Airport and they greeted one another with the awkwardness of those who have only met virtually. He had no car but insisted on paying for an Uber to take them to his cousin's flat in the Tempelhof District. His luck, he said, was that his wife's cousin, Diana, had married a Berlin man twenty years ago, and although widowed, she continued to live in their three-bedroomed apartment. Now, she offered a welcome refuge for Dmytrov, his wife and daughter. Anna and the baby were also welcome to stay, he said, it was the least they could do for Sasha.

They had all known Sasha since childhood, and Anna felt a flicker of irrational envy for their history: she wanted to belong to his community. Her sense of being the outsider abated when they clustered around to coo at the baby's dark eyes and chubby legs, eager to attribute a nose, a dimple, a smile to someone in the Vronskiy family.

'She has Sasha's smile,' Diana said in English, touching the downy face. Diana was fluent in five languages, and Dmytrov and his wife were improving their German and English, which had helped them find work in one of the many continental cafes peppered throughout the city. Having an affinity for languages, Anna admired their linguistic abilities and hoped one day her child might follow suit.

In a polyglot mixture, they swapped stories. Dmytrov's extended family had been the Vronskiy's neighbours in Donetsk until 2014, when many had relocated. When the Russians bombed Mariupol this year, Dmytro's wife and daughter had been out of the area, visiting a friend on the western side. Hearing the news, Diana offered them immediate refuge, and they obtained a visa to travel to Berlin. But under martial law, Dmytrov had no choice but to stay. He used his car to help evacuate people caught up in the bombing, bumping into Sasha who was doing the same. He spoke of the death of his many friends, some with hands tied with plastic cable ties, some who had experienced torture before they died. He struggled to keep his voice even, describing the scenes in a whisper as his face reddened. His wife put an arm around him. They had lost childhood friends, she said with sorrow and anger, and even those with whom they had petty arguments were now regarded as friends in heaven.

Two months of rescuing the living and burying the dead had frayed his nerves. He remembered Sasha coming to see him, explaining he had to get his sick father to a hospital in a safer district. Under the broken roof of Sasha's house, they drank the remains of their vodka, while Dmytrov confided his intention to sail to a neighbouring country. It was then that he and Sasha swopped letters to be posted to loved ones if they made it abroad. Dmytrov's wife never received a letter, which did not bode well for Sasha's survival.

When Dmytrov's car had sustained damage, he had opted to walk to the coast, dodging soldiers and bombs, arriving at a harbour to find no available boats. The army was closing in, so in desperation, he swam to Moldova's border, fighting the cold, black waters.

'I got your text,' said Anna. 'It's incredible you survived.'

'He thought he would die of hypothermia,' said Diana, and everyone in the room pressed their hands together, speaking in several languages at once.

He described stuffing his documents and phone into a waterproof ziplock bag, and strapping it around his neck.

'A miracle they didn't deteriorate,' said Anna, and with heartfelt thanks, she explained how receiving Sasha's letter gave her the hope she needed, because her husband, Alex Faver, had insisted he was a Russian agent. There was a roar of laughter. The man they knew would never help the Russians, they said, and Dmytrov's eyes clouded with memories.

'When we were boys, Sasha was the brave one. He went to army for two years, but I am afraid to fight.'

'We're all terrified. We've all read about the war crimes in Bucha and felt the fear. The Russian army is barbaric.' She clasped his hands.

For the rest of the night, they drank, ate and took it in turns to cajole the baby, everyone declaring their support for her search for Sasha. After compiling a list of places for her to contact, they left her to sleep on a makeshift bed on the floor, and she fell into a dreamless sleep, with the child's sweet breath beside her, feeling a sense of love and community.

In the morning, she put the little one in a sling and trod the Berlin streets with Dmytrov acting as her guide, visiting various charities and charitable foundations for information. Some receptionists gave her a friendly welcome, and paid a compliment to the baby, but with a terrible monotony, they looked at their lists and shook their heads. There were so many people searching for loved ones, they said, as they took her details and offered to contact her if they received anything. War wrecked buildings and displaced families, and in the resultant chaos, hard facts were like diamonds in a mine.

Once or twice, a pinched-faced refugee would follow them out of a building, offering the services of people who would search for Sasha if she had the money to pay, but Dmytrov counselled against it, saying he doubted anyone asking for payment in advance was genuine. After her experience with fake texts, she didn't argue.

When they had gone to every place on their list, they made a final stop for Anna to feed the baby. It had been a dispiriting day, but Dmytrov suggested they return via Tiergarten, where he showed her the refugee tents of Afghan and Syrian refugees.

'Diana says they clear them all away. Too many. But I don't know where they go.'

And you are the next wave of refugees, thought Anna.

'The British complain about the boat people, who come from Calais tents, crossing the Channel on dinghies, but they don't know about these tents in Berlin. Sometimes I think the whole world is on the move because of war.'

They walked on through a district where gleaming Audis and Mercedes sat in front of modernised office blocks and restaurants.

'And here's where the rich live,' he said.

She nodded. 'There's always a rich district to taunt the poor.'

But he didn't understand the word 'taunt', and she encouraged him to talk about his future. He held the dream of all those displaced: if he could not return home, then he wanted freedom, a place of peace, somewhere to call home, good employment, a school where his daughter could play in safety. Why, he wondered, did the Russians never want peace?

At one side of the cafe, a man in a black suit sat, scrolling on his phone, and a sense of disquiet sneaked into her. She clutched the baby in the sling. Was this the same man as the one in the car outside her Whitstable home? She needed to be on her guard.

At Tempelhof, she looked around at the green scene peppered with multicoloured lycra joggers, and mentioned her plans to get an appointment with the Ukrainian Embassy in order to ask about entering Ukraine. She also wanted to take the U-Bahn to the 1936 Olympic Stadium, the place where her parents died in 1991. He approved of her ideas, but said he couldn't take another day off work.

'What was Berlin like with the Wall? The schoolbooks do not say much in Ukraine.'

She knew only what she had seen in English history

books, and from the look of the modern city, she suspected there would be no remaining scuff marks on the Olympic pavement, or blackened streaks from the car crash from long ago. There remained a nagging disquiet that her mother was alive. Might she appear, an apparition on the site of her father's death, and offer an explanation? Crazier things seemed to have occurred in the last year.

Despite his best intentions, Alex had not released any files and she had not pushed. What if she hated what she read? A part of her wanted to forget *Frond Skis* and the nightmares, but a part wanted to understand. Kitty's advice had been to search her parent's history, and she wondered if it might give her leverage, so she carried one volume of Anna Karenina with her, wrapped in her backpack. If the suited mystery man considered her worthy of attention, perhaps the book could be traded for Sasha's life. British intelligence must have picked it apart, but it was something to consider as a bribe to the Russians.

The following day, having oriented herself around the city, and checked her appointment at the Embassy that afternoon, she set off for the Olympiastion. The same man appeared walking nearby, and she wondered whether she should challenge him. But the streets were crowded, and she felt safe in her visibility with a child strapped to her chest. As she crossed the wide Berlin roads, and queued at the Ampelmann traffic lights, his ever-present figure followed. From time to time, she stopped at a shop window and glanced to one side, or stayed behind a tram; or crossed a cycle path; or lingered near a glittering cafe; or dawdled next to a U-Bahn sign, flicking her line of vision to catch sight of his shadow. There he was, looking up at the sky or down at his feet or pretending to make a call on his mobile. The sign for the U-Bahn was in front of her. It was one train line to the Olympiastadion. A year ago, she would have felt too much fear to fulfil this pilgrimage, but now she was prepared.

FORTY-EIGHT
berlin

AUTUMN 2022

THE NAPPIES and supplies in her backpack weighed her down. She stopped at a cafe, and attended to the baby's needs before placing her back into the sling. Outside, the man examined a shop window. Wriggling her laden shoulders, she texted Alex with details of her journey and a follow-up request for her parents' file.

Safe with Berlin tourists and commuters around her, she put one hand into her pocket, while the other encircled the baby. A sudden memory of her mugging on the London tube gave her a flutter of fear, but with a beauteous clarity, she recalled the first meeting with Sasha; his bravery and their immediate attraction.

Nearing the U-Bahn entrance a hand grabbed her shoulder, and she wheeled around in anger and alarm. 'What?' she said, registering the man's heavy leather gloves. He apologised in accented English, addressing her as Mrs Faver, his face half hidden by a scarf, above which his blue eyes shone like steel.

'I did not mean to shock you. I am here to help. You seek your mother?'

Her arm tightened around the baby. 'Who are you?'

'Your brother, Stephen, sent me. He wishes to assist you.'

'Stephen's in Moscow.'

The man pointed his gloved finger at the road. 'No. Please, I take you to him. My car is nearby.'

'No.' She tried to walk on, but he blocked her way.

'Please. No need to worry, Mrs Faver. Your mother also asked me to collect you. I am here to help you. She wishes to see –'

'I don't believe you. If she wanted to see me, she'd be here.' Shoving him aside, Anna made for the U-Bahn steps, but the man followed, catching her backpack, forcing her to stop. Pedestrians streamed past them, annoyed that they blocked their way.

'Mrs Faver!' he said. 'Please.'

But that was no longer who she was, and she shrugged him off, kicking out. Hanging onto the backpack, he pulled her to the kerb, as people shrank from the altercation, and a black car slid to halt nearby, ignoring traffic.

'Go away,' she said through gritted teeth, 'or you'll regret it.'

She covered the baby's head by pushing it tightly to her chest and the infant squealed in shock. With her free hand, she pulled out a canister and sprayed a short burst directly into his eyes. The effect was immediate. He doubled up in pain, yelling and plucking at his face with his leather fingers. There were footsteps and the sound of a scuffle behind her, and she began to run towards a shop until she heard the familiar voice of Alex shouting her name.

Turning, she saw her would-be attacker guided into a

blacked-out limousine by a second man, while Alex snarled something that sounded like Russian abuse. The driver spat, returning the sentiments, before slamming the car door and pulling away. Anna checked her crying child's eyes, but they were clear, unlike her own, which were smarting with the blow-back. She buried the canister in her pocket. 'Oh my God. Who was that?'

Breathless, Alex puffed out a laugh. 'What the hell do you have in your pocket?'

'You don't think I'd traipse the streets of Europe without protection, do you? I'm not that Anna anymore.'

'So I see.' He hugged her swiftly in relief. 'Is it a legal pepper spray? It looked terribly powerful.'

'Don't ask,' she growled.

He made a face, pulling her out of the stream of commuters to check the baby, but her cries were subsiding. 'I got your text. I'm here on business. But I was worried they'd target you, so I had your phone tracked.'

She was tempted to swear, but he cut her off.

'We've authenticated the five missing volumes of Anna Karenina.'

The baby quietened, and she took a breath. 'So why were those people targeting me?'

'They know we have five volumes, but they don't know we have them all.' He took her elbow and squeezed her arm. 'I'm booked into the Radisson Blu on the River Spree, and there's someone I want you to meet.' He studied her side pocket for a second. 'But promise you won't spray me with whatever's in that thing.'

'Not today,' she said curtly as she stepped into his yellow-cream taxi waiting nearby.

. . .

As she expected, he had booked into an expensive hotel. They arrived at a beacon of modern architecture that complemented the glass bridge over the River Spree. Inside the Radisson Blu, a huge central atrium stretched upwards, allowing natural light to flood every floor. The Tiergarten tents – the other Berlin – flashed through her mind like a guilty secret as they went into the luxurious hotel lobby. An internal glass lift, a contraption that would have slotted into a Hollywood movie, took them to the fourth floor, and with mounting curiosity, she followed Alex along the hushed, carpeted corridor to his room. This was the secretive side of him, and she suspected, the real Alex. The man she had married was a mirage, although the same could be said of her parents and her brother. In their own ways, they were all people living by a different set of rules to the mainstream. And what of Sasha? Her conversations with Dmytrov and his family had convinced her that despite their different backgrounds, they had no hidden agendas. That was the simplicity and purity of their love.

With the flash of a keycard, Alex opened the hotel door to reveal an autumnal sun. She blinked for a moment, settling her vision. At the far end of the room, in front of picture windows overlooking the river, the plump silhouette of a man sat in a plush chair. Stepping out of the bright shaft, she saw a face creased by a thousand strokes and gnarled hands settled on his belly. Despite a walking cane at his side, underneath the smart suit, his shoulders appeared broad and firm.

His returning gaze devoured her and the baby with such unnerving intensity she had to look away. Alex urged her inwards, insisting she take the infant out of the sling and get comfortable before introductions. The luxurious suite held a bedroom, half hidden behind an open door, and in one corner was a drinks cabinet, a kettle and the paraphernalia of all hotels in addition to nibbles and half eaten sandwiches.

'Who is this?' She felt reluctant to address the stranger directly as she peeled off her coat.

'I am Maxim Popov,' the man said in accented English. He leaned forward as if to rise, one hand on a brass-topped cane; then seemed to think better of it, settling back to place the stick across his knees. 'You are Anna. You look exactly like your mother.'

She shot a silent question to Alex, who urged her to listen. 'He's a Russian who's helping us. A defector, although not current GRU, but he's offered us a great deal of relevant information. We think of him as the next Oleg Gordievsky.'

'Oleg who?'

She noted the man's trimmed, ridged nails. 'You trust him? Was he one of those men on the street?' She could not hide a note of incredulity.

'Yes to the first question. We trust him. But no to the second.' Alex's mouth crooked. 'Those men were a by-product of his defection. I trust him because his motivation in helping us is personal, not political or economic. So please hear him out.'

'Does he know where Sasha is?'

'Yes,' said Maxim.

Anger flared inside her. 'What have you done with him? Tell me!'

Alex soothed her. 'Please.'

Unperturbed by her reaction, Maxim assured Anna he wished no harm and had done everything he could to help. His accent was thick, but his command of English fluent. 'I also have information about your mother.'

'Again! My mother! Is she always to be used like a carrot to the donkeys?' She spat and if the baby hadn't been in her arms, she would have hurled swear words, but instead she lowered her voice. 'You're the second person to say that to me today, and I don't think they were wishing me a long life. Have you really seen my mother and Stephen?'

'Stephen is safe in Moscow.'

His expression was unreadable; impossible to determine if he thought that good or bad news.

'Although I haven't been to Moscow for twenty years,' he continued, his hands clasped, like a man with a rehearsed speech. 'He is well. I know this for a fact.' He urged her to sit down opposite him on the high-backed brocade chair, and she eased into the seat, keeping the man under observation, while holding the baby close. Alex placed glasses of water on the table between them like a conference secretary, and suggested he hold the child, in order for her to concentrate on Maxim's information. Reluctantly, she agreed, watching her little one examine Alex's face with the seriousness of a diplomat.

Maxim began.

One of her mother's philosophies, he said, was a desire to create a fairer world by promoting a communist doctrine. There were many people in Britain who thought like her in the sixties and seventies. She had been a student of Professor John Blount, and their mutual political views led to their marriage, which was why USSR recruited them both. Maxim outlined her father's travels under the guise of research, and how he and Annaliese slipped into East Berlin with false papers provided by Russian agents.

'I know this,' she interrupted, impatient with his lecture; then seeing Alex's expression, she pursed her lips.

'Annaliese accompanied him on these trips and, using the unique editions of the Anna Karenina volumes as identifiers to meet foreign agents, handed over microfiche obtained in England. John and Annaliese weren't thieves,' he insisted, 'but couriers.'

Wondering if the distinction was relevant, given theirs was a traitorous act, Anna kept her silence with difficulty. Her parents' behaviour pained her, although she could not connect it to her shadowy memories of her childhood.

'In the eighties,' he continued, 'as the military became increasingly computer literate, the books changed usage. They developed codes, set within the pages in order to deliver passwords necessary to crack messages about NATO movements. There were also spaces to secrete flash drives. This continued until the collapse of the Soviet Union.'

With white knuckles, he hesitated before admitting to a long affair with her mother, and then paused, as if the words bunched in his mouth.

Unable to meet his eyes, Anna stared at the carpeted floor with a sense of revulsion. How could this old man and her glamorous mother have slept together? She tingled with anger, but his deadpan expression did not change.

'The purpose of the car crash,' Maxim continued, 'was to enable Annaliese to escape the KGB by declaring herself dead. She did not wish to continue working for a Russia that had lost its way, and according to the doctors, John Blount was dying and had months to live. When the Berlin Wall came down, and the Soviet empire collapsed, new organisations within Russia sprang up, redefining agents' roles. KGB became GRU and the new foreign wing was the

SVB, but none of this interested her, and I respected her choices,' he said.

He paused again, and she realised he was wiping away a tear.

'I loved her. Believe me, I loved her. And of course, she loved you and Stephen very much, but she felt her priority was to protect you both. Intelligence agencies often threaten families to ensure the loyalty of their operatives. So after glasnost, we thought the best plan was for her to leave her children and start a new life under a different name. It would be too easy for them to track her down if she lived with either of you.'

'She lived with you?' Anna could not hide her incredulity. 'But Stephen –'

Maxim muttered something in Russian, fishing inside his jacket pocket to withdraw a folded A4 envelope. 'She was not with me, and Stephen's involvement was not our fault.' He stretched out a hand. 'Please, read. This is a letter she wrote. It took over a year to reach me.'

Alex rocked the baby as Anna put tentative fingers on the offering. She moved away to sit beside a desk that afforded sufficient distance between them.

FORTY-NINE

berlin

AUTUMN 2022

INSIDE WERE THREE ITEMS: a small, embossed business card in the name of *Lisa-Anne Gordon, Realtor, member of The American-Russian Society* with New York contact details. The second item was a larger card with a black rim, dated in the last two months, giving details of the same woman's funeral. The caption asked for donations to the church on the Lower East Side, Manhattan. Anna felt her heart thump as she read on.

The third item was a smaller envelope addressed to the Russian embassy in Paris and inside, a brief letter dated over a year ago.

'You said your name was Maxim. This letter is written to someone called Aleksey Kassvich.'

'A Russian diplomat working in Paris,' said Maxim. 'He was a friend she had met at an investors' event for Russians buying New York property. Her job was to act as an intermediary, transferring roubles to dollars.' He sighed, as if the thought pained him. 'She would not have done such work willingly. She hated capitalist business projects.'

With dread, Anna scoured the page before raising her eyes to glare at him. 'This letter asks him to find Vronsky. She says she doesn't know his real name, or where he lives. What do you know about this?'

Alex interjected. 'Aleksey disappeared after making a public comment expressing regret for Russia's invasion of Ukraine, but before that, he sent the letter to a man working in the Kremlin.'

Maxim nodded. 'Unfortunately, I knew this Kremlin contact, but did not realise the depths of his deception. His name was Stepanov, and although I had made no secret of my desire to find your mother, he always maintained ignorance of her whereabouts.' The old man breathed in deeply as if to absorb the magnitude of his discovery. 'Stepanov deceived me and her. He made promises that her children would be safe, but he broke them. I want to believe she wouldn't have left her Vronsky without him pressurising her.'

The room shrank. *Frond Skis.* Her old nightmare clutched at her heart, and she felt the blood rush to her face, infusing her voice with a toxic anger. 'Who is Vronsky?' The paper trembled in her hand. 'Tell me now! Who is he? What's his connection to my parents?'

Confronted with her rage, Maxim's impassive face melted momentarily as his stick clattered to the ground. He waved a hand for Alex to ignore it. The brass top glinted in the sunlight like a clue.

'Hear him out, Anna,' said Alex as Maxim's eyes creased with pain, the wrinkles forming a thistle-like mass across his face.

'Believe me, I was as shocked as you.'

She crumpled a corner of the cream envelope. 'Did you kill Vronsky?'

His hands reached out as if to touch her, then retreated into baby-like fists. 'No, Anna, no.' He pressed his lips together and released a breath. 'It is me. I was Vronsky. I never told her my real name, but two months ago, when I tracked her down, we spoke for hours on the phone. I was in Berlin and she was in New York. She was in hospital about to have a heart operation and had a premonition of her death. I wanted to be at her side, but she was due in surgery within hours. So we talked honestly and openly. For the first time.'

'Why didn't she contact me?' Anna's nails bit into her palms.

He stooped to pick up the cane, and grimaced as his back twinged, but Anna felt no compassion.

'Why would she speak to you and not to me?' she demanded. 'Why keep Stephen in the dark? Why not contact him?'

He put his head to one side. 'She didn't know about Stephen until it was too late. And she was ashamed to have left you both. As you get older, you look back and see things differently. She was too sick to face your anger, but to me, she acknowledged her errors. As did I. We made the wrong choices in life.'

'How can we believe anything this man says?' Anna spat the words to Alex, dropping the letter to the ground.

'We did a DNA test using a hair from Simon.'

'My son? Simon?' Her anger mingled with outrage. 'Without my permission? How dare you!'

'Anna,' Alex rocked the baby as if to calm them all, 'we

couldn't take his word for it. We had to obtain proof of paternity before speaking to you. Why risk distressing you if it turned out to be false?'

'What!' She gagged. This white-haired man, this strange Vronsky, this person with his belly wrapped in an expensive suit was not her father, nor a grandfather to her children. He was nothing to do with her. He was the enemy. A Russian, part of a brutal regime, and her mother would never have slept with such a man.

'He's lying. You're lying, Alex. You've lied about so much. How dare you take Simon's DNA without my permission. How dare you try to prove this twisted story. Give me back my baby.'

Keeping a firm hold on the child, Alex moved away, and she stamped a foot, aware her fury was too great to clutch the little one without causing distress. Twisting her hands, she wanted to attack him, but a series of disjointed sobs welled beneath her breastbone.

Maxim rearranged his features into a neutral expression, although his voice belied a greater emotion. 'Please hear me out. When Annaliese and I spoke after thirty years of absence, we did not make a video call. Both of us agreed to remember each other as we had been, so we chose a phone call.' He clutched the cane. 'But her voice was unmistakable, and we spoke openly. She admitted to denying you were mine because Stepanov advised her to do this. He told her of my history; of my work for the KGB. He told her I was an assassin, a side of me she had not known. And she could not come to terms with this. So when Stepanov asked your mother to go to America as a sleeper agent under a new name, she agreed in return for the safety of her children.' His face creased. 'It is hard for you, a child of peace, to recognise the way things were in the Cold War. Once an agent, always an agent, and once a traitor, always a traitor. She was at risk of being arrested and imprisoned by British intelligence. I'm sure Mr Faver will confirm this.'

Alex nodded as he continued to rock the child.

'The Service never lets you go. Your mother and I had discussed ways to escape, and I thought we had agreed on a plan, but she did not trust me.' His eyes closed as he gathered his words with care. 'Perhaps she was right. As a younger man, I was loyal to the Kremlin. But she was also wrong, because she trusted Stepanov. And new Russia is a copy of Soviet Russia. Years later, Stepanov was instrumental in sending people to entrap Stephen into helping the GRU.'

'Stephen didn't mention –'

'Marsalek was his emissary; Wirecard was the trap.' At her expression, the grim smile returned. 'Yes. I have since found out it was Stepanov's doing. His son boasted of these things.' His hands slid up and down the cane as his eyes misted with memories. 'Despite our differences, your mother and I loved each other; we had a passion for each other. And I have lived long enough to understand such things are rare. Before she died, we wept over the decisions that could never be undone; the loyalties that were misguided. Family should have come before politics. She told me she had come to London once or twice to see you both from across a street, or a park, but was afraid to make contact. What if her cover was blown? What would happen to you both? And what could she say to you? The lies trapped her.

'When she heard about Stephen, her greatest fear was that they would move to involve you next, to destroy your life, the way they had destroyed his. In her thirties, she had thought communism worth fighting for, but in her last days, she realised to change the world, you must first love the people closest to you. Only with love in your heart is your life worth living. She made me question my upbringing. I was taught to do my job, be patriotic, and if people suffered it didn't matter. I don't even know where my own mother is buried, and I saw that I had lost the love of my life, Annaliese, and the chance to see you – my only child. Russia demanded everything from me but it didn't give back anything of value.'

The tears prickled in her eyes and she wiped them away with impatient anger. Listening to him was like reaching for her mother, only to watch her fall into an abyss. 'Why tell me this now? She's dead, and all the time I was trying to puzzle out the Anna Karenina books, I could have flown over to speak to her. Are you here to torture me? Is that your motivation? You were a torturer, weren't you? All Russians are. And as for your leaders, old men in power learnt nothing from the past.'

With difficulty, Maxim's fingers clutched the brass top of his cane. 'Some months ago a woman in Mariupol told me I was an onion grabber. It is a story by Dostoevsky. Perhaps you know it? And I considered the term a compliment compared to my true nature. I was not a man who had spent half his life doing good and half doing bad. No. My heart was black. But your mother insisted that while I breathed I had a chance to help you; to redeem past actions; to balance my soul.' A ghostly smile broke across his face and then he frowned. 'It was fanciful – for how could I do that? I was surrounded by troops and chaos, and I was part of the problem. A Russian in Ukraine. And then, by the grace of the universe, I saw an onion on a string: a young man, flagging me down near Mariupol.' He placed a hand on his heart. 'He was brave. Not only did he refuse to leave his dying father, but after his father died, he dug his grave, and then went to help evacuate other people. I followed him, desperate to know more about you, and he came to a group of wounded women and children. He could have saved himself. He could have run away, but he faced the Russian soldiers, speaking to them quietly. I thought they would shoot him, but something in his words stopped them opening fire. Instead, they looked in my direction. I was holding a semi-automatic, draped in a Russian flag for protection, so they told me to shoot the civilians, and took him prisoner. Before he left, he begged me to send you the letter he'd given me.'

Her head drooped. 'Yes. I got it.'

'Of course, I was the enemy; the assassin – but Sasha Vronskiy looked into my eyes and told me his love for you would outlast the war. He knew nothing of the promise I had made to your mother, but he had faith in me to do the right thing or so he said. His humanity pierced the black steel of my soul, even though it was naive to think that protecting him or you against my own government would be easy –'

The word *naive* jogged Anna from her black grief. 'Wait. Stop giving me puzzles. So you know where Sasha is?'

Maxim turned the cane around in his hands, his lips pressing together as if she had not spoken. 'I did not shoot the civilians, I helped evacuate them. But the truth is, to negotiate with the devil, you need something to trade. By chance, as much as foresight, I had kept the Anna Karenina volumes locked away for thirty years in a safe deposit box in Berlin. The same leverage you carry in your backpack, according to Mr Faver.' He nodded at her expression of surprise. 'So to assist you, and to give Annaliese peace in her grave, I took what little power I retained, and became a traitor to my country. All I asked was that the father of my grandchild was released as part of any negotiations. I did this for you, Anna. For you and your mother. Because your young man is right and Russia is wrong. Love will outlast war.'

FIFTY

berlin

AUTUMN 2022

WITH ONE ARM raised in a triumphant wave, Jogi burst in through the door, his hair dishevelled. Despite the charged atmosphere in the room, he sank into the hotel armchair with a grin, crossing his legs and picking dirt from his creased slacks. Caught between rage and sadness, Anna went to ease her sleeping baby from Alex's arms, and thrust her face into the child's warmth. 'Tell me where her father is,' she said to Maxim, ignoring Jogi.

'Twenty-four hours, we've been travelling,' said Jogi, 'but we're here now. Boy wonder is having a shower, and I must smell like a teenager at a rave.'

Alex laughed, his knees bending in relief. 'Like you'd remember.'

Jogi looked from face to face. 'Haven't you told her yet?'

Anna stood in front of the window. The view outside was of a sparkling glass walkway arching over the River Spree, but her mind was elsewhere. *Frond Skis.* She hated the man called Maxim, and she hated Jogi's levity, and all the people who had lied to her. But hatred fought with love as she clutched her child.

'He's coming,' said Jogi, raising eyebrows. 'Aren't you happy? And by the way, we've extracted a further eighty prisoners of war from that Russian hellhole, Taganrog prison. Notorious. Their families are ecstatic.'

A light shone into her heart, and she struggled to kick her thoughts into gear. She had maced a man for the first time in her life, and come to a hotel suite to talk to a Russian who turned out to be her father. Her brother was forever beyond her reach, and her mother had died without ever making contact. From deep inside her, love pulled on inner strings to find a strength she did not know she possessed.

'Maxim brought us five Anna Karenina volumes. Michel provided one, and you had the last two. Without the set, we couldn't de-code the names and make a deal.' Alex spoke gently at her side. 'Maxim helped identify Russian agents, and negotiated the return of some Taganrog prisoners in exchange their agents, including Stephen. It was for you, Anna. Because you two have your whole life in front of you.'

She did not turn from the window to look as the door swung open. What if the love she had felt back in England was all a trick of sexual secrecy? What if she was like her mother, and would easily abandon those she loved? What if the whole of last year was nothing more than a game of *smoke and mirrors*? An espionage gone wrong? How could she fit the puzzle of her past and future life together?

now...

She turns and looks, and he is in the doorway; a tall man, glistening with damp, in clothes that hang from his shoulders. His cheekbones protrude on his gaunt face, made thinner by the shaved scalp revealing his physical suffering. The silver pin is still prominent, a stripe at one corner of his eye, but other more recent wounds are evident, including a crust around his jaw and scabs on his wrists. Beneath the anonymous grey tracksuit, his shrunken body limps forward, an old soul behind his beautiful eyes.

Yet, it is Sasha. It is all Sasha, and she shrieks. Alex takes the baby, so that, unencumbered, she can throw herself into his arms. They encircle one another: hands, elbows, noses to collar bones and lips pressed together with kisses, forever kisses, unable to let each other go, struggling to believe they are reunited. Kisses mingle with tears as he murmurs in Ukrainian, and she copies his words, learnt from recent lessons. Of course, she has no doubt he is her soulmate. No doubt at all. And she is his.

Are you real? Yes, it's me. You have returned. Are you alright? I am strong now I am with you. Did you suffer? I lived for you. I lived to see you again. I belong to you. And you belong to me. I will never let you go again. I will never let you go.

They talk over each other and into each other's hearts, and murmur in each other's ears, because the rest of the room has vanished. Only when the child cries do they pull apart, and Sasha's face lights as he sees his daughter for the first time. He takes three paces towards Alex who passes the baby into his arms, and immediately the infant stops grizzling to stare up at him in awe and wonder.

'Is she real?'

'Yes, she's yours.'

Anna presses herself to them both, kissing his knuckles. She must maintain physical contact, or he will prove to be an insubstantial dream and dissolve.

Maxim stares, the poker face wavering. 'I promised,' he murmurs, but the couple are too wrapt in the child to pay attention, and Alex presses a hand on the old man's arm.

'You did it,' he says. 'Annaliese will be looking down with happiness. And we have more work to do. It doesn't end here.'

'I know,' says Maxim. 'There is a long road...'

But Sasha and Anna aren't listening, pressed together in a trio of love.

Jogi sniffs his armpit critically. 'Alex has never explained to me, Maxim, how you knew Sasha was linked to Anna. Was it the last name, Vronsky, like in the book?'

Maxim turns his palms upwards. 'I see a photograph, and she has a chain with a crescent moon. I gave it to her mother, who must have left it in London before she fled. And of course, she looks exactly like Annaliese.'

Holding the baby, Sasha limps to the old man. 'I am grateful.' He speaks in English for Anna's sake.

'Despite orders, I promise I didn't harm them. I don't

know what you said to the commander of that unit, but I waited with the the civilians until the Ukrainian army came. Then I made my way to Germany.'

Sasha nods. 'I asked the Russian commander if their mothers and daughters were safe. He asked for a trade in return for not killing the civilians.'

'What did you trade?' Maxim said with clear curiosity.

'Nothing. I told him in another life, we were all brothers. Why were we killing each other?'

The room falls silent. Even the child sucks her thumb in contemplation.

'There were so many I could not save –'

'Do not be guilty. The guilt is mine.'

Maxim links his fingers together, while Anna glowers. Sasha turns to kiss her. 'He helped me bury Papi and he delivered the letter.' His fingers go to her neck to extract the chain bearing the golden moon and she clutches the ornament. 'This. He recognised this.'

'I am old KGB. A Chekist,' Maxim murmurs. 'Now I see the important thing is family and when my countrymen take Ukrainian children to turn them against their parents, it is a scar in my heart.'

Jogi cuts through everyone's sadness. He is the harbinger of cheer. 'Bloody nightmare to expedite Sasha's paperwork so quickly. And we've arranged for his leg operations to take place in UK. So you'll be out of action for awhile, Vronskiy. They won't send you back to the front because you're the only surviving member of your family, and we'll find you some counselling. Those prisons are...'

He does not need to finish his words. The room flinches and Sasha hugs the child more closely, before switching to English for the room. 'I will go back to my country, but in prison, I dream to be here. Thank you. All of you.'

Maxim looks embarrassed, or as embarrassed as a poker-faced man can look. 'There is a vineyard from me that will be yours, Anna, and I have the details of your mother's estate.'

'I don't want your money,' spits Anna. 'It's tainted.' The words *assassin* and *father* ricochet in her conscience, but Sasha hugs her.

'We have a future,' he says. 'One day there will be peace, and we will have each other. The war must end.'

The old Russian tips his head on one side, ill at ease. 'May I ask? What is the name of my grandchild?'

And for the first time that day, Anna laughs, telling Sasha how she swore to wait until she found him, so he could name their daughter. She lists a few of the endearments used thus far, which range from Ukrainian to English to French. Bemused, Sasha repeats the words watching the child wrap a tiny hand around his bony finger.

'So what is her name, Sasha?' Anna kisses him. 'Tell us.'

Joy and sorrow mingle in the hotel room. It is like the North Sea on a day when the dark waves crash on the shore, but the sun sparkles overhead. A day where everyone is aware that peace is possible, but easily broken and must never be taken for granted, for always there are those who would throw bombs and kill.

In the 1990s, Berlin and Eastern Europe were hubs of optimism, but also a shifting community of opinions, hopes and fears. In 2022, as war spreads, old men sitting behind desks hanker for an imaginary past and a fleeting power, casually destroying the lives of others. But we must hold onto a hope that the wars will end, evil will turn to ash, and people will embrace love over hate.

And as Sasha and Anna huddle with the baby in a Berlin

hotel room, they are proof that love completes the puzzle of our existence. The past cannot be undone, but we can hope that the future for Anna and Sasha and their child will be blessed by a new dawn.

Sasha kisses his baby daughter, and she squirms at the bristles on his cheek, scraping her nails across his chin with a smile. 'I think we call her Nadiya,' he says. 'This is Ukrainian for hope. And with you and me and Nadiya, we will live with Hope, in dignity.'

Anna hugs them. 'Nadiya. Yes. Always Nadiya.'

U24.gov.ua instagram reports
President Zelenskyy speaking in an interview with The Axios Show

For each man in the world, the priority is his family. His family is country, because family is a part of your world. And your world is your country.

bibliography

The Cold War, a Beginner's Guide by Merrilyn Thomas
Published 2009 Oneworld Publications.

Invasion, Russia's Bloody War and Ukraine's Fight for Survival by Luke Harding
Published 2022 Guardian Faber.

The Language of War, Hi! How are you? redacted I am fine, thanks, how are you?
By Oleksandr Mykhed
Published 2024 Penguin.

Christo Grozev, a Bulgarian investigative journalist,
YouTube, and Guardian newspaper lecture in 2025
A history of how he uncovers Russian spies.

@strategywoman on Threads,
A social media look at the culture, history and art of Ukraine.

Hot Money: Agent of Chaos (FT podcasts)
The life of Jan Marsalek
Pushkin+ on Apple Podcasts. July 2025.

acknowledgments

My thanks to my many beta readers and writers' groups for their encouragement and thoughts.

Thanks to my structural editor, Tom Bromley who gave insightful advice on how to position a dual timeline novel. (reedsy.com)

Thanks to my invaluable proofreader in New Zealand, Victoria Kennar. vkproofreading@outlook.com

And last but not least, thanks to my wonderful cover designer, Neil Hart.

neiljhart23@gmail.com

This novel is written with love to Ukraine in their David and Goliath fight. May the spirit of the Ukrainians never be dimmed, and all aggressors fail.

about the author

Justine Gilbert has lived in USA, Italy and England. Currently, she lives on the Kent Coast of England with three chihuahuas. She loves - in no specific order - reading, dogs, her children and grandchildren, and of course writing stories that are close to her heart. World events inspire her to write novels about ordinary people caught up in extraordinary times.

You can find out more about her on her website
www.justinegilbertauthor.co.uk

also by justine gilbert

Daisy Chain

Montecatini

If you have enjoyed The Anna Puzzle, or any of my novels, please leave a review on Goodreads or Amazon.

Thank you.

Printed in Dunstable, United Kingdom

77110231R00231